# A WRAITH BENEATH THE TIDES

*A Beyond the Tides Novel*

## EMILIA JAE

EM'S BOOKISH REALM PRESS

Copy & Line Edits: Tabitha Chandler

Cover & Chapter Headers: Charlotte Slegers (@charlotteslegers)

Map of Rymelle: Andrés Aguirre Jurado (@aaguirreart)

Title Page Art: @mooondance_studio

Art of Esmyra & Draevyn: @pandacapuccino

Half-Face Goddesses: @IC_Illustration_

Hardback ISBN: 979-8-9888968-8-3

Paperback ISBN: 979-8-9888968-7-6

# A Wraith Beneath the Tides

## Beyond the Tides | Book One

### Emilia Jae

TO THE FIERCE DAUGHTERS OF THE WORLD:
*may you never lose your wildfire.*

# AUTHOR'S NOTE & CONTENT WARNING

The Beyond the Tides Series is an adult romantic fantasy that contains content and themes that may not be suitable for all readers.

Sensitive content includes violence (including gun violence), gore, explicit language, sexual content, and on page death from the character's point of view.

The characters are all morally gray, including the FMC. Esmyra Blackwood is a pirate and siren shifter, who sometimes does questionable things. She is a borderline villain, and an anti-hero at best.

Reader discretion is advised.

This is book one in the series.

# Pronunciation Guide

## Characters & Creatures

Esmyra (Esmi) Blackwood - Ez-meer-ah / Ez-mee
Draevyn Rowe - Dray-vin
Cyrus Blackwood - Sigh-riss
Atlas Rowe - At-lus
Elowynne Everhartt - Elle-oh-win
Syrena Aeress - Ser-ee-na Ay-ress
Azarian - Az-air-ee-an
Kraken - Crack-en
Krechuums - Krech-ooms
Grindylows - Grin-dee-lows

## The Gods of Rymelle

Kaelypso - Kay-lip-soh
Naerysa - Nay-riss-ah
Irah - Eye-ra
Vydenne - V-eye-denn
Villaem - Vill-aim
Asyris - As-eye-rus

## The Kingdoms of Rymelle

Maerinys - May-rin-ese
Lephyrin - Leff-eye-rin
Sumnae - Soom-nay
Terrana - Ter-ah-na

# GUIDE TO THE GODS

*Kaelypso & Naerysa*

Goddesses of the Sea
Sunken Kingdom of Maerinys
Magic: Siren Shifters & Water Manipulation

*Irah*

God of Rage & War
Mortal Kingdom of Lephyrin
Magic: None (Human Kingdom)

*Vydenne*

Goddess of Illusion
Elven Kingdom of Sumnae
Magic: Mind Manipulation

*Villaem*

God of Agriculture & Growth
Woodland Kingdom of Terrana
Magic: Woodland Shifters with
Weather and Earth Manipulation

RYMELLE
SUMNAE TEMPLE
SUMNAE
SUMNAE CAPITAL
IEPHYRIN TEMPLE
IEPHYRIN
IEPHYRIN CAPITAL
TERRANA TEMPLE
TERRANA
TERRANA CAPITAL
ANCHORAGE COVE
MAERINYS
MAERINYS CAPITAL
THE CAVE
MAERINYS TEMPLE

# Prologue

L ight, bright and blinding, erupted from the castle spires. The man cast a panicked glance behind him as he raced through the flooding streets of Maerinys. Seawater seeped into his leather boots as his calloused hands nervously clutched a screaming infant to his chest.

Dodging terrified citizens and leaping over the gods' destruction, he forced his steps to carry the treasure he held as far as possible before they were engulfed with the kingdom.

His run turned desperate, fighting for the survival of not only himself but for who lay in his arms. Bricks fell from the sky, tumbling around him as the ground trembled.

Maerinys was sinking quicker now.

Alarms rang from the conch horns posted at each spiraling tower of the city—a warning of what was to come. A warning of what he'd helped cause.

Cries of both men and merfolk surrounded him, filling his ears until the deafening noise of the depths swallowing the kingdom was nothing but a distant buzz.

The resistance of the water forced the man's run to slow. Breath heaving, he hid behind a building as cracks splintered through its bricks.

The infant's shrieks had ceased, and he risked a peek at her porcelain-like face. Eyes as blue as the brightest lagoon met his own, and he hugged her tightly once more while the flood grew to his knees. The pirate lord knew he held a life more valuable than any gold and was willing to risk his own for it.

All he had to do was make it back to his ship, where his crew awaited his return.

"He went this way!" The call stunned him; its source only feet away.

He had never been a fearful man, but he knew death would be a better consequence than whatever would be placed upon himself and the blue-eyed babe if they were caught.

Willing his feet to carry them once more, he pushed through the resistance of the incoming tides until he reached the secret, hidden entrance to the kingdom's capital city—a system of caves that led out to a small isle off the coast, where a pinnace was tied off, waiting.

The waves were chest high as he held the baby above his head; the water splashed up into the man's face, pouring down his throat as its salty tang stung his nostrils. He stormed through the cavern, running through the darkness as fast as his feet would carry them. Even a mile into the underground cave, the roar of the waves filled his mortal ears, and when a loud crashing sound echoed, he dared to look back.

The cave began *collapsing*. The ground trembled and crumbled beneath his boots as if sinking alongside Maerinys, separating them from the way they came. It filled him with the fear of all gods. He gritted his teeth as he surged forward once more, racing for what seemed like miles until he reached the other side. Sharp, jagged rocks met them beyond the cave's mouth. Then, in the distance, his eyes fell to the pinnace, its small white sails rocking violently in the waves.

The pirate's reputation was one of merciless brutality, but he handled the infant with a surprising gentleness as he placed her in the boat and heaved himself over its ledge. He gripped the oars and began rowing them towards the open sea as the water surged in from all directions, racing towards Maerinys.

No matter how hard he rowed, no matter how direly his muscles strained, the currents were too great. Every row away from the kingdom somehow brought them closer to its sinking center.

Peering into the depths beneath them, scales shimmered under the surface as merfolk fled their home.

The man's eyes bulged, his jaw hanging open in disbelief as what began as a ripple in the waves grew rapidly—swallowing everything with it. A whirlpool greater than any he had ever seen surged, trapping them in its swirling cascades as it ripped the oars from his grasp, shattering the wood in tiny splinters.

The pirate lord had always known his death would be at the hands of his greatest love—the sea. If it weren't for his new plans, he would've welcomed it wholeheartedly, greeting the roaring waves as if they were a long-lost lover calling his name, beckoning him to her depths.

Malicious shrieks and hisses filled the air as sirens were dragged towards the sinking kingdom alongside them. Even the strength of their powerful tails couldn't save them from the riptides. The screams of terror from the citizens of Maerinys echoed in his ears, competing with the thunderous sound of the roaring sea.

The moonlight hid behind the mistiest of clouds, encasing their drowning world in near darkness. Merlights flickered from where they remained on the spiraling towers until, one by one, they snuffed out.

Sucking in a sharp breath, he waited for the sea to take their lives, when suddenly, a force as great as the gods strained against the swirling tides. Their small boat was shoved out of the whirlpool's grasp, as if the ocean itself was protecting them. The conjured currents dragged them away until they reached the peak of the pool, and the castle's highest spire was all that remained of Maerinys—right before pure, untapped power burst from it as striking as the midday sun.

His eyes slammed shut, shielding the babe on instinct while their pinnace rocked with the waves.

And then, as quickly as the storm struck, it vanished. The sea fell eerily silent and still.

Slowly opening his eyes, they worked to adjust to the darkness and found that the once great kingdom of the sea had ceased to exist, leaving nothing but a few bubbles in its wake. The man couldn't catch his breath, his chest rising and falling rapidly as he tried to comprehend what he just witnessed.

Suddenly, the babe erupted in an ear-shattering screech. At the same moment, a piercing pain ignited within the pirate's chest, as if someone had plunged their sharpened blade directly through his heart.

A roar of agony burst from the pirate lord's throat, matching the infant's. It was unlike any pain he had ever felt, fully believing his soul was leaving his body, tearing him apart as it ripped free of his ribcage.

With a sharp rip, he tore open his shirt and placed his palm over his heart. The man's eyes widened, blinking through what he thought was a trick of the hidden moonlight. He lifted his palm to his face and found it covered in a black substance, seeping from an unwarranted wound carved into his chest.

It was blood. *His* blood. Only it no longer held its crimson hue and appeared as decayed as his heart now felt.

The hazy clouds of mist cleared from the sky and he peered down at the trembling infant that rested in his other arm. His jaw gaped as his eyes landed on the reason for her shrieks of pain.

She didn't possess the black bleeding mark above her heart as he did, but instead, designs now marked her flesh, resembling burns. Swirls and intricate rune patterns trailed down her arms and spine.

His thumb traced over them, surprised to find the marks weren't raised or hot to the touch. It was as if they were inked into her newborn skin.

"Blackwood!" His name echoed through the air, rolling off the calming waves.

His gaze whipped in the direction of the noise to find *The Night Wraith* floating toward where they remained in the dangerous, open water—its onyx-hued wood and navy sails gleaming in the moonlight.

Glancing down at the infant once more, his throat tightened. Glimpses of what he had done and who he had betrayed by taking her flashed across his mind. But it wasn't just about stealing her, regardless of whether that was part of the plan or not. It had become about *saving* her, and in turn, the sea.

Once *The Night Wraith* reached them, a rope-woven ladder was cast down and he eagerly began his ascent—worried about the possibility that something else could rise up and pull them down to the depths alongside Maerinys.

Walking along the uneven, cobbled streets of Lephyrin's kingdom, Esmyra Blackwood seamlessly merged into the bustling madness of its capital city.

Adorned in a billowing blouse and breeches, Esmyra hid her weapons and stolen wealth beneath a floor-length, hooded cloak, tucking her midnight hair in its confines. She had removed her favorite jewelry, leaving it aboard her ship, *The Night Wraith*, that waited miles offshore while her crew ravaged Lephyrin unseen.

The kingdom was nestled on the coast, surrounded by jagged mountains that stretched endlessly. Lephyrin's skyline was dominated by the spires of its castle as the midday sun filtered through maroon banners strung across the market's buildings, bearing the sigil of House Rowe.

It was rare they ever made port, but months at sea would drive anyone to near madness—even the crew that sailed under the command of the fearsome pirate king, Captain Cyrus Blackwood.

The pirate lord turned self-proclaimed king had sailed Rymelle's seas for nearly one thousand years, putting fear as great as the gods into those who sailed those same waves—thanks to his daughter, Esmyra. A woman burdened by the weight of what she considered a curse, bound to the sea and its depths.

Lephyrin's air was filled with the clang of a blacksmith's hammer, the cheerful bartering of civilians, and the laughter of children chasing each other between the madness. Merchants bellowed their wares from sun-bleached stalls, their hands waving toward gleaming fruits, bolts of dyed silk, and sparkling trinkets.

Esmyra's hood was drawn just low enough to shadow her other-worldly eyes. She smiled faintly to herself as she walked, fingers trailing lazily over wooden stalls and overloaded carts. The crowd parted and shifted naturally, as if the world itself made room for her as she passed by.

Her first lift was a ripe plum, plucked from the edge of an old farmer's cart while his attention was stolen by a beggar woman demanding a lower price. Esmyra took a slow bite of the fruit as she turned from them, savoring its taste.

She made her way past a few more carts, and her attention was snagged on a stall of shimmering jewels. Her hand brushed over delicate charms until, between heartbeats, a dainty gold bracelet vanished up her sleeve.

Coins always came easier, their pouches hanging too loose on merchants' belts. She bumped into men throughout the market, swiping the small sacks from their sides as she moved to steady them. All they saw was a beautiful woman as they looked down at her, too distracted to notice her stealing from their pockets.

By the time she reached the market's far edge, her cloak was heavy with stolen goods. She took one last bite of the plum before tossing the pit into the dirt.

No one would know what had been lost until the sun began to set. By then, she'd be long gone.

While strolling back through the streets, Esmyra's eyes caught on a small boy sitting on the ground in a narrow alleyway. She tried to ignore him, but his hollow cheeks and sunken eyes betrayed the hunger gnawing at his stomach.

"Ugh," she grunted to herself as she quickened her steps, making her way to him. "Where are your parents, boy?" Her voice was as soothing as the breeze rolling off the harbor.

The boy trembled, the scent of his fear stuffing itself in Esmyra's nostrils. The torn, weathered cloth he wore as clothing fell from his bony shoulders as he lifted his lifeless stare to hers. "They were executed by the king's order. Three moons ago."

Esmyra's eyes narrowed on him. "Are you lying to me?"

The boy shook his head, never breaking eye contact as he admitted, "I'm sure my time with the noose will be soon."

Esmyra's lips parted. She never gave a damn about anyone who wasn't aboard her own ship, but occasionally, she would come across a child that tugged at her immortal heartstrings. The starving, orphaned children who wandered the streets of Rymelle's kingdoms would've once been her fate if it weren't for Cyrus Blackwood.

She let out a sigh. "I'll make sure you don't starve tonight."

A surge of fury flooded her veins toward those who wore the crown in Lephyrin's looming castle. They would never know hunger. They would never know the struggles of those who lived in the shadow of their wealth. Meanwhile, mere children were wondering if today would be their last, dying of either violence or starvation in their city's streets.

Esmyra swiftly funneled back into the crowd like a wraith and snatched a loaf of bread from a nearby vendor's cart. Before the merchant could protest, she was gone, the freshly baked baguette tucked securely under her arm.

She waded through the opposite way of the masses and halted in front of the child, offering the bread to him. He looked up at her, wide-eyed and nervous.

"It's for you." She placed the bread in his lap.

"But it's stolen," he countered. "They'll take my hand for this."

"Not if I take theirs first," she whispered with a wink. "You let me worry about them. Now, get out of sight and *eat* before you collapse."

"Why are you doing this?" he asked.

She blinked. "Someone helped me once, so this is me giving it back." The gold bracelet she had swiped slid down her arm and fell into her palm. Her lips pressed into a thin line as she glanced at it and tossed it into his lap alongside the bread. "Take that while you're at it. Spend it wisely."

The boy took a hesitant bite of the baguette. "Thank you, miss."

She gave a stiff nod before lifting a finger and pointing down the nearest alleyway. "Thank me by living. Now, go."

Esmyra was relieved when the child listened and turned from her, disappearing into the shadows.

The theft, however, hadn't gone unnoticed.

The corners of her lips tilted as she turned to face three guards rushing through the crowd. Their armor glinted in the midday sun as they gave chase, screaming at her to halt.

Esmyra pointed to her chest and glanced from side to side, as if they could mean anyone else. "Surely, you can't mean me." Her voice feigned innocence, and when their steps didn't falter, she grinned at them defiantly. "Well, let's have a little fun then, shall we?"

Esmyra took off in a sprint through the labyrinthine alleys, dodging carts and leaping over crates, laughing at their attempt to capture her.

They had no idea who or what she was. A brave, knowing man would halt his efforts—a wiser man would *run*.

When a narrow gap appeared between two towering warehouses, barely wide enough to squeeze through, she dashed between them, her cloak catching and tearing on the withered bricks.

Esmyra willed her skin to shift, blending in with the bricks at her back as an octopus would within coral—all that would've been seen were her clothes, clinging to a phantom form.

Once they ran past her shadowy alcove, shouting their slurs and curses for a thief, she emerged on the opposite side, where the streets were much quieter. Breathing heavily, she leaned against the cold stone wall, a triumphant smile playing across her lips as she caught the whisperings of courtly gossip. She snickered as she ducked behind an abandoned street cart and listened as a few women walked past, camouflaging herself once more.

Any information she and her crew gathered while making port was vital—it was their only lifeline to the latest happenings in the realm since they were typically adrift at sea for weeks at a time. Everything she knew was *The Night Wraith*, crewed by men and creatures of every kingdom as they served their cursed captain.

"Has your husband sent a letter home yet?" one of them asked the other as they strolled by wearing gowns made of expensive silks and lace.

"The last I heard was they planned to make port in Anchorage Cove," the other answered.

Esmyra's brows furrowed as she listened.

The woman cleared her throat before continuing. "It makes me nervous. He mentioned King Rowe is trying to learn more about Maerinys, but to send our husbands to the most dangerous island of Rymelle is unsettling. Even if the Phoenix is leading the mission."

*Lephyrin's Phoenix is going to be in Anchorage Cove?* Esmyra's eyes flared.

"Maerinys? Isn't that forbidden?" the other asked, stopping in her tracks.

It was. Everyone in Rymelle knew that to so much as mention the sunken kingdom, Maerinys, resulted in punishment from their king—the realm's law stated it was demanded by the remaining gods. It was as if they wanted to erase the fourth kingdom of Rymelle from history.

People rarely questioned it aloud, and when they did, it often resulted in the loss of their tongue.

The crew of *The Night Wraith* had sailed the majority of Rymelle's seas, but still, there was so much uncovered about Maerinys. The unknown of it all only piqued her curiosity all the more.

Esmyra allowed her skin to shift back into its normal hue and stood from behind the cart. "It is," she announced, startling them. "Forbidden."

The two women exchanged horrified glances, caught in the act of speaking of their king's treason against the gods.

One of them narrowed her eyes. "Hasn't anyone told you it's rude to listen in on private conversations?" she spat.

Esmyra smirked as she moved around the cart, clasping her hands behind her back as she stepped up to the woman. She gestured to their surroundings. "Doesn't appear to be in private to me."

The woman's jaw locked, eyes roaming over Esmyra in disgust. "You will back away from me, or I'll scream for the guards."

Esmyra leaned in closer, and the woman arched her back in response. A second later, the world shimmered, and a slight tightening tugged at Esmyra's eyes as they shifted—her once round pupils morphed into slits, dilating as the woman's stare remained locked on hers.

"You will tell me all you know of King Rowe and his plans." Esmyra compelled the woman with only a glance of her eyes, her demand wrapping around her victim's mind like ribbons before she sank her talons in.

The irresistible command had the woman's back straightening, and Esmyra grinned as goosebumps lined her collarbones.

"My husband spoke of King Rowe hunting for gold and riches beyond comprehension left behind in Maerinys."

Venom-fused talons slipped from Esmyra's fingertips with ease while she inspected them as if bored. "Interesting. Considering it's all likely tarnished from being lost in the sea, anyway." She met the woman's frozen gaze again. "Imagine risking the wrath of the gods for something so unknown?"

"Yes. The concern of the sailors is the wrath of gods," she admitted.

Esmyra sucked on her tooth before saying, "And these sailors are in Anchorage Cove? How long will they be there?"

The other woman gasped out in horror, and Esmyra raised a talon at her in warning as her gaze held steady on the one she compelled.

The woman blinked. "The last I heard, they were headed there. They are not to return until they find evidence of Maerinys. So, for only the gods know how long."

"Aye, that's very interesting," Esmyra admitted, straightening her blouse and cloak.

Millions of people had perished and drowned with their homes, but King Rowe was a tyrant, and all he cared about was the possibility of uncovering troves of gold and treasures.

"You will *never* speak of this interaction." She glanced at the other woman, who wasn't compelled, and she nodded rapidly in agreement. "*Say it,*" she demanded.

"I will never speak of this interaction," she echoed, her eyes glazed over.

Esmyra smirked. "Such a good girl." She crossed her arms and gestured to the crowd beyond with her chin. "Now, get out of my sight."

The woman blinked and turned from her, doing as she was told, and the other followed after her with hurried footsteps.

Esmyra's gaze trailed them until they disappeared into the masses once more, their nervous whispers fading with them.

Why would the king risk the wrath of the gods? Surely gold couldn't be the only answer. Her mind spun with everything they had revealed, and with a quick glance in each direction, she weaved through the jostling crowd in search of her crew.

Making port in Lephyrin would be much shorter-lived than she originally planned. However, now that she held the knowledge of the king sending his Phoenix out to sea—*her* sea—in search of forbidden, unfathomable treasures, she knew she had to get back to *The Night Wraith* to inform her captain of what King Rowe was up to.

And how they would beat them to it.

CHAPTER 2

*Esmyra*

Esmyra's tail stirred the water as her webbed fingers held onto a cluster of jagged rocks off Lephyrin's coast, watching the docks as her crew snuck away. Once they boarded their pinnace, they quickly rowed out of the harbor and toward the sea, where *The Night Wraith* awaited in a cove.

She dove back into the water and soared beneath the surface, the sea embracing her. Esmyra's long, midnight hair swayed gracefully like flowing ink while her cerulean tail shimmered with iridescent scales that matched those shielding her bare breasts. Upon touching the seawater, the markings her skin had carried since birth shimmered, creating a subtle glow that bathed her surroundings in a turquoise light.

On land, the birthmarks resembled fiery red burns searing across her arms and down her spine, but beneath the ocean's surface, they transformed as she did, as if they were delighted to be returning home. Esmyra never knew how or why it occurred and gave up on answers long ago.

Unbeknownst to her crew, she followed in the small boat's wake, gliding just below the surface. Her tail, a sleek blade of muscle, cut effortlessly through the water, barely forming a ripple.

Within the sea, Esmyra was stealth incarnate—a wraith beneath the tides.

As she chased after her crew, her mind reeled with everything she compelled the woman to say. The king was after treasure, willing to risk angering the gods over it. If the mortal king refused to cower away from the gods, then she decided there was no reason she shouldn't either.

There were three great kingdoms remaining within the Realm of Rymelle. Each territory had its own race, all of whom were servants to their ruling god. In return, the god bestowed gifts upon their inhabitants.

The elven Kingdom of Sumnae possessed gifts of mind and sight, which were given by worshipping Vydenne, the Goddess of Illusion.

The nymph and woodland Kingdom of Terrana possessed extraordinary gifts that allowed them to manipulate the elements of weather and soil by the God of Growth, Villaem.

And lastly, Irah, the God of Rage and War, was the ruling god of the mortal kingdom, Lephyrin. While his subjects possessed no gifts of magic, they were avid warriors and fighters—a race of destruction.

Rymelle once consisted of *four* kingdoms, one of them being the sunken Kingdom of Maerinys. Legends claimed the kingdom sank when the sea goddesses, Naerysa and Kaelypso, vanished without a trace.

It was that which resulted in the remaining gods to retreat behind the veil. They chose to no longer walk the same soil as their subjects, and instead observed from beyond.

But they were never far, always keeping a watchful eye.

Esmyra believed it was also how her father was easily able to claim the sea as his all that time ago—the absence of the sea goddesses allowed for an easy conquest. And with the power of his secret weapon, there was no one to challenge his claim, aside from herself.

The crew rounded the first bend in the land, now out of sight from the docks, and she poked her head above the surface alongside the pinnace.

"Esmyra, why'd ya have us leave so soon? We'd barely been there half a day before you rushed us out."

Esmyra floated onto her back, her eyes roaming over the elven male. She observed the sharp tips of his ears as they poked out from the confines of his golden headscarf, a testament to the kingdom he abandoned to sail the seas on *The Night Wraith*.

It was uncommon for her father to take in outsiders to man the ship of nightmares. But every now and then, if there were survivors from their attacks who didn't cower beneath Captain Blackwood's gaze, they would be offered a position on the crew, granting them power and stability in the sea. If they declined the generous offer, they would be granted an instant death instead.

A violent one.

It was why *The Night Wraith* was crewed by every race that inhabited the Realm of Rymelle. Neither Cyrus or Esmyra cared of the powers or appearance of who they sailed with—what they cared about was loyalty. Show loyalty to their captain and they were untouchable in the seas, break his trust and they would find themselves sent to the depths faster than they could feel regret.

"I'm sorry, Riven, but is there a reason you deem it necessary to question my orders?" The edge in her tone made the rest of the crew straighten, remaining silent in their seats as she gripped the edge of the boat, grinning up at them.

"Of course not!" There was a slight panic in his voice. Esmyra tilted her head to the side in challenge. "It was just a question, is all. We had been set to remain in Lephyrin for a few nights, and I'm sure Captain will want an explanation."

"Aye, and who's acting captain in Cyrus's absence?"

"You, Esmyra."

She pursed her lips as her stare drifted over the crew. "Information regarding the king was presented to me, and the captain will need to know immediately. It may derail any plans we had for the foreseeable future. That's all I'll grant you, and you're barely even deserving of that." She winked, and Riven visibly relaxed.

Esmyra sighed. Each second that ticked by made her more eager to present her findings to her father. "I fear I've lost my patience for your slowness."

A few laughs rang out from the crew.

"Well, by all means...a little boost would be appreciated," Jak, a male of woodland descent, called from the front. He was one of the few Esmyra genuinely enjoyed the company of, deeming him the closest being she had to an actual friend.

With a subtle smirk tilting her lips, she lowered her hand to the churning water beneath the pinnace. Her eyes began to glow, exuding an ethereal, icy light as she summoned her powers to wield the tides. The waves instantly responded at her will, and the water around the pinnace surged, propelling the small boat swiftly through the currents as she held on tight, being dragged alongside them.

The crew quickly tightened their grip on their oars and lifted them to ensure they weren't ripped from their grasp as they soared over the waves.

"*Kaelypso's tits*!" Jak bellowed with a laugh as the crew gripped the rail to avoid flying overboard, the wind whipping their hair violently. "A warning would've been nice!"

"Your challenge *was* the warning," Esmyra mused, and a few wicked chuckles escaped them all as her powers glided them through a narrow channel, veiled by creeping mist and towering cliffs.

The cove opened into a tranquil lagoon, its waters a glassy emerald, while the air was heavy with the scent of salt and damp earth.

The crew finally reached their anchored ship and found Captain Blackwood waiting at its bow. Before they climbed up to the deck to meet him, Jak offered Esmyra his coat to hide her bare body as she shifted back into her mortal guise.

Their captain didn't greet them willingly, nor was there kindness in his eyes as they roamed over each of them individually, halting on Esmyra.

His dark gaze met hers with a mixture of irritation and concern beneath deeply furrowed brows. Cyrus stood with his arms crossed, the edges of his long coat billowing in the wind. "Back already? What in all fucking gods happened out there?"

"Father," Esmyra greeted as she stepped forward, water pooling at her feet while the crew shifted uneasily around her. "We need to speak. I overheard information in Lephyrin that I think you'll want to know, and we need to move fast if we're in agreement."

Blackwood lifted a single brow. "Aye? You *overheard* something?" His tone made it clear he knew that wasn't necessarily the case, and she had to suppress a grin. "And what news might this be?"

Esmyra let out a huff through her nostrils. "It's matters that would best be discussed in private, Captain." She flashed him a menacing smile.

His jaw locked, eyes raking over the crew once more. "Get to your stations and ready the ship."

Cyrus turned on his heel and strode toward his office with Esmyra a step behind him, leaving the crew to tend to their own.

Blackwood's office was carved out of the ship's stern, lined with tall windows that arched across the back wall. Esmyra confidently strode towards the center of the room, feeling the intensity of her father's gaze as he took his seat at his massive, weathered desk. Its surface was scarred with dagger marks, scorch trails, and ink stains, while maps and charts lay scattered across it.

She took in the sight of her father—hair black as night, similar to her own, only he had eyes that nearly matched. His face bore the lines of a man who had spent a lifetime beneath the sun at sea, but now it was etched with the unmistakable shadow of rage. Esmyra stood before him, unyielding, challenging him as he tried to make her feel small.

"Do you have an explanation for me, or shall we get on with punishment for your defiance?"

An annoyed cackle slipped from her. "Defiance."

"Do you have another word for disobeying orders? You were to remain in Lephyrin for three days. Loot what you could. Stay hidden... Get *something* of value in the slightest. Yet you stand before your captain empty-handed."

Esmyra didn't always see eye-to-eye with her father. While she enjoyed the thrill of looting, she truthfully never wanted to deal with the politics of actually being in charge. It was the reason she never challenged him for the title of captain.

"I'm the acting captain once the crew touches the soil of the realm." Her tone held every bit of the defiance he accused her of. "Since you're physically unable to step on the land, the call was mine to make. I deemed it necessary to return upon hearing news of King Rowe and what he's planning."

"You're the first mate of *The Night Wraith*." He pounded his finger on the wooden desk three times. "You're second-in-command and—"

"Second-in-command or *weapon*?" she cut him off, her temper showing as the gills on her neck flared.

Esmyra thought of all the power she held within herself, and how the fearsome Cyrus Blackwood would be just as any other ancient, washed-up pirate who sailed the seas. For if it weren't for her influence to control the tides and the minds of men, he would be nothing— *have* nothing.

But the realm didn't know that.

"Esmi..."

His nickname for her had always been her weakness, but she knew its use came at a cost. A trip of guilt for what she had thrown in his face so carelessly.

She let out a huff as her nostrils flared, but her eyes softened when they met his. "Tell me I'm wrong. Look me in my eyes, Father, and tell me I'm not used as a mere tool for your bidding."

Cyrus was once a man, a human born into the Kingdom of Lephyrin, who quickly made his way from a privateer to no longer being a sword for hire. And then, over nine centuries ago, when the Kingdom of Maerinys sank to the depths, the man was gifted eternal life. But it wasn't a gift at all.

It was a curse that bound him to the sea, bestowed upon him by the gods for all his wicked deeds.

The captain leaned back in his chair, scratching at his beard. "Esmi, you know why things are the way they are. The reason they always have been and always will be. I cannot set foot on land."

She lifted a brow as a smirk played across her sharp lips. "You could," she mocked.

He scoffed and let out a harsh chuckle. "Aye, and what would you have me do?" He stood from his seat and slowly walked toward her. "Have my lungs mimic as if they're drowning in the sea? Have a misty haze plague my eyes, just how it would be beneath the tides? Or become repulsed at even the mere thought of food, having it only taste like salt and brine?"

Cyrus towered over her now, grinning as she listened to the reminder of all his curse entailed.

Esmyra had heard this speech countless times throughout the centuries. She was well aware of the reason he never set foot on the realm's land. But it never deterred her from provoking him whenever he became entirely too irritating.

"All I was saying is that you could—for you would not perish." She crossed her arms.

He barked out a harsh laugh as he took a step back from her, both not knowing if they should continue to argue or laugh off the disagreement.

"Aye, Esmi. I would only be driven to madness within mere minutes." Chuckles rumbled from him as he made his way back to his desk, shaking his head.

Esmyra often wondered how remaining aboard *The Night Wraith* for centuries hadn't forced him into insanity already. She always believed herself to be a slave to the depths, but it was her father who truly was. While she could shift from a mortal form to that of a siren, he remained as he was: heartless, brutal, and *trapped*.

"Madness aside, will your stubborn ears listen to why we've returned? Or do I have to incite obedience?" She winked at him, the world sharpening as her pupils shifted from round to a vertical slit.

"You wouldn't dare." The teasing in his tone vanished.

It was the one rule for her aboard his ship—her power was to never be used against him, though it often crossed her mind.

Esmyra lifted a brow as she placed her hands on her hips.

"Fine," he huffed. "What is it that made you return here so *eagerly*?"

She clasped her hands behind her back and stalked over to the desk before hopping on it, sitting atop his maps and weaponry that were strewn across the wood carelessly.

Esmyra combed through every detail she heard, recognizing that her father often refused to sail near any waters in the south, but he hardly ever gave a reason as to why. She didn't think it would cause any harm to leave that little tidbit out, knowing he would only care about the riches the king was after. Her only desire was to prevent the king from claiming the treasure, since he would only exploit it for his own selfish gains.

"King Rowe has his Phoenix sniffing out lost gold," she said before picking up an apple from his desk and taking a bite. "Rumors claim they're headed to Anchorage Cove."

"The Phoenix?!" Her father's eyes slowly widened as her lips tilted up. "Draevyn Rowe? You're sure?"

She only gave a curt nod, accompanied by a menacing gleam in her eyes.

"And you want to do what, exactly?" he asked with a raised brow. "Beat them to the gold?"

"Aye." Esmyra leapt down from the desk and leaned over it, looking him in the eye. "We're going to rip it from their grasp, and rid the realm of the Phoenix while we're at it."

This time, he was the one who smirked. "You are your father's daughter." He paused for a moment, his onyx eyes raking over her. "Ready the ship."

He pulled a dagger from his hip and slammed the blade into the map sprawled across the table, the weapon making its mark exactly where they now intended to sail. "Well, let's give Lephyrin's Phoenix a *warm* welcome to our headquarter port, shall we?" His words dripped with wicked anticipation.

"Aye," she answered, her grin matching his. "Let's."

Beneath the dim candlelight, kohl-lined, sapphire eyes stared back at Esmyra through the mirror. Lifting her hand, she gently placed it on the edge of the once intricate champagne frame, which now more resembled a tarnished piece of rubbish discarded by a king.

Her gaze wandered over every visible aspect of her appearance—from the blue-black hair that fell in waves down to the center of her back, the multiple silver rings that hung from her ears, and the ridiculous layered dress that had a corset cinching her waist into near nothingness. She pulled on a pair of knee-high leather boots she had swiped from a closet down the hall and worked to lace them up over the hosiery that clung to her legs.

As she stared at the stockings, she thought they appeared to be better suited for fishing than attire, but this was supposedly what men sought when searching for a woman to take into their bed. Not that she would know, for she hadn't had a desire for it in centuries. Any man or male who dared get too close to her found themselves beneath her spell, and their method of approach determined whether she offered them mercy or forced them to fall upon their own blade.

Taking a step back, she stood in the center of a rented room in the Kraken's Alehouse—a rundown tavern in the center of Anchorage

Cove, the boisterous haven for rumrunners and criminals of the sea. The music and rowdiness of the rooms below shook the floor and rattled the walls as the pub filled with guests.

It sounded like home.

The skirts of her dress flowed down to her feet, and she bunched up one side, tucking it into its belt to show off the fishnets hugging her muscular thighs. Bending the knee of her exposed leg, she angled it to the side and let out an aggravated huff as she continued to nitpick everything that clung to her curves.

"Well, Esmi, you look like any other brothel's daughter down there," Jak joked from where he sat across the room, watching her.

She turned to him, giving him an unamused look, and all he could do was raise a brow at her in challenge.

"Your presence here is hardly necessary. Any of you, for that matter," she grumbled.

Once *The Night Wraith* reached Anchorage Cove, they opted to anchor their ship around the bend to avoid being seen by the Phoenix's crew, who had already disguised themselves to blend with the crowd of the isle. Esmyra's plan was to compel Captain Draevyn Rowe for information needed—pry whatever she could from his mind before disposing of him, simultaneously eliminating one of their largest threats.

Jak stood and stalked toward her. "No one should deem themselves able to go up against the Phoenix alone, Esmyra. He's dangerous. Just as dangerous as you are."

She let out a sharp laugh. "I'm not afraid to play with a little fire, Jak." She shot him a malicious grin, to which he rolled his eyes.

Draevyn Rowe wasn't just any mortal prince—he was a *fire-wielder*. The only one known to exist in all of Rymelle.

Lephyrin's king loathed being considered the weakest of all races and kingdoms. Rumors claimed that when his second son, Draevyn, was born, barely a year after his heir, he brought them both to Irah's temple and bartered for their gifts. It's been said that the god's asking price was to place a piece of his violent soul within the infants. The king eagerly agreed, anticipating the fear it would instill in other kingdoms.

And it worked.

Atlas, the firstborn and heir, was granted the power of shadows and smoke, renowned for blinding enemies and casting them into darkness. Draevyn, however, received Irah's raging flames, granting him the renowned name of Lephyrin's Phoenix.

She'd heard whisperings over the years that Draevyn often took to the sea on voyages to meet with the other kingdoms, likely to ensure they remained in line when it came to their trades. While Draevyn wasn't the heir to the kingdom, he was still royalty. Though kingdom gossip claimed he had no desire for his title and only made appearances in Lephyrin when a threat presented itself.

King Rowe didn't have hired goons out looking for a lost kingdom of gold. Esmyra knew that since the king had his own son out searching, he must not trust anyone else to look for answers. Regardless of the fact that it was forbidden by the gods, he couldn't have the other kingdoms catching wind of this—it would put them all at even further odds with their struggle for power.

"This isn't a fucking game." Jak's voice cut through the room like a blade.

She stepped up to him, and though she was a foot shorter, she made sure to make him feel significantly smaller by staring at him down the bridge of her nose. "You forget your place, Jak."

"A bit difficult to do such things. However, I'm the only one ever looking out for you, Esmi. All gods know your father is barely capable of it."

Her brows furrowed as she stared up at him, her chest heaving. "A foolish waste of time, if you ask me."

"Well, luckily, I didn't ask you. Everyone needs help sometimes. Even if they're too stubborn to admit it."

She took a step back to get a better view of him, her eyes roaming his body as his stance remained rigid. "Do you truly think there is any scenario where he would have the upper hand on me?"

"Draevyn is the *Phoenix*. He's no normal man," he challenged.

"And this is unknown territory to him and his men," Esmyra shot back. "In no realm would he win in a fight against me. It also won't even come to such things. The plan is to compel him for the information the moment he stands before me."

Jak's nostrils flared.

"Besides, water beats fire every time." She winked.

"Aye," Jak whispered as he rubbed his temples. "The crew should all be in their places by now, scattered about the room and blending in. I'll go join them so we don't arrive together."

"Good riddance," she growled.

Grinning, he gave her a quick wink. "Try not to kill anyone when they stare at you, gorgeous," he said before leaving the room.

After one last glance at herself in the mirror, she huffed out a breath and followed Jak's footsteps toward the door that was nearly falling off its hinges. Obnoxious, drunken voices and deafening music slammed into her the moment she pulled it open. Her feet carried her down the rickety, creaking stairs until she halted near the bottom.

Laughter and shouts filled the air of The Kraken's Alehouse, mingling with the music of a drunken fiddler by the door. Lanterns hung from iron hooks throughout the room, while the bar itself was a massive slab of dark wood spanning the back wall. Scattered throughout the room were rough-hewn tables littered with dice, mugs of ale, and the occasional pile of coins or gems gleaming in the lantern light—the pirates of Rymelle filling nearly every seat.

Esmyra's eyes drifted around the room until they finally landed on the king's son, huddled in the back corner with a few of his men. She took the last step off the staircase, the untucked edges of her layered dress drifting over the sandy, ale-covered floorboards.

With each step she took into the room, the distinct scent of rum and salty sea air wafted through her nostrils as she surveyed the motley crew of pirates and rogues who occupied the tavern. Some eyed her with curiosity, while others leered with unmistakable desire as she approached the center.

Leaning against the worn wooden bar, she caught the eye of the stout barmaid, who gave her a subtle nod. Esmyra knew she'd recognize her, even beneath the disguise—the crew of *The Night Wraith* had been here enough. Without a word, she reached into a small pouch tied to the belt of her dress and placed a few coins on the counter before her.

The barmaid's hand swept the coins into the folds of her apron before handing Esmyra a pint of ale, and she took a swig as she turned away from the counter.

A graceful, lethal hum fell from her lips, echoing softly between the rhythms of the playing music. It was a soft, melodic song that wrapped itself around her victims' minds and held them hostage until she could strike. While she could only ever compel her victims with her eyes, her siren's song would hold them in a lucid trance. Their movements and breathing slowed, their world would sway, and their wills would be dimmed to a mere flickering candle flame.

A tavern was the perfect place to cast it, where the crowd was already drunk or nearly there, giving the same effect.

Weaving through the crowd, she continued her symphony of manipulation. For in a world where trust was a rarity, Esmyra was more than aware that the greatest power of the realm lay in the art of deception.

Easily slipping into the role, she toyed with a lock of her hair as it cascaded over her shoulder, beckoning to the men who gazed at her with coy grins. With each table she passed, she gave a flirtatious look or playful smile, her humming arousing desire in the eyes of the onlookers.

Her gaze locked on Jak as he played his role with ease on a stool near the tavern's door, acting as if he were numerous ales deep as his hands trailed up a true courtesan's skirt. Esmyra shot him a quick smirk while subtly lifting her mug of ale in approval, and he gave her a dip of his chin before returning his attention to the woman in his lap. As her gaze wandered about the tavern, she found the stations of most of her crew, knowing they all secretly watched her whereabouts, waiting for an order or the need to strike.

When she turned to aim for Draevyn, a massive hand clamped down on her waist, pulling her forcefully against its owner's clammy body. Esmyra's face bounced off his chest, and her eyes instantly shifted as fury surged through her at the unexpected touch of a man.

"Come here, darlin'. I'll give you a cock to sit on," the drunk man slurred over the music and laughter surrounding them.

"Release me," she demanded, her voice stern.

"No can do," he taunted as he held her in place.

She lifted her head from his chest, not bothering to will her eyes back into their human form, and stared up at him. The moment his laughter slowed, he glanced down as he clutched her to his sweat-covered front, and all signs of amusement fell from his filthy face.

It sent a jolt of satisfaction through her. Her stare quickly found a few members of the crew, all of their eyes locked on them. She took note of the wrath on Jak's face while he watched her, completely ignoring the woman kissing the nook of his neck.

"W-wi-*witch*," the man stuttered out, locked in a trance of fear.

Esmyra tilted her head to the side and tsked. "Not quite." She flashed him a wicked grin as the tips of her canines elongated for only a second before returning to their usual length. She could feel the man's heart pounding rapidly in his chest.

"What is the meaning of this?" A deep voice holding a near growl made her eyes flare, and she shifted them back to their usual form.

Draevyn Rowe now stood before them, hand on the hilt of his sword as it hung from its sheath.

The drunken man then shoved her into Draevyn, who caught her on instinct in his arms. When she turned to face the drunken fool, he ran off, pushing through the crowd a moment later.

"Coward," she hissed before peering up into the Phoenix's gold-flecked, whiskey eyes. Her stare drifted down to one of his hands that refused to loosen his hold on her waist.

"Are you alright?" he asked as his eyes roamed over Esmyra's body.

Curiosity struck her then. Draevyn was *worried* for her. He thought he was rescuing a damsel in distress...when the only person he rescued was the foul man who ran off.

*How delightful.*

"Yes. Thank you for helping me," she answered as she kept her breathing heavy, pretending to be unarmed and frazzled.

She straightened her stance as he leisurely removed his hold on her. Once his eyes were through inspecting her, Draevyn offered a curt nod. "I will be on my way then, miss."

He moved to turn around. Eyes flaring, Esmyra reached out on instinct and draped her hand delicately over his shoulder, turning him back to face her before pressing her chest against his.

Draevyn gave her a knowing look with a forced tilt to his lips and let out a huff. "Though you're very beautiful, I'm afraid I'm not interested in your services. Perhaps you should call it a night. I would hate to see you end up in the wrong bed. One of a man much more brutal than myself."

Esmyra licked her lips seductively and didn't miss his stare drifting to the movement of it with a slightly raised brow. He looked as if he was silently pleading with her to not challenge his bluff.

"I think you're much more brutal than you lead on, Captain." Her voice was like smoke and honey.

His eyes widened, and this time, when he smirked, she sensed it was more than genuine.

Suddenly, a drunk, cloaked passerby slammed into their sides, spilling his ale all over both of them as he stumbled about without mumbling an apology. Esmyra didn't have to look to know it was Jak, as if he were urging her to get a move on.

Draevyn grabbed her wrist lightly. "Gods, this place is a fucking nightmare. I have a table in the back. Come with me so I can at least get you out of the center of the madness."

Esmyra had to suppress a grin as the Phoenix brought her to a secluded corner. He escorted her to an empty booth, only a table away from where his crew lay in wait, and gestured to the seat. She slid in a moment later as he sat across from her.

The captain waved to the barmaid, and she brought over two mugs of ale. This couldn't have been more perfect—the more booze the man gushed down, the easier it would be to pry his secrets from him. She would hardly need to make a scene, though his crew remaining so close posed a small issue.

Esmyra felt the eyes of her crew digging into her back. With subtle glances around the room, she caught several of their pistols hidden and aimed directly at Draevyn and his crew members.

Draevyn's gaze found hers, and the siren within her thrashed. It was as if it recognized him—or recognized the threat he was. Her pulse hammered in her ears, not fully understanding what was happening within her.

"Have a name, love?" he asked.

Her eyes glided over him for a few moments before answering, "Esmi." She opted for her nickname, and she wasn't entirely sure why.

"Esmi," he mimicked, as if working to taste the name on his tongue. "Well, Esmi, where were we? Ah, yes. How is it you know I'm a captain?"

Esmyra's stare roamed over him, taking in the Phoenix's disguise. He wore a filthy, loose-fitted shirt, rolled up to his elbows, showing off numerous scars. She recalled his worn leather belt, strapped with numerous weaponry—a cutlass, daggers, and two pistols. And then her stare lifted to the bandana tied loosely above his brow as his dark hair poked out beneath. Its fabric was a deep scarlet color, possibly to resemble the countless blood he'd spilled or the flames he wielded.

Draevyn Rowe's disguise was certainly a convincing one to the untrained eye, until her stare fell to his hand resting on the table.

Her fingers gently danced across the table until they trailed along his own resting atop the splintering wood, her touch tracing over his ring. "You wear the mark of a king, Captain. Was an easy guess." She winked, and his eyes flared as if he was just now realizing he forgot to remove one of the few things that could give his identity away. "Tell me. What's a man such as yourself doing in Anchorage Cove?"

He cleared his throat, and she leaned back in the booth, making sure her bottom lip pouted outwards as her breasts peaked in his direction. His eyes drank her in as he gulped down a sip from his mug.

"You don't have to do all your acting around me, love. Don't waste your efforts. My statement from before remains." Another swig of ale. "Bold of you to continue to try to throw yourself at a known man of the king."

Esmyra's jaw locked, and she placed her hand on her lap beneath the table as her talons threatened to extend at the sudden surge of anger. "And what efforts do you speak of?" Her voice feigned innocence.

"For one, I can tell you're no true member of a brothel. At least not of this isle, and if you are, well...you aren't very good at it." Her brow furrowed. "Men were ready to throw coin at you left and right, yet you didn't take any of them on their offers and instead continued to waltz right by. In *my* direction, may I add." All hints of seduction dropped from her face. "No need to act with me. Now, why is it you wanted my attention? Consider it received."

*What the fuck?*

Her eyes darted back and forth between his, trying to think of where to steer the conversation. Aggravation flooded her.

The way the man looked at her, challenge in his eyes yet a hint of lust, made her believe seduction wasn't entirely off the table. Perhaps he was just looking for something a bit *more*.

Now, she could play this one of two ways—force her way into his secrets as planned, which would surely end in a blood bath with both of their crews lingering. Or she could attempt to get aboard his ship, where even more secrets regarding the crown could emerge.

She didn't hate that new idea. A burst of excitement surged through her at the thought of uncovering more of Lephyrin's treachery and wielding it against their tyrant king.

Esmyra swallowed, praying to the lost sea goddesses that her acting would be convincing. "A man of the king may not be as cruel as those who reside at this isle. Would you not agree, Captain? Many eyes and hands have felt entitled to my body."

His brows furrowed slightly. "If you're truly in this line of work, then there's not much I can do for the behavior of the men in Anchorage Cove. Perhaps a new way to earn coin would better suit you."

"Do you have a ship in the harbor, Captain?"

Draevyn cleared his throat. "I do." His voice was rough, as if irritated by her question.

Esmyra swallowed and hesitated before asking, "And what would you charge a mere woman like myself to board your ship to start a new life somewhere?" She paused. "Not all ships are safe for such things."

His stare softened as he looked over her once more, and that was when she knew continuing to play the damsel in distress would be the best approach. Draevyn leaned back in his seat and let out a sigh as he scratched at his facial scruff—a dark brown color that showed hints of red in the lantern light, much like his hair. "I wouldn't charge a woman coin for refuge or seeking safe travels to a better life."

*A better life.* As if women in the line of work she was claiming to be had a better life in his kingdom, using their bodies and any form of drug they could get their hands on to make their lives more bearable.

A false smile leisurely climbed her lips. "Then you are very kind."

His smile moved to match hers, but then turned menacing. "I wouldn't say that, love. But if you're looking to leave this isle, I'll grant you safe passage to another port. We leave just after dawn. We were only passing through."

"And what brought the king's men here in the first place?" She pushed, and his smile dropped.

"That's the business of the crown."

"Aye," she whispered. "Of course. Apologies, Captain..." she dragged out the word, wondering if he would provide his name willingly, but he only gave her a wary look. "Do I get to know my soon-to-be savior's name? You know mine. 'Tis only fair I know yours."

He cleared his throat. "Captain will do for now."

Esmyra's lips twitched into a smirk. If he wished to play games of the mind, he would soon learn that she never lost. "Aye...*Captain.*"

# CHAPTER 4

# Esmyra

The first light of dawn painted the sky in hues of pink and gold, casting a soft glow over the beach where Esmyra sat alone. With her legs drawn up to her chest and arms wrapped around her knees, she gazed out at the endless expanse of the ocean, lost in thought.

Her thoughts plagued her every so often. Despite how much she enjoyed her life and the tales men spoke of her while out at sea, a sense of incompleteness clung to her. It was an aching void in her chest that nothing seemed to ease.

The daughter and weapon of the realm's most notorious pirate, whose reputation spread far and wide across every sea. But in private, she was simply Esmyra—a slave to her father's will. A monster that lingered beneath the tides, feared by all men and creatures alike.

The gentle rhythm of the waves lapping against the shore echoed in her ears. As the sun continued its ascent, her thoughts turned inward, reflecting on the life that had brought her to where she was. A life of thieving and deceit, of lies, bloodshed, and ruin.

What had driven her father to where he was today? The most feared man that sailed the sea, damning anyone who stood in their way. He wasn't always so ruthless when it came to using her abilities. His curse bound him to the salty coves, while she was condemned to remain a lonesome monster of the deep he sailed and ruled over. Some days, she saw the sea as nothing but a cage for them both, no matter how much it felt like home.

She always felt that the monster was more so something inside of her. Something she couldn't necessarily control, just waiting to break free. While the monster reveled in being a weapon, Esmyra occasionally felt remorseful for all she'd caused—that small bit of humanity she had left. It was a constant inner battle within herself, never knowing which way to lean.

The siren within her felt like sharing her skin with a shadow, pacing just beneath the surface of her flesh. She could feel it there, forever awake, coiling tight around her spine.

The worst part was that, on most occasions, she didn't mind it— when the fury sparked hot or the fear in someone's eyes made her pulse quicken in anticipation. Some days, she yearned to lean into it, aching to see how it would feel to let go.

Because the truth was, she wasn't sure where Esmyra ended and the siren began anymore. The lines had blurred over the last few centuries.

Footsteps sounded behind her, and she blew out a breath of premature annoyance, already knowing who and what was coming.

Jak sat beside her then, gazing out at the sea along with her. "I swear you just keep getting stupider."

She cackled. "Personally, I think it's genius."

"So it would seem," he let out on a breath.

"This ensures we can uncover everything occurring within Lephyrin. Just the fact that he has his son looking for the lost ki—" she cut herself off. "The treasure they spoke of."

"Captain will want you to just sink the ship."

"And that's also my plan," she admitted. "After I make sure I've learned all of his knowledge."

He huffed before turning to face her. "You could've done that in the tavern."

Esmyra's jaw tightened in irritation—mainly because he was right, but something in her was screaming to do what she intended now. "It would've been much more difficult. His entire crew was sprawled about, surrounding the two of us. If it became known he was under a trance, all hell would've broken loose. We were trying to be discreet. Also, imagine all the secrets on their boat. All the things I would never think to ask."

"So what's your plan, Esmi?"

She didn't want her father to realize the treasure they were after was in the very waters he vowed to never sail in—if he had trusted her with the reasoning of why, then maybe she would've hesitated. But the unknown of it all made her only want this more.

"I'll get aboard the ship, and once I have Draevyn alone, I'll pull whatever information from him I can and then dive even further if there is anything of value in his quarters or office."

"I'm coming with you."

Her neck snapped in his direction. "Absolutely fucking not, Jak."

"Relax there, gorgeous," he said as he pushed himself to his feet. "They'll never know." A second later, Jak took on his woodland form of an owl—his feathers several shades of shimmering silvers with piercing gold eyes.

Esmyra scoffed. She had always been jealous of the fact that the woodland shifters' magic absorbed their clothing. Meanwhile, whenever she shifted, she was entirely nude.

He gently landed on her shoulder, and she gave him an incredulous look, trying to hide a laugh that was begging to come out of her. "The answer is still no." A moment later, the bird took off, soaring through the sky and towards the harbor of Anchorage Cove.

"Bastard," she whispered to herself.

Calls from the dock in the far-off distance caught her attention, and she shaded her eyes from the sun, watching as Dracvyn's crew walked along the wood that stretched out over the harbor and toward their awaiting ship, *The Odyssey*.

This hadn't gone according to plan, but if Lephyrin's men desired to harm her while aboard, the consequences she'd inflict upon them would make hell appear gentle.

CHAPTER 5

*Draevyn*

"Ten coins says she doesn't show, Drae."

Draevyn stared into the streets of the rundown port, ignoring Samwell, his first mate.

"You told her to be here at dawn. Well, it's dawn, and still no sign of her. She likely just wanted your cock and presented you with a sob story from boredom when you declined her offer."

A breathy laugh left Draevyn. "If she's a true courtesan, she would've moved on into the next man's lap without hesitation." He turned to Samwell just in time to watch his shrug. "She was watching us. It's clear we were her target. I'm just not entirely convinced the reasoning was to leave the isle."

Truthfully, he knew this was madness. A man like him should know better. Was she bait in another man's pawn? It wouldn't be the first time a beautiful face sent a man straight to ruin. Too many tales began this way and ended in blood—or, in his case, ash.

When Draevyn laid eyes on Esmi in that tavern, it was akin to a bolt of lightning through the chest, waking him from a deep slumber. Her stare...gods help him. It had been haunting him since the moment they parted ways, as if her piercing blue gaze was seared into his soul the moment they locked eyes.

And then her *voice*. Her voice was like velvet gliding over his skin.

36

She was trouble—*that* he was certain of. Trouble, however, always seemed to beckon him into its grasp.

"And you think bringing her aboard is wise?" Samwell asked, snapping him from his trance. "Perhaps she knows who you truly are and thinks you could be an in with the crown."

"She doesn't strike me as the type." Draevyn sighed. "I also never told her my name. If she proves to be a dangerous person, it's not as if she could do much against an entire crew of men."

"All women want is a rich, powerful man. One that you scraped up from the depths of this gods-forsaken pirate haven is no different." Samwell chuckled. "All this aside, we're still no closer to finding this lost kingdom of riches your father has had us on the hunt for."

When Draevyn didn't answer, he continued. "You were certain that answers would be found at Anchorage Cove if any part of Maerinys is still reachable. We received nothing but threats...and a few added scars from said threats." Samwell glared at the gash down his arm.

"It's hardly my fault you were caught off guard in the middle of a tavern of criminals." Draevyn raised a brow. "But maybe you're right and she's not coming."

They made their way to the edge of the dock, and the moment Draevyn's foot touched down into the pinnace that would bring them to their awaiting ship, a call drifting on the wind stopped him in his tracks.

A woman with long, black hair was running toward them down the dock, her slender hands lifting the hem of her dress before stopping in front of them at its edge.

Out of breath, she huffed at them, "No five-minute leniency with the crown, I see."

Draevyn smirked. "You were told dawn."

Esmi lifted her hand to shield her eyes from the now blinding sun. "Aye. Apologies, Captain."

"*Aye*," Sam mocked her, and she shot a dagger-like glance in his direction. "Perhaps you should learn to speak a bit more proper if you wish to start a life beyond brothels there, miss."

He jumped down into the awaiting boat.

Her stare narrowed on him, but then a smile graced her face, though there was a tightening around her eyes. "I shall do my best to learn the more common way of speaking." Esmi gestured to the city behind her. "'Tis a bit difficult given the circumstances previously dealt. Would you not agree?"

"And is there a reason your hair is soaking wet while you made us wait for your arrival?" Samwell spat.

She grinned. "Went for a swim."

Draevyn stayed silent, watching their exchange.

*Esmi has fight in her.*

A curious thing for someone who was supposedly desperate to escape the life she claimed she had here. Though he was sure being here for a long while would make anyone more rough around the edges.

However, he couldn't shake his suspicions about her ulterior motives. His curiosity compelled him to ignore his better judgment and delve deeper. She was hiding something. He could see it in the way her hands hung loose at her sides while her eyes remained sharper than any blade.

Draevyn moved to stand at her side on the dock. "Arms out, love."

Her gaze shot to him. "Excuse me?"

"Did you think that just because you're a beautiful, young woman, that we wouldn't expect treachery from you? I need to check you for weapons... Captain's orders, I'm afraid." Draevyn winked.

"You *are* the captain," she growled.

"Something to hide?"

"Hardly." Her voice became lethally sweet as she lifted her arms out at her sides. "Do your worst, Captain."

*Gods,* this woman was already trouble.

He carefully guided his hands down her curves, being sure not to linger on any part. Moving down her arms, he tugged her sleeve up, and his eyes caught on a swirling red mark adorning her skin, resembling a burn.

Esmi ripped her arm from his grasp. "You may pat me down,

Captain, but if your eyes wish to remain on my bare skin, that will cost you." A threat lay beneath her words, catching him off guard.

"And would the cost be coin or my hand?" Draevyn taunted, but when her brows furrowed and the corner of her lip curved, it snapped him from his trance. He cleared his throat. "Apologies, Esmi. Ladies first," he said, gesturing to the awaiting boat.

Sam extended his arm toward her, but she didn't even offer a glance in his direction. Instead, she leapt down and took her seat along the bench without another word. His first mate gave him a wary look, as if he could already sense the trouble within her, just as Draevyn had.

He blew out a breath through his nostrils and took his place on the opposite end from Sam, and they began rowing back to their ship, *The Odyssey*.

With each heave of the oars, Draevyn watched Esmi sitting across from him.

"Ever been out at sea, miss?" Samwell interrupted the silence.

"Oh, yes, many times," she answered, gazing out at the sea.

The slight widening of her eyes made Draevyn raise a brow. Perhaps her story about being trapped in Anchorage Cove wasn't necessarily true.

"And when was the last time?" he interjected, his gaze locked on her as suspicion swirled in his gut.

"Many years ago," she answered calmly, all signs of her panic gone once more.

She looked his way and smiled, but an icy chill ran up his spine the moment they locked eyes. He immediately averted his gaze, feeling an odd uneasiness beneath her stare.

Once they reached the starboard side of the ship, the crew sent down a rope-woven ladder, dropping it into the pinnace so they could climb aboard. Samwell went first, easily climbing until he swung his body over the rails and onto the deck. They continued to watch the few other crew members among them until only Draevyn and Esmi remained.

"You know the rules. Ladies first," he cooed, and she gave him a look that made him believe she wished to give an eye-roll instead. "I'll catch you if you fall."

"Men," she huffed, and then turned to face him. "That won't be necessary, Captain." She stood from her seat and easily climbed the rope in her heeled thigh-high boots. Esmi quickly reached the top and perched herself on the rail. She gazed down at him with a smirk before swinging her legs over in tandem and disappearing over the rail's ledge.

"What a woman," Draevyn breathed before following her lead.

The moment Esmyra faced the crew aboard the ship, all eyes were on her, as if they had never seen a woman among them. A whistle shot out from the far edges of the crew, and her gaze whipped in its direction. She wanted nothing more than to reveal her true self, but doing so too early wouldn't prove useful.

The man who mocked the way she spoke on the dock was eyeing her warily, as if he could sense who and what she was. Or, perhaps, he just believed the usual bullshit that most pirates had—that having a woman aboard their ship would only anger the gods.

What men failed to remember was that the seas were once ruled by not one but two goddesses, Kaelypso and Naerysa.

Draevyn threw his leg over the rail and then stalked up next to her. "Everyone, this is Esmi. We'll be escorting her to our next port. You'll treat her as a guest of the royal house."

She subtly glanced down at the ring adorning his finger, which contained flames wrapped around an intricately drawn R—the seal of King Barrett Rowe.

Her eyes flicked back up to him to find that his gaze was now on her, watching her intently.

"All hands on deck!" he bellowed, his eyes never leaving hers. The crew leapt into action, dispersing across the ship to their designated assignments. Moments later, the sails unfurled, and the ship was soaring across the waves.

Esmyra seemed to be the only one who noticed a small shadow fly overhead as it eclipsed the sun, and she watched as the owl landed atop the crow's nest.

"Showoff," she muttered, suppressing a grin as Jak hid in plain sight.

She stood before the captain with her arms crossed behind her back, the sea breeze blowing her thick, black hair around her face as the gulls called their songs overhead.

"And is there an assignment for me, Captain?" she asked sweetly, almost taunting.

He sucked on his front teeth. "Come with me. I'll give you a tour of the ship."

Draevyn offered her his arm. Esmyra raised a brow in suspicion, wondering how this would all play out since she barely had a plan. She didn't have time for this—or the patience. However, if there was any chance of getting Draevyn alone to compel him, it may lay within these next few moments.

She linked her arm through his, and they started at the bow before circling around until they were at the stern. He brought her to the quarterdeck, where his first mate manned the wheel in his absence. She took note that it was the irritating man who was aboard the pinnace with them.

Esmyra offered a smile, but it went unreturned, and for a brief moment, she imagined shoving him overboard.

"May I steer the boat?" she asked as her fingertips played along the rough wood of the wheel.

"Absolutely not," the man answered.

"Samwell," Draevyn scolded, releasing his hold on her arm.

Samwell gave him a wry grin. "Draevyn."

Her eyes flared as the name finally slipped from someone, even if it wasn't the captain. While this whole time she knew exactly who and what he was, she had to play these next few moments carefully.

"Was that necessary?" Draevyn shot at Samwell.

"You alright there, Esmi?" Samwell taunted her. "You look as if you've seen a ghost."

When she lifted her chin to meet their stares, she found that Draevyn's whiskey eyes were watching her beneath furrowed brows—the gold in them shone brightly, mimicking the blaze held within him.

Esmyra knew she wasn't the only predator aboard this ship, but she needed to make sure that he believed *himself* to be the only one.

"Esmi." Draevyn's voice came out as a deep growl, snapping her out of her trance.

"Yes, I'm fine, of course. Though I'm happy to finally know my savior's name."

"Hm," he grunted out. "Sam, take her to the galley, where she can be put to work. And keep your mouth shut while you're at it."

The fucking *galley*? He planned to put her to work in the kitchen? She knew men were the most moronic of creatures, but even she hoped he would've been slightly more original.

Irritation surged in her. She *really* didn't have time for *this*. She could practically hear Jak's mocking laugh from up above.

If only her father could witness this now.

Samwell escorted her below deck and to the kitchen, where their cook was hard at work, chopping vegetables for the stew that nearly overflowed the pot atop a roaring fire.

"Tommy," Samwell greeted.

"And who be this, Sam?" the older man snapped, barely giving them a glance over his shoulder.

"Your new assistant. Captain's orders, I'm afraid." Samwell placed his hand between her shoulder blades and gave her a small shove into the room, which had Esmyra clenching her teeth to reel in her anger. "We're providing her safe passage to our next port."

"Drae's picking up strays now in pirate coves? What's gotten into that boy..."

Samwell cleared his throat. "My thoughts exactly."

"You know," she interjected. "I'm right here."

"Well aware. Now, be a good little lady for Tommy here, and

perhaps you'll survive the journey across the sea." Samwell turned his back to her and stormed back up the steps.

"Was that a threat?" she called up to him, but went unanswered.

Letting out a huff, she wondered if all this trouble was worth it. She should've just compelled Draevyn at the damn tavern and risked being caught. Her crew could've easily slain his—but then she would never find all the answers she sought regarding Maerinys.

"Was no threat, lady," Tommy called, making her turn back toward him. "Sam is all talk. He's just protective of the captain, is all. Besides, I'm sure you're aware by now that you're under the protection of the crown while aboard."

"Aye," she answered. "It appears so."

Esmyra stalked over to Tommy and rolled up her sleeves, the crimson runes covering her arms on full display. "What can I assist you with, Tommy?"

His eyes traced over the markings. "That's quite the mark, missy. How long did that take? And with such an odd color."

She cleared her throat and surprised herself by giving him an honest answer. "I don't remember. Was a long time ago, I'm afraid."

His stare drifted up to her face. "You don't look a day older than twenty-five, darlin', but it's none of my business."

"Just good genes, perhaps," she offered.

He let out a chuckle and gave her a wink. "Aye, perhaps."

There was something oddly comforting about Tommy. He reminded her somewhat of her father when they were behind closed doors, when he could let his ruthless mask fall—something she rarely did herself.

Once silence blanketed the galley, aside from the soft sounds of his knife hitting the cutting board, she grabbed the handle of another and began chopping in tandem alongside him. She couldn't remember the last time she ever participated in something so...*normal*.

Perhaps she never had.

Hours came and went while down in the galley with Tommy, and he told Esmyra of his times at sea. How he was once a self-proclaimed pirate turned privateer and offered his services to the crown after the great Captain Cyrus Blackwood and his crew ravaged his last ship, just before an unknown creature beneath the waves sank it down to the depths beneath the cover of night. He was left marooned on an island until he was found by Lephyrin's sea fleet days later.

The siren within her grinned, but Esmyra flinched—the man's words describing the sea monster forced an odd feeling resembling guilt crawling up her spine, knowing that monster was her.

"I wasn't aware that a ship under a king's command would harbor such men," she stated as they finished cleaning the pots and pans.

He lifted a brow as he looked her way. "And what do you mean by that?"

She gave him a knowing look. "The captain is the *Phoenix*. It isn't assumable that he would sail with the likes of...*privateers*." A quick wink was shot his way. "Once a pirate, always a pirate, I'm afraid."

Tommy's brows furrowed, and he placed the pot he was drying down on the counter. "I gave up that life long ago. And you listen here, darlin'...if you know what's good for ya, you won't go around saying those kinds of things."

"And what things might that be?"

"What you called the captain. We don't speak of that name aboard his ship. It was a name placed upon him by no choice of his."

*Did the Phoenix fear his flames?* She wondered if such a thing was possible. Draevyn Rowe was the only creature in known existence who wielded power just as great as she did—somehow even more destructive. His flames were rumored to incinerate everything in their path. Only half a thought from him would have anything turned to ash in mere seconds.

So why would he loathe his name?

Footsteps stormed down the stairs, catching both of their attentions. Samwell appeared in the doorway. "You're relieved of babysitting duty, Tommy. Hope she wasn't too much trouble."

"She was a breeze compared to what you menaces were like when you were young." He waved her off. "I'll see you in the morning."

"Aye, Tommy." She turned toward Samwell and shot him a glare as she made her way to him. "And where will I be going now?"

She was praying to the lost goddesses that it was somewhere away from people. She had to scour the ship for anything useful and rummage through Draevyn's mind while she was at it. However, the bastard had yet to come anywhere near her.

"Captain set up a little room for you to sleep away from the crew. Felt like you'd be more comfortable that way. Now follow me," Samwell called over his shoulder.

Her brows furrowed as he stalked up the galley's stairs. The infamous Phoenix was far from what the rumors had described, and everything he'd done since they met had contradicted those claims.

Samwell directed her to a room on the deck with a tiny cot on the floor. "It's all we could do on short notice. Now, don't leave this room. It's dark and the sea can play tricks on you. Someone will fetch you in the morning."

Esmyra snarled. "Fetch."

"I would assume that's a better thing than what I'm sure you're accustomed to in cove brothels, no?" A lift of one of his brows, accompanied by a dark smirk, gave away his mocking amusement.

The death grip held on her temper was slipping. "Do you have a problem with me aboard this ship, Samwell?"

"To be determined."

"Is the captain your lover? Are you upset I moved to seduce him last night?" she taunted.

He huffed out a laugh. "No. He's my friend and the captain. Just making sure he doesn't do anything foolish because he laid eyes on a beautiful, mysterious woman in a foreign isle."

Esmyra took a step closer to him and watched his body tense, as if he had to force himself to resist taking a step back. "Are you always threatened by women, Samwell?"

His eyes roamed over her slowly. "Only the ones I can't read. And so far, you're at the very top of that list."

The corners of her lips curled at his answer.

"Stay in the gods-damn room," he barked and then slammed the door in her face.

The room plunged into darkness, but her wicked smile remained. With only a blink of her eyes, the tiny space was illuminated with a subtle teal light as she finally allowed them to shift.

CHAPTER 7

*Esmyra*

For what seemed like hours, Esmyra impatiently lay on the poor excuse of a cot, staring up at the ceiling as she plotted her next move.

She should have known her attempt at seduction wouldn't work —Draevyn was a *prince* and a frustratingly handsome one at that. One who likely had several women waiting for his return home. He would never have to pay to be with a woman when they constantly threw themselves at his feet.

Esmyra huffed through her nostrils as her mind raced, desperately searching for answers she knew her father would never provide on the lost kingdom and its gods.

All she knew of Kaelypso and Naerysa was that they had been lost to men since before she was born, when their empire drowned in their own sea. She had only ever heard whisperings of them while docked, and so rarely at that. Whenever she questioned her father about the goddesses, his answer was always that they abandoned this world after forsaking their creatures...creatures that she stemmed from.

Esmyra knew Cyrus wasn't her true sire, but he had raised her since she was a mere babe. And it left her with endless unknowns.

Sometimes, when her crew was asleep, she would sit perched atop the bow of *The Night Wraith*, imagining what the realm would be like if the twin goddesses were found. Perhaps they would make no difference in a world of men on land. But what of a woman connected to the sea in a way that defined her very existence? A woman who shifted as one with the waves, forever wading through its currents.

She'd likely never know but had accepted the harsh truth of that long ago. Siren shifters supposedly went extinct when they were hunted down by men following the loss of their true home. And even then, the description of them in Rymelle's legends weren't identical to Esmyra herself—while they could still shift and walk on land, their song could only be used while in the sea, and all it did was lure men to them. They couldn't manipulate minds the way she could with a single glance. They also hadn't possessed the power to control the tides, nor would their skin camouflage when threatened.

Esmyra lifted her hand from where it rested on her stomach—the teal glow that cast from her eyes illuminated her skin as if it were an iridescent pearl. Her fingers splayed out, and in the dimness of the room, delicate webs materialized between them, while her nails elongated into razor-sharp talons.

She wondered where she'd come from—if it was Maerinys or somewhere beyond their realm entirely. Who were her parents, and *why* did she have all these powers no texts held knowledge of?

Esmyra stood and tiptoed over to the small door. As it creaked open, she glanced through the crack and discovered the deck was empty, indicating that most of the crew had likely gone to bed.

Once deemed safe, she took her first step beyond the room and waltzed along the starboard side. A quick glance up at the crow's nest had her eyes directly on Jak as he sat perched on its rail in his owl form. She could only imagine what was going through his head as they locked eyes—and she knew it was likely laughter at her expense.

The sound of waves crashing against the ship drowned out the noise of her footsteps as she turned to where the captain's office lay in complete darkness. Her hand reached for the intricate doorknob and slowly pushed it open.

The room was dark, illuminated solely by the moonlight seeping through the windows. She silently closed the door behind herself before stalking towards the desk that lay in its center.

The space was fit for a traveling king. Shelves lined the walls, full of ancient books and rolled scrolls. Draevyn's desk was covered in numerous maps, that of each kingdom and the sea that separates them. Wasting no time, she began rummaging through the drawers but found nothing of interest—only extra feathered quills and pots of ink.

She slammed the last drawer shut in frustration. This couldn't have all been for nothing. Huffing out a breath, she twirled a lock of her hair as her eyes roamed over the desk a final time, her fingers tracing over the thick paper and flipping through the small pile. Unexpectedly, her attention was drawn to one of the pages, showcasing an aged map of Rymelle.

Placing down the other pages, she brought the unfamiliar parchment toward her.

"What in the name of all gods is this?" she whispered to herself. Her eyes roamed over every mark of ink. Lephyrin, Terrana, and Sumnae were marked where they had always been, displaying symbols of their royal house. But in the south...lay *Maerinys*. The symbols surrounding the small kingdom were that of the sea—tentacles emerging from the waters and *tails*...scale-covered tails that resembled her own.

Her finger traced over the name.

*So this was where Maerinys was.* If this was what once lay in the southern seas, why would her father refuse to sail them? He'd always told her the currents were deadly towards even the strongest of ships, forbidding her from going there and getting sucked into its riptides.

But she now heard it for what it was—an excuse.

A new suspicion that she wasn't the only one keeping secrets plagued the back of her mind.

Her eyes drifted over the unfamiliar markings and area, where a cluster of rocky caves was circled over many times in ink, just east of the lost kingdom.

This must've been it, what King Rowe had found so far. Perhaps

Draevyn was out searching for this cave, thinking it may lead to the kingdom in the depths. However, a human could never survive a swim so deep. She had to wonder why they would even bother, and all for just a bit of gold.

Footsteps sounded just outside of the office door, and Esmyra quickly rolled up the map and stuffed it into the folds of her dress before tiptoeing to the far corner of the room, hiding in the shadows.

The door swung open, and Draevyn strolled through the room with a loud sigh. Gaze set on the candles atop his desk, their flickering flames burst to life as he took his seat.

Her eyes flared, watching his fire-wielding in use for the first time. She was thankful their small flames only cast a subtle light, but she carefully pressed her back into the wall, willing her skin to shift and blend into the shadowy corner.

She was thankful for how dark her clothing was.

Esmyra watched him curiously as his eyes moved over the contents of the desk. Her heartbeat kicked up, knowing he was likely looking for the one item she had taken.

"Drae!" a voice called from the deck, and his attention moved to the doorway. Samwell stormed through a moment later. "She's gone."

Esmyra's eyes narrowed, jaw ticking.

Draevyn cleared his throat. "What do you mean, she's gone? She must be here somewhere."

"I checked her room to make sure she stayed put, and *of course,* she didn't. I walked the entire deck, went below with the crew, even woke up Tommy to see if he'd heard or seen anything of her, but nothing. She's dangerous, Captain, and I don't trust her. You brought aboard a woman from the most well-known pirate and criminal haven, believing a sob story of her wanting a better life. It was a lie. She's up to something and we need to find her."

Esmyra's lip curled back, anger burning in her throat as he spoke of scouring the ship for her. The first mate was a problem, and it was becoming entirely clear that she would never get the captain alone with Samwell constantly lurking about. She would have to make his death happen sooner than anticipated.

"Esmi's around here somewhere. We're in the middle of the sea, Sam. Where could she even go? You likely just missed her. I'm not entirely sure why you feel so strongly about her when you've known her for mere hours. She's done nothing to you."

Her eyes shot back to Samwell, who fixed his stare down at his feet. "It's just a feeling, Drae. You don't feel uneasy around her? You don't *sense* it?"

The corners of her lips curled wickedly.

"Sense what exactly?"

The first mate blew out a breath. "I'm not sure I know how to even describe it."

Draevyn laughed. "Seems to me that perhaps you've read too many folktales regarding women aboard ships."

He scoffed. "I don't believe that shit. Regardless, be careful. We don't know what she's capable of. Are you sure she isn't elven? She could be playing a trick on your mind."

"She's an unarmed woman aboard a ship full of men she doesn't know. I spoke with Tommy, and he likes her. Quite a bit, actually." Her vicious smile turned into something much softer at the mention of Tommy's approval. She wasn't entirely sure why it mattered to her. "Perhaps she just didn't feel like being cooped up in the closet we gave her for a room and wanted to take a stroll. She'll turn up. Go to bed, Sam."

"Whatever you say, *Highness*," Samwell taunted.

"Get the hell out of here with that," Draevyn said with a barely amused chuckle.

Esmyra's brows furrowed at their effortless banter after arguing only seconds before.

His friend went to turn but then threw over his shoulder, "Why are you up, anyway?"

"Just wanted to check something. I'll head back shortly."

With that, Samwell took his last few steps out of the room and closed the door behind him.

Esmyra's gaze moved to Draevyn, who was already looking back down at his desk, seeming at ease. But then his voice broke the silence.

"Is there a particular reason you're in my private office so late in the evening, Miss Esmi?"

Surprise bolted through her like a strike of lightning. Not once had he looked in her direction, and even now, his eyes remained on the contents covering his desk. She didn't move—she even held her breath, hoping he would think he was mistaken.

"I don't have all night, love. Come on out of the shadows. You know who I am, which means you also know of my brother. I've grown up around shadows my entire life. You cannot hide from me."

As if in response to his words, the flames of the flickering candles grew more intense, bathing nearly the entire room in their warm light. She willed her skin to return to normal before he could witness its transformation, blowing her cover further.

With her lips pursed and arms placed behind her back, she hesitantly strode into the center of the room. "When did you realize?"

Draevyn let out a breathy chuckle. "The moment I stepped into the room. Now, are you going to answer my question regarding why you're in my private office unattended?"

This couldn't have been more perfect. She finally had the prince alone.

"And yet you didn't rat me out to your loyal little dog. Why is that?" she challenged.

"Don't question me to avoid what I have asked you now twice." His voice radiated an authority that normally would've had her clawing out the man's eyes. She wasn't sure why she couldn't bring herself to do it.

Esmyra smirked, but the amusement was fading from his features. "Was out for a little stroll and got sidetracked. Must've gotten lost." She dragged out the last three words.

"You're trouble, Miss Esmi."

"You sense this, yet you don't listen to your friend. Why is that?"

Draevyn leaned back in his chair and folded his hands behind his head as his eyes leisurely raked over her. "Perhaps I like trouble. It keeps things interesting. But, while I have you here, I need to know the truth. Why exactly did you choose to come aboard my ship?"

Her skin heated beneath his gaze. "Is safe passage no longer believable because I became a little curious, Captain?"

"I'm not entirely sure I ever fully believed that's what you were after."

Esmyra chuckled softly, a bit of menace beneath it. "You *do* enjoy trouble, princeling."

He let out a sound that was half laugh and half scoff. "Princeling would be my brother. I've told you, it's Captain."

"But you're also a prince."

"Only in certain eyes." Draevyn stood from his seat and moved to circle her. With every pass he made around her body, he inched closer until his breath grazed her nose, before finally coming to a stop directly before her. His whiskey-hued stare bore into her, the gold flecks in them dancing like flames. "Give me the truth. I won't tolerate any more lies slipping from your pretty lips."

She sucked in a sharp breath at his sudden proximity, loathing that he noticed as he took a step around her once more—only she knew this predator's dance he was attempting.

The tiny hairs on her arms stood at attention and she went on high alert as he became silent behind her. "And if I don't have the proper answer?" she asked, her eyes shifting as she readied herself to attack.

All she had to do was force his stare to meet hers and she could compel him. Her siren song began slipping its way up her throat.

Draevyn brought his lips to her ear. "Then I'm afraid the only things awaiting you in Lephyrin are the gallows, love."

Esmyra moved to strike, but he was faster. The ice-cold touch of cuffs clamped around each of her wrists faster than she could blink, and she let out a sharp hiss at the contact.

Horror seized her then.

A sudden depletion of power left her motionless—her eyes refused to shift, talons wouldn't extend, and her connection to the sea beneath the ship was severed. Her throat tightened, eyes darting back and forth as she repeatedly tried to summon her magic.

"What the fuck is this?!" she barked over her shoulder. Esmyra thrashed in his hold while unrelenting panic overcame her for the first time in her life.

"Now, I'm afraid since you didn't find your original quarters suitable the first night, we'll need to move you down to the lower levels." He leaned down to her ear, sending goosebumps along her neck. "While you appear human, you can never be too careful. These cuffs are precautions."

Esmyra scoffed as she tried to pull out of his hold. "I assure you, I'm human." The words came out in a growl.

"Well, then these cuffs act like any other."

Draevyn bent down and effortlessly heaved her over his shoulder before stalking through his office, out the doorway, across the deck, and down the stairs with her in tow. They passed the sleeping crew, though she was sure to wake them all as she continued to kick, bite, and scream the entire way down to the holding cells.

Once in the ship's prison, he rummaged in his pocket for keys and opened the single cell door, throwing her in as he ignored her efforts to shove out of his hold.

Esmyra couldn't feel her power—there wasn't an ounce of it left in her. She felt utterly *mortal*—drained and weak.

The cell's barred metal door was slammed in her face, and her fingers coiled around them as her breaths became heavy with fury, staring into Draevyn's eyes. "*This* is how you treat women aboard your ship?" The words dripped with venom as they left her, and she imagined tearing his pretty little eyes from his skull.

"No, Esmi. This is how we treat *prisoners*. And until you can give me a believable answer, this is where you'll remain. I can't have you sneaking around the ship at night if you won't even provide me the smallest of answers when I've only shown you kindness since we met. Kindness that no one else would give."

"Do not speak my name as if you believe it holds power against me, Prince Draevyn Rowe."

His jaw ticked at her words and she gave him a menacing grin from behind the bars.

Esmyra's stare drifted down to the cuffs locked on her wrists.

They were strange looking. The cuffs possessed a silver sheen, but with crimson-hued crackles etched into the surface, mimicking spider-like veins.

"They're made of velsinyte," Draevyn admitted as he watched her. "They were the only ones I had on hand in my office, and while harmless to humans, they're very uncomfortable. Apologies, they're all I had on hand."

*Velsinyte?! What the fuck is velsinyte?*

Esmyra cleared her throat. "Yes, they're wretched." She stuck her hands through the bars. "Release me."

He raised a brow. "I believe you're missing a crucial word, love."

"Release me...Captain?" she tacked on, annoyed.

"I was thinking a 'please' should be in there."

Esmyra clenched her teeth, patience wearing extremely thin. "*Please* release me, Prince and Captain Draevyn Rowe, from these velsinyte bindings."

He huffed out a laugh. "Absolutely not. You're more trouble than anticipated."

Draevyn tucked the keys into his pocket. "I'll be back to check on you in the morning, and hopefully by then you'll want to work with me a little, so you won't need to remain down here until we reach the next port."

He turned from her, but her words stopped him in his tracks. "And my trip to the gallows?"

"To be determined," he said over his shoulder without looking back and then stalked back up the stairs.

Esmyra hissed at his back and then frantically tried to twist her wrists in any direction possible to free herself from the cuffs.

*Velsinyte.* She had never heard of such a thing. How had they affected her? Her magic...it was entirely gone. Her connection to the sea was cleaved straight through, and it left her nearly gasping for air.

Her throat tightened as she shook her head in denial.

*Gods,* was this how it felt? To be so drained, weak, and...*powerless.*

She became disoriented, unsure if it was an effect from the cuffs or her surging panic.

Esmyra was about to snap her wrist in an attempt to break free when the sound of wings filled her cell. She glanced up through the bars and found Jak now standing before her in his human form.

"What in all gods happened to you?!" he whisper-shouted. "I watched you walk into his office and he followed in shortly after. I saw him drag you out with cuffs, but I assumed you were just fucking with him until you had a better moment to strike." He crossed his arms as he stared at her, frowning. "You're still cuffed?!"

She nearly threw herself into the cell door. "Get these fucking things off of me!" The words rushed out of her as she shoved her clasped wrists through the bars.

Jak's eyes flared. "Holy gods, Esmi..." He moved to grab the stone-like metal and hissed when his skin brushed against it. "What the hell are those made out of?"

"He said they're made from velsinyte. Whatever the hells that is. They completely depleted my power in seconds...it's as if I'm now..."

"Mortal," he finished for her, and all she could do was give a small nod.

"How can something drain someone of their power?" he asked, his lips parting as he took a step back from her, looking horrified.

"I have no idea," she admitted, breath heaving.

Jak kicked at the bars, the loud *ting* barely registering. They both heaved, pulled, and tried to pry it off its hinges, but nothing worked. Regardless of whether or not they could free her of the cell, there were still the cuffs to deal with.

"His pocket," she whispered, and Jak met her stare.

"Draevyn took the keys with him when he went upstairs."

"We need help, Esmi..."

"No... *No.* No, we don't." The thought of her father finding her this way had her wanting to crawl out of her skin. "Just go get the gods-damn keys and free me so I can sink this fucking ship."

He took a hesitant step backwards, his eyes locked on hers.

Esmyra knew then he wasn't going to obey her. "Jak...don't you fucking dare bring my father here."

"It's a good thing I followed you, gorgeous. Just try to forgive me, okay?"

"Jak, wait—" she shrieked, reaching through the bars.

But she was too slow.

Jak shifted to his owl form in the blink of an eye and swooped up the flight of stairs, out of her sight, and leaving her in the dark.

Powerless and alone.

# Draevyn

Draevyn sat at his desk, fingers idly tracing the rim of his untouched glass of rum. The ship swayed gently beneath him, the distant creak of wood and the subtle waves filling the silence of his cabin. The scattered candles flickered and surged with his every thought, casting shifting shadows across the scattered parchments that cluttered his desk. His mind, however, wasn't on the journey ahead or the orders from his king.

It was on Esmi.

He'd done what was necessary. That was what he told himself, anyway. He couldn't explain it, but he just knew in every fiber of his soul that she was dangerous. To start, she was a liar—*that* he already knew just from her saying she was seeking safe passage and was later found rummaging through his things. Not to mention how she aimed for him in a tavern full of criminals. He wasn't entirely convinced she didn't know his real name either, before Sam had given it up to try and scare her.

And even that hadn't worked. Draevyn had become so used to people fearing the Phoenix, that expecting the terrified reaction had become second nature...

Only she hadn't cowered away.

Had he made the right choice? When he'd looked into her eyes before shutting the cell's door, there was something else lingering in her stare alongside her defiance.

*Fear.*

Esmi hadn't shown fear when she found out she was aboard the Phoenix's ship, yet she had when he put her in a cage for only a single night. Should he have left her in the cuffs? Were the cuffs and the cell too much together?

Draevyn exhaled sharply, raking a hand through his dark hair. It was too late for doubt, and he couldn't go back on his word now. Dawn wasn't far off at this point, and he could release her come sunrise and apologize. He'd spent his entire life making hard decisions, and this was no different.

His father would've done worse.

The thought curled bitterly in his stomach. The king had always been merciless, especially when it came to exploiting Draevyn and his powers. The second son and unwanted heir. He had spent the majority of his youth drowning beneath expectations he could never meet, forever compared to his shadow-wielding older brother. Meanwhile, Draevyn had secretly been the stain on the Rowe name, the reckless disappointment, if his father's cold gaze and brutal words were any indication.

Nothing he said or did had ever been enough to fix the damage he'd caused to his family when he was younger, though the realm would never know that. To an outsider looking in, Draevyn was the ruthless Phoenix—Lephyrin's protector and executioner.

He found solace in the sea, though. It offered an untamed freedom, far from the iron grip of his father's throne. But even aboard *The Odyssey*, away from the castle's suffocating halls, the old wounds never truly faded. The truth was, Draevyn hated himself more than anyone else ever could for what he'd done when he lost control that day nearly twenty years ago.

With a sigh, he reached for the keys in his pocket, running his thumb over their worn edges before carelessly tossing them onto his desk.

A sudden rush of shouting shattered the quiet.

Draevyn's head snapped up, the bellows of his crew sounding more urgent and panicked.

"SHIP AHEAD!" Sam's voice echoed.

"They're closing in fast!" bellowed another.

The heavy boots of his men thundered beyond his office door, the hurried clatter of weapons being drawn following in their wake. Draevyn was already moving, shoving back from his desk and slamming open the cabin door. The salty night air rushed in as he strode onto the deck, his eyes scanning the midnight horizon.

The ship was nearly upon them.

It loomed out of the mist like a phantom, its sails catching just enough moonlight to gleam like a blade in the dark.

"Where in the hells did they come from?!" Draevyn barked as he ran up to the quarter deck and took his place at the helm, gripping the wheel.

"They weren't there a moment ago, Captain!" Sam called out, panting. "It's like they rose straight from the damn sea! They blend in with the gods-damn night."

"All gods," Draevyn whispered, his jaw going slack as his mind raced. He whirled toward Sam. "*The Night Wraith*?" His voice barely hid the panic he desperately tried to shove down.

Sam swallowed. "Gods, I fucking hope not."

The ship closed the distance between them with impossible speed, as if a false wind had caught its sails. Then they came fully into view as the mist eerily cleared, rushed out by an unseen force.

Draevyn's blood ran cold at the sight as they ran back down to the main deck.

*The Night Wraith* rolled up alongside them, close enough now that the crew's taunting began.

"Best start praying to your god, lads," a man called out from the deck.

Cruel, raucous laughter echoed across the water. Draevyn's crew tensed, gripping their weapons, their knuckles white. He unsheathed his sword alongside his men, flames licking up the blade as he raised it high.

His stomach twisted as a figure came into view on their enemy's deck, the crew parting as the man approached them. Both crews fell silent, the only sounds were the waves rolling beneath their ships and the echo of the man's heavy steps.

Cyrus Blackwood halted at the ship's rail, silhouetted against the light of the moon as his long coat whipped in the night breeze. His long hair and beard were black as the night sky, and his depthless eyes somehow gleamed in the dark. He didn't join in with his crew's taunts, didn't twirl a sword or pistol in the air like some bloodthirsty criminal. No, he simply raised a hand and gave a small, lazy wave with his fingers, his mocking grin stretching ear-to-ear.

A high-pitched screech erupted through the air, and Draevyn's crew all glanced up toward *The Night Wraith's* crow's nest, where an owl swooped down and barrelled toward them, before circling their deck from above.

"You so much as set a single member of my crew on fire, Phoenix, and my beast will drown your men here and now," Blackwood called, his voice rolling off the wind.

Draevyn clenched his jaw, the veins in his neck straining as he tried to think of a plan that wouldn't be a death sentence for his crew.

"We need to be smart about this, Drae," Sam whispered, but Draevyn's eyes remained locked on Blackwood's crew and their grins.

He was right. Draevyn fucking loathed that he was right. All of Rymelle had heard the tales of Captain Cyrus Blackwood. He was rumored to be immortal, with a monster roaming the depths that obeyed his every beck and call. Draevyn wasn't willing to try and call the man's bluff.

"No mercy, boys!" Blackwood boomed, and a moment later, a roar of cheering sounded.

Out of nowhere, grappling hooks soared through the air from *The Night Wraith*, latching onto *The Odyssey's* railings, splintering its wood.

*Fucking Irah.*

"Brace yourselves!" Draevyn roared, his blade stretched out.

The pirates' boots slammed onto the deck, their steel blades flashing in the dim moonlight. The first blade came at him in a blur, and he barely raised his sword in time to block it. The shock of the blow rattled up his arm, but he shoved forward, twisting his sword and sending his attacker sprawling.

The fight exploded around him.

With a thunderous roar, his men met the assault head-on. Gunfire cracked through the air. Metal clashed against metal. *The Odyssey's* deck transformed into a chaotic battlefield, a maelstrom of flashing steel and desperate brawls, with the suffocating stench of salt, sweat, and blood.

Draevyn ducked beneath the swing of a broad axe and drove his cutlass up into the attacker's ribs, his flames roaring up the blade and incinerating the man from the inside out before twisting it free just in time to parry another strike.

Around him, his crew fought fiercely, but the pirates were relentless and brutal in their attacks.

Draevyn drove his cutlass through another's gut, yanking it free just as someone else came at him. He ducked, rolled, came up swinging, but it was endless. For every one he cut down, another took their place.

And through it all, over the chaos, Blackwood still stood at the center of his ship, smiling.

CHAPTER 9

*Esmyra*

The deck above was a storm of violence.

From the dark, damp belly of the ship, Esmyra grinned as she listened to it all—boots pounding against the wood, the clash of steel, the sharp crack of gunfire.

She tugged at the rusted cell's hinges bolted to the wooden beams, but it wouldn't budge. The siren within her thrashed. Esmyra wasn't meant to rot here while the men spilled blood above. She twisted her wrists, the cuffs biting into her already raw skin from struggling to break free.

A shadow flickered against the lantern's flame hanging from the wall, swinging as the ship rocked with the sea. A whisper of beating wings sounded, followed by the lightest tap of boots against the steps leading down into the brig.

*Jak.* Thank the gods.

"Didn't think I'd leave you to rot, did you, gorgeous?" He stepped into the subtle glow of the lantern light.

"Kaelypso's tits, it's about damn time," she growled, her fingers curling around the bars as she stared at the infuriating smirk on his face.

His grin flashed in the dark as he jingled a key between his fingers, gold eyes bright with amusement. "Had to let you sweat a little." He shrugged. "Builds character."

"Open the fucking door before I build character by clawing your eyes out."

With a low chuckle, he slid the largest, rusted key into the lock, twisting until it clicked. "Found these on his desk in the office," he admitted.

The cell door groaned open, and she threw her wrists in his direction before he could say another word. "Hurry!" she shrieked, desperate to get the cuffs off and regain her magic.

Jak's eyes flared, and he began rummaging through the keys once more, sticking them in the keyhole one by one until finally, the click of the lock sounded and the cuffs fell to the floor with a loud *clang*.

The moment they fell from her wrists, she sucked in a sharp breath as she was flooded with her power. It shot through her veins like a vicious crack of lightning, starting in her chest and bursting to the tips of her talons. She gripped the rusted bars to hold herself up as it nearly brought her to her knees. Jak watched her with concerned eyes. It was a look she had never seen him wear—at least not toward her.

"What did you say it was called again? Velsinyte?" His brows furrowed as he said the word, eyes narrowing on the strange stone-like metal.

"Aye," she answered, grabbing the cuffs from the floor. "And they're coming with us."

They barely made it a step toward the stairs before the room exploded.

*BOOM.*

A cannonball tore through the hull, sending splintering wood, embers, and smoke billowing through the brig. The blast threw them off balance, sending both of their bodies flying into the cage as the floor beneath them buckled. The ship groaned as *The Night Wraith* tore it to pieces and water surged through the shattered hull.

"Only one way out of here now, gorgeous," he shouted over the rushing water.

"Way ahead of you." She dug into the folds of her dress and handed him the parchment that she stole from Draevyn's office. "That may be the answer to all of our questions. Bring it back to our ship, but do *not* give it to Cyrus. Hold on to it for me until I return. Understood?"

Jak let out an exasperated sigh but eventually nodded.

"Get out of here while you still can," she ordered with a menacing lilt to her voice, her eyes flashing an icy light.

"I'll see you on the other side." Jak winked and morphed into his owl form, the parchment now clutched in his talons. With a few flaps of his feathery wings, he was soaring up the staircase and out of her sight.

Esmyra stood there in silence for a few moments, giving him enough time to escape the lower levels before she waded through the water a few steps away from the cell's door.

She reached for her power, welcoming its return as her fingernails elongated into claws. Webs formed between her fingers, and the previously dark cell became bathed in teal. She sucked in a sharp breath through her nostrils, the salty tang of the sea stinging them beautifully as her magic answered her call.

And then the ship began to tremble.

CHAPTER 10

*Draevyn*

The blood of both crews slicked the deck beneath Draevyn's boots. His men were barely holding against the ruthless tide of pirates cutting through them.

He wasn't sure how much longer his crew would last. The bodies were piling, the exhaustion settling in as they were attacked in the middle of the night. Blackwood's orders be damned—his men were already meeting an early fate. He wouldn't allow the rest of them to die without giving it his all.

Too many of his men were falling back, their formations breaking. The world seemed to slow as he watched one go down, a cutlass driven into his gut as his eyes went wide with shock. Another of his sailors was forced against the mast, the blade at his throat catching the moonlight before it slit through flesh and bone.

A sudden, vicious rage burned in his chest.

Draevyn's fingers curled tight around the hilt of his sword, his flames burning beneath his skin. He closed his eyes for half a breath and let his power surge free.

Flames licked at his fingertips, curling up his arms like hungry serpents. With only a thought, every enemy aboard his ship caught fire —they screamed in horror, rolling across the blood-soaked deck as they tried to put out the flames consuming their bodies.

*The Night Wraith's* crew began to retreat, and Draevyn felt a rush of pride roll through him as the pirates leapt off his ship and into the sea to put out the blaze. He cursed himself for not using his flames sooner, but he didn't want to risk Blackwood summoning his beast. *The Odyssey's* deck glowed with embers, the air thick with smoke as fire spread across the planks, catching the tattered sails above. But something was wrong.

Sam ran up to him, covered in blood and ash, as they turned to watch the pirates climb back up to the deck of their ship, standing alongside their captain, all wearing the same triumphant grin.

Draevyn's heart hammered against his ribs at the sight.

*Fuck.* Did he just doom them all?

And then, the sea surged on all sides of his ship, the waves slamming against the hull. All contents aboard began flying across the deck. Draevyn's eyes darted to the unmanned wheel, spinning frantically as it fought against the relentless waves.

"Sam!" he bellowed over the roar of the sea, leaping over fallen bodies and running up the stairs that led to the quarterdeck.

Once there, Draevyn gripped the wheel with all his might, his muscles straining against the pull of it as *The Odyssey* continued to be tossed around in a cloudless storm.

What remained of his crew were in a state of panic, running and yelling at one another as they raced to secure whatever they could as waves breached the starboard side.

Draevyn's barked orders were drowned out by the violent winds and crashing waves.

"Drae!"

He searched the deck to find Sam heaving himself up the stairs to meet him, grasping the railing with all of his strength.

Sam made his way to Draevyn's side. "Where the hell did this storm come from?!"

Draevyn glanced toward *The Night Wraith,* realizing that the ship had already put distance between them. The entirety of their crew was still on the deck, watching—*waiting.*

"Is it even a storm?!" Draevyn bellowed back. "There isn't a single fucking cloud in the sky. What could be causing this?!"

He frantically looked in every direction. It was the oddest thing he'd ever encountered. The sea...the distant waters were calm, but chaos surrounded their ship, as if the ocean itself was working to bring them to its floor.

A larger wave breached the deck, sending the crew slamming into the opposite railing, some flying overboard as their screams echoed through the air.

"Holy gods," he breathed.

"Do you have orders, Captain?!" Sam screamed over the madness.

Draevyn's throat tightened, his heart feeling like it would explode in his chest. "Get to the pinnaces." The words were barely audible.

"Captain?!"

"The pinnaces, Sam! Now!" he roared, running past him and down the stairs. Sam caught up to him a moment later, and they both worked to help the fallen sailors back onto their feet as they continued to be tossed around by the violent waves.

"To the pinnaces!" they screamed, and everyone ran to untie the small boats from where they were restrained on *The Odyssey's* sides.

Tommy stormed up to them then. "Where be the girl? This is Blackwood's monster at work!"

Draevyn's eyes widened, a sudden fear gripping him as his head snapped towards the stairs, where a rush of seawater was already pouring down them. "Fuck!" he roared and whipped back towards Sam. "I'll be right back. Make sure everyone left board those boats!"

"Draevyn, don't you fucking dare!"

"She'll drown! I just put her down there to scare her, Sam. It wasn't meant to be a gods-damn death sentence!"

Draevyn blocked out Sam's scolding screams as he leapt down the steps and sprinted through the kitchen and bunkers to reach the final set of stairs, where the holding cells appeared to be completely submerged in water.

"All gods," he gasped before running down as many as he could, before sucking in a sharp breath and diving into the flooded room.

Draevyn waded through the water, barely able to see anything beneath its darkness. He was already running out of air by the time he reached her holding cell and found a gaping hole in the ship's side—Esmi nowhere in sight.

*Fuck.* The cannons.

His throat tightened, a sickening feeling crept in at the thought of her drowning because of him.

Once at the top of the holding cell's stairs, Draevyn let out a gasp for air. Soaked and heavy, his captain's coat clung to his skin, weighing him down as he rushed back to the deck.

The main deck was empty, save for the dead bodies, and Blackwood's ship was already sailing nearly a mile away. The last of the pinnaces were lowering into the raging sea when he locked eyes with Sam.

"Wait!" he ordered. "Drae, over here!"

Draevyn moved to bolt toward them and then whipped back in the direction of his office. "Hells. The map," he grumbled, running as fast as he could.

Barreling into his office, the seawater was up to his knees. He frantically combed through his desk, where they had stored months of research on the lost kingdom, only to realize the most important parchment had vanished.

The map of the kingdom and where it once lay.

"Fucking Irah!" he roared as he picked up a candelabra and whipped it across the room.

A vision worked its way into his memory. Of a woman who made her way to him in a tavern—a *pirate* tavern—the prior night, claiming to seek refuge, followed by going back on her words and rummaging through his belongings the moment his back was turned.

And then, finally, her reaction to the velsinyte cuffs.

They nearly brought her to her knees, but they wouldn't have affected a mere mortal.

"That's impossible," he whispered as his eyes darted back and forth.

No, it couldn't have been. Even if the woman possessed magic, the cuffs remained locked on her wrists when the ship began to sink.

Draevyn clenched his jaw as he stormed back towards his office door and ignited everything aboard that could still catch flame. A raging, flickering orange hue lit their surroundings, sending black smoke into the sky.

"Drae, hurry!" Sam called as he coughed through the smoke, the rest of the crew also screaming for him.

A deafening roar erupted, filling his ears, and he turned just in time to see an enormous wave rearing up from the depths, towering over the ship as if it were formed from the wrath of the sea goddesses themselves.

Only…it wasn't a wave at all. He blinked through the sting of the splashing seawater numerous times, but the vision before him remained.

If it hadn't been for the flames now engulfing the ship, Draevyn wouldn't have been able to see what was attacking them.

A shudder rippled through the ocean as something far more sinister than anything he'd ever seen rose from the depths. Emerging from the abyss was a colossal creature of legend—a *kraken*, but not the kind he'd heard of in sailors' tales. This beast wasn't made of flesh and bone but of the water itself, its massive tentacles swirling and coiling around his ship.

*No… This can't be real.*

The roar of the ocean drowned the crew's shouts of terror as the kraken's tentacles wrapped around the ship as if it possessed a tangible form. Draevyn stumbled back, holding the railing as his mind reeled at the impossibility of it all, disbelief gripping him by the throat.

He turned back to face the others and found nothing but fear in their eyes as they took in the same sight.

Chaos reigned, and he knew he wouldn't get to the pinnaces in time to join the others. But he would be damned if he allowed them to drown alongside him.

With a single point of his chin, the rope securing them to the ship ignited into flames, quickly burning to ash before sending the small boat plummeting down to the water. Their screams echoed over the roar of the storm and flames, but he held onto the hope that he'd given them a chance to escape.

With a deafening groan, the ship's timbers splintered under the pressure of the kraken's tentacles as they squeezed relentlessly, crushing the vessel's hull as if it were made of mere driftwood.

The kraken's watery form twisted and writhed, an embodiment of the ocean's wrath, and Draevyn's jaw fell open as the churning sea swallowed his ship. His flames were extinguished, casting the surroundings back into utter darkness as his disbelief turned to a grim acceptance. He let out a shuddering breath—there was nothing he or his flames could do to stop what was occurring.

With nowhere else to go, he braced himself for the deadly blow of the water-formed beast by gripping the ship's rail, ready to go down with his home as any captain would.

One of its enormous tentacles crashed down upon the deck with a thunderous boom, splintering what remained of the wooden railings and deck. The vessel lurched violently and the timbers snapped as water cascaded over the gunwales. With a groan, the hull gave way under the strain, and the mast snapped like a twig, landing in the sea as a tangled mess of ropes and canvas.

And then, with one last tremor, the ship submitted to the embrace of the sea. Draevyn's roar of defeat was drowned out by the crashing waves as water poured down his throat.

Within minutes, *The Odyssey* slipped beneath the waves with a mournful wail, disappearing into the dark depths, dragging him with it.

Beneath the turbulent surface, Esmyra watched as the ship succumbed to her fury. She couldn't tear her eyes away from the sinking vessel as it fought against her summoned monster —the *true* monster of the sea that all sailors feared, conjured by her powers.

The ship was fully submerged, and she searched through the swirling debris, watching for the panicked, flailing movements of the drowning crew. Among the sinking wreckage, a lone figure caught her eye—a single man thrashing in the water as he fought against the merciless current, being dragged down by the weight of his coat.

Her glowing eyes flared as she realized it was the *prince*.

Esmyra had called upon the creature conjured of waves, drawing it to the ship that held her as its prisoner. Yet now, as she watched the single drowning man, a flicker of remorse tugged at her black, immortal heart.

Her fingers twitched. Some part of her, something buried deep in her soul, itched to move—itched to *save* him.

The thought startled her, the siren within thrashing to react for reasons she couldn't comprehend.

She curled her webbed fingers into fists, forcing herself to stay in place.

Esmyra glanced to the east, where the underside of several lifeboats cast shadows on the surface. While what remained of his crew was safe, Draevyn's descent to the depths was swift and unforgiving.

*I showed you kindness when no one else would*. His words from hours prior filtered through her mind. But then the bastard locked her in a *cage*, trapping her behind bars with velsinyte cuffs bound to her wrists.

Nothing was worse to her than a cage—she was to be as untamed and relentless as the sea.

Esmyra floated there as she watched his body go still, sinking further. Her eyes then drifted down to the hand clutching the velsinyte cuffs she'd stolen.

For a brief moment, she hesitated, torn between her instinctive desire to let the sea claim what it was due. But that impulse to intervene continued to weave its way into her.

*Ugh.* With a forceful flick of her tail, she swiftly propelled through the water toward Draevyn, her movements agile and serpentine.

Once Esmyra reached him, she wrapped her arms beneath his and drew him close. The stupid princeling was significantly heavier than he appeared. The weight of his coat had his body sinking as if he were made of stone. Esmyra floated around him, being sure to keep one arm beneath his to avoid them sinking further, and then one of her talons sliced up the back of the fabric, severing it in two before shoving it down his arms. The remnants of his jacket fluttered down to the depths as she gripped him once more and rushed them both toward the surface.

As they emerged from the water, she cradled the unconscious man in her arms, his limp form draped against her own, and her eyes softened, emotions swirling through her she barely understood.

The sun began its ascent on the horizon, casting the settling waves in vibrant, warm hues as she called off her beast. The conjured kraken burst into nothing but violent bubbles that rose to the sea's surface as the ocean swallowed what remained of *The Odyssey*.

She glanced over her shoulder to where the pinnaces floated nearly a mile away to the east, and then to where *The Night Wraith* floated in the west.

Esmyra swam his body to a large piece of floating debris and laid him across the splintered surface. Heaving herself up next to him, she swept his dark hair out of his face, the markings on her arms returning to their usual crimson hue as the seawater rolled off her skin.

Exhaling heavily, she moved her gaze to the man notorious for his violent, blazing ruthlessness—yet he had displayed only the opposite in the single day she'd spent with him.

Lowering her head, she placed her ear atop his chest. It remained still, refusing to rise and fall with his breaths, his heartbeat fading with each passing second.

"Don't die on me after all that, you stupid princeling," she hissed as that odd feeling within her continued to stir.

Her hand reached out and gripped his cheeks, tilting his head toward the sky before she carefully pried his jaw open. Extending a talon towards his chest, she directed the seawater within his lungs to expel itself. Slowly, the water emerged from between his lips in thin streams, snaking through the air while levitating above his unconscious body.

But he still wasn't breathing.

"Hmm," she huffed out. Esmyra stared at the dying man, wondering if she should even bother trying to save him from what she'd caused. She had one last idea, and if it didn't work, she would accept his fate and swim back to *The Night Wraith*.

For if Draevyn were alive, he would never be able to resist a siren's song—it would pull him from this sleep of death, force him to open his eyes, and listen to her so she could compel him if desired.

Esmyra began to hum, her voice a soothing call on the sea wind. She hovered over his body as the tune fell from her lips, her tail swaying back and forth behind her while the sun lifted into the sky in unison with her words.

Her long, midnight hair fell around her shoulders like a dark, wet veil, allowing water droplets to fall silently on his skin. As Esmyra hummed, the surrounding water stirred, swirling lazily around them.

Draevyn's eyelids fluttered, his lips parting as he drew in a shaky breath before he started choking, gasping for air as his hands flew to clutch his neck.

Esmyra tilted her head, her humming fading into silence as her lips curved into a small grin. She swiftly reached for the velsinyte cuffs and dove back beneath the waves, leaving Lephyrin's prince behind without a backward glance.

CHAPTER 12

*Esmyra*

Esmyra glided through the currents, surrounded by the sea's pulse. While in the vast expanse of the underwater world, she knew it was her true home, but the loneliness was suffocating. She occasionally wondered, if her kind never went extinct, if she would even desire to return to *The Night Wraith*.

Swimming up to the underside of her ship, she scaled the outer wall with her talons, using only her upper body strength to heave herself up to the rail, where she perched herself atop the wood, her hair covering her nearly bare breasts.

The deck appeared empty, the crew likely beneath the lower levels preparing for the day at sea after the night's battle. She turned to the waves once more, dreading having to face her father's fury for disobeying orders once again.

"Esmyra."

"Kaelypso's tits!" she shrieked as she turned toward where the voice came from.

Jak was glaring at her from only a few feet away, leaning back on the railing carelessly. His light brown hair reflected a golden warmth from the rising sun.

An irritated snarl worked its way across her lips. "Jak. Shouldn't you be up in the crow's nest keeping watch? Or has your laziness over-taken what remained of your usefulness?"

He let out a laugh. "You're in such deep shit, Esmi."

Water slid down her face from her soaked hair as her eyes flared. "You didn't speak of the map yet, did you?"

He offered her his hand before she swung her tail over the railing as it separated into two sleek legs.

Jak didn't hesitate when he took his jacket off and placed it over her shoulders, as he typically did. She slipped the velsinyte cuffs into the coat pocket a moment later.

"No." He nervously scratched the back of his neck. "But returning here without you set him in a fit of fury." Jak rubbed at his temples with one hand as he wrapped his opposite arm around her shoulder. "And then having to tell him we needed to rescue you…" He let out a low whistle. "Good luck. That's all I have to say."

She scoffed. "This is exactly why I told you not to do that!"

"Well, I may have let it slip that you lost access to your powers…"

Esmyra's steps halted as her jaw popped open. Her eyes shot to her friend, and a light cast on his face as her eyes shifted. "You. *What*?!"

Jak raised a brow. "Bloody hells. How else was I supposed to get them there?! They know you likely could've handled it on your own."

"I can't believe this," she whispered as her eyes went vacant.

"You can't expect me to lie to my captain regarding everything. I kept the map a secret. Was that not enough? His word is still above yours, Esmyra. However, he surprised me when he received the news of your capture. He seemed worried."

She looked up at him through furrowed brows. "Ridiculous. Nothing can touch me."

"Aye, well…"

Her jaw locked, eyes narrowing on him. "Well, what?"

He let out a breath. "Well, it's a bit obvious now, at least to the two of us, that thinking you're invincible is a dangerous illusion."

She shoved out of his hold and jabbed her finger into his chest, her talon extending just enough to poke a hole in his shirt. "You were supposed to cover for me! Please tell me you didn't speak of the cuffs."

Jak opened his mouth to protest when a booming voice echoed across the ship.

"*ESMYRA.*"

Both of them jumped at the sound of the captain's voice.

"Aye, but a bit hard to *cover* for someone who is unclear with instructions while also not the first in command," Jak whispered in her ear. "He only knows you managed to get locked in a cell. He holds no knowledge of how. But you're going to have to tell him *something*."

She turned in the direction of the booming voice and found Cyrus standing in the doorway of his office beneath the quarterdeck.

"Father," she greeted.

"In here. Now." He didn't even wait for a response before turning on his heel and stalking to his desk.

Esmyra's eyes drifted up to Jak. "Any chance you'd like to join me?"

"It's cute that you think I have a death wish."

She snarled. "Ugh. Well, I don't know why he's reacting so ridiculously."

"Cyrus thought there was a chance he would lose you." Jak bent down and whispered into her ear, "The parchment is in the front inner pocket of the jacket, should you need it."

Esmyra's hand instinctively lifted to touch her chest where the pocket was sewn, and the map crinkled beneath the pressure of her touch. "You didn't look?" Her eyes remained on her father's office as she asked.

"It wasn't my business. If you needed or wanted me to know, you would tell me. Though I hope it's worth whatever you're shoving your nose into."

She let out a huff in response.

Tightening Jak's coat around herself, she started toward her captain's office. The sound of her friend's footsteps echoed behind her as he made his way towards the crow's nest atop the ship's mainmast.

Esmyra slammed the cabin door behind her and stormed towards the middle of the room, her father's furious stare boring into her once again. Crossing her arms, she let out a low growl as they stared each other down.

"Your continued defiance is becoming rather bothersome, Esmyra. There's no other word for your behavior these past few days." A grin formed on her father's mouth as he leaned back in his chair. "Does the title of first mate no longer suit you?"

She averted her gaze to the floor, refusing to look him in the eye. "Aye, well, let's not forget the true reason why I possess such a title in the first place."

His eyes narrowed in on her. "Perhaps you're right, and a shift is needed."

Esmyra's jaw locked at his words, knowing he would never demote her. It was all a power play, a show to her that he was always the one in charge, even if she held all his power in her talons.

"Now tell me. What is a suitable punishment for a daughter and first mate? What good are you if you're out getting captured while disobeying orders?" he asked as he scratched his beard in contemplation. "You were to compel the prince at the cove, rummage through his mind, and be rid of him. And suddenly we have to come *rescue* you?" His breathing turned heavy as his voice rose. "What the fuck happened?!"

*Punishment.* How did you punish a being who already felt trapped and alone? She knew the only way to derail the situation— and demotion—was if she played the only card she had.

And she hated every gods-damn second of it.

Esmyra crossed her arms behind her back and stepped up to his desk as she said, "I think you'll find that punishment won't be neces- sary once you lay eyes on the reason for my *defiance*, as you love to call it."

As he raised a brow, she reached into the coat's pockets and threw the velsinyte cuffs and rolled-up map on the desk before him. The sound of the metal clinking echoed off the walls.

Cyrus shot her a warning look. "And what be this? Handcuffs and unreadable parchment?"

"Oh, don't get your beard in a knot." She gestured to the parchment with her chin while a grin crept up her face. "See for yourself."

With a grunt of aggravation and a bit of amusement, he unraveled the paper. He raised a brow and looked back up at her. "A map of the kingdoms."

"Aye, the *four* kingdoms."

"Why would this matter to me? I've told you many times that the Kingdom of Maerinys was lost just before you were born."

Her eyes shifted as irritation surged. She huffed out through her nostrils and pointed to the circled cluster of rocks just a few miles east of where Maerinys sank.

"I believe King Rowe has uncovered a way to get to the sunken kingdom. While in Anchorage Cove, I decided there may be more secrets hidden on the Phoenix's ship and compelled my way onto it when his mind held next to nothing," she lied. "I found this in Draevyn's office before—"

"And how exactly did you become the Phoenix's prisoner aboard his ship?" He cut her off.

Her mouth popped open as her spine straightened. "Really? Out of everything you've heard from Jak and myself...*that's* all you care about?"

"Of course it is!" he boomed as he stood from his seat, but she didn't flinch. "My greatest asset was captured by the enemy. My *daughter*, who can compel any living being to do as commanded with only a hum from her voice or a glance with her eyes! I had to come save you and lost several members of the crew doing so. I would like to know how that fucking happened, Esmyra."

She refused to answer. All she could manage was to stare at him down the bridge of her nose, chest heaving.

Cyrus huffed out an aggravated breath as he rubbed his temples. His gaze then landed on the cuffs. "And why did you put these here?" He leaned back in his chair again as he lifted the heavy stone-like metal, examining them.

"They're supposedly crafted from a substance called velsinyte."

Her captain choked on air, letting out a few coughs as his strained gaze found hers once more. "You're *sure* that's what these are? How in all gods did you get in possession of these?!"

Esmyra placed her hands in the pockets of the coat. "Stumbled upon them on the king's ship."

He stood from his desk then. "Esmyra, this isn't a game. If these are what you speak of, they are very...dangerous. Especially for you." His eyes went wide, face growing more pale by the second as he seemed to put it all together.

"I had never heard of such a thing until—"

"Until what?" he cut her off.

She swallowed, a tightness forming in her throat. "Until they were placed upon my wrists."

"Kaelypso's depths, Esmyra!" he roared.

Her hands flew out at her sides as she screamed back, "Draevyn caught me sneaking into his office, and when I couldn't think of a clever enough excuse as to why, he clasped those cuffs on my wrists and threw me in the cell beneath the ship."

"So, he knows who and what you are, then," he guessed.

"He didn't have the slightest clue. I had to hide the fact that they nearly brought me to my knees."

"For the love of all gods." Cyrus bowed his head—whether it was in disappointment, shame, or worry, she wasn't entirely sure.

Esmyra cleared her throat, and after a few silent moments passed, she asked, "What is velsinyte, and why did it affect me the way it did?"

A huff of air left his nostrils as he pursed his lips. "You're a creature of magic we don't understand. Velsinyte, to most, is a substance of mortal legends. There were rumors that a weapon was forged by the gods themselves, and it had the ability to deplete magical beings of their power."

Her head rapidly shook back and forth as she tried to take in his words. "I'm not a typical shifter. I've spent *centuries* in the realm's libraries when we make port. Every text I've found has made that clear."

"Yes, well...magic of sorts runs through your veins, so it appears the substance works on you all the same. Magic is magic. It calls to its kin."

She involuntarily rubbed her wrists as the words flowed from him, feeling the phantom touch of the cuffs lingering on her skin.

"Why was the prince in possession of these then? Why carry them on his ship? Does he not fear mutiny among his crew? His ship was full of nothing but mortals," Esmyra wondered aloud.

"Perhaps he was hiding them from his own kin, fearing that they may use them on *him* one day. Or his enemies."

Her eyes flared. "Rumors claim that Draevyn and Atlas together are a force. Flame and shadow make for quite the opponent. I would bet coin on the enemy."

"Aye, well, we may never know now that his body lay at the bottom of the sea," he said as he took the cuffs and shoved them into the drawer of his desk.

Her eyes widened as she held her tongue. She would let him believe that...for now, at least.

Esmyra tapped the circle on the map. "We'll sail here and search for the lost kingdom and its gold. The humans are fooling themselves. They cannot possibly get down there without gills. We'll take the treasure for ourselves before they even come close to it."

She smirked as her gills fluttered out in a display from the sides of her neck.

"We will do no such thing. Do you wish to risk the wrath of the gods?"

Esmyra's brows furrowed. "You're afraid... Genuinely afraid, aren't you? Tell me, father, is it of the southern waters or the gods?"

Cyrus's nostrils flared, the veins in his neck straining as he stood before her. "I don't want you near there. Now go find some clothes and get some rest."

Her mouth popped open at his sudden dismissal. "So you're abandoning what the king is searching for just because it lay within the southern waters? It's a dead, sunken kingdom, Father."

His jaw ticked. "Get to your post, Esmyra."

"But—"

"That's an order," he barked.

Her lip curled back. However, she knew fighting him further on this would do no good, at least not in that moment.

Esmyra turned on her heel and stalked out of his office, slamming the door before crossing the deck. She then perched herself atop the bow of the ship, where the sea breeze whipped her hair around her face.

If her father refused to search for Maerinys, that only meant that she would once again need to keep secrets from her captain and crew, and search for it on her own.

As the sun completely set on the horizon, she prayed to the lost sea goddesses that it would be worth it.

# CHAPTER 13

# Draevyn

As Draevyn neared the castle, the grand doors swung open, and the guards announced his return home. He stormed past them, aiming for his father's throne room.

Draevyn's anger surged, his flames igniting each torch he passed as he made his way through the halls.

The castle was busier than usual, full of faces he didn't recognize. Mortal women and nymphs stalked about the halls, arm in arm in their intricate dresses, ducking out of the way or gawking at him as he passed.

A growl slipped through his lips each time it occurred—their whispers echoing in his ears. *The Phoenix.*

He went to turn the last corner when his chest slammed into another's. "Fucking Irah," Draevyn huffed, but when he went to apologize, his eyes met his brother's.

Atlas grinned. His brother's face was almost a mirror to his own. If it weren't for Draevyn's well-kept beard, they would appear as twins —and where flames flickered in his brown stare, wisping shadows lurked within his brother's grey eyes.

"Brother," he greeted him.

"Atlas." The corners of Draevyn's mouth lifted.

They stood in silence for several seconds before Atlas reached out and clasped him on the shoulder, pulling him in for a hug as a few deep chuckles left them both.

"What in all gods happened to you, Drae? I hate to say it, but..." He let out a laugh. "You look like hell swallowed you and spat your ass right back out again."

Draevyn raised a brow as he searched for the words to describe the nightmare of what happened after leaving Anchorage Cove.

"Hell would've been kinder to my flames, Atlas."

"Ah, so the depths then!" he boomed as he wrapped an arm around Draevyn's shoulder and began guiding him down the hall. "I see you're in your usual enthusiastic spirits."

Draevyn blew out a breath from his nostrils. "May I have no moments of peace anywhere in my life?"

"Oh, come on, Drae. It couldn't have been that horrible. You just haven't found the kingdom yet. Sure, Father will brood over it and be his typical raging self, but it will blow over. It's not as if you lost your ship."

Draevyn stopped dead in his tracks at those words, and his brother stumbled as he halted alongside him. Letting out a loud breath, he turned to Atlas and said, "There's much to discuss."

Atlas barked out a laugh. "You're shitting me? Holy balls of Irah, you actually lost the ship?" When Draevyn's face showed no signs of amusement, all of his own dropped. "Oh gods, what happened?"

He rubbed his temples. "It's a long story, and one I certainly don't feel like repeating. So let's find the king, shall we?"

Atlas gave him a curt nod and their steps continued toward the throne room.

As they walked in, the grand hall of the castle was adorned with tapestries depicting Lephyrin's triumphs, threaded in vibrant maroon and gold. Guards were posted about the room, all in a perfectly still stance as their eyes followed the brothers making their way to the king.

"Your Majesty," Draevyn began, his voice echoing through the great hall as they came to a halt at the foot of the dais.

Their father sat on a gilded throne, his rotund frame spilling over its armrests. The king's crimson robes strained slightly at the seams as his golden crown sat tilted atop his thinning, dark hair. Round and flushed, his cheeks puffed out, framing a sneer that warped his thin, cracked lips. His dark, beady eyes were locked on them as he twisted one of his several golden rings around his fingers. Draevyn's eyes drifted to his father's forearm, halting on the scarred, mutilated burns beneath rolled-up sleeves. His throat tightened at the sight, and he immediately averted his gaze to the floor.

King Rowe stood, his heartless eyes narrowing. "Draevyn, you were told not to return to Lephyrin until you found what we needed. I trust you've obeyed said orders and come bearing the news that the cave's entrance has been found."

"My ship has been lost at sea," Draevyn admitted, each word heavy with the weight of failure.

A murmur of disbelief rippled through the assembled guards, their faces pale with shock. But while King Rowe remained composed, his cheeks flared with heat, giving away his irritation.

"And how could this have happened?" he demanded. "I've received no reports of storms at sea."

Draevyn bowed his head, anticipating the bellowing tantrum his father would throw once he spoke the words aloud. "It wasn't a storm we encountered, Your Majesty." He paused as his father's eyes narrowed on him. "It was *The Night Wraith*."

A few low gasps erupted from the guards, horrified whispers following them.

Draevyn glanced at Atlas standing beside him, watching as the color drained from his face.

The king leaned closer to the edge of his throne. "Blackwood?! You're sure?"

"I am." Draevyn dipped his chin. "I saw him with my own eyes. Fought his crew alongside my men, but it wasn't enough. *The Odyssey* was lost to the depths, along with half my crew."

"And why in all hells did you not light that bloody ship on fire?!" King Rowe barked, brows furrowing.

Draevyn cleared his throat. "He said if I called on my flames, he would call his beast, and my crew would be lost. I played fair until I couldn't, and by then, it was too late."

The king let out a few lifeless chuckles. "You took the word of our realm's most brutal criminal? What the fuck is wrong with you?"

Draevyn's jaw ticked, trying to keep his retort in. The truth was, technically, Draevyn went back on his word first, and that was why he met Blackwood's beast.

His father didn't give a damn about anyone besides himself. He would never understand the brotherhood that Draevyn shared with his crew, nor would he show them the same loyalty, feeling the need to keep each of them safe.

Draevyn had prided himself on always making his best effort to be a man of honor, but perhaps the king was right in a way.

He bowed his head in shame. "It was a mistake. It won't happen again."

His brother placed a hand on his shoulder. "Tell us what happened."

Draevyn sucked in a sharp breath. "Regardless of Blackwood going back on his word, *The Odyssey* took on several cannons and was well on its way to the depths before he called his beast on us."

The king leaned closer again, his beady eyes raking over Draevyn. "You saw the beast? You're sure it was that?"

Draevyn gave a curt nod. "We've never witnessed anything like it before—tentacles the size of our castle's spires rose from the sea and consumed us out of nowhere. Despite our best efforts, the ship was swallowed and dragged to the depths."

Truthfully, the realm wasn't even sure what the creature was. Only that it was colossal and sank ships within minutes. Draevyn knew better than to try to explain to his father that the monstrous creature was forged by the sea itself. The king would call him a liar—it had always been his assumption of Draevyn and the one thing he swore to never be.

King Rowe's eyes flared. "Tentacles?! You believe the beast he's tamed is a *kraken*?"

Draevyn blinked. "Correct."

"Those monsters are nothing but legends and ghost stories told around ships' decks," he barked.

"Well, let me assure you...it appears some legends hold truth."

The king's jaw clenched, his hands balling into fists at his sides. "This failure is unacceptable, Draevyn. You may be my son and the captain of our sea's armada, but that can change at any moment."

*Right*. How could he fucking forget?

"So Blackwood got away? And his monster?"

Draevyn cleared his throat. "Unfortunately, yes."

His father let out a low growl as he pointed his stubby finger down at Draevyn. "The beast that haunts the depths needs to be destroyed. And *you* will be the one to do it."

Draevyn had laid eyes on the creature made entirely of the sea itself. It would be impossible to defeat. If Blackwood could conjure the kraken at will... He didn't even want to consider what that meant for all who sailed those same waters. He barely made it out alive himself.

He lifted his stare back to his father's. "I'll add it to the never-ending list of your requests of me and my crew."

"Speaking of the crew...what of them?" the king demanded. "How did you make your way back to Lephyrin without a ship?"

Samwell, Tommy, and what remained of his men stayed down at the docks, awaiting Draevyn's command on what the king would demand of them next.

Draevyn blew out a breath and turned to Atlas, who silently watched their interaction. "Those who survived the attack made it to the pinnaces before the ship went down. The only near casualty from the beast was myself."

"Drae," Atlas interjected, but the king was unfazed.

"And how did you survive, then?" his father questioned.

His jaw locked as he stood beneath the king's gaze. "I was lucky to have washed up on some of the larger pieces of debris. A ship of merchant sailors found us floating in the middle of the sea not long after. They dropped us off in Lephyrin's harbor an hour ago."

"Lucky indeed." He paused, his eyes raking over Draevyn as he scratched his beard. "Well, since you're here, you may as well stay until the end of the month. Your brother is to take a bride and create a marriage alliance with one of the other two kingdoms of Rymelle. Families of each court from Terrana arrived a few days ago, and the elven of Sumnae are on their way to Lephyrin as we speak. Our people will want their Phoenix present for it. After that, we can discuss a new strategy as to how you will go about finding Maerinys."

Draevyn's eyes flew to his brother.

"We have much to discuss," Atlas said, his jaw ticking.

The king stalked down the steps of the dais, clasping his hand on Draevyn's shoulder before shaking him. "Don't disappoint me again, boy."

Draevyn gave a curt nod before turning on his heel to head for the doors.

"And *Captain*..."

Draevyn reluctantly turned to face the king.

"You will not be welcome back in Lephyrin until you've found the entrance to the lost kingdom and rid us of that beast once and for all."

Without another word, Draevyn left the room, feeling like the disappointment his father believed him to be, as Atlas followed after him.

He strode through the corridors of the castle, his anger surging once more, blatant for all to see as the torches lining the halls flared as he passed. Atlas's shadows simultaneously worked to snuff them out.

"Do you wish to talk about it?" his brother asked as he remained two steps behind him.

"There's nothing to discuss," Draevyn growled. "The king wishes for me to remain out at sea. Never to return home until I defy the gods and find a non-existent entrance to a kingdom that disappeared centuries ago." He let out a breathy, hate-filled laugh.

"And is that what *you* wish?" Atlas asked.

Draevyn stopped in his tracks as they arrived at the entrance to the gardens that were encased within the castle walls.

"It's never mattered what I wish, Atlas. I've always loved the sea, prefer it honestly, but to be told to never return home because of an impossible hunt..." He shook his head as he took his first step into the garden.

"You know why he never wants you to be here, Drae," his brother said, following him.

Unsurprisingly, the gardens were filled with more females from the other kingdom, all gawking at Atlas as they passed. However, whenever their stares glanced towards Draevyn, fear clouded their eyes.

"And why is that?"

"It's because of your gift granted by Irah." Atlas chuckled. "Childish, really. Meanwhile, he flaunts you as Lephyrin's protector to those outside the castle walls."

Their father loathed being human—only seeing it as a sign of weakness in a world of gods and magic-wielding beings.

In his insatiable hunger for power, the king had bartered his own sons' souls when they were just infants to the malevolent god that ruled over them with a flaming fist. The coward offered his children as a sacrifice, demanding to be bestowed gifts by Irah himself. Irah deemed their father unworthy and placed the gifts upon Atlas and Draevyn instead, leaving their father speechless and resentful toward his heirs—until he decided he could use his sons as his kingdom's weapons.

The king of Lephyrin went through extraordinary measures to ensure the entirety of the realm believed that was exactly his plan when he went to Irah's temple all those years ago. He would never allow the other kingdoms to know he wasn't deemed worthy.

Atlas had been gifted Irah's shadowy tendrils of darkness—where Draevyn was bestowed with his fierce flames and the rage that came along with them.

Their mother, when she was alive, never forgave the king for what he attempted to do. And neither had Draevyn, for if he never had this *gift*, his mother would still be alive.

One day, when Draevyn was only nine years old, he was hiding from his father in his mother's personal chambers. When the king found him there, he attacked *her* for defending her son and hiding him away for being scared.

The first crack of his father's hand on the queen's cheek had her letting out a screech of agony as she used her body to shield Draevyn behind her. He screamed, begged, and cried, but nothing would stop the king's fists from slamming into his mother's face.

*"He is to protect Lephyrin one day. You will not make him soft!"* the king screamed at her before gripping her by the throat and throwing her against the stone wall. Her hazel eyes had met Draevyn's as the king continued to berate her, seeming to plead with him to run away.

Perhaps he should've. But he couldn't leave his mother alone with the monster his father had become. And then a single tear slipped down her cheek as she whimpered beneath him, taking his relentless assault.

In a desperate attempt to save his mother, Draevyn lost control of his flame, setting fire to everything in the room. He didn't know how to stop it, and couldn't put them out. With each ravaged breath, the flames grew, consuming everything in sight. The more Draevyn panicked, the more his parents screamed, the larger the blaze surged, nearly engulfing the room.

The king ran from the room just before part of the ceiling collapsed—but not before a lick of fire raced up his forearm, mutilating its flesh. But Draevyn and his mother became trapped inside, suffocating from the smoke.

Draevyn screamed for her, trying everything he could to lower the flames, but he could hardly see with the tears lining his eyes. The blaze rose and flared alongside his emotions.

The king returned several minutes later with Atlas in tow, and Draevyn would never forget the look on his brother's face as he took in the scene. Atlas had managed to snuff the majority of the fire out with his shadows before the guards took over.

But by then, it had been too late for the queen.

*"It's okay, my boy,"* were the last words his mother ever said to him.

She was brought down to the infirmary with the best healers of

Lephyrin working to save her life, but there was nothing they could do. She succumbed to her injuries that night, and nothing was ever the same again.

That was the day the king no longer looked at Draevyn with love in his eyes but with fear and hatred. And shortly after, King Rowe started using the velsinyte cuffs on his own son without anyone's knowledge.

He had just been a boy. A gods-damn child trying to save his mother from her abusive husband, learning to wield the blaze that he was still barely able to keep at bay. Draevyn remembered the surging panic, the tears stinging his eyes, and the disgust in his father's stare as if it happened only yesterday, instead of eighteen years ago. He knew it would haunt him for the remainder of his life.

The heavy, magic-absorbing cuffs were often used as punishment, or if his father believed Draevyn's emotions were surging too greatly. The king stated it had been to protect everyone around him, making his son feel like the demon that Irah placed within him—the Phoenix the realm made him out to be.

Upon reaching their twenties, the king spread fearful rumors of the immense power the brothers possessed, cautioning that those who dared challenge the Lephyrin crown would be met with the wrath of King Rowe's Phoenix—his fire-wielding son who loved nothing more than to burn his enemies alive, or those who dared to cross him.

Draevyn hated it, and he hated *him*—his monarch and sire. However, in the world of gods, men, and beasts, they all had a role to play. His purpose was to serve as the king's monster and weapon. It wasn't until Draevyn challenged him on the reckless use of his power that the king sent his son out to sea, after his father searched and searched for those gods-damn velsinyte cuffs he loved so much—only to find they had vanished.

And now, they lay at the bottom of the sea.

"Are you listening to me?" Atlas said with a laugh, snapping him out of his trance.

Draevyn blinked. "Afraid I missed it. What were you saying?"

"How about you go clean some of that seawater out of your ears,

Drae?" He shoved at his brother in a way they used to when they were just kids running around the castle, playing tricks on the staff, and ignoring their mother's pestering to behave.

"What I said was, he's just jealous of your gifts. The stubborn old bastard. Sometimes I'm jealous of them, too. I wouldn't mind playing with a little fire every now and again."

A quiet chuckle left Draevyn. "If we could, I would trade gifts at any moment."

Atlas grabbed his arm, and their stares locked. "That day wasn't your fault, Drae." He pursed his lips before offering him a smile. "Besides, you're much more responsible than I would be if I were to possess that power," he said, trying to lighten the mood.

Draevyn gave his brother a look as they exited the gardens on its opposite end. "You're the most responsible moron I know," he heckled.

A loud laugh left Atlas. "I missed you, brother. It hasn't been the same around here since Father sends you out to sea so much. I know you prefer to be out there most days, but sometimes I swear he may still fear you." He shook his head as if it would shake the thought from him.

Draevyn opted to change the subject. "So, responsible moron, what's this he spoke of regarding you taking a wife?" He cocked an eyebrow at him as he gestured to the ladies, who were pretending to be looking in any other direction than where they were.

"Gods, don't remind me. They all flocked here for a fun little masquerade, and I'm to choose a bride by the end of it." He rolled his eyes.

"Annoyed you'll finally have to be tied down?" Draevyn mocked.

Atlas huffed through his nostrils. "A bit of that. And a bit of the fact that it must be done on that night. I would rather court a few beautiful women before deciding, but Father has insisted on forming stronger alliances, though I cannot fathom why it matters. Rymelle's kingdoms have been at peace for centuries."

"Indeed," Draevyn said as he scratched at his beard, but he knew if the other kingdoms heard of him searching for Maerinys, it could put them all at odds. "And why the masquerade?"

"Tradition of other kingdoms, apparently. They all wanted to ensure every daughter had a fair chance."

Draevyn snorted. "Interesting."

Atlas shot him an unamused look. "Yes, well, they believe it would be more fair to the ladies and kingdoms if I were to pick someone not entirely for beauty."

"A tragedy, really."

"Indeed," Atlas groaned. "Will you be staying for the ball?"

"It appears I must." Draevyn scratched at his beard and smirked. "I'm not sure what will become of you if I leave you here to the women who've been eyeing you like you're their last meal." He winked.

"Nothing of decency, brother, *that* I can promise," Atlas admitted with a menacing smile. He sighed a moment later. "But if you insist... how typical of you to ruin my last bit of unmarried fun."

"I'm sure you still have time for plenty of it," Draevyn said with a laugh as they stalked up the staircase that led to their shared wing of the castle.

# Esmyra

Esmyra had been stewing in her thoughts for days, her mind reeling about everything she'd uncovered and the endless unknowns that kept presenting themselves to her. Her father had been avoiding her since their argument in his office.

She stood at the bow of the ship, watching as the waves beneath them crashed into the hull, when a hand fell atop her shoulder, startling her. Esmyra whipped around in a near hiss when she locked eyes with Jak.

"Kaelypso! You know better than to sneak up on me like that, you *fool*."

"Aye. Doesn't mean it's never not funny to watch something scare you for once," he teased.

"Oh, shut up and go back to your crow's pit."

"Crow's *nest*, Esmi," he countered with a laugh.

Esmyra waved her hand before turning her gaze back to the sea. "Semantics."

Jak placed his elbows on the ship's rail, watching the waves alongside her. "Are you done moping around yet? Gods, I thought it was boring without you here, but this is almost worse."

"I'm just very frustrated with him lately," she whispered, pursing her lips.

"Well, I'm always frustrated with him. And you. And the crew, yet here I be! Every damn day..." He turned around to face the deck and leaned back on his elbows as his eyes bore into the side of her face. "And did I mention *you?*"

"I will not hesitate to shove your ass overboard, Jak."

"Ugh. Beautiful, reckless sea woman." He winked as she glared at him. "You know you'd just have to come rescue me because you can't stand to have conversations with anyone else aboard most of the time."

"Aye, well, I'll just have to learn to grin and bear it, I suppose."

Jak sighed. "Give the man a break that he didn't jump at the chance to go on a treasure hunt with you immediately. You know that eventually he's going to have us turning around to head that way. The captain doesn't know how to handle his anger sometimes, and he feared losing you, now knowing something out there can weaken you."

A sad huff left her as she turned to meet his stare. "Scared of losing his daughter or weapon?"

Jak rolled his eyes. "You know the real answer to that. The *great* Captain Blackwood is feared amongst all in every kingdom. While his methods sometimes aggravate me when it comes to using your power—he loves you with everything he has." He paused. "And that's a lot of fucking loot."

They both let out chuckles as he attempted to lighten the mood, but their amusement was interrupted by the click of boots echoing from behind them. When they turned to face the noise, they came face-to-face with the captain. His mouth was set in a hard line, yet his eyes gleamed with sorrow.

"Esmi," he started and then turned to her friend. "Jak, get your ass back up into the nest. The sun is nearly set, and it's getting dark."

"Aye, Captain," he answered before morphing into his owl form and flying up the mainmast of the ship, leaving them alone together for the first time in days.

Esmyra's eyes narrowed on her father. "That was hardly necessary."

"I know you may still be upset with me, but we need to speak. There's a reason I don't want you anywhere near Maerinys."

She tilted her head in confusion.

Cyrus gestured toward the back of the ship with his chin and turned on his heel, leading her to reluctantly follow him across the deck and back to his office.

Shutting the door behind them, he said, "Take a seat behind the desk, would you?"

"Why?" she asked with an arched brow.

"It's where you're to be one day, and I'd like to show you something."

Esmyra's brows furrowed at that. A moment later, he swiped away all the crowded junk atop his desk to reveal a larger version of the original map of Rymelle, with Maerinys included.

"Aye, Father, this is the same thing I brought to you, only... bigger."

"It plays a key role in what I'm about to tell you." He sighed. "I told you that I found you when you were only a baby, left alone in the streets of Lephyrin."

A laugh left her. "Aye. You also said I would be good for bartering." She leaned back in his chair and placed her boots atop his desk as she crossed her arms. "Only when the time came to sell me, that big ole black heart of yours couldn't do it." She smirked.

Sadness lingered in his eyes. "Aye, that's what I've told you for many years. But it wasn't the truth."

Esmyra's grin dropped at his words, her throat tightening from dread.

Cyrus sucked in a sharp breath. "I found you in Maerinys."

She ripped her feet down from his desk and leaned across it, staring at him, jaw agape. "*What*?!"

"I'm sorry, Esmyra. I'm sorry I lied, but it was to keep you safe."

The ringing in her ears was deafening. "Safe from what, exactly? You found me in the kingdom of the sea and lied about it my entire life. Why would you even lie?!"

She had a feeling she stemmed from the kingdom somehow, given her siren form, but never thought she was ever physically there.

The reason for his lie dawned on her a moment later.

Cyrus Blackwood was a pirate—the self-proclaimed pirate *king*. All he wanted was power over the seas. He was a mere mortal when Maerinys sank. That was nine centuries ago...the same time he 'found' her—around the same time he'd been cursed by the sea goddesses themselves.

Or so he'd said.

"You...you *stole* me. Didn't you?" He flinched at her words, and she stood from the desk. "You didn't find me in the street. I wasn't a child you saved from a life of poverty, disease, and hunger." That lie was the reason she had a soft spot for the children suffering in Lephyrin. "My 'father' stole me from my *true* family."

"Esmyra, no. It's not what you're thinking. There's so much more to it than that."

"How?!" she screeched as the roar of the waves around them grew louder. Her eyes shifted from the sudden rush of anger as her talons extended, embedding themselves into the wooden desk, splintering it.

Panic etched itself into his face. "If you would just let me talk."

Esmyra lifted her webbed, taloned hand and pointed it at him. "You've had *centuries* to talk. Now, it's *my* turn." She walked around the desk and sized up the man she called father. "Let me make sure I'm understanding this correctly, shall we?"

His onyx eyes were locked on her, unblinking.

She tilted her head to the side in a predatory manner, but the captain didn't back down. "You didn't happen to stumble upon a baby in the streets of the kingdom, no. You knew exactly what I was, and *that's* why you took me. You raised me as your own and morphed me into your personal fucking *weapon*."

"Esmyra." His voice was strong—bone chilling and radiating with authority—the voice of the captain. "Enough with the witch hunt for what you want to believe. Now, I've made mistakes, but keeping you *safe* will never be one of them. Do you hear me?"

"Safe?" The word left her in a confused whisper before her eyes lifted to his. "Safe. From. What?"

Cyrus pressed his lips in a thin line as his nostrils flared. His stare went from blazing with rage to reflecting only deep sorrow.

A chuckle left her, but it was devoid of warmth. "You're rummaging through that little brain of yours in search of more lies." She waved her talons in the air with each word.

An odd feeling settled into Esmyra's chest—it was pain, heartache even. The one person in all of Rymelle who she believed deep down in her soul would love her unconditionally was the same person who had lied to her all her life, keeping her compliant and hidden from her truth.

"You're despicable," she whispered right before storming toward the door.

"Esmi, wait," he demanded, grabbing her arm.

She whipped around to face him as one of her hands remained on the door handle. "Just tell me one thing, *Father*, just one."

The veins in his neck strained. "Aye."

Esmyra swallowed thickly, her heart rate refusing to settle. "Did you know what I was when you took me? Did you know that I was a monster?"

"You're not a monster, Esmyra." His pleading eyes roamed over her. "I may have used your abilities to my advantage, but you've never been what you're speaking of. If anything, 'tis I who be the monster in the sea."

"Answer the question, Captain."

She scented his fear, mingling with an immense sadness before he finally spoke. "I knew exactly who and what you were." The tiny bit of hope she'd clung to in these last few minutes evaporated as the words left him. "But I raised you. Regardless of the blood running through our veins, you're my daughter. My chosen first mate and heir to the sea. I would choose you over this"—he gestured to their surroundings—"any day."

Esmyra's eyes were stinging, and it was an odd feeling she'd so rarely experienced—*tears*. "I don't believe you." Her voice was barely above a whisper.

She shoved out of his grasp then. "I'm not the heir to the sea, Captain." She paused as his eyes flared, his brows slowly creasing. "I *am* the sea. The storm. The depths. The monster within."

Esmyra quickly rushed past him, through the room, and ripped the map of the realm from the desk. Rolling it up, she glanced back at him and found he was standing in the doorway, gritting his teeth.

"Esmyra, what are you doing?" His voice boomed, and she could tell the death grip held on his temper was slipping.

"Something I should've done before even coming back here," she admitted, stalking back toward him.

"And what be that?"

She whirled on him. "I'm going to find the hidden entrance to Maerinys before Lephyrin does, and when I come back, we are going to get to the bottom of all of this. No more lies."

"Absolutely not," he challenged. "Not only am I your father, but I am your captain. You will not leave this ship. You are to *stay here!*"

Esmyra tilted her head to the side once more, her voice coming out lethally sweet. "Afraid of what will become of the great Captain Blackwood without your beast to aid you in your bidding?"

His jaw ticked, and he moved to rip the map from her hand in answer.

But she was quicker.

"*Esmyra!*" Her name was an echo behind her as she took off into a sprint across the ship's deck, map in hand.

Cyrus was yelling, no longer as her father, but as the captain—his voice commanding and echoing over the roar of the waves beneath the ship. She could practically feel the booming of it rumbling the floorboards beneath her feet as they touched down with each stride. She desperately worked to tune it out, knowing that if she stopped now, she may never get another chance.

When Esmyra reached the rail, she didn't yield, nor did she look back, before diving over its edge and into the sea.

The fire crackled in the hearth of Atlas's room, filling the chamber with the scent of burning cedar as Draevyn sat in the settee, enjoying the silence. The warmth should've eased the cold in his bones, but nothing had chased it away—not the change of clothes, not the wine in his hand, not even his fire-fueled blood could remove the icy chill running along his spine every time he thought of her. Of Esmi.

Atlas lounged in his high back chair across from him, one leg slung over the other, a goblet of wine in hand. "So," his brother drawled, watching him over the rim of his cup. "What *exactly* happened on this little trip of yours? I want the details. And I'm hoping some of them are dirty." He fluttered his eyebrows.

*Well, so much for silence.*

Draevyn rolled his eyes. "You're a pain in the ass."

Atlas uncrossed his legs and leaned closer to him. "Oh, come on. I'm sure it wasn't all terrible. I mean, thank the gods you're okay, but—"

"Except for Kaelypso and Naerysa, for they clearly were doing their best to bring me down to their depths," Draevyn cut him off.

"Ballsy to speak ill of the goddesses, Drae." Atlas huffed out a laugh, but when Draevyn didn't join in on the amusement, his brother's face turned serious. He rubbed his temples. "Alright, for real this time. What happened?"

Draevyn sighed and told him the story of how they sailed out at sea in search of Maerinys, of the woman he met in Anchorage Cove, and of the fight that ensued on the deck of his ship once Blackwood found them. And lastly, of the massive creature formed entirely of water that sank his vessel to the bottom of the sea. By the end, Atlas's face had paled.

"You were serious about the kraken?!" Atlas gasped.

Draevyn shook his head rapidly, refusing to meet his stare. "I can't find any other explanation for what I saw with my very eyes. The crew believes it to be a freak wave, but I saw it for what it truly was before it snuffed out my flames. Tentacles were crawling up the sides of my ship, reaching into the sky before bringing it down."

"And you said they were made of the *water*?" Atlas interjected.

"Indeed."

"And how did the crew not witness this?" his brother asked.

Draevyn swallowed, knowing his reaction before he admitted, "I turned the ropes holding the pinnaces to ash. They crashed back down into the water before I could even see the full extent of what we were up against. No one mentioned anything of seeing Blackwood's monster. Only a wave without a storm."

"You did *what*?!"

"It was to give them a chance at survival," Draevyn said with a shrug. "And a captain is to go down with his ship."

"That's such bullshit, Drae," Atlas snapped. "You're a *prince*. As your future king I fucking forbid you from trying to do anything moronic like that again." He had never seen Atlas get serious so quickly. "It's a miracle you didn't drown! What if you never made it back to Lephyrin?"

Draevyn didn't know how to tell his brother there was barely anything for him to come back to Lephyrin for besides, well, him. Their father had condemned him to the sea, and it felt more like home than his own kingdom did. Regardless of how much his flames resented water.

Atlas blew out a breath. "This woman you found seeking refuge... She drowned?"

Draevyn cleared his throat. A wave of regret rolled through him at the thought of locking her in a cell without any way to escape as the water rushed in. "She did. All she was looking for was a way to a better life, so she said anyway. And all it did was damn her to the depths."

"You can't blame yourself for that, Drae," he assured him. "It's not your fault.

That didn't make him feel any better about it—it was his fault she perished in the sea. His fault she didn't have a chance to escape on a lifeboat with his crew. He tried to do a good thing, for *once*. Something greater than what the *Phoenix* was always known for—death, destruction, and ruin.

He wanted to bring someone peace. Just once.

Draevyn glanced towards the open doors that led out to the balcony overlooking Lephyrin. The curtains that were pushed off to the side fluttered in the breeze as it rolled through. "Wasn't it, though?"

"It wasn't. And I don't want you to hold onto that blame. The blame for that was Cyrus Blackwood and him alone." Atlas let out a few aggravated huffs. "And that little *beasty* of his," he growled.

"Perhaps you're right," he lied, knowing he would forever hold the blame, just as he did for his mother's death.

Atlas leaned back in his chair, his eyes raking over Draevyn. "You told Father that you washed up on a cluster of debris. Is that true?"

He nodded. "I was knocked unconscious, lungs filled with water, when I suddenly came to and choked up what nearly killed me. I could've sworn I heard a voice sing me back from the vale."

The vision slammed into him then—of him sprawled out across half-shattered wood, coughing up seawater before gazing into a pair of icy blue eyes hovering over him. However, the moment his vision cleared, they were gone. He'd imagined them—imagined *her* being the one who saved him.

Atlas laughed. "Drae, were you drinking a bit of rum before you were shipwrecked? Or perhaps you slammed your head."

Draevyn stared into the fire, watching its flames flicker and burn. "Do you believe in sirens?"

His brother stilled for only a second, but then the easy grin returned, and he took a sip of wine. "Are you asking if I believe in ghost stories? Myths and legends? I must admit, I do love a good tale. Usually when it's told by a drunk sailor at the taverns trying to justify why he ran his ship into the rocks."

Draevyn let out a sharp breath, shaking his head. "I'm serious."

"So am I." Atlas leaned forward, studying him now. "What? You think a *siren* saved you?"

He hesitated, his fingers tightening around his goblet as he sank further into the settee. "I don't know."

"No one has seen or heard one's song since they were hunted down a few centuries ago." Atlas hummed, setting his goblet down on the tea table before him. "Let's say I do believe sirens never went extinct. If the stories hold any truth, it would've eaten you." He barked out a laugh as he dramatically raised a hand into the air. "Feasted on your sun-kissed, sea-salt-tainted flesh."

"If she was one, then I don't know why she didn't kill me," Draevyn admitted.

His brother snorted. "Well, maybe she liked your face."

Draevyn scoffed as he stood from the settee. "Oh, piss off."

"I mean it!" Atlas stood alongside him. "You've always had that whole brooding, stormy thing going on. Maybe she was intrigued."

Draevyn rolled his eyes in answer.

"And it's not possible it was the woman you lost or thought drowned?" Atlas asked.

Draevyn thought for a moment—his mind flashing back to the scene of the hole in the bottom of the boat, where her cell had been. "It couldn't have been her. She drowned before the ship even went down. Their cannons shot straight through the brig."

"Well, perhaps it was luck, then. Or Irah looking out for you while you were no longer in his territory," his brother assumed.

"The bastard has never done anything for me before," he countered with a scowl, and all the candles in the chamber surged with flame.

Atlas sighed and walked over to Draevyn, clasping him on the shoulder. "Once the crown is passed down to me, your time being sent out at sea will be over." He blew out a breath. "Gods, I've been wanting to surprise you with this, but I swear every time I see you, the fire in your eyes has somehow dimmed more and more…"

Draevyn shrugged out of his brother's grip. "What are you going on about?"

Atlas cleared his throat. "When I'm sworn in as king, I want you to be my advisor, Drae. It'll be a way for us to rule together. I'll be Lephyrin's first power-wielding crown, and I can't picture myself there if you're not standing alongside me."

Draevyn's eyes widened. Atlas wanted him as an advisor? He never saw himself having anything to do with the crown again, let alone help a ruler make decisions. Draevyn ruined everything he touched, and he would never allow himself to doom his brother's reign.

When he went to speak, a knock sounded on the chamber's door.

"Come in," Atlas groaned.

The door opened to reveal a guard standing in the doorway, giving a deep bow. "Prince Atlas, your presence is requested in the gardens by our guests from Terrana."

Atlas turned to Draevyn with a raised brow, a mischievous grin forming. "Better days are to come, brother. Now, would you like to accompany me in entertaining our beautiful guests?"

"It appears I don't have a choice," he grumbled.

Draevyn followed him without another word, yet he found himself picturing those better days he spoke of, along with a pair of icy blue eyes he couldn't get out of his mind.

The hour-long monotonous conversations in the garden were Draevyn's personal version of hell. So much so that when his father's guards approached them, he felt a twinge of relief.

"Captain Draevyn." He and Atlas gave each other knowing looks before turning to face the guard.

The man could barely contain his unease as he faced their intense gazes. Individually, they commanded respect, but when they stood together, their power was palpable.

"Do you have something you wish to say?" Atlas challenged with a raised brow.

"The king demands your presence in the throne room at once," the man answered.

"What for?" Draevyn asked. "We were there only a few hours ago. Surely he—"

"Surely he has a reason, Captain," the guard cut him off. "Your king demands you as an audience, and I'm here to collect you."

Draevyn's jaw clenched.

Atlas took a step toward the man. "Not only is he a captain, but he is also a *prince*. You will speak to my brother with respect, regardless of how the king treats him. He is royalty. Draevyn is above you in more ways than one, you measly little *guard*."

Draevyn thought his brother's defense of him was barely merited, knowing the guard's unpleasantness was likely demanded by the king.

"Very well. Apologies, Prince Atlas."

Atlas scoffed. "Your apology isn't even directed at the correct man. Do better. We'll meet our father in the throne room, but you're dismissed."

He went to step around the guard, but the man stopped him. "He's only requesting Captain Draevyn."

Atlas's shadows surged then, his eyes becoming a swirling haze of grey as he bent down and looked into the gaze of the now terrified guard.

An audience of onlookers formed around them.

Atlas lifted a hand as shadows danced around his fingers, exuding from his palm. "Are you now saying I cannot accompany my brother to a throne that is to be mine one day?"

"Of c-course not, Prince," the man stuttered.

"Then remove yourself from my sight." Atlas's back straightened as the darkness drew back into his palms. Draevyn watched on with a smirk, enjoying the show alongside everyone else.

The man couldn't get away fast enough, nearly tripping over his own feet as he backed away.

When Atlas turned to Draevyn with a wide grin, he let out a huff of a laugh. "Was that necessary?"

"Just because you've accepted the way people treat you, doesn't mean I have to, Drae," he answered as they moved toward the throne room.

Draevyn's eyes softened at the words, knowing his brother meant well. Atlas always meant well, looking out for Draevyn as the protective older brother he was—especially after that dreaded day he'd lost control of his flames.

The remainder of their walk was in silence until they reached the doors.

King Rowe looked anything but happy to see the two of them together. "Only one of you was required."

"Yet here we both stand," Atlas challenged. "What is it you want with Draevyn now, Father?"

The king's cheeks flashed a deep red. "Watch your tongue, *boy*. You are the heir. *I* am the king. It isn't what I'll be demanding of your brother, but what I demand from the captain of my armada."

Draevyn stepped around Atlas. "Is there something I can assist you with, Father?" He could feel Atlas's disappointment in him as he stood at his back.

"The elven high families of Sumnae have arrived, and they brought news."

"And what might that be?" Atlas chimed in.

The king pointed a chubby, swollen finger at his heir. "One more outburst and I will have you removed, Atlas!" He returned his gaze to

Draevyn. "A ship was spotted several miles away in the sea, anchored between our kingdoms."

"A fishing vessel, perhaps?" Draevyn guessed.

"No." A wicked grin grew from ear to ear on the king's face. "They stated it was *The Night Wraith*."

Draevyn's brows lifted in surprise. "And Blackwood didn't move to attack?"

"Perhaps there were too many ships from Sumnae for him to try to challenge them," Atlas wondered aloud.

Draevyn knew that couldn't have been the case, knowing the beast could take out as many ships as its master desired.

His eyes lifted back to the king. "What are you asking of me?"

"I think you already know, boy."

A heavy exhale escaped Draevyn's lips as he grasped the horrifying truth: his father was sending him on a suicide mission. It was the perfect way to eliminate him for good.

"Are you out of your fucking mind?!" Atlas boomed.

"Remove yourself! Now!" King Rowe bellowed back.

"He's your *son*!" Atlas screamed, his voice bouncing off the walls. "No one can survive an attack from *The Night Wraith*. It's a miracle he did the first time, and the elven were lucky to have arrived unharmed! Yet you send one of your heirs to fight an unwinnable battle in the sea."

There was a weighted silence in the vast room as the echoes settled. Draevyn worked to hold his tongue, processing what he was about to be ordered to do. He knew there wouldn't be a way to defeat a creature made of the sea—not when his power derived from flames.

"If we're the kingdom to finally bring down Blackwood, we'll be the most respected and powerful in the realm! Do you have no faith in Lephyrin's Phoenix?" the king challenged his heir.

"I have all the faith in the realm and every god that rules over the kingdoms. It's *you* I have no faith in. All you seek is more power and influence. Let us not forget that Irah didn't deem you worthy of being granted such power. It was *us* he did." Atlas gestured to both himself and Draevyn.

A cruel smile spread across the king's face as he stared down at them both. Draevyn's hands balled into fists at his side as he watched, trying to suppress the flames dancing along his fingertips.

"You forget your place, Atlas," the king stated calmly. "He's not my heir, *you* are. And though he *is* my son, he's also the captain of my sea fleet. It's his duty to our kingdom to rid us of any threats."

Draevyn stepped in front of his brother. "It's quite alright, Atlas. His decision is made. As is mine." He paused for a moment as he forced his eyes away from his brother's and turned his attention back to the king. "My crew will ready the ships and we'll leave at dawn."

Before anyone could say another word, Draevyn turned on his heel and stalked back toward the doors, slamming them behind him as he took his first steps toward what would surely be his demise.

CHAPTER 16

*Esmyra*

smyra's tail cut through the water with swift, powerful strokes, her turquoise scales shimmering in the dim light filtering through the ocean's surface.

She clutched the soaked, weathered map, its edges frayed and disintegrating from the seawater. Her eyes darted between the map and the underwater landscape, but it was essentially useless while she was beneath the waves.

Her mind was a whirlpool of frustration. She should've trusted her instincts more and gone alone to begin with, before bringing this to her father, knowing he had always been wary of the southern seas.

Relying on his approval had only delayed what she set out to do. But no, she *had* to stick to tradition and involve the captain, didn't she?

Esmyra was his first mate and greatest asset, yet he didn't even trust her instinct about what she was about to uncover. All because he'd been lying to her for centuries about the truth of where she came from. *Everything* she knew was based on a lie. She had nothing without trust, and the one person she had put all her faith in had fed her nothing but false truths her entire life.

If she didn't find the sunken kingdom before the humans of

Lephyrin did, she may never know her true lineage. Or even where she truly belonged.

The stakes were higher for her now, extending beyond simply upsetting the gods.

Her swim halted, and her fingers tightened around the map as she gave it one last glance. Above the surface, the sun gave way to the moon, and her midnight hair flowed around her like swirling ink, while her tattoos and eyes emitted a faint glow in the darkness.

The parchment finally disintegrated entirely in her grasp and floated away in the current. She huffed out a breath through her gills and her tail propelled her forward once more—regardless of where she ended up, she knew she needed to swim to the southernmost part of Rymelle.

All these years, he had lied to her. The only person in the entire realm she trusted—aside from Jak. To Rymelle, Cyrus Blackwood was the most feared pirate in all the seas, but to her, he was simply her father.

He raised her aboard *The Night Wraith*, and that was all she'd ever known. It was her life for nearly one thousand years—longer than any creature in Rymelle typically lived. It wasn't until the past few centuries that she ventured out to experience everything the world had to offer on her own, except for the southern seas. Whether it was out of boredom or curiosity, she wasn't entirely sure. However, what she found was a bleak reality of impoverished kingdoms ruled by corrupt royals—Lephyrin being the worst of them.

If the menace king of Lephyrin became the wealthiest in Rymelle, on top of having his shadow and flame-wielding sons, he could become the most feared and powerful king, even without possessing a drop of magic himself. She *refused* to let that happen. She would rip his plan out from underneath him and put the power back into the hands of his own people—making them richer than their tyrant king.

Esmyra swam south for days, pushing her body to its limits.

As she became increasingly frustrated by the need to rest, she hitched a ride on a sea turtle's shell, gliding through the water until it abruptly turned around and sped off.

She released her hold the second it began to drag her back toward where they came, bubbles erupting around them. The creature swam as fast as it could in the opposite direction, leaving her behind—and alone.

"Thanks a lot," she huffed, as she waved her webbed hand through the water.

She circled back and found the cause a moment later—only a few feet ahead lay an underwater cliff, dropping off in complete darkness.

With caution, she neared the trench, gripping its ledge as her fingers curled around the rocky edges.

*What in all gods is this?*

Even with the glow of her stare, she could barely see a few feet below the trench's cliff. This must've been it—where Maerinys sank to its doom. Esmyra wasn't a fearful woman, but something was gnawing at her insides, screaming that whatever lay at the bottom of the darkness wasn't just a lost kingdom.

But she had made it this far. It would be foolish to turn back now.

Esmyra gulped and began to scale down the wall of the trench, gripping its jagged edges with her talons.

She was on high alert, unable to see much of her surroundings. But the further she descended to the bottom of the sea, she realized the brighter the markings on her arms glowed. Her eyes flared as she rotated her forearm, examining it. They had never glowed *brighter* before. The tattoos that more resembled burns always appeared the same—a rusted red on land, and a dim turquoise beneath the tides, matching her scales.

*Kaelypso's tits, what's happening to me?* She blinked multiple times before continuing her descent, only this time, she released her hold on the wall and began swimming as fast as she could down into the darkness.

The walls of the trench loomed menacingly on both sides, adorned with ancient coral and scuttering sea creatures. Her heart raced as her every breath and movement became intensified by the suffocating silence.

She halted and hovered where she was. The walls were expanding outwards—the once narrow trench was now easily a mile wide.

The quiet was interrupted by a deep, resonant rumble as it echoed through the water, sending a shiver through her fins. The sound was unlike anything she had ever heard—low and malicious, reverberating through the depths. It sounded like the ocean itself was growling, a guttural, primal noise.

Esmyra's senses heightened as she froze, her eyes widening while she scanned the trench for any sign of danger. But all she was met with was a labyrinth of darkness. The rumbling intensified, drawing nearer, accompanied by the rhythmic swish of something massive displacing the surrounding water. The vibrations sent shockwaves through her very scales.

A distant and enormous shadow caught her attention as it ripped through the undisturbed water. The creature's body surged with a terrifying speed, its scales reflecting the faintest glimmers of her light.

Her gills hitched, fear gripping her by the throat as she took in the beast's size. It was a *sea serpent*—a behemoth of the deep, known as a myth of Kaelypso's creation a millennium ago. Before Esmyra became the monster of the depths, *this* was the creature that sailors feared. And now it was circling her like prey.

The siren within her thrashed as if it recognized what was hovering before her.

*This couldn't be happening.*

Esmyra twisted her tail sharply, the water parting around her as she searched for a place to hide. Its low, guttural growl vibrated through the water, making her heart race so fast she thought it would burst.

There was nowhere to swim to—nowhere to hide. And now here she was, levitating and glowing like a fucking beacon.

Its serpentine form stretched far beyond her line of sight. A dragon-like head emerged from the darkness, eyes shining like twin orbs of liquid silver, cutting through the darkness with a sharp, predatory glint. Rows of razor-sharp teeth lined its gaping jaw, and its navy scales made it effortlessly blend in with the trench's gloom.

Esmyra's mind raced, thoughts fragmented and frantic. She knew if she remained still, she would be as good as dead. Yet every instinct screamed that if she fled, the movement could cause it to attack sooner. She was fast—but even she knew she couldn't outswim a dragon of the sea.

Its eyes remained locked on her, as if it were trying to decipher what she was—or if she was a threat. Her heart thudded even harder, her gills flaring as she struggled to maintain her false composure.

*Think, Esmi. Think.*

Just as she was about to make the dash to the surface, or at least out of the trench, the sea serpent surged towards her with its gaping maw. She extended her arms and sent a powerful jet of currents towards the beast, aiming for its exposed throat.

The monster sensed the attack and twisted its enormous body with a speed she never thought possible for its colossal size. Her jaw dropped as she watched the jet of water glide off its scales. The beast let out a deafening roar that reverberated through the trench, its sound making the walls tremble.

What in all hells was she going to do?

As she looked up at the sliver of the trench's opening, she reached out her hand and felt the surrounding water come alive with pulsating energy, answering to her call as she willed it. In response, the currents violently swirled before wrapping around her like a protective veil.

Her power summoned a vortex, a destructive, swirling maelstrom, and sent it spiraling towards the creature. With a violent thrash of its tail, it easily evaded her attack, slicing the damn thing in half.

"Shit," she hissed, distracted enough to accidentally drop her shield.

It lunged at her once more, its mouth aiming to swallow her whole. Barely avoiding the snap of its teeth, she propelled herself towards the surface, her heart catching in her throat.

How in all gods could she kill this thing? And how long had it been stuck down here? Had the goddesses damned their creature to the darkness of this trench, or was it here for a reason? Guarding something.

She didn't dare look down as she raced through the water as fast as she could, feeling the monster right on her tail. Knowing she would never make it in time, she summoned a barrier—a solid wall of water that she thrust between herself and the beast. The creature slammed into it, momentarily stunned by the impact.

Esmyra conjured a barrage of sea blades, launching them at the serpent's eyes. When the beast tried to escape the attack, it twisted to the side, crashing into the rocky wall, and caused massive boulders to break off and drift down to the ocean floor. The deadly sharp sea-blades struck, embedding themselves in the creature's scales and forcing it to recoil in pain.

The serpent's body whipped through the water, thrashing violently, shattering the surrounding coral formations that lined the jagged walls.

Esmyra knew this was her last chance at escape, and her eyes beamed brightly as she summoned the full force of her power. With a battle cry, she released a massive pulse of energy. The shockwave propelled the serpent downward, back to where it came from, as it erupted in a bellowing roar that echoed through the trench.

Using what was left of her energy, she soared upwards. The force of her tail sent her spiraling past the edges of the trench's opening, through the open water, and up toward the surface.

The dim, bluish glow of the deep brightened as she ascended, the sunlight filtering down in golden shafts. With a final, powerful thrust, she broke through the surface, her head emerging into the open air. Droplets of water scattered like diamonds in the sunlight as she arched out of the sea, her long hair flipping with the movement, sending a showering spray flying in all directions.

Esmyra was gasping for breath, scanning the area frantically, when her eyes caught on a small island in the distance, to the east. She glanced down beneath her, the darkness of the water concealing everything below her tail.

Was this how sailors felt when they sensed she was stalking them?

With that thought, she didn't waste a moment before swimming toward the island. Worry worked its way through her gut as she realized that for the first time in her life, she sought refuge on land while fleeing from the sea.

Esmyra crawled onto the rocky surface of the small, mountainous isle in the middle of the sea. No sand met her bare feet, only cold, slippery stone.

Not far from where she heaved herself up, a cluster of jagged rocks appeared at the top of a small hill, and it didn't take long for her to realize this was all the isle bore. She was thankful it seemed uninhabited, considering she stood there entirely bare.

Something caught her eye, and she glanced down at her arms, where her *still* glowing markings remained, radiating their vibrant teal as seawater beaded down her skin.

They had never glowed above the surface, only ever in the sea.

She lifted one of her arms to her face, rotating it curiously with a raised brow.

*That's interesting.*

When her focus returned to the isle, she noticed a dark, narrow entrance within the rock formations. It seemed to beckon her, shrouded in shadows and overgrown with seaweed. The lapping of the waves on the rocks echoed softly as she walked through the gap, entering a spacious cavern. Its entrance was illuminated by beams of sunlight filtering through crevices in the rocks above.

This was what she was looking for—it had to have been.

As she moved farther into the cave, a chill ran down her spine while she climbed over the slippery rocks. Inside, the air was cold and damp, carrying an earthy, metallic scent that tasted like blood on her tongue.

Stalactites hung from the ceiling like menacing teeth as she ventured deeper. The darkness of the cave seemed to swallow her, and she willed her eyes to shift. She couldn't explain it even if she wanted to, she just *knew* she was exactly where she needed to be—as if her soul was humming in response to where she now stood.

Her thoughts were a tangled mess of what this could all mean.

*What in all gods could be in here?* Her pulse quickened with every step.

Her eyes squinted as she approached one of the far walls, noticing strange, weathered symbols carved into the stone.

The tunnel was beginning to narrow, and just as she considered turning back, her gaze fell on a passageway partially obscured by moss draping the cave's walls. The tunnel seemed to lead even deeper into the heart of the cave. She squeezed her way into the tight space, the jagged edges of the cave's wall scraping against her bare skin.

The ceiling grew lower, forcing her to stoop to avoid hitting her head. After what felt like an eternity, the passage widened, opening into a hidden chamber.

"This is it. This must be the secret entrance to Maerinys," she whispered to herself.

Grinning, she turned around, her long strides carrying her quickly out of the cavern, through the tunnels, and back to the sea.

She'd *found* it, what the humans were searching for—what was forbidden by the gods themselves.

Knowing the sunken kingdom could be reached, she had to get her crew there before King Rowe's men discovered it. Everything would be theirs for the taking—she even hoped to find answers regarding who or what she was.

The sea breeze blew her midnight hair around her face as she reveled in the warmth the sun brought her skin. With a hesitant glance towards where the monster waited in its trench, she dove back into the sea, shifting midair before crashing into the water and soaring north just below the surface.

Back to *The Night Wraith.*

Back to her father.

And, hopefully, back to the answers she longed for.

It had taken her days to find the hidden cavern in the sea, and nearly just as many to make her way back. She first swam to Anchorage Cove, where the crew frequently made port, and when she didn't see *The Night Wraith* floating in its harbor, she continued her way north, closer to Lephyrin.

Her frustration grew with each passing hour as she swam beneath the waves and still couldn't find her ship. She wondered if her father was trying to punish her, knowing just how furious he would be upon her return for disobeying his orders.

Again.

Esmyra sent out a pulse of power, and the water rippled around her from its force. She was met with resistance in all directions from objects and creatures within several miles of her, but one reverberation slammed back more intensely than any of the others, and she knew it must have been a ship.

After swimming for several miles, Esmyra came to a sudden halt as the underbelly of *The Night Wraith* came into view. Her brows lifted in confusion when she noticed it was anchored in the middle of the sea—something the crew had rarely ever done, if at all.

As she neared her anchored ship, a sense of unease washed over her. The vessel was eerily silent, even from where she hovered in the water, and no lantern lights flickered on its deck. A tightness caught in her throat as dread slithered through her veins.

Esmyra's head breached the surface, her eyes locking on the onyx ship as the moon hung low in the sky, casting a glow over the calm, dark sea. "Gods-dammit," she muttered, and with a final, powerful thrust of her tail, she reached the ship's side and shifted to her human form.

Grasping the rope ladder, she climbed up and heaved her legs over the rail. Once her feet touched down, seawater rolled down her skin and puddled on the wood.

Where was everyone? Moving cautiously across the deck, she tried to cover her naked body with her arms as her senses were on high alert.

The scent of iron filled the air, mixing with the salty tang of the sea. Reaching the mainmast, a horrific sight stopped her in her tracks—bodies lay strewn across the deck, lifeless and marked by brutal wounds and burns. Crimson puddles stained the wooden planks, pooling around the fallen.

Esmyra's breath caught in her throat right before she took off into a sprint and knelt beside the piled bodies of her crew. "No. No. No. No!" she screeched over and over again, refusing to believe the sight.

Blood rushed to her ears, her vision turning blurry as she knelt there, unknowing of what to do.

Esmyra turned every body, and each male's burnt, crisped skin was more unrecognizable than the last. She noted it was a fraction of the crew, and the rest remained unseen. Searching every face that lay intact, relief eased into her as she realized her father wasn't among them—nor was Jak.

She clenched her fists, fury and sorrow welling up within her as she pushed herself to her feet. Whoever had done this would pay. They would pay for it with their lives. The lives of their loved ones and anyone they held dear.

Esmyra forced her way across the ship, being careful to step over the bodies littering the floor. She stormed across the deck and found that her father's office was also empty. Eyeing his coat hanging next to the door, she took it and wrapped it around her bare body before leaving the darkened room.

Her gaze drifted to the stairs that led below deck, and Esmyra's talons extended as she grabbed a pistol from a fallen sailor's belt. Silently moving towards the hatch, she descended the steps, each creak of the wood under her feet echoing in the stillness.

In the dim light of the galley, she noticed the signs of a struggle—overturned tables, broken crates, and more blood seeping into the wooden planks of the floor.

*Who the fuck could have done this?*

When she found that this section of the ship was empty too, she had no leads on where the rest of her crew could have gone.

Were they thrown overboard? There weren't any bodies floating in the sea when she arrived. Her father's curse prevented him from dying, but what if he'd been taken? The fearsome Captain Blackwood was left defenseless by his greatest weapon, and he may now be in the hands of the enemy.

And when the enemy was all of Rymelle, whose inhabitants they had taunted for centuries, it was anyone's guess on who could have done this. The prize on her father's head or capture was one of the most hefty in all the realm.

*But they were burned,* she thought. No—*no*, she couldn't think that way.

Lephyrin's mortals would never be brave enough to attack *The Night Wraith*.

Jogging up the stairs, she nearly gasped at the sight of Jak as he stood above the bloodied bodies—the *one* male left living.

Her eyes fixated on him, shifting as her thoughts spiraled. What if it hadn't been an attack at all? What if this was a mutiny?

Esmyra hardly recognized his expression and stormed toward him, her lip curling back as she lifted the gun and shot three times.

*BANG. BANG. BANG.*

The sound echoed across the water and filled the midnight air, but Jak just barely dodged the bullets. When the pistol emptied, she tossed it carelessly to the side as she continued to advance on him.

Jak locked eyes with her. "Esmi, wait!"

"No," she bellowed, blinded by a haze of fury.

Her taloned hand wrapped around his throat as she slammed his back into the mainmast. Jak's gold eyes were bulging from his head as he desperately tried to get air into his lungs.

"If you try to shift to get out of this, I will slice your wings from your fucking body," she snarled.

"Please listen to me!" The words were barely understandable as they left him, his lungs straining for air beneath her hold. "Esmyra!" he gasped.

Her grip tightened, hand trembling slightly before letting him go, shoving his body away from her. Jak whimpered as he stumbled off to the side, nearly losing his footing.

"What in all gods was that for?!" The look on his face showed pure horror.

She stepped up to him as twin daggers conjured of water levitated on each side of her head, their blades aimed directly for Jak's eyes. Her stare began to glow, illuminating his body as he trembled in fear.

The siren beneath Esmyra's flesh no longer saw a friend standing before her, but a threat. Her captain and half her crew had disappeared as the other half laid slain beneath her feet. Someone was responsible, and ironically enough, only one person was alive to speak of it.

"You have thirty seconds to tell me what you know before I gouge your eyes out, Jaky boy." She reveled in watching a shiver roll through his body at the sound of her voice, knowing just how serious the threat was.

"Lower the blades," he pleaded, but she just raised a brow. "Esmyra! I'm your friend."

"I have no friends," she stated simply, and his body jolted at the words.

He blew out a breath as his spine straightened. "You know that's not true. Don't become the monster he nearly formed you into."

"Fifteen seconds, Jak." Esmyra's voice was a lethal calm.

"Okay, okay!" He was panting once more, holding his hands up in surrender. "When you left, he sent out half the crew to search for you."

"Why?" she demanded.

"Why do you think?! You ran, Esmyra! Even I had no idea where you were going."

She blew out a huff through her nostrils and lowered the water-wielded blades. "Start from the beginning. What happened when I left?"

His posture relaxed slightly, but she could tell he was still on alert, waiting for her to strike. "We waited two days, and when you didn't return, he sent half of everyone out. We anchored here to know where to come back to. He didn't want to wait until making port somewhere or anchoring in a cove. The captain wanted us on the hunt immediately."

"And were you here when this occurred?" She gestured to the lifeless bodies.

Jak rapidly shook his head. "No. I arrived here hours ago and immediately flew off to try to find the source."

Her throat tightened, and she stared at him, unblinking. "And did you? Find the source."

"Aye," he breathed, hesitantly pointing up to the main mast of the ship.

Her stare followed the movement, and her lips parted at the sight of the words slightly charred into the sail's canvas.

*Pirates of Rymelle, Be Warned.*

"Lephyrin's ships now sail back to their kingdom," he finished

The water-blades fell to the deck with a subtle splash. Her lips parted as her eyes went distant. "And who was aboard these Lephyrin ships, Jak?"

Jak's stare darkened. "I think you already know."

Now the burns that marked her crew's flesh made sense to her, when everything else appeared untouched by flames. The Phoenix purposefully left *The Night Wraith* intact as a warning to the realm's pirates.

This was her fault. This was *all* her fault. Not only did she leave her father and crew defenseless, but she was also the only reason the Phoenix survived the sinking of his ship.

She saved him for his kindness, only for him to turn back and use it against her.

Her gaze met Jak's. "Do they have him? Does the Phoenix hold my father captive?"

"Aye," he answered without hesitation. "He be strapped to the center of the ship at the mainmast—not even held in a cell below deck. They were already nearing Lephyrin when I soared back to look for you."

Her stomach dropped. They were going to bring her father to the king, but that wasn't even the worst of it. They were bringing her father on *land*. His boots would no longer be on the deck of a ship in the sea but rather on the soil of the realm he was cursed against.

Panic clawed at her throat. He wouldn't be able to breathe. Wouldn't be able to see or eat.

Without another word, Esmyra stalked to the bow of the ship, and Jak wordlessly followed, keeping a few steps back. When she halted at the tip, she climbed atop the rail, balancing on it as she stared out at the water. Her father's coat fluttered in the night breeze, billowing behind her.

She lifted her arms straight out over the sea as her hair fluttered around her face. The winds picked up as her power surged in all directions—the waves becoming more violent as every second passed. And as the sea became a wild storm, she forced her arms out straight at her sides, sending a shockwave through the entire ocean, calling what remained of her crew back to her.

Breath heaving, she leapt down, and when she made eye contact with Jak, an almost prideful smile tilted his lips. "And what be our next move...*Captain*?"

Esmyra's eyes narrowed at the title. With her father gone, she was now acting captain. Her word would now be law aboard *The Night Wraith*.

Meeting his gaze again, she pursed her lips before saying, "I think it's time to teach the Phoenix what happens when his flames get a little wet. Aye?"

As pinnaces surged in from the distance, as if carried in by the force of the waves, Jak's menacing smile grew to match hers. "Aye."

A day later, the bustling sounds of Lephyrin's capital buzzed around Esmyra as her crew blended seamlessly with the rowdy night crowd.

With a nod, she signaled them to move. They navigated through the labyrinthine streets of the kingdom, Esmyra's sharp eyes scanning for any sign of the city guards.

The plan was simple: infiltrate the castle, locate her father, and slay the fire-wielding prince. Her talons ached with the need for revenge.

"The streets will be nearly empty tomorrow evening, yes?" a guard called to another as they waltzed past them without a second glance.

Curiosity got the better of Esmyra, and she moved to follow, despite Jak's hesitance as he stood guarding her back. She pressed herself against an alley wall and watched, listening.

"Tomorrow is the ball where the prince is to choose a wife, and everyone whose family name holds value will be there." The man grimaced, turning his nose up at a beggar sitting on the side of the road. "The castle will be open to all sorts of beings from each kingdom of Rymelle. Unfortunately, we'll still have to deal with the lot that frequents these parts of the city."

Esmyra grinned, seeing a possible way into the castle.

She turned to Jak, who crossed his arms as he leaned up against the brick building they hid in the shadows of. "I'm not going to like this, am I?"

"Care to play a little dress-up?" She winked.

# Draevyn

A cascade of candle-lit chandeliers cast a warm, golden glow across the grand ballroom's marble floor. The air was filled with the melody of a waltz as couples swirled around the dancefloor, their laughter and conversations filtering through the air. The room was alive with the shimmer of silks and the flash of jewels as nobility from every kingdom in Rymelle mingled for the first time in centuries.

Draevyn rolled up the cuffs of his navy tailored jacket adorned with gold embellishments. The truth was, he had never felt more out of place.

This wasn't him—it was Atlas. He didn't belong here and hadn't in a long time. Not where he was forced to wear a smile on his face, shake hands, and politely nod at everyone who walked by. His brother lived for events like this, always seeing them as a way to meet beautiful women and take as many as he could to his bed, usually all at once. But Draevyn had never been that way.

Of course, he'd had women in his life before, but none he ever took seriously. Why would he bother when he barely made port in recent years? He often found that women were more interested in his flames and what his status could do than they were in *him*.

It was just one more thing Atlas reveled in, loving the attention more than the air he breathed. However, his brother possessed power that he assumed could cause pleasure and be made use of in the bedroom, while all Draevyn's power contained was destruction.

Women of his past acted fearless when toying with the Phoenix's flames until they found his love scorched their hearts.

To Draevyn, the gilded walls of the room resembled a prison more than a palace. He lingered near the tall, arched windows, where the darkness of the night pressed in on the glass. Every now and then, people would glance his way—curious lords and hopeful women—but his gaze would slide past them as if they weren't even there, dismissing them without a word.

His fingers twitched at his sides, his mind far from the twirling figures and the shallow conversations surrounding him. Draevyn's frustration was ready to boil over, contemplating slipping away from the scene of glittering masks and empty smiles and never looking back.

As he skirted the edge of the dance floor, his gaze landed on a familiar figure in the center of the crowd. Atlas was at the heart of the festivities, surrounded by a group of Lephyrin's women and females of other kingdoms, who were all laughing and vying for his attention. Unlike Draevyn, his brother thrived in the spotlight—his smile came easy and his charm effortless as he moved from one conversation to another.

Their eyes met across the room, and Atlas's grin widened as he raised a glass in a silent toast, inviting him to join. Draevyn gave him a subtle shake of his head as a smirk formed. It wasn't as if it would be difficult to slip into the role expected of him, to wear the same false smile and play the part his brother seemed to relish. However, as the years had passed, his patience for such things had withered away.

The night was intended for Atlas to take a bride and future queen of Lephyrin. Draevyn wouldn't dare step into the madness of the room and risk the females thinking he also desired that when the only thing he had grown to long for was the sea.

His brother watched him for a moment longer, a glimmer of understanding in his eyes as he dipped his chin. A moment later, Atlas excused himself from the group of women and strode in Draevyn's direction.

He let out a huff and opted to meet his brother halfway.

"Good of you to show," Atlas taunted. "I was beginning to think you slipped away the moment Father's eyes wandered from you."

"And miss you selecting one woman you'll be spending the rest of your life with?" Draevyn raised a brow. "I would never miss that kind of entertainment."

Atlas scoffed as he aggressively patted Draevyn on the back and pushed them both toward a table lined with endless kinds of imported wine and baked goods. He poured them each a glass and handed one to him. "You enjoy wounding me. Why don't you stop being such a gods-damn stiff and go speak to one of the beautiful women here tonight? As much as I'm up for the challenge, I don't think I have it in me to bed them all."

Draevyn sent the entire glass of wine down his throat, needing the liquid courage to have this conversation. "I have no desire."

"Petty conversations and pleasantries, I understand. All you must do for that is smile and nod. However, you're still a man, Drae." Atlas let out a low laugh. "Unless you've been bedding women in every port you sail to, I believe it would've been quite some time for you, no?"

"You're just as nosy as the women you're courting, do you realize that?" Draevyn grumbled, but his brother only barked out a laugh.

Atlas shook his head. "One day, you'll learn to have a bit of fun." His eyes then drifted to the dais, where the king sat, watching them both with narrowed eyes. He sighed. "It appears I'm not doing my duty enough, judging by Father's stare."

Draevyn suppressed his smirk. "Better hurry and choose before he decides for you."

"Fucking Irah," Atlas huffed and then placed his empty glass on the table. "Well, off I go to offer myself over to a sea of women." He winked. "The invitation remains if you care to join me, brother."

A moment later, Atlas disappeared into the crowd.

The crew of *The Night Wraith* were on edge as they planned to infiltrate Lephyrin's castle to rescue their captain—who was undoubtedly suffering from agony as each moment passed. Esmyra desperately tried not to think about what he must've been going through, recalling everything he told her it entailed. How his lungs likely felt as if they were filled with water, barely able to catch his breath as his vision turned blurry with a haze that mimicked that of the depths.

With the castle hosting a royal ball, the guards and security would be preoccupied, creating an opportunity for her crew to enter and seize anything of value, but their priority was to recover their captain and aid him in his escape—and kill the princes while they were at it.

But first, in order to do this, they needed to blend in. The crew had intercepted a convoy earlier that day—a carriage carrying the finest clothing for noblemen and women attending the ball.

Esmyra's usual wardrobe of billowing blouses and high-waist trousers had been replaced by a gown of crimson, its fabric glistening like blood in the low light. She looked every bit the regal debutant, save for the pistol strapped discreetly beneath her dress—not that she would need it, but she often kept additional weapons if her crew found themselves in need of it.

And sometimes, she just liked to use them for fun.

She found the transformation of her crew hysterical. They had resembled nothing more than sea rats only an hour prior and now appeared as if they belonged in the halls of any royal palace.

With their disguises in place, the crew of *The Night Wraith* made their way up the winding path to the castle. The structure loomed above them, its towers piercing the night sky like jagged teeth while torches flickered along the outer walls.

As they approached the grand entrance, Jak offered her his arm. "You're looking absolutely devastating in that dress." He leaned down and whispered in her ear. "It mimics the color of all the blood we'll spill."

Esmyra gave him a knowing look. "If I didn't know you prefer the company of other men, that might've made me blush, Jaky."

A low chuckle rumbled from him. "Only most nights, love. Not all of them." He winked, and she rolled her eyes.

Truthfully, Esmyra was the same way when it came to inviting others into her bed. She never cared if they were male or female. She only needed to be able to tolerate them...which was the reason she hadn't bothered with anyone in centuries.

The ball had begun hours ago, and as they approached, the end of the line of guests came into view as they were vetted by the guards. As Esmyra's eyes drifted about the area, she spotted nearly ten more guards scattered about.

"Idiots. There's barely anyone out here anymore," Jak observed alongside her.

"They likely don't believe anyone would be reckless enough to attack an event like this."

He snorted in response. "Foolish mortals."

"Aye," she breathed and then subtly glanced over her shoulder to address the six crew members accompanying her. "I count ten armed guards. Take them out subtly, and I'll take care of the man at the door. Jak and I will find my father, and the rest of you are to be scattered about the ballroom. Find both princes and be sure to have eyes on them constantly. Once we retrieve our captain, I'll come back to compel the princes out to avoid making a scene. And we'll kill them once we have them alone."

Esmyra planned to make a statement with their deaths. If Draevyn thought he could leave a warning to the realm's pirates charred into her sails, she would send her message right back to the king, written in his sons' blood.

"Aye," they murmured in agreement.

The males at her back dispersed, cloaked by the darkness of the night and hidden easily from mortal eyes.

Esmyra took the lead up the steps of the castle, her hands lifting the front of her gown as she hummed a calming melody. Jak was only a pace behind her, his hand pressed against the small of her back. Once they reached the door, the guard stopped them, as planned.

"What is your purpose here?" The man's voice was stern, unwelcoming.

Neither of them reacted to the guard or his question. Instead, they kept their heads bowed, looking towards the ground as the tune of her voice seemed to wrap around them all.

"You will look at a man when he speaks to you. Surely, as a lady of nobility, you were taught that. If you weren't, then you have no place here this evening. This is an invitation-only event." He paused for a moment, observing them. "And enough with your *humming*!"

Esmyra's stare lifted to his as she batted her kohl-lined lashes at him. She recalled how the darkness of the pigment made her blue eyes appear brighter, more enchanting. The man's stare locked with hers, and her eyes shifted. Once round pupils morphed into slits, mimicking a serpent's.

His body stiffened as he fell into her trance—eyes vacant and fixated on her. It was as if he were frozen in time as he succumbed to her spell.

"Now, now. Is that any way to speak to a woman?" She tsked and shot Jak a grin. Her eyes traced up and down the man. "Tell me, do you hold knowledge of a prisoner recently taken to the castle?"

"Yes." The man couldn't help his answer. She felt his mind writhe beneath her grasp, trying to fight her magic, but he was no match for her power.

"Good boy," she cooed. "Now, where would he be held?"

"The dungeons."

*Typical.*

She let out an annoyed breath. "And where be the dungeons?"

"Can't get in the locks without the key," he stated.

Esmyra glanced up at Jak, who watched with a curious expression. His light brown hair fluttered in the night breeze as his mouth twisted into a scowl. "Locks shouldn't be an issue."

"Aye, but we can't be wandering about all night."

Her attention returned to the guard. "Do you know where the dungeons are?"

"Yes."

Footsteps sounded from behind them, and her crew met them at the top of the staircase.

The side of Esmyra's lip tilted upward as she lifted her hand and gestured to the door. "By all means. After you, sir."

The man turned on his heel and mindlessly stalked through the grand entryway without another word.

Esmyra's crew moved through the throng of guests in the ballroom with ease, taking in every detail—the layout of the room, the positions of the guards, and the location of the two princes.

As Esmyra and Jak followed the guard through the corridors of the castle, the distant echoes of the festivities became muffled. The man stared blankly ahead, silent as he led them down a hidden staircase.

"This is significantly farther than we anticipated," Jak whispered, but all Esmyra could do was hush him.

Her mind was consumed with rescuing her father and seeking retribution against the Rowe family. The weight of knowing that she was to blame for his capture had her stomach twisting in knots, tormenting her.

Down in the lower levels, the air grew cooler, tinged with the musty scent of damp earth and stone—a stark contrast to the warmth and fragrance of the festivities on the upper levels of the palace.

The guard brought them to a halt before a massive iron door, reinforced with heavy bars. Jak pulled a dagger from his boot and shoved the blade into the lock, twisting it until it popped open. The door creaked open, revealing the darkness of the dungeons beyond, only lit by a few scattered torches. A wave of cold air rushed out, blowing the loose strands of Esmyra's hair around her face.

She turned to the guard. "And this is it, then? The prisoner, Cyrus Blackwood, is in here?"

"Yes," he answered. "For the time being. For the king wishes to present the realm his newest capture, showing that he rid the sea of its monster."

Esmyra froze as Jak's wide eyes met hers.

"King Rowe wishes to show Blackwood to his guests this evening?" Jak asked.

"Yes. Once the feast has ceased and the dance commences once more."

"Fuck," Esmyra muttered.

If they weren't able to leave the castle before the guards came down here for their prize, there was a chance that none of them would make it out.

Her eyes lifted to Jak. "Be rid of him," she demanded.

The sound of steel tearing flesh filtered through the air as Jak slit the guard's throat. His lifeless body fell to the ground with a subtle clatter of his armor.

Esmyra turned on her heel and stalked down the dungeon corridor as her gown dragged along the floor, Jak following alongside her.

The dungeon walls dripped with moisture, and the floor was uneven, slick with dirt and filth. The air was thick, every breath she took in was tinged with the scent of rot.

"Father," Esmyra called softly.

"Captain!" Jak echoed.

Labored breathing caught both of their attention, and her eyes narrowed on a cell only feet away. "He's here!" she said before sprinting to it.

Esmyra fell to her knees, her throat catching at the sight of her father slumped against the wall, wrists bound. "Father," she choked out.

"About time," he rasped, though his eyes appeared unseeing.

"We had to take the scenic route," Jak joked, and Esmyra scoffed. "You ready to get out of here, Captain?"

Cyrus stood from his crouch and slowly made his way to the barred door of his cell, rubbing his wrists as the rusted shackles cut into his skin.

He turned to Esmyra. "How did you get here?"

"Nevermind that! This is my fault, and now I'm going to get you out." The words rushed out of her frantically.

When her hand reached for the door, she immediately pulled it back into her chest at the sight of what circled the lock of his cell.

*Shadows.*

Swirling tendrils of darkness weaved their way through and around the lock in a sort of spiral motion. "What in all gods?" she whispered, her eyes darting back and forth before lifting back up to her father.

"The crowned prince was brought down alongside me, and the king instructed him to bind me here with magic."

Esmyra's back straightened slowly, her muscles stiff as her jaw ticked. "All locks can be picked and broken."

"No, Esmi. I don't think this one can."

Her chest rose and fell quickly, feeling as if the walls were caving in on her. "No! I will not accept that." She ripped the pistol from the strap of her thigh and aimed its barrel at the lock, emptying every bullet in the gun.

*BANG. BANG. BANG.* The noise bounced off the walls, its echo lingering. As the subtle cloud of gunpowder cleared, the lock came back into view—appearing untouched.

"Esmyra!" Jak gasped.

"Someone surely heard that," Cyrus warned, anger and worry swirling in his tone.

"Let them come! Every last one of them will pay for this," she seethed. "I will rip this door off the fucking hinges." Her fingers wrapped around the bars while she violently shook them, fully believing she could break it off the stone wall herself.

Her lips parted then, and she observed the odd stone bars her hands now curled around. It brought an odd sensation to her skin, and she recognized its unbearable touch.

"All gods," she whispered as she took a hesitant step back. Her eyes wandered up and down the cell door. "It's carved from velsinyte."

"What?!" Jak gaped.

"Esmyra, listen to me! You need to get out of here." Cyrus's breaths were labored, and a gurgling sound slipped through each word as if water had filled his lungs.

A moment later, shouts erupted from above as guards funneled down the staircase.

She pressed her face through the bars of the cell, ignoring the subtle burn that tingled the flesh of her cheek. "I found the entrance to Maerinys," she whispered, and his hazy eyes flared. "I found the entrance and I will uncover everything that remains in the lost kingdom and rob King Rowe of its glory. And then, I will come back for you. Perhaps I can barter—"

"Esmyra." His voice morphed from concern to pure, terror-filled rage. "You cannot seek out Maerinys. There's nothing there for you, and it's dangerous. Leave me here to rot. *The Night Wraith* is yours, and you're now its captain. I should've been dealt this fate centuries ago. This is my price for living the life I chose. Do *not* throw yours away for the likes of me."

Her fingers loosened their hold on the bars and she took a step back as her eyes remained on her father. "I'm not throwing my life away—I'm putting it to good use. I'm the only being who can likely even access what remains of Maerinys."

"Esmyra!" he tried to scream, scolding her, but her name ended in a violent cough.

Her eyes softened, lips parting. Nausea rolled through her at the sight of the most feared pirate in all of Rymelle unraveling so quickly.

"Esmi, we need to get the hell out of here," Jak urged. "If they throw us behind these bars, we'll never get him free." He reached out and grabbed her arm, but she instantly shook out of his hold, shooting him a dagger-like glare.

"Not without him."

"Esmi, I don't think there's anything we can do right now." Jak's voice was soft, a bit of pity within it.

She watched as the shadows continued to swirl around the lock, taunting her.

The footsteps of armored boots were growing louder by the second.

"Shift, Jak, and fly out of here the moment you can."

His golden eyes grew wide as his jaw fell open. "What?!"

"I'll be fine. Now go! Stay in the shadows of the ceiling, and do *not* be seen."

His eyes darted between her and their former captain. "Is that an order from my captain or a request from my friend?"

"An *order*," she said through her teeth. "I'll see you on the other side." Her voice softened on the last few words.

Jak's chest was heaving as he looked back and forth once more between her and Cyrus. "Gorgeous, reckless woman," he breathed, and a moment later, the man who stood before her now flapped enormous wings, taking his owl form before he soared up through the shadows of the ceiling.

She turned to her father for a final time and pressed her face through the velsinyte bars, welcoming its sting. "I will find a way to free you from them. Mark my words."

Cyrus cupped his daughter's cheek with a calloused hand. "Just get out of here safely." Each word seemed more difficult than the last.

"They have much more of this substance than ever anticipated, and we know it weakens you. Only the gods know how Lephyrin is in possession of it. But you *cannot* be put behind these bars, Esmi."

A single tear slid down her cheek, and he wiped it away with his thumb. "I'm very proud of you. Please forgive my lies. They were for a good reason."

The raw, scorching pain in her throat made her choke back the sobs begging to escape from her father's words.

The light of the guards' torches now shone brightly down the hall, and Esmyra slipped into the shadows of another cell further down as she willed her skin to camouflage against the stone, slowing her breathing to avoid being heard or caught.

The clattering of boots halted.

"Gunshots were heard, Blackwood," one of them spat. "And one of our men lay dead at the gateway. Throat slit."

*Kaelypso's tits.* Everything was happening so quickly in her rush to set him free that she'd forgotten about that.

"Perhaps the guard slit his own throat to put himself out of his misery for working for your cunt of a king," Cyrus retorted.

Esmyra's grin grew ear-to-ear at his words.

"You will mind your tongue when you speak of my father, *Black-wood*. Or I'll have it cut out."

Esmyra's eyes flared at the crowned prince's voice, trying to hold in her fury to avoid her eyes shifting and giving her whereabouts away with their glow.

"Well, *Prince*," Cyrus began, his tone full of disgust. "It would be a bit hard to cause gunshots and the slitting of throats when I'm bound and without weapons in a fucking prison cell. While my eyes have halted their use, I'm sure yours work just fine."

She carefully peered around the corner of her cell's wall and watched as the prince stepped up to her father's cell. With a subtle wave of his hand, the tendrils of darkness guarding the lock dispersed, seeking refuge back into his palm.

The cell door opened with a grating screech just before Atlas said,

"Seize him." He then waltzed past all the guards, aiming for the stairs that led to the main floor.

Esmyra's eyes narrowed, a snarl creeping across her lips as she watched the men, their faces hardened and cruel, enter her father's cell. His heavy chains clinked with every step as they forcibly dragged him away.

She counted her heartbeats as the guards dragged her father away, holding still even after the sounds of their footsteps long since faded away. She reached into the fold of her gown and placed her mask on her face before rushing after them to get to the main floor of the castle. She raced through the cells, past the dead body of the guard, and up the stairs from which she came, moving silently through the dimly lit corridors.

Voices echoed faintly from a nearby chamber. Esmyra paused, pressing herself against the wall as she strained to listen. The conversation was urgent, filled with tension. She inched closer, careful to remain hidden in the shadows.

"A body was found in the dungeons. It was a guard who was originally stationed at the main entrance of the castle. Be on alert. Protect the heir at all costs. He slipped back into the party without anyone realizing he was gone. Blackwood is being held and guarded a few chambers away and will only be removed once the king is ready to bring him before the crowd."

Esmyra's fists shook at her sides. How would she sneak him out of here? Her song was strong, but not strong enough to hold an entire room under its grasp. And even then, all it did was slow everything down, setting them in a lucid trance. She needed someone to look her in the eye for a full compulsion to take place.

Once she reached the main floor, she stalked down the hallway that led to the ballroom when another voice caught her attention.

"You, there!" the voice called, and she halted her steps. "Where are you coming from?"

Esmyra steadied her breathing, not allowing the panic creeping in on her to consume her thoughts. She gracefully turned to face the guard, her crimson gown twirling around her feet. "Apologies, sir. I took a wrong turn and have found myself lost. I was only following the voices back."

The man's harsh eyes softened a fraction before they traced over her body, noticeably halting on her curves. Her jaw locked as hunger crept into his stare, repulsed at the feelings his eyes betrayed. He took a step closer as he released the pommel of his sword.

"And what kingdom might you be from?"

Esmyra didn't hesitate when she said, "Terrana."

If she said Sumnae, his eyes would immediately drift to her ears and would realize a point didn't grace their tips. If she said Lephyrin, he would've asked her what house she stemmed from, and she couldn't risk that either.

He snorted at her reply. "A woodland, then." The hunger was working its way back into his beady eyes. "And what might you shift into? Do the markings on your arm mean something of your kind? Or were you burned as punishment for wandering about foreign castles?"

Esmyra glanced down, not realizing her gown's sleeve was bunched up just enough to have the markings of her wrist show.

"That's a bit rude, no?" Her head tilted to the side in a predatory manner.

His hand reached out and aggressively clutched her arm. "Tell me, miss. Ever been filled with a man's cock?"

Esmyra's gaze calmly drifted down to where the man held her in his grasp and her eyes shifted as a humming melody made its way past her lips. When her stare lifted back up to his through the slits in her lace mask, the man's face paled. "Tell me, sir...ever been caught in a siren's song?"

A clean slice to the throat would end him simply, but she didn't want him to meet his end in such a common, quick manner. That would be too kind—this man deserved a death far worse for thinking a woman's body was owed to him.

Her talons shot out from the tips of her fingers, and faster than the man could blink, she swiped them across his face.

The man began to scream as she released her venom, allowing it to seep into his blood.

"You will be silent," she commanded.

He obeyed as her magic gripped him, squirming in soundless pain as the venom ate at his flesh and eyes.

Grabbing him by the arm, she dragged him down the hall. Halfway down the corridor, she opened a door to a dusty, narrow closet. Without a second thought, she shoved the man into it, leaving him to rot in the dark.

Esmyra cleared her throat and straightened the front of her gown. Lifting its hem, she strode around the corner, aiming for the ballroom to find her crew and break her father free.

# CHAPTER 20

# Draevyn

The grand ballroom had somehow grown even more crowded, with people of all kingdoms still finding their spaces about the room. The guests danced as the orchestra played, only taking brief breaks to guzzle down the wine provided by the king.

Draevyn lingered on the fringes of it all, one hand braced on the stone column behind him, the other swirling a glass of that same wine he'd barely touched. He refrained from rolling his eyes at all the encounters he continued to observe, all while counting down the minutes for the night to end.

He locked eyes with Atlas as he reentered the room from a side door. His brother gave him a subtle nod, making Draevyn's jaw lock in irritation at their father's plan. He recalled the malicious gleam in the king's eyes as he explained what he planned to show the entire realm. Atlas's princely smile fell back into place before he wove his way back through the masses as if he never left.

Draevyn sighed, his gaze wandering aimlessly over the crowd, when suddenly, someone caught his eye.

Standing alone in the entryway of the ballroom was a woman unlike any he had seen. Her onyx hair cascaded down her back in soft waves, and her scarlet gown shimmered with every subtle movement. It hugged her in all the right places before spilling into an elegant train as her bright eyes pierced through the confines of the lace mask adorning her face.

But then his gaze fell to her skin as it glowed with the warmth of the room's light. His heart nearly stopped in his chest at the red runes trailing up her wrists just below the hem of her sleeve.

He had seen those markings before—would never be able to forget them if he tried.

A tightness formed in Draevyn's throat, shock rolling through him. He thought he'd damned the woman aboard his ship to the depths. She should've drowned, but there she was—standing before him across the room, clear as day. He knew without a doubt it was Esmi, as if a force tugged at his soul directly toward her.

Draevyn watched her curiously as she glanced in all directions before forcing her way through the crowd. A shrill shiver raced down his spine at the way her gaze was locked on the king as he sat on his throne.

Something was off. How was she here? How had she escaped the sea? And how had she even entered the castle? Surely, a woman who stemmed from a brothel in Anchorage Cove had no way of gaining an invitation legally.

*Blackwood.* Had she somehow escaped with them when his ship sank? The last time he'd seen her was the night they were attacked, but he had since taken revenge on the crew of *The Night Wraith*, leaving no survivors.

Draevyn straightened, his jaw locking as he set his glass on a nearby table.

He pushed through the crowd, getting more aggressive with each step, knowing he needed to get to her before she reached the king. He caught quick glimpses of her between the dancers as he navigated around them, shoving his way until he finally cut off her path, halting her. As if commanded, the surrounding dancers gave them space as they stood in the center of them all.

"Esmi," Draevyn greeted, his voice steady despite the way his heart raced. Her eyes widened, sharp and calculating under the lace mask.

Her lips parted as she looked him up and down. But then a grin formed on her perfect face. "Hello, *Draevyn Rowe*," she purred, her voice a velvet whisper against the music, gliding along his skin. "I must admit, I'm surprised you remembered my name. Or recognized me in a mask." Her last few words had a bit of a bite to them.

She felt threatened. But why?

"Would be rather difficult to forget the name of a beautiful woman who I once promised refuge. Especially since I mourned her death when I thought she was lost to the sea by my own doing," he challenged. "And even more difficult to forget those unusual markings of yours."

Her eyes drifted to her wrist, and a snarl quickly worked its way across her lips. "Do my markings offend you, Captain? Or do they merely mimic what you desire to do most to those inferior to you?" she retorted viciously.

Draevyn's eyes flared, rage surging within him. He was grateful that the synchronized flickering of the torches and candlelights went unnoticed by those in the room—aside from her. The hateful smirk twitching the corner of her lips gave her away.

A growl worked its way up his throat as she stared up at him, her eyes mimicking a fierce storm. Before he could say anything, she spoke once more. "Now, are the markings on my flesh the reason you halted me in the center of the room? If not, I will have to dismiss myself before your father's eyes burn a hole through my own."

He blinked before glancing over his shoulder and back toward the dais, where, sure enough, the king was watching them through narrowed eyes.

Draevyn faced the woman he still found difficult to read, eager to solve the puzzle she had become in his head. He wasn't about to let her slip through his fingers a second time.

His hand reached for hers. "Will you spare me the agonizing torment of a speech from the king later this evening and dance with me for the remainder of this song?" His voice wasn't kind, nor was it gentle as he asked. It resembled more of a demand than a request.

Esmi lifted a brow as her eyes narrowed in on him before drifting over his shoulder to the dais. "And what do I get in exchange, little princeling?"

Her fire flooded Draevyn with amusement. She was clearly unafraid of Lephyrin's Phoenix. "I've told you before, the princeling is my brother." He gestured with his chin to Atlas, who was several feet away in the crowd. Draevyn leaned down and put his lips beside her ear, her scent of the fresh ocean breeze and aquatic florals washing over him.

It was intoxicating.

His calloused hand brushed over her flesh, and her eyes widened, followed by a slight curl of her lip. He was surprised to find that the scarlet markings weren't raised or rough to the touch as true burns would be—they were just as soft as the rest of her skin.

Draevyn drank her in once more before reaching for her hand and pulling her into him. He couldn't help but feel as though a woman whose flesh bore the mark of flames but was as wild as the sea stood before him for a reason.

"And, *little wildfire*, what you would receive in exchange would be a pardon from the gallows for breaking into Lephyrin's castle."

He expected her to balk at the threat—fight him, or maybe even a slight flare of her eyes to give away some sort of panic.

Instead, she gave him a feline smile—one that made every hair on the back of his neck stand on edge as their chests remained pressed against each other's, her delicate hand in his. "Was that a threat, Captain?"

"It certainly was," he answered as he took his first few steps into the dance, guiding her along with him.

She hummed in response, as if she didn't have the time or patience to even bother with a reply.

"Just as last time, I stand before you, wondering if you're merely trying to distract me from your true intentions." He winked. "We must stop meeting like this."

"Oh, I'm sure you have some cunning scheme of your own," she said, tilting her head slightly. Her smile was a blade's edge, sharp and enigmatic as she brought her lips to his ear. "But tell me, is your plan worth risking everything for?"

His brows furrowed, pulse quickening as he wondered if she somehow knew about Blackwood.

"Now, you'll understand what it's like to be helpless, and you'll question how you thought you and your king could live so lavishly while giving so little to your people," she finished.

Draevyn's jaw locked, his heart slamming against his ribs.

The music ground to a halt and the king's voice echoed through the grand ballroom. "Everyone! The time has come for us to bring out a gift to you all... Someone the Kingdom of Lephyrin has captured and plans to rid our world of before you all this evening."

Draevyn ignored the beginning of his father's speech as he focused on Esmi's words. His eyes narrowed on the mysterious woman. Their gazes met and goosebumps trailed up his arms.

*Something's not right.*

Draevyn tried to shove out of her grasp. But he was too late.

He was unable to blink—barely able to breathe. To him, the world now began and ended in her vicious smile.

The last thing he saw was Esmi's eyes as they shifted.

CHAPTER 21

*Esmyra*

**K**ing Rowe stood upon the dais at the far end of the ballroom, a golden goblet raised in his hand. The music stopped and the whispers of the court fell away into an eerie hush.

Esmyra's grip on Draevyn tightened as he thrashed against her mental hold. She could feel him trying to ignite her siren's spell in his flames, but his features remained in a distant daze beneath her grasp.

Esmyra moved her gaze from Draevyn toward the king, her pulse quickening beneath her calm facade. She came to this castle for a reason, but now she feared she'd dallied too long.

"Lords and ladies of all kingdoms!" the king boomed, his voice echoing through the grand hall. "Tonight is a night of celebration, not only for my son choosing his bride and future queen but for the justice the Realm of Rymelle has long awaited."

Her heart stilled as blood rushed to her ears.

"Tonight," the king said, his eyes gleaming with satisfaction, "we have captured the scourge of the seas—the infamous pirate, Captain Cyrus Blackwood."

Esmyra scanned the room and found that every member of her crew already had their gazes locked on her, looking for orders. She thought she would have more time to reconvene with Jak, but that was out of the question now. The king was about to put her father on display for the realm to see.

Guards were posted everywhere, and the shadow-wielding prince was at his father's side. They were surrounded by too many swords. Without being in the sea to summon the full extent of her power and being unable to place the entire room in a trance, she was stuck—her *father* was stuck, and it was entirely her fault.

She swallowed hard, her thoughts racing. She had to find a way to save her father. He was the only family she had, the only person who knew what she truly was beneath the guise of her wicked beauty. The only one who had ever understood her. His lies barely mattered to her anymore, not at that moment. She'd recklessly left her captain and crew unattended and abandoned them for days, and now he was captured by the realm's most vicious king.

The clink of chains forced her out of her thoughts as the guards dragged her father into the hall and put him on display on a tall, wooden structure that was wheeled in beside the dais.

Gasps rang out in every corner of the room as they took in the sight of Cyrus as he stood as a prisoner of the Lephyrin crown. Black-wood was beaten and bloody, his form haggard. He gasped for air as his cursed lungs betrayed him, but only his crew knew why. His clothes were torn to shreds, appearing more like a beggar man dragged in from the streets than the feared pirate king.

Esmyra was desperate to act, to spring into motion and free him as she held Draevyn in a trance. Her magic flared as her mind churned with possibilities—if she could break the spell she held on the prince to incite chaos, perhaps she could lead her father to *The Night Wraith*. But she had entrapped her greatest threat in this room beneath her spell. If she were to release her hold on him, she would risk him igniting her entire crew in flames the second a move was made.

Cyrus's eyes met hers then. He had seen her, standing at the center of it all, the king's son her puppet. A flash of understanding passed between them. There was no anger in his gaze—only regret and a father's love.

"You no longer need to fear the seas of Rymelle! For Captain Cyrus Blackwood is now my prisoner, and his beast that answers only to his call is nowhere to be seen!"

Esmyra rolled her eyes at that. She gritted her teeth as she watched the king rub his rotund stomach in satisfaction while he guzzled down his wine in celebration.

The king's voice rose again, cutting through her thoughts. "We end this here and now!"

A noose lowered from the ceiling, halting directly before her father's throat. Her eyes flared, and her vision sharpened as they shifted, losing what was left of her composure. She then saw the makeshift stage for what it was—a replica of the gallows.

Gasps of horror rang out in all directions, but they were accompanied by cheers of triumph. Cheers to end her father's life.

The king was bloody *mad*. He had to have been. This ball was only held for his son to find a bride, and now, it would hold an execution—or an attempted one. His curse wouldn't allow death to claim him, but this would only cause him more suffering.

Esmyra's eyes flew to Jak, and he was moving before she even had to give him a signal, shoving his way through the crowd to get to her, but everyone was in too much shock at the scene occurring before them to notice.

The guards dragged Cyrus forward, and she could see the hatred etched into the faces of those around her as they cheered for him to meet his end.

There would be no mercy.

Her breath caught in her throat. She had to do something.

The knotted rope was tightened around her father's neck.

A tear slipped from her eye as he gave her a look that seemed to say, *leave me here and run while you can.*

"I'm sorry," she breathed, shaking her head. "But I cannot do that." Disappointment crept into her father's stare at her refusal to abandon him here.

Jak reached her then, eyes frantic. "Do you have a plan?" he huffed in her face.

Her taloned nails slid from the tips of her fingers as she glanced side-to-side, watching her crew also make their way to the center of the crowd.

"I have one, but it's *mad*," she whisper-shouted.

"Well, it's all we've got, Esmi."

Her eyes moved to Draevyn, who stood frozen under her trance, his magic thrashing against her mental hold. "Get ready to run," she whispered to Jak. "With him."

It all happened so fast—the creak of the guard pulling the gallows' lever filtered through the room as she dropped her hold on Lephyrin's Phoenix and shoved him into her friend. Any word Draevyn moved to say died at the edge of his tongue as Jak slammed a pistol into the side of his head, knocking him unconscious.

Time slowed as gasps erupted from all sides. She reached for a dagger strapped to one of the guests beside her, ripping it from his sheath faster than he could notice.

And then she was running.

"*MOVE*," she bellowed, and the crowd parted for her.

Esmyra watched in horror as her father's body fell, the crowd waiting with bated breath for the inevitable snap of his neck. With all her might, Esmyra gripped the dagger's hilt in her hand and hurled the blade toward the platform. Time continued to slow as she watched the dagger spiral through the air until it sliced through the noose above her father's head.

The rope never went taut, and the sound of snapping bones never came, as Cyrus's body dropped to the ballroom's marble floor.

Chaos erupted.

Screams came from all directions as the crowd dispersed, desperately seeking a way out of the ballroom, but Esmyra could barely hear them over the blood rushing in her ears. Men swarmed her father as the king bellowed blubbering nonsense, his plump face red and riddled with rage. His guards shielded him and his heir, rushing them off the dais and out one of the side doors.

Esmyra's feet were moving a moment later, bringing her closer to the front. Her crew sprang into action, weapons drawn as they fought through the panicked masses.

Soldiers and the king's guards stormed toward them from all sides, and the crowd surged in a frenzy, people of all races trampling over one another in a desperate attempt to flee.

She shoved her way through the madness, dodging the wild flails of lords and the flashing swords of soldiers. But the mob was thick, pushing and shoving as people scrambled in every direction. The clash of steel, panicked cries, and barked orders filled the air.

"Esmi, look out!" Jak screamed.

A soldier's blade swung, narrowly missing her throat as she bent backward to avoid its sharpened edge. She turned and kicked the soldier in the chest, sending him toppling into the sea of bodies.

Gunshots went off, and more screams sounded.

She whipped around, eyes glowing as an aggressive grip held firm on her arm. Her glare landed on Jak as he shot at the onslaught of guards hurtling toward them.

"Where is Draevyn?!" she hissed through clenched teeth.

"Likely halfway to *The Night Wraith* by now." Jak's eyes lifted over her shoulder and shoved Esmyra to the side as he lifted his pistol and shot a guard who was racing toward them. "I knocked him unconscious and handed him to Riven, Alec, and Ren. They slipped right out the doors the moment the screams ensued. Riven used his magic to sneak past any lingering guards so they wouldn't be seen."

"Genius," she whispered.

*Gods, I love elven magic.*

Her eyes snapped back to where her father fell, finding he was already back in the hands of the guards, being shoved out a side door of the ballroom.

*Fuck.*

A cry rang out above the chaos. "Seize them! Don't let them escape!"

"I'm going after him," she rushed out.

"Esmyra!" Jak gasped as he tugged at her arm. "We have the

Phoenix as leverage. We couldn't get to the heir, but we need to leave. Now."

"Leave me," she whispered. "I'll go and make sure they know *exactly* what leverage we have and what we seek." A growl worked its way through her. "No one will be leaving this kingdom by sea and live to speak of it until they return my father to me."

She shoved out of his grasp and took off in a run, pushing her way through what remained of the crowd to follow the guards and her father.

The masquerade ball was a chaotic bloodbath. Frantic guests in ornate masks fled in every direction, their once-impeccable gowns torn as they stumbled over upturned tables and broken bodies. Esmyra raced through the mayhem as everything she had come here for unraveled before her very eyes.

She swallowed her panic.

Ducking beneath a fallen banner, her heart stammered as she halted to catch her breath in the shadows near an archway. The sounds of clashing steel and panicked cries echoed through the corridors.

Esmyra smoothed her hair back and took a deep breath, willing her breathing to calm, knowing the chaos would work in her favor if she played her cards right. No one would notice one frightened woman in a sea of fleeing nobles.

Pushing forward, she wove her way through the remaining guests, her demeanor calm and composed despite the surrounding madness. She caught the eye of a guard—tall, broad-shouldered, and still clutching his sword with trembling hands as he stood at the base of a staircase.

*Perfect.*

She staggered toward him, feigning exhaustion and fear, her voice breathless. "Please...*help me.*"

The guard's eyes widened at her disheveled appearance. "My lady...are you hurt?"

"No," Esmyra whispered, her tone soft and pleading. She let her hand graze his arm, her touch delicate. Her eyes met his. "Can you help me get out of here?"

Her voice carried the slightest hum of power, the magic beneath the surface so subtle he was oblivious to being pulled in as she discreetly worked a hymn into her words.

His grip on his sword loosened as his eyes softened, gazing into hers as they shifted. "Yes...yes, of course," he said, his voice growing more distant as the enchantment took hold.

Esmyra offered a soft, grateful smile, satisfaction rolling through her as she felt the control settle in. "Thank you," she breathed, taking his hand in hers. "But...before we go, I need you to take me somewhere."

The guard blinked, his brows pulling together. "Where?"

"What I seek lies in the upper chambers of the castle," she whispered, leaning closer, her lips almost brushing his ear. "Do you know where King Rowe sleeps?"

A subtle nod was her answer, and she suppressed her grin.

"'Tis vital. You must take me there."

He hesitated for a moment, and she sensed the rational part of his mind trying to fight through the fog of her spell. But it was no use. Her power held him too tightly. With a nod, he sheathed his sword and motioned for her to follow.

"This way," he said, his voice monotone, like a puppet whose strings she'd taken hold of.

Esmyra followed him up the grand staircase, slipping away from the chaos below. The further they ascended, the quieter the sounds of the main floor became.

The guard led her through a set of double doors, their heavy wood creaking as they opened to reveal a private hall, where at its opposite end she could make out an elaborate door of what she assumed to be the king's chambers.

"No private guards at the door?" she whispered aloud.

"No, miss. The royal family was taken to a safe room under heavy guard until the madness below subsides."

"And he's to return this evening?"

"Indeed. I suspect he will be up once the castle is cleared."

"Aye," she answered with a sly smile.

Esmyra stalked down the hallway, her gown billowing behind her on a phantom breeze. The door to the king's chamber opened with ease. She turned to the guard a final time as he stood at her back. "Return to your post at the castle staircase. Speak of this to no one," she commanded.

The man's back straightened, and without a word, he turned on his heel from her and marched down the hall from which they came. Once he left her sight, Esmyra waltzed through the chamber's doors.

The room was luxurious, though far from welcoming. Rich tapestries adorned the stone walls, and the massive bed was draped in silks the color of her crimson gown. The only source of light in the abandoned chamber was the fire crackling low in the hearth.

She crossed the space swiftly to find that beyond the first wall, the room expanded to a small study fit for a king, where endless books and parchments covered a large wooden desk. The room's shadows embraced her as she moved towards it, hidden from view of the door. Pulling out the chair that more resembled a small throne, she sat at the king's desk as she awaited his return. Her heart beat steadily as she listened for any sign of movement in the corridor.

Truthfully, she barely had a plan. Compel him was the obvious choice. Force him to release her father to her, and then they would be free, but not before she slaughtered him for the attempt on her father's life. And then she would do the same to his fire-wielding son being held on her ship.

It wasn't long before the heavy tread of boots approached, followed by the creak of the door. With a wicked grin, Esmyra silently crossed her legs on the king's desk, her scarlet gown flowing down to the floor as she waited.

"Just guard my fucking door along with my heir's," the king barked.

A throat was cleared. "And what of Captain Draevyn? He's yet to be found. Likely chasing after the culprits, perhaps?"

Esmyra had to suppress her snort.

"Draevyn can handle himself. Protect my *heir*. That's a fucking order!"

A moment later, the door slammed, and the room was silent once more, aside from the small crackling embers of the fireplace. She watched from the shadows of the study as the king came into view, pouring himself a glass of wine on a small bedside table before throwing it down his throat.

"Fucking mongrels, these other kingdoms," he grumbled, and her brows furrowed. King Rowe shoved out of his finery coat and carelessly threw it aside before walking up to the fire, staring into its flames.

Esmyra sat perfectly still as she observed the king. Her anger brewed at the sight of him standing there, unguarded and entirely alone. It would be easy to kill him—nothing, really. It would barely even take half a thought. But he held what was most important to her, the only family she had, and if she killed him in this moment, there was a chance she would never find a way to free her father—not with those velsinyte cells in play.

"Highness," she greeted, her voice smooth as velvet.

The king stiffened, his body slowly pivoting to face her as she remained sitting at his desk in the dark. Esmyra lifted a hand and gave him a dainty wave.

"Who are you?" he demanded, voice booming. "If you're here for a cock to suck, you will need to leave. The castle was under attack tonight, and I have no interest in entertaining a common whore in my bed."

Esmyra tsked in disgust as she stood. "No need for such nasty words, King," she said, her tone gentle but firm as she watched his stare drift to the door, likely ready to call for his men. "I'm not here for your cock...though if you keep this up, I may just pin it to the wall."

His jaw ticked as she took a confident step toward him.

"However, I'm not here to provide entertainment, either," she continued. "And you will not call for your guards that stand just beyond your door."

The king's sharp gaze narrowed on her, suspicion etched into every line of his face. "Who are you? How did you get in here?"

She stepped closer, the glow of the fire catching the strands of her dark hair as her lips curled into a knowing grin. "My name is Esmyra," she said simply. "And I'm here because we both hold something the other wants."

He barked out a harsh laugh. "And what exactly is it that you think I want, *Esmyra*?" he spat her name as if it brought his tongue a bitter taste.

Esmyra tilted her head, her eyes shimmering in the firelight as she took another step forward. "Power over the realm. Wealth greater than any kingdom. And perhaps...*your son* returned to you?"

Liquid fire lit in the king's stare, and for a moment, she wondered who the phoenix in the royal family truly was.

"My son?" he growled.

He pivoted to face the door, but she was in front of him in an instant. Her voice lowered to a seductive whisper, laced with her magic, as she gazed into his frantic eyes. "Perhaps I should've introduced myself properly a moment ago. My name is Esmyra *Blackwood*, and I have come to retrieve my father. You will not call for your guards. You will remain as you are."

The king took a hesitant step back from her as he gazed into her shifting eyes, their glow casting across his stout face. "Blackwood has a daughter?"

His eyes looked her up and down curiously, and then he took a step *into* her, catching her off guard. "And if your eyes are any tell, a daughter with power. *Extraordinary* power, it seems—one believed to have been lost to our world. Now tell me, have I found the *true* beast of the deep that answers to Blackwood's call?"

Esmyra's heart pounded against her ribs, each thump echoing in her ears, as she desperately tried to use her compulsion on the king. Her magic reached out again, trying to grip his mind, but it was like water slipping through her fingers or trying to hold air. No matter how aggressively her power lashed out at him, it wouldn't work. The man remained entirely normal—alert and knowing, refusing to fall under her spell.

It had never occurred before, and something she certainly wasn't prepared for.

The king lifted his hand directly before her face. A ring carved from stone adorned his middle finger. Her heart sank with dread when she realized what it was.

A ring of velsinyte.

"How—" she stuttered, but he cut her off.

"I heard reports of a gunshot ringing out from the dungeons before they brought your father up to me. What's wrong, *Esmyra*? Couldn't free daddy as easily as you believed?" His smile grew cruel, and he turned to walk back to the table to pour himself more wine, as if turning his back to her wasn't a fatal mistake.

"You know, we knew Blackwood didn't possess magic, but have heard the legends of his possible immortality, so we imprisoned him behind velsinyte to be safe," he continued. "Can never be too careful, being the only kingdom of ordinary men and all."

Panic was nearly suffocating her—a feeling she was clueless about how to overcome. She tried to calm her racing heart, but it was no use.

Could she get close enough to somehow remove the ring from his finger? She wasn't above biting it off.

"You're right, I won't call for my guards. No true threat stands before me. Though, you aren't hard on the eyes. I may just change my mind regarding the invitation to my bed."

Bile crept up her throat.

"Release my father," she demanded, her voice smooth as silk

despite the tension that coiled in her chest. "And I will return your son to Lephyrin."

"The question there would be if he returns in one piece."

"And that entirely falls on you and how long you risk testing my patience. Which is wearing thin, if you would like honesty."

The king's lips curved into a thin, cruel grin. "Considering the only son worth saving was with me only moments before I arrived in my chambers to find the likes of you, I'm assuming you're the reason no one can seem to find Draevyn."

Did the king not care for his second heir? Her eyes darted back and forth as her mind raced. He watched her as he took a slow, deliberate sip of his drink.

"Do you take me for a fool, siren?" King Rowe's voice was sharp, his tone laced with a hint of amusement. "You think you can bargain with me when I hold your father's life in my hands?"

"Just as I hold your *son's*," she hissed, lip curling back. Esmyra took her first step to circle him, and when he took one to match, they began a dance. "My father is immortal. Cursed centuries ago to feel as if he is suffocating if he steps on land. Holding him here does nothing but prolong his anguish." She paused. "And my annoyance."

"Ah, so the legends hold truth then." He shrugged. "Then it appears he'll remain a tortured prisoner."

"Do you not have a single desire to see your son again? Your greatest weapon?" As soon as Esmyra spoke the words, something in her softened. She realized then that she and Draevyn had something in common. They were just weapons to their fathers.

"Perhaps he's just waiting for the opportune moment to roast you all alive before he comes crawling back here with his tail between his legs."

A click of her tongue echoed in the chamber. "Ah, so the king of Lephyrin believes to be the only one in possession of velsinyte."

The amusement dropped from his face. "You don't hold such a weapon," he spat. "It's impossible."

The cruel smile he wore only a moment ago now adorned Esmyra's lips. "I wouldn't be so sure. Aren't you at all curious about how I was able to entrap your Phoenix? Of course, I could hold him beneath my song, but I stand before you here and now. He's aboard *The Night Wraith*. And I promise you, any attempt to retrieve him, and I will have your men dragged to the depths faster than you can say *oops*."

A moment of silence stretched between them. Esmyra's heart continued to race, though she refused to let it show. This was no ordinary negotiation—if anything, it was her first worthy opponent.

The king's beady, age-lined eyes roamed over her. "You can shift into a full siren form, no? That's how you drag ships beneath the tides?"

"You think I'll bare all my secrets to you, *King*?" she hissed.

"If you wish to have your father returned to you," he countered. "I'll make sure every guard and soldier's finger in Lephyrin wears a velsinyte ring by morning. Your magic will have no bearing on my kingdom."

"Not your sons, though?" she mocked. "They're beings of magic. Of your doing, I might add, if rumors are to be believed." She took a step towards him, but he didn't match it back. "It would snuff out their power too, and well...you can't afford that, now can you? So, who's to say I won't waltz into Atlas's room and enchant him next?" She cocked her head to the side, flashing her teeth. "Your heir has quite a reputation for being easily seduced."

"I should gut you like the fish you are," he threatened, a growl radiating in it.

"You'd have to catch me first." Esmyra winked before striding to the fireplace.

His nostrils flared as he watched her lift a trinket from the fireplace and twirl it around in her hand carelessly, staring him down. "Answer the question. Can you shift and breathe beneath the waves?"

"Aye," she answered carelessly, before tossing the trinket into the flames, sending embers flying.

"Then perhaps we may be able to strike a bargain."

"I was willing to make a trade, not strike a bargain." Esmyra took a step closer to him. "You stole something from me, and I'm here to take it back by any means necessary. If anyone in Lephyrin wishes to leave by ship, the sea will claim their life. That I can assure you."

His stare was calculating as he watched her, leisurely looking her up and down. "It must be lonely, no? Being the only one of your kind left." Esmyra flinched at the words, and she hated that he witnessed it. "Now, we can do this tiring little dance of yours, or we can barter. The choice is yours, really."

Her nostrils flared, teeth clenching so hard she thought they might shatter before she said, "I'm listening."

"I'm sure you're familiar with the sunken Kingdom of Maerinys..."

Esmyra's jaw locked, knowing exactly where he was headed with this. "Aye," she answered.

"An abundance of treasure sank to the depths alongside the kingdom hundreds of years ago. Retrieve it for me, and your father will be returned to you."

"Interesting that you have more interest in gold than your son's well-being," she challenged.

The king said nothing, his gaze cold and unyielding.

She huffed out a breath before continuing. "Why do you seek this gold? Surely it makes no difference to a *king*." Her voice was a near growl.

Greed crept into his gaze as it grew distant. "It's not the gold I seek, but what it represents. To restore balance in the realm. When not only *you* lack magic but also your people, you must compensate in other ways to gain respect."

"You compensate with cruelty."

The king clenched his fists. "And what of my sailors? If you wish to speak of cruelty, how many have I lost due to them voyaging across the sea and coming to meet the likes of you? Is that not cold nor cruel? You're no better than me, *siren*."

"That doesn't concern me, King Rowe. The sea claims who it will."

He swirled around what remained in his glass, watching as he created a whirlpool of red. "My terms are quite clear, Ms. Blackwood.

Your father will remain locked behind bars of velsinyte until you bring me proof of this sunken kingdom holding what I seek," he said.

Her eyes narrowed beneath furrowed brows. "You don't care about your son at all, do you? You only want—"

"My son understands the risks of his position," he cut her off. "But I will make it known to you here and now that Draevyn is not my priority, nor is he even my heir. You were foolish to use him as a bartering tool."

"And if I refuse?" She cocked her head to the side in mockery, trying to reel in her temper, though her talons extending gave her away.

"Try all you might to retrieve him. I can only hope to have you behind those very bars one day." King Rowe took a step up to her and lifted his hand to brush his knuckles against her cheek. "A gilded cage for such a pretty prize."

Her lip curled in a snarl. "You are foul."

A laugh left him as he took a small step back. "Not as foul as those I could sell you to."

Her eyes flared, lips parting in horror.

Esmyra would kill this king one day. Once her father was freed, she would inject her venom into his body and watch him squirm beneath her. And only once death was sure and near would she flay the skin from King Rowe's bones and end his reign.

"So what will it be? Take to the depths and retrieve what I seek? Or end up just as your father did?"

A hiss slipped from her, animalistic and as cruel as the words he spat at her, but all it earned her was a mocking laugh. Esmyra's eyes landed on the door, where she knew several guards waited on its other side, and she took her first step toward it.

"You forget what lies beyond our small barrier, seawitch," he called, his tone full of amusement.

Once she reached the door, she placed her hand on the intricate golden handle and glanced over her shoulder. "Oh, I've forgotten nothing."

A hymn left her lips, then—a haunting, otherworldly melody of seduction that wrapped around her and glided through the room in only seconds. As she peeked through the doors, she found all five guards stood at attention, held beneath her song. A vicious smirk spread across her face at the sight of them.

Esmyra pushed the double doors of the chamber open wide, each of them slamming into the walls on either side as she tauntingly looked each guard in the eye before turning around to face the mortal king—his guards stood at her back, their gazes fixated on their monarch.

It was the first time King Rowe showed the slightest hint of fear—the scent of it stuffed itself in her nostrils, and she reveled in it.

The siren within her purred as she imagined herself covered in his blood once she skinned him alive for the pain he inflicted on her father. But the matter of those pesky shadows swirling the lock came to mind, and she knew she couldn't risk Cyrus's escape on such a gamble.

"I don't take kindly to being threatened, Your Majesty. You will do well to remember that when you look back on this night and feel nothing but regret."

King Rowe's lips trembled as she mentally commanded each of the guards to pull a dagger from their sides and slit their own throats while under her spell.

The king's eyes flared as crimson poured down the fronts of his men, each dropping to the tile floor at Esmyra's feet, armor clanging as blood pooled around their bodies.

He lifted his stare back to her, and her lips tilted into a sharp smirk, but she knew there was nothing but the promise of vengeance in her eyes.

Sucking on his teeth, a rough chuckle slipped from him. "Well played, Esmyra Blackwood." The words were a whisper on his lips as he brought the bottle to them before emptying what remained.

Esmyra turned from him, her scarlet gown billowing around her as she stormed down the corridor. Satisfaction rolled through her, and she became eager to return to *The Night Wraith*, where Draevyn Rowe was secured in her crew's grasp.

# CHAPTER 23

# Draevyn

The dim, swaying light of an oil lamp cast flickering shadows across the dark room. Draevyn groaned, his head pounding as he slowly came to consciousness. The air was thick with the scent of salt and damp wood, mingling with the metallic tang of blood—his blood, he realized. He blinked, trying to focus through the disorientation as the cold shackles bit into his wrists.

Draevyn hadn't felt so drained in years. *What the fuck happened?*

One moment, he was dancing with a beautiful woman, and then the next, he was here. His eyes slowly widened as the face of the woman he'd been with came rushing back to his memory.

*Esmi.* The brothel worker from Anchorage Cove. However, he still didn't necessarily believe that story, especially considering where he currently found himself.

The room was entirely too dark, playing tricks on his senses. He tried to summon fire in the palm of his hand but went unanswered— the usual warmth wasn't brought to his skin, and his flames didn't flare in his chest. Frustration worked its way through his veins. He tried again, but his magic failed to ignite once more. Not even a single ember would spark.

An unbearable, sinking feeling settled into his gut. He closed his eyes tightly, mentally preparing himself for his throbbing headache to worsen as he faced the inevitable—what his reality had become.

Draevyn lifted his bound hands, and through the darkness of whatever hellish cell he had been placed in, his vision slowly focused on the stone-carved cuffs encircling his wrists.

"Fucking Irah," he growled, nostrils flaring as his flames thrashed against the cuff's hold. The last time he saw the cuffs was aboard his ship, right before it sank to the depths, where he'd left them on Esmi's wrists.

*This was her doing.* He didn't know how she managed to remove herself from the cuffs, but knew deep within his soul that she was responsible for this.

As Lephyrin's sea captain, he had grown accustomed to the waves and their sounds over his years at sea. His jaw tightened, knowing he was now held prisoner on a ship, far from the protection of the crown.

Draevyn rested his head on the wall at his back, and through the dim light of the oil lamp, a figure came into view, just outside the barred door of his cell.

The man was of average build, not small, but nowhere near as broad-shouldered and muscular as Draevyn. Even in the darkness, he could tell his skin was tanned from years at sea beneath the scorching sun. A small bronze hoop hung from his left ear and his brown hair was cropped short on the sides while slightly longer on the top of his head.

The man said nothing, just stared through narrow eyes.

Draevyn straightened, the chains connecting the cuffs clinking as he moved. His mouth was dry, his throat parched. "Where is she?" he demanded.

The man didn't answer immediately. Just kept staring, his golden eyes gleaming in the low light like an owl perched in the realm's trees. "You're in no position to be making demands," he said simply.

"I know she's behind this. Did she sell me off?" When he went unanswered, he continued. "Her name is Esmi, or so I was once told, but that may be just another lie in her web." The man lifted a brow as Draevyn pushed himself to his feet, despising how drained his body felt from the cuffs.

The pirate reached into his coat and pulled out a rusted key, sliding it into the lock. "'Tis your lucky day, *Phoenix*. Captain's been waitin' for ya to wake up." He opened the door with a creak, stepping aside to let him out. "And the captain should never be kept waiting."

"The captain?" Perhaps she wasn't on the ship after all and *had* sold him out. Had she been a trap, cunningly cloaked in a beautiful form? He may never know, and the thought of that was somehow more irritating to him than the situation he found himself in.

He loathed how much of a mystery this woman was. A woman who showed up in his life unannounced, who conveniently appeared whenever chaos ensued.

Draevyn hesitated for a moment, his eyes narrowing as he sized up the man before him. But he knew he had no choice. With his hands still bound and his power drained, he was in no position to resist. So, he may as well see who had managed to capture him and what their intent with him was.

The man grabbed Draevyn's arm the moment he was beyond the cell door and shoved him toward the stairs. They made their way through the narrow, dimly lit halls of the ship, the wooden boards creaking beneath their feet. The distant murmur of the crew, the clink of bottles, and the occasional burst of raucous laughter sounded over the crashing of the sea.

Draevyn glanced down at the death grip the pirate held on his arm.

How was he going to get out of this? Had this been his father's doing since velsinyte was involved? They believed themselves to be the only kingdom in possession of it. Was the chaos that ensued at the ball just a disguise to have him disappear without a trace? He wouldn't put it past his father. In fact, it was the perfect way to have him removed from Lephyrin.

The sun threatened to blind him as they reached the top of the stairs and took their first steps onto the main deck. Once Draevyn's eyes adjusted to the brightness, they flared. The crew stormed around the deck in all shapes and sizes, creatures of all kinds.

"What in all gods?" he whispered, brows furrowing. He'd never seen anything like it, convincing himself it was just a trick of the sunlight as his senses adjusted.

Pirates, while abiding by their laws, still typically remained with their own kind and race.

"This way," the man ordered, right before kicking Draevyn in the back of the knee, nearly sending him to the onyx floorboards.

The moment he noticed the hue of the wood, his throat tightened, knowing he was aboard the notorious ship that terrorized Rymelle's waters.

The last time he stood atop this deck, he had ignited everyone aboard in flames before capturing its captain. But how could he be aboard *The Night Wraith* now? His father held its captain as a prisoner beneath Lephyrin's castle.

At last, they reached a wooden door stained the same color as the vessel, with a tiny, circular window of scarlet-hued stained glass adorning its center. The man knocked twice before pushing it open without waiting for a response. He shoved Draevyn inside, where he found himself in a large, dark cabin.

The walls were lined with maps, assorted weapons, and ancient bound texts. A grand wooden desk sat at the far end in its center, and behind it, in a tall, imposing chair, sat Esmi.

Draevyn nearly choked. An infuriating smirk played across her face as she stared at him from the other side of the room.

She wore a tightly laced corset, while a low-cut, ruffled shirt peeked out from underneath, her breasts spilling over the top of it. Her pants were crafted of black leather, hugging her muscular legs, and tucked into knee-high boots perched atop her desk—one ankle crossed over the other.

Her long, dark hair fell around her face while a tricorne hat sat tilted atop her head. Its brim shadowed her piercing blue eyes as she gazed at him tauntingly while silver hoops glinted in her ears.

Draevyn's heart raced wildly, confusion creeping into him as she confidently sat at the captain's desk as if it was where she had always been—where she belonged.

The corners of her lips tilted, but the subtle smile didn't meet her eyes. "Welcome aboard *The Night Wraith*, Draevyn Rowe."

CHAPTER 24

*Draevyn*

"The captain has spoken to you." The man shoved at his back, sending Draevyn stumbling into the center of the room. "You *speak* when you're spoken to."

Draevyn swallowed thickly, not knowing what to do or say as he struggled to process it all.

A captain for a captain. A pirate for a prince. The reality of it all settled into him rapidly, and his fingertips ached—the flames ready to burst and ignite this entire ship, if it weren't for the gods-forsaken cuffs encircling his wrists.

"That's quite alright, Jak," Esmi said from the chair, her unwavering gaze still fixated on Draevyn. "He's our guest." Her smile turned feline.

"You have an interesting way of treating your guests, Esmi," Draevyn said, working to keep the irritation from his tone.

She lifted a single hand to inspect her nails, that more resembled talons. Draevyn eyed them with a raised brow, certain he would've noticed those before. "You may address me as Captain or Esmyra." Her voice was stern, leaving no room for argument, but he didn't give a damn.

"So there was a bit of truth behind your web of lies when we met in Anchorage Cove."

169

The man, Jak, kicked the back of his knee and sent Draevyn down to the floor with a grunt. "I don't appreciate your tone to my captain."

"And I don't fucking appreciate being held as a prisoner in the middle of the sea," he snapped, shooting Jak a glare. He turned back to the beautiful, vicious woman before him as she watched their encounter. He pushed himself to his feet as he said, "You owe me an explanation."

Esmi cackled as she lifted a pistol up from the desk, twirling it in her hand. "I owe you nothing, Phoenix."

Draevyn swallowed, sweat licking up his spine, thinking for a moment she might shoot him right then and there. But there was something in her eyes that made him think she wasn't done toying with him. She wanted something—the question was *what*.

"Was this your plan all along?" He bared his teeth at her. "Capture me as a bartering chip for something you desired more? How are you in possession of velsinyte?"

Her eerie eyes roamed over him. "I stole them, of course."

"From the castle?"

A malicious giggle slipped from her. "From you, princeling. After you placed me within a cell on your ship." The tone of the last few words betrayed her fury.

Draevyn's eyes darted back and forth as his thoughts swirled with how such a thing was possible.

"Right before I sank it to the depths," she finished.

His jaw gaped, bound hands balling into fists as they hung in front of him. "How." The demand erupted through clenched teeth.

Esmyra grinned tauntingly, right before her eyes flashed an other-worldly glow. The room lit up in a hue of teal, and the displayed weapons and stained glass windows about the room glistened in its light. But it was gone as quickly as it came.

"What in all gods?" he whispered, stumbling back a step from the predator sitting in the captain's chair. He knew now with absolute certainty that she wasn't who or what she originally claimed to be... So what the fuck was she?

Esmyra stood from the desk, her eyes remaining locked with his as she cocked her head to the side. "Walk with me, Draevyn."

She never gave him a chance to respond as she strode past him, the heel of her thigh-hugging boots clicking off the wood floor. Jak opened the door for her, and she waltzed out onto the main deck, leaving Draevyn no choice but to follow.

Jak grabbed him by the arm, guiding him to follow her, but Draevyn ripped it from his grasp.

"Now, now, you two." They both turned to face Esmyra as she watched from the bottom of the stairs that led up to the quarterdeck. "He's going to be a good boy and cooperate. Aren't you, Draevyn?" His nostrils flared at her words, and Jak let out a harsh laugh. "Besides, where's he going to go?" She gestured to the open water that surrounded them before making the trek up the stairs.

"You heard her." The words were a whisper in his ear—too close for comfort—as Jak stalked past him and followed his captain.

Draevyn slowly turned toward the bow of the ship, watching the crew as they worked, paying no mind to the shackled prisoner standing in the center of their deck.

Males of all beings worked in tandem. He could only assume those bearing markings of the woodland kingdom were the shifters, while those with the pointed ears stemmed from Sumnae, the kingdom of the elves. There were even a few that bore no markings, appearing as ordinary men from Lephyrin. His eyes narrowed on each person they passed over while the crew continued to ignore his existence.

Eventually, he looked up at the quarterdeck, where Esmyra held the ship's wheel with a single hand, her midnight hair flowing on the sea breeze as she stared down at him. It was as if she were begging for him to be foolish enough to defy her and make a move to flee.

Draevyn knew his odds of escape barely existed and was interested to see what information she would give if he cooperated with her instead of fighting her every move. So, he shoved down his pride and moved toward the stairs, praying to Irah that he could manage reeling in his anger long enough to find a way to free himself.

At the top, he took note of Jak hanging back by one of the smaller masts, watching Esmyra intently before his golden eyes slid to him with pure hatred. He couldn't blame the man—last time he was aboard this ship, he burned everyone alive at his father's orders.

But how was there already a crew manning it once more? Where had Jak been that night? Surely he'd known Esmyra for some time to be so clearly devoted to her as his captain. Perhaps they were lovers, and this was all just a pawn in their little game he now found himself in. A burning sensation surged in his chest at the thought of those two sharing a bed.

Draevyn took a step up to Esmyra and gazed out at the vessel, watching the crew just as she was, the stone cuffs biting into his skin. "Is this where I'll receive an explanation?"

"I already told you, Draevyn Rowe. I don't owe you anything. In fact, consider yourself lucky to be alive."

Draevyn stared at her, hating how gorgeous her face was. It was alluring, wicked even. It was as if her beauty alone could beckon any man to her—combine that with her voice that more resembled a poisonous honey, and she was absolutely...*lethal*.

"I can't help but think this wasn't your original plan."

Esmyra's jaw locked, veins in her neck straining as she turned to face him. He grinned at her sudden change in demeanor and took it as his assumption was correct.

Esmyra lifted a finger toward his face, and a talon leisurely slid from the tip of it, its sharpened point halting just below the fragile skin of his throat.

"You're a prisoner aboard *The Night Wraith*. Shackled and bound without your flames to aid you. Just because I'm allowing you to freely stride about, doesn't mean I won't throw your ass right back into the cell and let you rot until we arrive at our destination. If anything, it means I don't deem you as a viable threat."

Jak snorted as he remained several feet behind them, hands tucked in his pockets.

A silence fell between them before she turned her attention

forward once more. The only sounds were those of the working crew and the waves colliding into the ship.

"Well, *Esmyra*," he spat her name just as she did his. "Is there anything I *am* allowed to know?"

"That your father is a tyrant, cunt of a king." She huffed through her nostrils. "And a cowardly one at that."

"On that much, we agree."

Her brows furrowed at his words, the skin of her nose wrinkling slightly. He could've sworn a subtle smirk curved the edge of her lips along with it, but it was gone so fast he considered it a trick of the blinding sunlight.

"Interesting," she said. "Your relationship with your father."

He watched as the dark curls continued to flutter around her face beneath the hat. "Not really. We tend to just stay out of each other's way."

Esmyra cackled under her breath. "Interesting indeed."

"Now, about our destination you spoke of...where exactly is that?"

She scoffed. "Jak, take him below. I've tired of his presence."

Draevyn's nostrils flared, working to silence the growl building in his throat. He thought he found a crack in her hard exterior, only to be proven wrong about her once again.

"Aye, Captain," Jak answered as he pushed off the mast's pole and grabbed Draevyn by the arm.

"Well, that didn't take long, Phoenix."

Draevyn clenched his teeth at Jak's words. He *despised* the nickname the realm gave to him.

"I give it two days before she sends you to the depths," he finished.

Jak aggressively led him down the first flight of stairs, across the deck, and then back down into the prison cells of the ship, locking him in once again, with his only source of light being the oil lamp rocking with the waves.

Perhaps the man was right, and he had pushed his luck too soon. He saw the slightest bit of freedom, and he ruined it. Only the gods knew how long she would keep him down here or where they were even headed. He was locked back in his cell with even more questions than he had when he left, and he loathed it.

Draevyn could only hope that she took the chance to let him free once more, and he wouldn't make the same mistake twice. Watching Atlas with women over the years had taught him a thing or two.

If Esmyra wished to play a game of power, then she would find that he didn't intend to lose.

CHAPTER 25

*Esmyra*

Esmyra sat at her father's desk, studying the old map of the realm beneath the light of several scattered candles. It had been nearly a week since Jak escorted Draevyn back to his cell beneath the ship, and she hadn't visited—had no desire to. He was in no position to ask her questions, demanding information as if she were the captive and he the captor. All it did was prove that he didn't take her seriously, and the thought of that nearly had her ripping out his throat with her teeth.

It was a mercy for her to lock him up once more. Though she knew he would need to be removed from his cell in only a matter of days, knowing they were nearing their destination—the cave she believed led to the underwater kingdom.

But she couldn't get the thoughts out of her head about how he agreed with her views of his father, his *king*. And so quickly. As if it weren't even a second thought. The Phoenix agreeing to it would be considered treason if it met the ears of anyone on Lephyrin's soil. She pursed her lips, wondering if anyone was aware of how he felt.

A knock sounded at the door, and before she could answer, Jak pushed it open and strolled through alongside Ren and Riven. She arched a brow at the three of them as they stumbled in through the doorway, drunk.

"Can I help you, gentlemen?" she greeted, a bit of playfulness in her tone.

"Captain!" Ren shouted, taking a step toward her desk with a half-empty bottle of rum in his hand.

"We're just checking in on you," Jak added with a boisterous laugh. "And Ren has a question."

She tried to hide her smirk as she turned her attention back to the stag shifter. "Well, I don't have all night, Ren."

He bowed deeply, nearly in a mocking manner, as his head almost bounced off the floor near his boots—or maybe he was just that drunk. "My favorite scary lady of the sea," he began.

"Scary lady of the sea?" She crossed her arms, trying to hide her amusement. "Not quite as fearsome as I would've hoped." He scratched the back of his neck as she chuckled softly. "On with it, Ren."

"Right! We're out of rum," he rushed out.

"Oh, and whose fault is that?" Esmyra snorted as Jak and Riven turned their attention to Ren as he bowed his head. "Kaelypso's tits. Well, you're shit out of luck until we make port," she said with a laugh.

Ren grinned. "What if we send dear ole Jaky-boy here out to fly and get some?"

Jak looked wholly unamused. "I can't carry it back in that form, you idiot."

Ren summoned a ball of fog in his hand, the gift of his woodland magic, and threw it at Jak's face. All it earned him was a swift punch to the gut that had him barrelling over.

"Gods, you're all exhausting. We'll discuss it later." She let out a subtle laugh as she pointed to the door. "Go to bed, the lot of you."

Ren and Riven turned toward the door and left as commanded, yawns escaping each of them as they made their way below deck.

Esmyra leaned back in her chair as Jak gazed at her from the center of the room. "Is there something you wish to say?"

He stumbled toward her, and her eyes narrowed on him.

"Gods, spit it out," she demanded.

"Why did the mortal prince call you Esmi?"

The question certainly wasn't one she anticipated. She stared at him beneath softly furrowed brows. "Did that upset you?"

Jak took another step toward her. "Very few beings in this realm are allowed to call you that. Your father and I being the only two. So, how did he know it? Why?"

"Is that jealousy I sense?" Her voice was sweet, but a lingering bite hid beneath.

Jak scoffed, the longer parts of his chestnut hair swaying as he turned away. "Of course not." He paused. "Call it...aggravated curiosity."

"And why would this make you aggravated?" She challenged her newly appointed first mate. "And you speak of this days later, I might add. Been holding onto this, have we?" She cocked her head to the side.

"Aye," he huffed before facing her once more. "Just rubbed me the wrong way, is all. He's undeserving of it. He doesn't know you. Not the real you, anyway."

"Aye," she echoed, her eyes softening slightly. "I needed a name to give him at the tavern in Anchorage Cove. It was the only one that came to mind when I was put on the spot. You know that experience didn't exactly go according to plan."

"I'm just saying, any other name would've sufficed."

She snorted. "Next time, I'll lie and say I'm Kaelypso. Is that better suited for you?" she heckled.

His lips twisted in a taunting grin as he suppressed a laugh. "Very much so, thank you."

Esmyra shook her head. "You're drunk. Go to bed."

"Aye...Captain," he said with a wink before turning on his heel and aiming for the door.

Esmyra held her breath until she heard the click as it shut behind him. "*Men,*" she huffed before turning her attention back to the map.

It made her think of the man she locked up below deck. *Aggravated curiosity*, Jak had said. Perhaps that was exactly what had been working its way through her veins regarding all the mystery surrounding Draevyn.

Why the flame-wielder was sent out to lead the sea fleet of Lephyrin, why he called his father a tyrant, and why that same man also had no consideration for his son's life.

Esmyra's eyes fell to her father's pistol resting on his desk, and her fingers brushed over the intricate designs carved into it, the cool touch of the metal biting into her skin. "I will find a way to free you. I promise," she whispered, as if he could hear.

Her immortal heart ached thinking of him rotting in that velsinyte cell—gasping for air every second that passed as blindness drove him to madness. She huffed out a breath as her stare lifted to the ringlet of rusted keys hanging on the wall.

No, this wasn't her fault. Not entirely. And the other to hold blame was held within the confines of her ship.

Esmyra's teeth clenched before slamming her fist down on the wooden desk, rattling everything atop it. She stood and snatched the keys from the wall before stalking out the door and down the stairs.

Esmyra wasn't all that surprised to find Draevyn awake—his back leaning against the far wall of his cell as he sat on the floorboards, wrists still bound. His eyes lifted to meet hers, but he didn't speak. She received no greeting or acknowledgment of her presence, aside from a scathing look that appeared as if he wished to ignite her in his blistering flames.

She took a step up to the cells and crossed her arms, sucking on her tongue. "You've seen better days."

He huffed out a hate-filled laugh. "And whose doing might that be?"

"Well, that would be yourself. If you kept your mouth shut, perhaps I wouldn't have grown tired of your company so soon."

Draevyn's whiskey eyes narrowed, and she could've sworn she saw a flicker of his flames in them, even with the cuffs. "Forgive me for asking questions regarding my capture, Captain."

Esmyra leaned against the cell, allowing her talons to slide from the tips of her fingers as she pretended to inspect them. "Care to stretch your legs, Phoenix?" Her eyes fell to him again for a moment, and his brows furrowed. "Or should I say wings?" She winked.

Draevyn pushed himself to his feet, eyes locked on her as he stalked to where she leaned against the bars of his cell. She assumed he expected her to take a step away, but she remained as she was—within easy reach, even through the bars.

"And where's your loyal dog? I never expected to be in your presence again without him a mile up your ass," he said.

His words caught her off guard, and she snorted in surprise. "Jak's sleeping. As is the rest of the crew." She reached into her pocket for the keys and unlocked the cell. The creaking of the rusted bars echoed through the darkness of the small prison. "It's just you and me, Phoenix."

Esmyra turned her back to him, wondering if he would try anything, knowing they were entirely alone, but instead, he just remained standing at the edge of his cell, not one foot beyond it.

"Why do I feel like this is a trap?" he said, forcing her to turn back to face him at the foot of the stairs.

"If it's answers you seek, it would be in your best interest to follow." Truthfully, it was she who wanted answers, but she wouldn't mind a trade. Esmyra took a few steps up the stairs before calling back over her shoulder to him, "What better time to ask questions than beyond the presence of my *loyal dog*?"

With a dark grin, she stalked up the rest of the stairs.

Draevyn watched through the open door of his cell as Esmyra waltzed up the stairs, leaving him alone.

She was testing him.

He sighed and followed her up the stairs, through the galley and the cots of the sleeping crew. The stench of unwashed bodies, brine, and rum stung his senses, forcing him to hold his breath. It appeared the entirety of her crew was asleep, and she was letting him free, unguarded and unprotected.

It was brave of her, or perhaps more so foolish. Even being confined to the velsinyte, his strength surely outmatched hers.

Her midnight hair billowed behind her as she made her way up the last flight of stairs, leading to the deck, which he realized was nearly as dark as below once he reached the top. The only source of light came from the waning moon hiding behind eerie clouds, casting a silver glow atop the dark waters.

"I don't have all night, Phoenix," she called without turning to face him.

His eyes narrowed on her back. What was she trying to do? Throw him overboard? Once he caught up to her, he found her perched on the rail of the ship's bow.

Esmyra faced him, one leg crossed over the other as her hands gripped the rails near her thighs for balance. His eyes drifted to the starboard side, where lifeboats were strapped. Perhaps he could shove *her* overboard if he timed it right and make his escape. His only issue, still, would be how to free himself from the cuffs.

Her eyes gleamed with a predatory intensity beneath the moonlight.

"Well, Esmi—"

"You've already been told you may address me as Captain or Esmyra," she cut him off.

Draevyn cleared his throat. "Apologies, *Esmyra*. Old habits and all."

She tilted her head, studying him. The corners of her lips curled into a small, unreadable smile, but she didn't speak. His heartbeat picked up as they stared at each other. Every nerve and sense in his body screamed she was dangerous, but he couldn't pinpoint why— nor could he look away.

She was clearly some form of a shifter, with her retracting talons and occasional glowing eyes. But what kind? He thought of how he'd woken up after his ship was wrecked—how he could've sworn a voice sang him back to life.

Sirens had been extinct for hundreds of years, and he loathed his lack of knowledge of them. It wouldn't make any sense for her to be a siren when she ran a ship of the very beings those creatures fed off of.

"Well, you brought me aboard the deck for a reason, stating you would provide me answers to my questions. Was that the truth or just another lie? It appears you prefer your prisoners to remain ignorant."

"Careful, Draevyn Rowe," she started. "You seem to believe you deserve the answers you seek, and I can change my mind at any moment." Her voice was smooth, like the calm before a storm.

His teeth clenched. He despised being toyed with and could tell that was exactly what she was doing—playing little mind tricks on him. Perhaps sailors didn't desire women aboard their ship, not because it was bad luck, but because they were entirely too cunning.

"But tell me...why should I indulge you?" she asked.

Draevyn worked to ease the tightness in his jaw, remembering that the only way to win her little game was to play by her rules. "Because you took me alive. If it was revenge you sought for the death of your captain, you would've killed me back in Lephyrin. But you didn't. That means you need something from me. My question is what."

Esmyra's smile widened, though it didn't reach her eyes. "The only thing I need from you is for you to remain alive. And out of my way." She gestured to his bound wrists with her chin. "Hence the cuffs." Her tone was laced with a faint mockery, as if she found the notion amusing.

Draevyn shifted on his feet, his eyes remaining on hers. "What you speak of makes little sense. You need to keep me alive? What game are you playing?"

"Game? I don't play games." Esmyra chuckled, the sound devoid of warmth, as she leapt down from the rail and stood before him, unafraid as he towered over her. She leaned in, her face now just inches below his chin as she whispered, "Your father, though...he certainly plays his cards well."

Draevyn refused the urge to flinch. "So this is the king's doing, then? Was I traded for Atlas?"

Even if he were, he would be fine with it. He would expect it. Atlas was the heir to the Lephyrin crown, and he was nothing but a fire-wielding monster that his father only let loose when it was in his best interest.

"No," she said. "You were who I sought. To trade for my captain —who is very much alive, by the way. Rotting in your father's dungeons." The last few words left her in a growl.

Draevyn's mouth fell open. "Alive, you say?" He wasn't sure what exactly happened once he lost consciousness back at the castle, but clearly, something significant had occurred.

It hit him then. He had seen Jak's golden gaze before—back at Anchorage Cove. It was the eyes of the drunken man who had stumbled into them. He shoved Esmyra into Draevyn's arms, prompting him to bring her to a secluded corner for safety. Heat welled in his chest, anger igniting as he began to put the pieces together.

"You're picking certain truths to tell while omitting others," he continued. "We met before I captured your captain. You were targeting me for something else. Your *crew* was targeting me at that tavern, and our paths happened to cross again."

The tension between them thickened, the night air growing colder as they stared each other down. Esmyra's eyes bore into Draevyn's, searching for something—fear, perhaps. But he gave her nothing.

"Why did you let me aboard your ship that day in Anchorage Cove?" she asked, and the question caught him off guard.

"You were in need of help."

"Aye," she nodded, placing her hands behind her back as she took a casual step toward him. "Or so I easily made you believe. But what of your people? What of the mortals of Lephyrin rotting in their streets of famine and disease while their royal family stands by and does nothing to aid them?"

His brows furrowed, head flinching back slightly. "I don't know what you *think* you know about me, Esmyra, but I assure you, I'm rarely in Lephyrin."

"So I've realized. Regardless, you still hold blame." She circled him—a predator stalking its prey, and he felt with every bone in his body that was exactly what she was.

"I'm not following," he started, voice low as he stood still.

"You're right. You were targeted long before we met, Phoenix. *The Night Wraith* followed you to Anchorage Cove on word that you were headed there in search of information regarding Maerinys." She tsked. "Risking the wrath of the gods. Now tell me, is it bravery or stupidity that runs you?"

Draevyn's eyes flared, his flames bursting to life within him, but they still refused to ignite in his palms. He bared his teeth. "I knew there was something off with you. I should have listened to Sam."

"Ah, yes. Samwell was certainly onto me from the first moment I stepped foot on that dock. But you appeared unable to resist a damsel in distress." She snorted as she took another step closer, the wind whipping her hair around her face. "What a fucking *hero* you are."

Esmyra was sizing him up as if she were a man, an opponent in a little dance, seeing how far she could push him before he snapped. She emanated power in surging waves, as if she were one with the sea.

Draevyn had never balked before a foe, never yielded. Yet, Esmyra was the only being he'd ever come across who had his body yearning to kneel.

He lifted his chin. "Never have I been considered a hero. And I'm not entirely sure what *you* are, but know that I've faced worse than whatever lurks within your pretty flesh. It will take more than glowing eyes and shifting talons to put fear into me."

Esmyra clicked her tongue. "Such a liar, too, Draevyn Rowe. Your fear, though little, is evident—its scent stings my nostrils as we stand before each other. You're right to be wary of me."

She turned her back on him, her hair swirling in the wind as she took a step up to the tip of the bow, gently placing her hands on the rails as she stared out at the waves. "I'm well aware that you hold no knowledge of what I am." She paused, her shoulders rising as she drew in a deep breath. "But you will."

Draevyn watched her, how carelessly she put her back to him—as if he weren't a threat due to his bound wrists. His anger flared at her lack of answers, tiptoeing around everything he needed to know. He was a captain and a prince, though he loathed the second title nearly as much as "the Phoenix."

Esmyra was a pirate. Her captain was held prisoner by the crown. And now she was dangling his life in front of him, likely to get back at his father for what he did to Cyrus Blackwood. For some reason, she needed him alive. He no longer cared why, nor could he find a reason to idly stand by.

"We each seek the same thing," she said.

*Doubtful.*

Draevyn took a silent step up to her back as she continued to face the sea, his boots silent against the floorboards. All sensible thoughts left his mind as he saw his only chance to escape. A glance to the back of her head, followed by one to the lifeboats, and his decision was made.

One moment, his bound arms hung at his front, and the next,

they were lifted above his head and slammed over hers. Draevyn heaved his arms toward himself, the metal chains linking his velsinyte cuffs wrapping around Esmyra's throat as he forced her body into his chest.

He expected Esmyra to let out a gasp for air—to scratch, and claw, and bite, but she remained silent as the chains nearly crushed her windpipe. Her arms lay slack at her sides, barely fighting back as he worked to suffocate her.

But then Esmyra *laughed*.

A violent chill went down his spine.

It was a villainous cackle that crawled under his skin and buried itself deep in his bones. The sound was sharp, cold, and biting, like a blade. It coiled around his mind like a serpent, stirring up a primal fear as his fire-fueled blood ran cold.

"What in all gods?" he whispered as he tightened his hold, but she didn't so much as balk as he felt the tiny bones in her throat crack beneath his pull.

"You will regret this, Draevyn Rowe." The words came out in a struggle, but her voice was cruel, scraping down his mind like talons.

A bright, teal glow cast from her eyes, illuminating the sea before them. Her once sleek legs merged and bound themselves together beneath the hem of her skirt.

*Is that a fucking tail?!*

And suddenly, a sharp sting radiated down his arm as her talons dug into his flesh, drawing blood.

Then, excruciating agony followed.

Draevyn bellowed an unexpected, horrific noise of anguish into the air, his back arching. He'd never felt such pain, such *agony*. Every muscle in his body tightened as an overwhelming dizziness took over him. Fire never burned him, but he imagined the gaping wound in his arm resembled what his victims once felt when he burned them alive.

Esmyra slithered out of his grasp and onto the floor before her tail whipped out and tripped him, bringing him to the ground with her.

"Fucking Irah!" he bellowed as he lifted his arm toward his face.

Horror worked its way through him as he took in the sight of his skin sizzling, *melting*. "Esmyra! What is this?!"

She inspected the sharpened nails she had just maimed him with as he writhed in pain. "That was very rude, Draevyn Rowe."

"You're shitting me." His breaths came in rapid bursts as his vision darkened, feeling as if he would lose consciousness from the pain.

Esmyra cocked her head to the side. "Say you're sorry."

"Gods." His chest heaved, unable to take in air fast enough, fearing that one of these breaths could be his last. "I thought you needed me *alive*," he gritted out through his teeth.

She shrugged a single shoulder. "Accidents happen. New plans may need to be forged."

He couldn't believe this, and he wasn't willing to try to call her bluff. What in all gods was in her nails that made his arm feel this way? It felt like she sliced him with a poison-dipped blade.

"I'm sorry," he muttered through clenched teeth.

Esmyra crawled over to him, her bare, scale-covered chest spilling from the top of her blouse while she lay atop him. His eyes bulged as they fixated on her, the teal scales now covering her body, shock overtaking him at the sight.

Her tail swayed tauntingly behind her as her face hovered above his. "What was that?" she whispered, aiming her ear toward his lips.

The words snapped Draevyn from his trance.

"I'm sorry! Gods, can you fucking blame me? I saw an opportunity, and I *took* it," he spat.

The more he thought of it, the more horrified he became. What had gone through his mind to make him suffocate a seemingly defenseless woman? Only she wasn't defenseless at all. All of the thoughts he tried to shove down about her, deeming it impossible, had been true.

Esmyra was a...*siren*. A monster of the sea that the realm believed to be extinct.

She took those very talons and leisurely walked them along his chest until they reached the edge of his throat. For a moment,

Draevyn thought she would slice his flesh open and have him bleed to death beneath her.

"Okay," she finally said. "But only because I respect honesty."

Esmyra took his maimed forearm and brought it to her pouty lips, eyeing him with a bone-chilling cruelty, before sinking her teeth into it. Draevyn's eyes flared in horror as she sucked the venom from his body, drinking it in as if it were the finest wine.

"What the fuck?" was all he managed to whisper as the pain slowly subsided. His breathing steadied as the sky above grew lighter with the rising sun.

She dropped his ruined arm onto his chest and pushed herself up to hover above him. "This is what happens when you underestimate a threat," she hissed. "And now you know that's *exactly* what I am."

The orange hues of the sunrise behind her framed her in a fiery blaze—mimicking the flames trapped and thrashing within him.

*Wildfire, indeed*, he thought at the sight of her, but before he could say another word, she sent her fist into his cheek.

Draevyn's head slammed off the wooden floorboards beneath him, and then all he knew was darkness.

Esmyra peered through her spyglass toward the distant isle. Waves crashed against its jagged rocks, spraying saltwater into the air. She stood at the helm of *The Night Wraith*, her gaze locked in the direction of the cave.

She was furious with herself. She'd been foolish to release the prince and have him walk around the ship, forgetting what he was: her prisoner.

All she'd wanted was to play with him a bit and pick through his mind. The cuffs he wore, however, worked against her magic, removing the ability to compel him for answers. Even with his flame bound within him from the velsinyte, she never should've risked it, and it forced her to play the only card she had as he attacked her.

Esmyra didn't plan to let Draevyn know what she was until the most opportune moment, but now that it was out in the open, she had no reason to hide anything of herself or her reasoning behind why they were truly here.

Her stare drifted from the isle to the prince tied to the mainmast of her ship, still unconscious from the prior night, and then to the sea beyond—where a trench lay hidden beneath dark waters.

A shiver ran up her spine as she recalled the monstrous beast that waited within it.

"Esmi," Jak called as he stalked up the stairs. "You're sure this is it? Looks like nothin' but an abandoned isle to me."

Her knuckles turned a ghostly white from her death grip on the ship's wheel. "Aye. This is exactly where we were headed." She released the wheel and moved past him, taking the steps back down to the main deck. "Avast! All hands on deck," she boomed. "Get us as close to the isle as possible before releasing the anchor. The depths here are...substantial."

*Substantial.* She almost had to laugh at her lie as she envisioned the trench with a fucking sea monster awaiting them.

He followed after her, confusion etched into his sun-weathered skin. "Esmi, how do you even know?"

She turned to him, and he nearly slammed into her as her steps halted. Her eyes gazed into the golden hue of his as she said, "This is where I was...when everything went to shit."

Her friend's brows furrowed. "What's on that isle, Esmi?"

"It isn't what's on the isle that I fear." She paused, clearing her throat as the blood drained from her face. She leaned into him and whispered, "It's what's beneath us."

Jak's eyes widened slightly. "And what might that be?"

She turned to face the sea and swallowed thickly, the pure fear she felt at the sea serpent creeping back in. "A creature of myth."

"One worth fearing?" He lifted a brow.

"Aye," she whispered and then stalked over to Draevyn.

She put her hands on her hips as she observed him. His head and shoulders lolled as his body sagged against the ropes holding him upright, his brown hair hanging in front of his face as it was tousled by wind.

Esmyra sucked on her tongue as she considered what to do with him. She knew she would need to leave at least half of her crew aboard *The Night Wraith* to keep watch and guard the cave, but she also didn't trust them enough to not torment the prince until death either. Which meant she would need to bring him along, and the thought of it had her rolling her eyes, knowing he would make everything significantly more difficult.

"Jak," she called over her shoulder as her eyes remained on her prisoner.

"Aye, Captain?"

A corner of her lips lilted. "I'd say it's time to wake the sleeping prince. Would you all agree?"

Vicious chuckles sounded from the crew, and she took it as an answer.

With a delicate wave of her fingers, water levitated up from the sea —a small, swirling spiral she conjured effortlessly. It snaked over the rail of the deck and hovered above her shoulder like a guardian.

"Time to wake up, Phoenix," she whispered, right before she commanded the water to drench her prisoner.

CHAPTER 28

*Draevyn*

A frigid shock tore Draevyn from his haze of unconsciousness. Eyes flying open, he jolted awake, his chest heaving as ice-cold water dripped down his face and hair, soaking into his clothes. A tightness formed in his chest as he gasped for air, but the ropes binding him tightly to the mainmast made the act nearly impossible.

"*Fucking Irah!*" he bellowed, taking in rapid breaths.

His blurry vision cleared, revealing the ragged onyx deck of *The Night Wraith*. He slowly lifted his head to find the sky above was a grim, swirling gray, matching the waters below—both appearing restless and unwelcoming.

The sounds of malicious chuckles caught his attention, and he took notice of the crew—all of them grinning.

"Rise and shine, Draevyn Rowe!" Her voice cut through the headache throbbing beneath his eyes, and the memories of all that occurred rushed back to him.

A vision of glowing teal eyes, razor-sharp fins, and venom-tipped talons digging into his flesh flashed. And then he recalled nothing but darkness.

Draevyn blinked the water from his eyes, the salt of it stinging them as his muscles ached, struggling against his bonds. His eyes were locked on the very ones that now haunted his mind, only now they appeared normal—human, even.

But he took in the sight of Esmyra, maybe even for the first time, *really* looking at who stood before him. And he realized there was nothing human about her at all.

She was a snake hidden in the grass, waiting to strike.

"The prince looks cold," Jak stated. "Shame we ain't got a cozy fire for him."

"An even bigger shame he can't light one himself," Esmyra cooed, and laughter rippled through the crew, their eyes gleaming with amusement.

Draevyn's lip curled in disgust as his eyes drifted to his bound hands, still clamped between the velsinyte cuffs.

He clenched his jaw, trying to steady his breath, his mind racing for any chance of escape, but the ropes held firm. A smirk formed on her face as he lifted his stare to hers.

"You play dirty," he growled, his voice low and cruel.

Esmyra gave him a quick wink. "The dirtier, the better. It's more fun that way." Draevyn blinked at the words, but then she took a step up to him as she brought her lips barely an inch from his cheek. "I'm so glad you're awake. We've got a long journey ahead, and unfortunately for us, you will be coming along."

"And what journey might that be?" he snapped.

"A journey you're not privy to," Jak barked from behind her. "Not after you attacked her at your first chance of freedom."

Esmyra smiled, and her eyes remained on Draevyn as she called over her shoulder, "Now, now, there, Jaky. The Phoenix has only shown his true colors. And when someone shows you who they really are..." Her lip curled back as she cocked her head to the side. The pupils in her eyes narrowed into the thinnest of slits, making Draevyn's heart slam against his ribs. "You believe them."

Draevyn's nostrils flared, but he couldn't find words to speak.

Esmyra leaned up on her tiptoes, delicately draping one of her arms over Draevyn's shoulder. He suppressed the shiver that begged to ravage his body from her touch.

"And you best believe *me*," she continued. "For next time, I'll let my venom consume you from the inside out." She backed away from him, taking her place next to her first mate.

"I was right that night we met, Draevyn Rowe. You are *much* more brutal than you claim to be. After all, I showed you kindness when no one else would," she echoed what he'd spoken to her the night his ship sank, making his jaw clench. "But you mistook it for weakness. This is your only warning—there is *nothing* weak about me."

Who was this woman? Esmyra was a creature of myths—a siren of the sea. So, how and *why* did she live the life of a pirate?

She was challenging him, and he hated that he was incredibly intrigued by it.

"Apologies, Esmi," he said, a tiny grin forming.

"*Captain*," both Esmyra and Jak snapped in unison.

His eyes narrowed in on Jak. It was clear there was much more to her first mate than just undying loyalty. Draevyn cleared his throat. "Apologies, Captain," he corrected himself. "Now, am I entitled to receiving information for what you lot have planned for me? Or are we just sailing the seas in hopes my father will come to my rescue? If it's the latter, let me spare you the time you're wasting. He won't give a damn."

"So it would seem," Esmyra grumbled, placing her hands on her hips. "Do you see the isle behind me?"

Draevyn moved his gaze over her shoulder. "Indeed," he said through clenched teeth, not having a clue where they were.

"*That* is your daddy's doing. We're in search of the lost kingdom of Maerinys or anything left of it."

Draevyn's jaw popped open, and he couldn't help the breathy laugh that slipped out. "Listen, love." She lifted a brow at the nickname he gave to nearly every woman. "I'm sure he promised you all your share in the gold he's expecting you to retrieve for him, but—"

"I no longer have interest in whatever we find down there," she cut him off. "My only interest is to rescue my captain from the likes of your father. You just happen to be collateral damage in case he goes against his word."

Draevyn huffed a hate-filled laugh through his nostrils. "Then it appears I'm here for the ride."

Esmyra's otherworldly eyes looked him up and down skeptically, likely because he was suddenly being cooperative. It appeared that no matter where he wound up, he was destined to be someone's prisoner. Whether it be trapped beneath the suffocating hold of his father's command, or now a true captive of one of the most feared creatures of Rymelle's legends.

"Right," she barked. "Listen up, you lot!"

The crew snapped to attention, their grins and jeers gone as they focused on her every word.

"We'll be splitting into two groups. The first half of the crew will guard the entrance and our exit route of the isle, along with *The Night Wraith*. The second half is with me," she said, her gaze locking onto Jak, and he gave her a curt nod. "We go in, look for any gods-damn thing we can trade for Cyrus, and then we get the fuck out of here. Aye?!"

"Aye, Captain!" they boomed as they dispersed, speaking amongst one another on who would be where.

She turned back to face Draevyn as he watched her through narrowed eyes. Surely, he would remain on the ship, tied to the mainmast as he was now.

"Cut him loose, Jak. I want the lifeboats headed for the isle in ten minutes," she hissed before stalking toward her office.

Jak's glare nearly burned a hole in the side of Draevyn's face.

Draevyn offered him a mocking, closed-lip smile. "Have I done something to you?"

Jak scoffed. "Consider yourself lucky that my captain insists keeping you alive guarantees the return of Cyrus. If anyone else attacked her, they would've found themselves sent to the depths. If not by her, then by one of us."

Draevyn knew he shouldn't speak his next words, but he didn't give a damn. "Captain or lover?" His head tilted.

Before he could blink, Jak's fist struck his cheek, violently jerking his neck. The taste of iron filled his mouth as blood dripped from his bottom lip.

He was about to take it as his answer before Jak spoke once more. "It appears what they say about you is true."

"And what might that be?" Draevyn huffed, spitting blood at Jak's boots.

"That the Phoenix has never had a friend in the world. Nobody to care for him—guard his back. Though why would a fire-wielder need such things, I suppose?" Jak's grin was wicked as he unsheathed a dagger from his boot before slicing through Draevyn's bindings.

"I would imagine it must be lonely. And truthfully, I don't give a damn that it is. I can already see it in your eyes, *Phoenix*." He spat the nickname with disgust. "You see her as a monster. I'm the person who's made sure that's not what she becomes. A *friend*."

Jak reached out and gripped Draevyn's arm, heaving him into his chest before whispering, "Cross her again and I don't care about the consequence. I will slit your throat myself, even if it means letting Cyrus rot."

A moment later, he was shoved in the direction of the lifeboats.

The soft creak of oars echoed across the calm water, mingling with the distant cries of gulls, as half of the crew rowed a pinnace to shore.

Draevyn watched Esmyra as she stood at the prow of the small boat. Her silhouette blocked the blinding sun as her long coat fluttered in the light breeze, revealing flashes of weapons at her hips. He was confused about why she bothered, considering she was a weapon herself.

Her dark hair tumbled in loose waves down her back, but her eyes —those cold, predatory eyes—were fixed on the isle.

Draevyn sat in the middle of the pinnace, bound and bruised. His throat was dry, lips cracked from salt and thirst, but his mind was sharp with rage, his flames begging to burst to life.

The island's jagged outline was unwelcoming, appearing as if no life had ever lived on it. But it was the captain who held his attention, not the island. She hadn't spoken to him since Jak threw him into the pinnace, her silence more terrifying than any threat.

Yet here, now, she stood calm and poised, as if she wasn't conducting this search for the lost kingdom out of spite or duty to a king she loathed but from fear for her captain's life.

That had also confused him. Pirates were known to have an "every man for himself" code when it came to survival. Yet, this crew broke into Castle Lephyrin, plotted to blend in with the crowd, and kidnapped a gods-damn prince to get a member of their crew back. Captain or not, Draevyn assumed everyone was replaceable—even the captain of *The Night Wraith*.

Perhaps Jak wasn't lying regarding his feelings for Esmyra, and what he felt for her was only platonic. Perhaps it was the real captain who held the siren's heart, and that was why she was entertaining his king's proposal.

The oars continued to dip into the water, pulling them closer to the shore. Esmyra's voice cut through the quiet, low and commanding. "Hold fast."

The rowers halted, lifting their oars. The pinnace glided to a slow stop, rocking gently in the shallows. Esmyra turned then, her gaze finally falling on Draevyn. There was something unreadable in her eyes, a cold calculation mixed with something far darker—like a shark circling beneath the surface.

"Hope you don't mind getting a little wet," she said right before she leapt out of the boat. The splash of her boots echoed above the waves.

Two burly males moved toward Draevyn, dragging him to his feet. He lifted his bound hands to put space between them and himself. "I've fucking got it," he huffed before stepping out of the small boat and following after Esmyra.

Draevyn's eyes widened. He'd never seen anything like this island before. It was crafted of rocks and jagged stone, as if they were stacked by the gods and molded as one.

His eyes narrowed on Esmyra's back as Jak and the others fell in line behind her. "Are we in the right place? Perhaps the sea level is off and this is but a marker in the water, not an actual island."

Esmyra's steps halted, and she reluctantly turned to face him, a scowl forming on her face.

He squinted from the sun as he scanned their surroundings. "'Tis no life here, *Captain*." He hoped she sensed his mockery. "Perhaps you should invest in a proper compass."

The edges of Esmyra's lips curled up in a subtle, false smile. "Well, it's good we're not looking for signs of life. Would you not agree, Draevyn Rowe?"

He sucked on his tongue as he watched her, not enjoying the way heat rushed to his cheeks every time her sultry voice spoke his full name. "What is it your lot say?" His brow kicked up. "Aye?"

This time, her lips lilted a tad higher, as if she wanted to chuckle. "Aye," she echoed with a subtle dip of her chin. She turned away from him and began to climb over sharp-edged rocks and boulders, moving deeper into the isle.

"Keep up, Phoenix," Jak called over his shoulder. "It would be a shame if you slipped and cracked your skull."

The veins in Draevyn's neck strained at Jak's taunting as he watched them follow her, trying to do so himself, but his bound hands made it significantly more difficult to keep his balance on the slick stone. He had never worn the velsinyte cuffs for such a long period before, and not only had it snuffed out his powers completely, it also seemed to make him weaker.

Esmyra raised a hand, and the pirates fell silent, halting as their eyes locked on a massive rock formation ahead. The entrance to a cave yawned before them, half-hidden by crusted seaweed and the shadows of the cliffs. It was an unassuming place, but there was something about it Draevyn couldn't place, a weight in the air that made the hairs on his arms rise.

"This is it, gents," Esmyra announced as she turned to face them.

"You've been here before?" Draevyn asked. "How are you so sure?"

Jak pressed his lips in a tight line. "I hate that I agree with his question. This is truly where you went that day?"

"Aye," she answered proudly, placing her hands on her hips.

"How long ago were you here?" Draevyn asked.

Any hint of the amusement she held a moment ago fell from her face. She waltzed up to him and lifted herself onto her tiptoes. "It was the day you attacked *The Night Wraith* and slaughtered my crew," she spoke softly into his ear.

Draevyn ignored the chill that ached to run along his spine as he locked eyes with hers. "Was only returning the favor, love." He winked.

She flashed him her teeth before turning on her heel and stalking back toward the opening of the cave.

"Mind your tongue, Phoenix. Or I'll cut it out of your skull," Jak growled, twirling a dagger in his hand. But Draevyn only shrugged away the threat; the more he watched their dynamics, the more he realized Esmyra's word was law among their crew.

Jak could spit any threat he wished, but unless his captain gave the order, the first mate's hands were as tied as his own.

CHAPTER 29

*Esmyra*

Sweat beaded on Esmyra's brow, stifling under the long coat she forced herself to wear under the rays of the scorching sun. Even the males were sweating in their thin tunics, but she wasn't ready for them to witness what she knew beamed beneath her clothes.

She'd peeked under her sleeve when she first set foot on the island's stone as Jak, Ren, and Riven were forcing Draevyn to his feet to leave the pinnace. And just like last time, the markings adorning her flesh radiated their subtle glow as if she were beneath the ocean's surface, but this time, her skin wasn't even wet.

There was something about this island that called to her, like a thread wrapped around her heart, tugging her in its direction.

She ached to know why, but was clueless about any potential reasoning. But she knew in her very bones that the answers she'd sought her entire life could be answered within the confines of the cavern before them.

Esmyra stepped forward, inspecting the cave's entrance. Without a word, she motioned to her crew and stalked through.

It was just as she remembered: the air inside was cool, damp, and heavy with the scent of wet stone and brine. Droplets of water fell into unseen pools somewhere in the darkness as only small shafts of sunlight filtered through the crevices of the cave's ceiling.

She paused for a moment, her eyes adjusting to the gloom as the rest caught up to her. Esmyra glanced back, watching as they each took in their surroundings.

"Bloody unnatural, this place," Ren muttered, his voice hushed.

"It's certainly something of that nature," she answered, just as quiet.

"How far did you venture in when you were alone?" Jak asked as he stepped up to her, squinting through the darkness. He peered over his shoulder. "Keep up, Phoenix."

Esmyra rolled her eyes. "Your tormenting of him is becoming tiring, even to me. We don't know how long we'll be here. Let's not make *me* any more annoyed than I am."

"Forgive me for not being so...*forgiving* when someone attacks my friend."

Esmyra's eyes softened, but her stare remained ahead on their path. "You're forgiven."

She faced the others. Ren and Riven's stares drifted along the walls and ceiling while two others flanked Draevyn on each side, observing her silently. "Hopefully, we won't be too long, but we need to stick together. I never made it very far in here, but there's a small passage up ahead that will open to a larger cavern. Once we arrive there, we can form a better plan."

"And what if there be beasts, Captain?" Ren asked.

Despite her nerves about the trench, she lifted a mocking brow. "Beasts? Don't tell me you're scared, Ren."

"Something is off about this place, boss," Riven answered for him.

"Regardless, we need to keep moving. We've only just arrived." Her voice was firm, though quieter than usual. Even she couldn't shake the feeling that the cave was listening, waiting, or even watching them.

But she'd never known fear, let alone made it known. She absolutely refused to show them any hint of it now.

"Am I not a good enough weapon to ease your pathetic nerves?"

She crossed her arms as her hip jutted to the side. Jak let out a hushed chuckle, but neither of them answered her. "And, lucky for us, we have bait, if needed." She gestured to Draevyn with her chin, and he rolled his eyes.

She didn't wait for them to respond before her eyes shifted, lighting their way in the darkness.

Stalactites hung from the ceiling like the teeth of a massive, ancient beast. The echo of the crew's footsteps was unnervingly loud as they emerged from the narrow pathway and into the open cavern.

"Esmi, there are carvings along the stone," Jak announced.

She remembered them from before, though she couldn't read them.

"Aye," she said as she stepped up to the nearest wall, tracing her fingers along the unknown markings. "They appear to be a rune of some kind, or perhaps another language entirely."

"They look familiar," Ren interjected as he scratched the stubble on his chin.

Esmyra went to tune out their voices but felt eyes on her. She shifted on her feet as an uncomfortable feeling of being watched loomed over her.

When her stare lifted, it met Draevyn's.

His whiskey eyes were piercing, even through the darkness of the cave. She couldn't get a read on what he was thinking, but she didn't appreciate how his stare narrowed in on her. As if he were trying to see through her.

"Do you have something you wish to say, Draevyn Rowe?" she hissed.

His gaze roamed over her leisurely, sending a sinking feeling in her gut. And when his stare halted on her arms, she knew exactly what was going through his mind.

"For once, I agree with a member of your crew. The markings are very...*familiar.*" His eyes, even in the dimness of the cavern, darkened as he assessed her.

She didn't like it.

"Your usefulness is diminishing by the minute," she snapped, her posture rigid.

Draevyn only lifted his bound hands before him in a defensive gesture.

"What do you think these mean?" Jak whispered as he stepped up to the wall, running a hand over the worn carvings. "These markings seem ancient. Carved into the rock by men. Or something...*else.* Spirals, runes, symbols, none of us can decipher. And each of us stem from a different kingdom."

"What they mean, Jak, is that we're in the right place. We should keep moving," Esmyra said.

She led the way as they followed behind her silently. The path narrowed, forcing them into a single line, as it sloped downwards.

The sunlight that once pierced through the cracks in the cave's ceiling had dissipated entirely, leaving their only light source stemming from her eyes, illuminating the markings that grew more present the deeper they traveled.

"I think they're telling a story," Riven said from behind her.

"A story of what, though?" Ren added.

"We'll likely never know," Esmyra answered, even though she desperately wished it wasn't the truth, feeling as though they could hold answers she sought her entire life.

"They weren't carved by mortals. If I'm certain of anything, it's that," Draevyn added.

"Obviously," Jak hissed. "Your kind wouldn't be capable."

Draevyn let out a low chuckle, but there was no amusement in it. "A mortal, a siren, two woodland shifters, and an elven stumble into an ancient cave, and not one of us can decipher the markings on the walls."

"Your point?" Jak snipped.

"It's odd. While we all speak the tongue of Rymelle, it's clear that whatever creature carved these didn't. So, how old are they exactly?"

"Nothing your fragile mortal mind would know, I'd assume," Riven said, a bit of bite in his tone that typically wasn't there.

Esmyra turned to watch the bickering. Riven's white hair and grey eyes nearly glowed in the teal light, a stark contrast to the rich brown hue of his skin—but the elven's annoyance was clear on his face as he glared at their captive.

"Everything alright, Riv?" Esmyra called over.

"It appears the mortal prisoner forgets his place among us." He took a step up to Draevyn, but the prince didn't back down an inch. "Do you forget what us elves can do? What *each* of us can do?"

"Perhaps he needs to be reminded," Ren chimed in.

As his words rang out, violent winds brewed in the small space while a misty fog emerged, surrounding Draevyn on all sides. Jak and Ren each summoned their powers with a raised hand, taking Riven's tormenting as their cue.

Draevyn's eyes flared, a sweat breaking out on his forehead.

"Do you feel the blade of my magic scraping down your mind?" Riven taunted, his hand now stretched before him. "If it weren't for those damn cuffs, I would be in there, forcing you to see your fears."

Esmyra watched curiously as the veins in Draevyn's neck strained, his teeth clenching so hard she thought she might hear them crack even over the conjured, howling winds.

Nostrils flaring, Draevyn slammed his eyes shut. "Get out of my head, *elf*," he roared.

"Oh, just you wait until I can *truly* be in there, Phoenix," Riven cooed, grinning at Esmyra before dropping his hand.

Draevyn's body sagged as Riven released his hold.

The cave became eerily silent as the magic ceased—the crew members staring at their captive menacingly.

"What do you lot believe of mortals, anyway?" Draevyn snapped. "Do you believe us to be non-threatening just because we don't possess magic? Perhaps what we lack in power, we've gained in knowledge. We've survived this long somehow."

"I believe we've made it clear that *you* are a threat, Prince. Your hands are bound for a reason." Esmyra lifted a taloned finger in his direction as her vision sharpened from the slits of her irises dilating.

"We're not talking about me." His voice dripped with venomous hatred.

"And we weren't talking *to* you at all," she said matter-of-factly, earning soft chuckles from the crew.

"Speak when spoken to, Phoenix." Jak's voice echoed in the cavern.

The remark was met with silence, and Esmyra fought back a smirk as she swore she heard a deep growl brew in Draevyn's chest.

CHAPTER 30

*Esmyra*

Esmyra's boots splashed in stagnant water. Wiping her brow, she halted as the males accompanying her peered over her shoulder.

"Seawater?" Jak asked.

Esmyra sniffed the air, the brine in the air stinging her nose. "I would assume."

"How deep does it go?" Draevyn asked.

She faced him with a raised brow. "Does it look like I have any fucking clue? I've never been this far into the cave." Her words faded to a whisper. "We keep moving."

Draevyn snorted. "Well, forgive me for not knowing your magic has limits, *siren*."

Esmyra shot him a dagger-like glare before turning to Jak. "We should've brought a gods-damn muzzle for him."

"Esmi," Jak whispered, as if the others wouldn't be able to hear. "If this water keeps getting deeper, we won't be able to go much further."

"I know," she answered softly. "But we need to go as far as we can. Cyrus is depending on us."

The deeper they walked, the thicker the air became. Sweat beaded down their faces.

205

"Why don't you remove your coat, Esmi?" Jak offered. "It's too hot and only weighing you down."

*Gods,* she wanted nothing more.

Her eyes widened slightly, clutching the coat tighter. "I'm fine," she lied, feeling as if she might die of a heat stroke.

Jak stopped in his tracks, causing the others to in turn. He watched her warily. "Is something wrong? You've been acting strange since we arrived."

"Of course not, Jak. Let's just keep moving." She nervously tugged at the collar of the jacket as it stuck to her skin.

The water, once ankle-deep, now rose to their shins, bone-chillingly cold as it seeped into their boots. The cave was alive with strange sounds now: the occasional clatter of stones falling from the walls, the gurgle of water in hidden crevices, and a faint, almost subtle hum that seemed to vibrate through the stone itself.

A low thrumming rumbled beneath Esmyra's feet, as if the cave was breathing, pulsing with some ancient energy.

"Do you hear that?" she asked quietly, and she was answered with a few low hums of agreement. She gazed down the darkened path before them. "It's coming from up ahead."

Esmyra took off in a sprint, the splashes from everyone's steps echoing as they chased after her. The cave floor continued to slope downward, and the water rose again, cold and swirling around their knees.

The crew stumbled to a halt as the tunnel opened into a vast chamber. The ceiling here rose impossibly high, lost in the darkness, and the sound of rushing water roared all around them. At the far end of the chamber, a massive stone archway stood half-submerged in the underground pool they were in, the water rippling in strange, unnatural patterns that put even Esmyra on edge.

*Kaelypso's tits. What the fuck is that?*

She knew water. Wielded it—was one with it. Yet, she'd certainly never seen it do *that.*

Esmyra stepped forward, her breath catching. The archway was covered in the same ancient carvings, and something about the way the water shimmered beneath it made her skin hum. It was as if the pool wasn't water at all, but something alive, something waiting.

She couldn't shake the feeling that it had been waiting for *her*. The markings along her arms and spine warmed at the thought.

The crew shifted behind her, their unease palpable. The air felt thinner down here. The once humid tunnel had turned into a vast cavern that had an abrupt coldness sinking into their bones.

"Well, this is creepy," Ren said with a nervous laugh.

"Aye," Esmyra breathed as she scanned their surroundings, the hairs on her arms standing alert.

Jak stepped up to her, trying to catch his breath. "Everything inside of me is saying we need to turn back. Something's off about this place, Esmi. It doesn't feel right."

But Esmyra's eyes were fixed on the ancient archway, her nose wrinkling beneath furrowed brows. This was what they had come for —the path to the kingdom beneath the sea. She felt it in her very being, as if it were calling to her in her mind.

"We're close," she said, though she sensed they were standing on the edge of something dangerous, perhaps even deadly.

The crew exchanged wary glances but remained silent. They trusted her, that she knew, but they feared the cave. Truthfully, she didn't blame them; something inside herself felt a primal force lurking within the confines of where they now stood.

Teeth clattered behind her, and she found both Ren and Riven were huffing hot air into their hands for warmth at the sudden drop in temperature.

"Want to know what would come in handy right now?" Draevyn's voice echoed as he wore a smug look.

"So help me gods, if you say—"

"My fire? What will you do, Esmyra? Cut out my tongue?" He winked at her, and she blinked.

No one ever challenged her the way he did, and the bastard kept getting braver each time. She desperately tried to ignore the subtle heat pooling between her thighs at his sudden remark.

*That* certainly wasn't something she was used to.

Jak let out a huff. "Nice try, Phoenix. You'll remain in the cuffs."

"Even if it means your precious captain freezes?"

"I'll be fine," she snapped, though her eyes wandered back to her shivering crew, worry rushing through her. "We've come this far. Just a little further, and if we come across something too dangerous or a dead end, we'll turn back."

With a steadying breath, Esmyra moved toward the archway. The water lapped at her boots as she waded deeper; the males following close behind. The chamber echoed with the sound of their movement, and the strange humming grew louder.

"Gods, I can't fucking wait to get back to the ship," Riven said through chattering teeth.

"Aye," Ren chimed in.

"Knock it off," Jak interjected. "She wants to keep going. This is for Cyrus. Remember that."

Esmyra stared up at the carved stone and its meticulous markings. It was beautiful and ancient, the sight of it nearly took her breath away. This had to have been part of the lost kingdom—and it was *hidden*, locked beneath the earth, for no one to see or find again.

Esmyra's lips parted, heart racing as a roaring filled her ears. Her body felt like it was being controlled by something else entirely, her fingertips aching with the need to touch the archway as if it were calling her home.

*Touch it*, a voice urged in her mind, startling her.

The siren within her had never outright spoken to her before. It was more of an entity she could feel and sense. So why was this happening now? A rush of fear surged through her as the ancient voice echoed in her mind.

Taking a brief glance over each shoulder, she noticed all eyes were on her, looking more concerned than they had only a moment before.

Draevyn subtly shook his head as their stares locked.

*It calls to us. Touch the stone*, it urged again. She sucked in a sharp breath, an aching need to obey roiling through her.

Esmyra turned from him and gently placed her palm on the stone. The moment her skin made contact with the arch, she no longer felt the chill of the cavern air, and a lick of intense heat raced along her spine and down her arms. She gasped from the shock of it, but kept her hand in place.

"Esmi! What are you—" Jak's words died on his tongue as quickly as they raced out.

The rune markings carved along the stone burst with a vibrant glow as the ground began to tremble. At first, it was a subtle vibration, but within moments, the walls around them groaned, rocks tumbling from the ceiling.

The crew began shouting as the shaking grew more violent, but Esmyra's hand remained glued to the structure.

She could distantly hear their bellowing voices, begging and pleading for her to move, say, or do anything. But everything around her had evaporated, and all that stood before her was the entrance to her life—her *true* life. The life she should've always lived.

It called to her, beckoning her as if it were her own seductive song.

"*Esmyra!*" Draevyn screamed in desperation above all others, and she blinked through her trance.

Everything came rushing back to her at once—the collapsing walls of the cave, the roaring of water, and the tumbling of boulders sent her heart into her throat. She started gasping for air—her chest heaving as if she hadn't taken a single breath since she stepped up to the archway.

"Move, now!" Esmyra shouted, but it was too late.

With a thunderous rumble, giant pieces of the ceiling collapsed, sending a cascade of stones and debris crashing around them. Enormous waves and splashes erupted throughout the dark, open cavern.

"Esmyra, look out!" Draevyn roared.

Her eyes snapped up to the ceiling as an enormous piece of stone broke off, aiming for where she stood. Jaw agape, she took a hesitant step back, but shock froze her in place as the boulder fell, waiting for it to inevitably crush her beneath it.

One moment, she was standing, and the next, she found that her feet no longer touched the ground. Draevyn's body crashed into hers, shoving her out of the way of the falling boulders, but when they

both went to find their footing, the floor beneath their boots
gave way.

The world seemed to move in slow motion, with even the smallest
sounds and movements stretched out in time. The last thing Esmyra's
eyes caught was the horrified look on Jak's face as she fell.

And then she and Draevyn were through the archway's door.

The earth slipped out from under her as she tumbled down a
steep slope. The jagged rocks scraped at her skin before she began free-
falling alongside Draevyn and the rushing cascades of water. The
panicked shouts of her crew grew distant as the darkness swallowed
them from up above.

The fall seemed to stretch on endlessly as she plummeted through
the void until she was plunged into bone-chilling water. The icy
wetness jolted through her body like a sharpened blade.

She gasped as the cold enveloped her, disoriented by the sudden
drop. Webs formed between her fingers, and her gills emerged from
her throat on instinct as she kicked her legs to swim upward. Her head
broke the surface and she sucked in deep breaths, treading to keep
herself afloat in absolute darkness.

"Jak!" she called out, her voice echoing. "Ren! Riven!" But there
was no answer, just the sound of splashing alongside her heavy breathing. "*Fuck!*" she screeched as she began circling her surroundings.

With her eyes lighting the way, she swam toward the nearest edge,
her fingers brushing against smooth stone. Pulling herself up, Esmyra
climbed out of the water, soaked and shivering. Her ears strained,
listening for any sign of the others.

Bubbles caught her attention in the center of the underground
lake, and she remembered why she fell. Her lip curled back, aggravation seeping into her every pore. "This gods-damn prince," she hissed
before shoving out of her pants and long coat before diving back into
the water, using her tail to propel herself deeper to grab the drowning
man.

Again.

Esmyra swam through the lake, her senses on high alert. The
Phoenix was near—she could feel the sharp pulse of his heart as he

clung to this world, a trembling note that carried through the water. She followed that signal, diving deeper into the lake's depths.

But now, as she moved through the eerie, undisturbed water, something far more sinister stirred.

Ahead, a dark shape flailed beneath the surface, a lone figure struggling against something unseen. Her sharp eyes focused on Draevyn—his limbs jerked violently, his mouth open in a scream that was drowned out by the water.

But it wasn't the current dragging him down.

Pale, twisted hands clutched his ankles, pulling him deeper, toward the bottom of the lake.

*Grindylows.*

The vile creatures swarmed around him like ghosts in the depths, their dark, sickly green bodies blending with the darkness of the cave's water. Their hollow eyes glinted in the dim light cast from her own, and sharp teeth flashed as they tugged him deeper, where they would feast on his flesh.

Esmyra hissed as fury ignited through her. Grindylows were wicked creatures that haunted the darkest trenches of every sea, preying on anything their vile hands could latch onto. She swam toward them with powerful strokes, her tail slicing through the water as she closed the distance.

The sight was crafted from nightmares. Draevyn's face was contorted in terror as he fought, but it looked nearly impossible with his hands bound together. One of the grindylows clung to his neck, its bony fingers digging into his skin, while two more had wrapped themselves around his legs, pulling him even deeper.

Even beneath the surface, Esmyra's battle cry was ear-piercing as she charged into them. She grabbed one of the creatures by its scaly neck, yanking it off Draevyn with a forceful twist. It screeched, bubbles erupting from its mouth as it flailed in her grip, but she crushed its throat in her hold. The creature dissolved a moment later, becoming nothing more than a wisp of shadowy bubbles.

Another grindylow lunged at her, its claws reaching for her face, but she spun, dodging it with ease, and slammed her tail into its chest.

It flew backward, the water's resistance barely slowing it before its body crashed into the rocky wall of the cave and burst into shadows alongside its kin.

The remaining two clung stubbornly to Draevyn, refusing to release their grip. Esmyra charged once more, reaching for them. She tore one off his leg, hurling it into the darkness, where it vanished with a hiss. The last one, its fingers wrapped tightly around Draevyn's neck, shrieked as she gripped its bony arms, prying it loose with a growl of effort. She threw it aside, and it disappeared into the shadows of the lake, joining the others in retreat.

Draevyn's body became lifeless, no longer fighting as he descended further into the murky water. Nausea crept in as her heart raced. Esmyra wrapped an arm around his waist, pulling him close. His head lolled against her shoulder, the icy water turning his lips blue.

*Gods-dammit, Phoenix. Stay with me.*

With a final surge, she broke through the surface, waiting for him to gasp for air, but he never did.

Aggravated, she huffed, "Don't you fucking die on me. Your use hasn't expired yet."

She heaved him onto the rocky surface, sprawling him out next to the garments she tore off herself, and she didn't hesitate before pressing her lips to his, breathing air into his lungs.

Esmyra repeated the motion, dread taking over her as the seconds dragged on. Then, at last, a weak cough escaped him, and she dove out of the way. Draevyn sputtered, choking as water spilled from his mouth. The clattering of the chains binding his wrists echoed through the cavern. Draevyn's eyes opened slowly as his chest rose and fell with ragged breaths, his gaze fixed on her with a mixture of horror and disbelief.

Her spine straightened, eyes roaming over the vast darkness that surrounded them as he worked to catch his breath.

Angrily huffing through her nostrils, she locked eyes with him. "What the fuck have you done?!"

CHAPTER 31

*Draevyn*

Esmyra's lethal voice resonated with a promise that she may have saved Draevyn's life, only to be the one to end it herself.

"What have *I* done?! How about saving your gods-damn life!" Draevyn bellowed back at her, still trying to catch his breath as his body trembled from the freezing water soaking his clothes.

He stared in disbelief at the woman hovering over him, the water beading off her soft, *glowing* skin.

Why was it glowing?

*How* was it glowing?

"How about a thank you for saving your life!" he shouted as he sat up next to her, staring.

Esmyra's lips curled back, revealing her canines. "Saving me? If I remember the past few moments correctly, and I'm pretty sure I do, considering I was the only one conscious, *I'm* the one who saved *your* ass!"

Draevyn watched as her tail split, shifting into two sleek legs. His cheeks burned hot as he noticed she was now entirely bare. Watching her shift felt too intimate to be a witness to, even in the darkness. He averted his gaze, but his eyes drifted along her arms, brows furrowing at the markings that no longer appeared as burns.

"Neat trick."

"Glad you think so," she hissed as she struggled to shove herself into her soaked pants.

Draevyn let out a huff after a few moments of tense silence. "What happened?"

Esmyra pushed herself to her feet before walking to the water's edge, glaring up at the rock wall that seemed to stretch on for an eternity.

Was that where they'd fallen from? He barely remembered anything after he dove to save her life.

"In your once again moronic heroics, you doomed us both." Her voice was sharp, irritation filling every word as she rubbed her temples.

He looked around, noticing the others weren't alongside them. "Did they survive?"

"They better have, for your sake."

Draevyn stood and took a step up to her. "Interesting enough, the one person bound in cuffs, whose life is constantly threatened, was the only one who thought to save you."

Her spine straightened, and Draevyn's lips lifted in a subtle curve, knowing his words cut where he wanted them to. "Perhaps they're not as loyal to their captain as you believe."

Esmyra whirled. "You know nothing of them."

"Oh, I believe I know enough just by what I've witnessed in mere days. Pirates are known to be lethally selfish. Your crew is no exception."

She lifted a finger, her talon sliding out until it reached the skin of his neck. "*Acting* captain. Let's not forget where their true one lies rotting and who's the cause of him being placed there."

"That would be himself, Esmyra. For his crimes against the entire gods-damn realm. And you should be there with him, perhaps even more so."

"Don't you think I know that?!" she bellowed, her voice bouncing off the walls of the caves. Tiny pebbles chipped off the surrounding stone and fell into the pool at their feet. She took a step up to him, bringing her voice to a mere whisper. "I would trade places with him if I could."

"Foolish. You would only be put to death." His eyes narrowed on her, barely able to see in the cavern's darkness.

*Why did she care so much about the realm's most feared criminal?*

"It's better than him being tortured with every breath he breathes."

His jaw tightened at their continued dance. What did she mean by that?

"At first, I believed you to have an intimate relationship with your first mate. Yet, you speak of your captain as a lover," he said. "Interesting he would place a woman in charge in his absence."

A mixture of shock and something resembling disgust cloaked her features, evident by the way her jaw dropped and her brows furrowed. "That is vile! Is it so confusing to you for a woman to be placed in power?"

He shrugged a shoulder. "Not necessarily. It's the way you speak of him, is all."

"My relationship with my captain is *not* your concern. However, I will put an end to your mortifying thoughts regarding the love being anything more than familial."

Draevyn lifted a brow. "Familial?"

Esmyra turned from him, as if in dismissal. Cupping her hands, she lifted her chin and shouted, "Jak! Ren! Riven, can you hear me?!" She took a step closer to the wall. "Hello!" The word echoed.

"It appears they're not coming for you," Draevyn stated. "They likely think we're dead."

"Likely just you, *mortal*," she spat before storming past him in the opposite direction.

*Fucking Irah.* This woman was something else.

"And where are you going?" he growled, rolling his eyes with a sigh.

She half turned, her midnight hair dancing around her in the teal light as she moved. "I'm looking for a way out or a way further. We've come this far. If you would prefer to be eaten by the grindylows or whatever other beasts lurk in that water, then be my guest."

The grindylows proved there was *some* form of life down here.

After thinking it had been entirely abandoned and forgotten, creatures were lurking in the shadows and lakes. They'd been carelessly strutting around, and here he was...powerless in the cuffs.

The further Esmyra stepped away from him, the more oppressive the darkness became, thicker than any night. He found it suffocating —disorientating, even. He gazed into the darkness, and he could've sworn the darkness gazed right back.

Perhaps he should've let her die, be crushed by the stone, and he could've fought his way out. Then he remembered the three males tormenting him in a show of their power, and he realized that so long as he was bound in velsinyte, he was utterly fucked.

Draevyn stormed across the space toward her, praying to Irah that he didn't fall into some unseen crevice or walk off another cliff as she halted before a wall. He followed her gaze to the stone that bore the same carvings of the cave above, identical to her arms.

"This is pointless," Draevyn grumbled. "We're wasting time. We should be trying to—"

"Or, you can shut your mouth and let me think, Draevyn Rowe," Esmyra snipped, her fingers brushing against the cold, damp stone. Her breath caught the moment the pads of her fingertips made contact.

A shiver ravaged Esmyra's body while her feather-like touch followed the patterns, making his pulse quicken as he watched.

"I think it's clear these markings are deliberate and possibly ancient. Symbols of power. Perhaps even that of the gods," he guessed.

"Aye," she answered, the word barely audible.

"And I would love to know why they match the markings seared into your flesh," he said, suspicion lacing his voice as he took a step closer.

Esmyra didn't answer. In fact, she ignored him completely. It was as if he weren't even standing beside her. She was locked in a near trance, just as she had been before they fell down into this separate cavern.

Without a word, she pressed her palm against the largest of the runes, and Draevyn watched in awe as a strange warmth pulsed, exuding from her, mimicking his flames. The markings along the entire wall lit up—a vibrant crimson light spreading across the wall like veins of molten metal.

Esmyra's eyes were glowing, just as they always had when she put her power to use, but this time, it was brighter, nearly blinding, as her hand remained on the wall of stone.

Draevyn took a hesitant step back, lifting his bound arms to block the light as the markings continued to reveal themselves all around them. They glowed brighter, illuminating the entire cavern while his jaw hung open in disbelief.

*What in all gods is this?*

He slowly turned, circling around as his neck craned to follow the runes. When the lit markings met in the middle, and all were alight, the crimson light flickered and surged, bursting brightly. He shielded his eyes from the glare, and when it lessened, he slowly cracked them open once more.

His heart leapt in his throat.

The wall's runes were no longer the color of flame but matched the ones she bore atop her flesh—the entire cavern now bathed in a soothing, teal light.

The silent space echoed with a deep groan as the stone shifted, a crack violently splintering through it where she placed her hand. The runes hummed with life as an ancient doorway revealed itself to them —to *her*—summoned by her touch.

It was impossible. He had never seen anything like it in all his years. Never read of such things in texts or heard stories of it as a child. It was unfathomable magic and it was just conjured by his enemy before his very eyes.

Only, she looked as mortified as he felt.

"How did you—" Draevyn cut himself off as he took a step up to her. She was trembling, her hand still held in the air as if it was still touching the stone that had shifted away. "Esmyra?" he whispered.

She gasped and took a step back—like she'd just been placed back into her body, taking everything in from the last several minutes. He caught her as she stumbled into him, and when his hand brushed against her markings, he hissed. Heat, sharp and quick, scorched his skin.

*Wildfire,* he thought once more.

"Esmyra, can you hear me?"

Her breathing became erratic as she settled back into herself before promptly shoving out of his hold. He blinked in shock.

"Holy mother of Kaelypso." It seemed she couldn't get the words out fast enough.

"Did you say something for that to happen? To the stone?" he asked warily.

"No," she whispered as she stepped away from it and glanced up, slowly spinning in a circle, eyes wide. "I just...*touched* it."

"Same as the arch from above," he stated.

"Aye." Her full circle came to a halt, and she faced him once more.

"Let's stop touching things, huh?" he said, a hint of teasing in his voice, but all it earned him was a scoff.

"How was I supposed to know that would happen?" she growled. Her neck craned up as she took another look. "What do these even mean?"

"I was hoping you would have the answer, considering they mark your body."

Her gaze whirled to him, lip curling back. "Watch your tongue."

"It's the truth! And it's obvious. I'm surprised your moronic crew didn't put two and two together when we were up there with them." He gestured to the ceiling of the cave. "Why are they suddenly glowing? They were red, resembling burns until you pulled me out of the water."

She averted her gaze to the floor. "They glow teal when in contact with water."

His eyes flared. "Every time?"

"Every time," she echoed with a sigh.

Draevyn reached out, brushing his bound hands against her arm, and she swatted at him as she took a step away. "You're dry," he stated.

"Well, aren't you observant?"

"So, you're lying to me," he said, annoyed. He knew his flames would be sparking at his fingertips if his magic wasn't locked away.

Esmyra took a step up to him and shoved at his chest. "I'm not lying. There's something strange about this place. Strange and *ancient*. They glowed the first time I was here alone, as well."

He thought back to when they were all walking, and the sweat beading down her brow when she refused to remove her coat. "You didn't want them to see," he guessed.

"That's none of your concern." She crossed her arms and jutted her hip to the side.

Draevyn took a step into her, closing the small space that remained between them. "You know, Esmyra, you keep saying that, but I'm currently trapped in a fucking *cave* that looks like it will become my tomb. So, I think anything that occurs here is every bit of my gods-damn concern."

The fire inside him was blazing—there was something about her that constantly brought this out in him. His eyes roamed over her as his breathing settled, but she didn't back down an inch. Just stared up at him down the bridge of her nose.

Draevyn hated that he found it attractive—he wasn't even certain attraction was the right word for it. But someone who didn't see him as a terrifying monster, especially in his anger, was curious, to say the least.

"I don't have time for you," she huffed, turning on her heel and stalking toward the conjured doorway.

"Where do you think you're going?" he demanded.

A sharp cackle left her. "Obviously, our only way out of this hellhole is through this magical, glowing doorway."

The sass in her tone had him sighing, rubbing his temples before he slowly followed after her. "What makes you so certain that's our way out?"

"Kaelypso's tits, Draevyn!" she groaned as her arms flailed out at her sides. She looked over her shoulder at him. "Just trust me for once."

Draevyn's lips twisted into a sneer. "Trust you? You're the one who dragged us into this cursed pit."

She let out a chuckle that he thought may have been genuine. "Aye, well, now I'm finding our way out of it. And let's not forget we have your *daddy* to thank for it."

They both stepped up to the newly revealed passageway, and he could've sworn he heard her heart pounding. The light from the runes illuminated the tunnel beyond, showing smooth stone floors and walls, far too clean to be natural—a pathway carved by ancient hands.

"This place..." Draevyn's voice softened. "It certainly leads somewhere, judging by the craftsmanship."

For the first time since the night on his ship, they shared a look that wasn't laced with hatred. The surrounding cave hummed with power, the ancient markings glowing brighter, inviting them deeper into the tunnel.

Esmyra nodded. "Then let's see what's waiting for us."

They stepped through the entrance, and he snickered. "Whatever lies ahead can't be worse than you."

Draevyn didn't miss the subtle smirk that tilted her lips.

CHAPTER 32

*Esmyra*

The gleaming carvings on the passage walls stretched into the dark, seemingly endless as they walked. The runes were a mystery that gnawed at Esmyra, leaving her desperate to know why they matched the markings she was born with.

Her father had kept her from Maerinys for a reason, and she couldn't shake the feeling that this may have been why. Esmyra never had answers for her runes or the magic behind how or why they glowed. She had scoured countless libraries and ancient scrolls, searching every kingdom for a clue to the marks her body bore, but nothing of use ever revealed itself.

There were no other creatures known to have them—it was just another thing she was utterly alone in.

Draevyn walked beside her. They'd been silent since entering the tunnel, mostly because she wasn't quite sure what to say.

*Everything inside me is screaming to turn back*, Jak's last words echoed in her mind.

Had Jak, Ren, and Riven perished in the tumbling rocks? Were their bodies splattered across the cave floor miles above them? Nausea twisted in her gut as that image appeared in her mind. She would never forgive herself if that were the case.

First, her father was captured due to her absence, and now this. If

221

only she had turned back, found another way into Maerinys—even if she once again had to face the wretched beast hidden within the trench beyond the isle. But no, her recklessness had cost her, and this time, it was the only family she had left.

The three idiots she did nothing but scold or scoff at—the people she held closest to her immortal, rotten heart, aside from her father.

It was too much for her to bear, feeling as if she was on the point of breaking—no, *erupting*—into something she didn't know she would be able to pull herself out of.

Esmyra always felt like there was something else inside her, sleeping as if it were dormant, waiting to awaken. It was what she considered the siren within, but since being in this gods-forsaken place, she felt it all the more. No longer in a heavy slumber, but now watching and waiting for the opportune moment to claw itself out.

The stone had reacted to her touch. Not once, but twice—both times revealing something hidden. The wall's markings matched her own, no longer glowing solely beneath the tides, but as they neared Maerinys as well, serving as a map and guiding her.

Esmyra was certain it wasn't a coincidence, and she couldn't shake the thought of why her father forbade her from these waters or Maerinys.

And Draevyn—the dreaded, violent Phoenix—had saved her once again. And then she'd saved him in return.

She glanced up at Draevyn, whose eyes remained forward, lulling with each step.

How long had they even been in the cave? Hours? A full day?

"Are you tired, Draevyn Rowe?" she asked.

He sighed, as if hearing her voice exhausted him further. "We've been walking for hours, have fallen over cliffs, fought off creatures trying to drown us, and have discovered that you seem to be some kind of key to this eerie place. And this is all after I was kidnapped as your prisoner, sleeping on a dirt-covered floor." He glanced at her, but there was a subtle amusement in his whiskey eyes. "No, I have all the energy in the world, Esmyra..." He dragged out her name.

She lifted a brow.

He continued. "Do you have a family name? You repeatedly speak mine, which is irritating, by the way. So I would love to return the favor."

"That is—"

"None of my business?" He cut her off. "How predictable."

She grimaced. "You're an incredibly annoying captive. I should've brought a muzzle with me. Perhaps I'll slice a piece off your shirt and stuff it down your throat."

"Or perhaps you could just take off your own and use that. I wouldn't fight that as hard." Esmyra nearly lost her footing as he said the words with a wink. He walked past her, not sparing her a second glance.

Heat rushed to her cheeks as her heart skipped with a weird fluttering sensation. She loathed the effects he and his words had on her body.

"*Alive*, Esmi. You need him alive," she whispered to herself as she stared at his back.

They walked in silence for several minutes when a fork appeared in their path—the runes halting, not lighting either way.

"Shit." She blew out a breath.

"Which way, Captain?" he asked mockingly.

She slowly pivoted to face him, popping her hip out. "I'm *thinking*." A roll of her eyes had him grinning.

"Why don't we just rest here for the night," he offered when she wouldn't take his bait. "If it even is night."

Her shoulders slumped. She was hoping to be out of this cave by now, on her way back to Lephyrin with some shred of evidence for King Rowe. Now, here she was, stuck miles beneath the surface with his annoying son, with no way to reach any of the others.

"We don't have time to rest," she said, voice stern. "Every moment down here is another moment Cyrus suffers."

"Esmyra, stopping to rest our bodies will probably be more beneficial than anything."

She needed him to stop talking reason and to just listen to her. The last thing she wanted to listen to was the logic of a man.

Her jaw locked when her eyes met his. "Feeling mortal, are we?" She gestured to the cuffs.

"Only thanks to you," he grumbled.

"Gods know how long we've been down here. Not to mention, I'm starving." She tried to peer down each path, but each plunged into nothing but darkness. Esmyra huffed. "Fine, we'll rest here for a few hours and decide which path to take when we're ready."

She waltzed up to one of the walls, placed her back against it, and slid down until she reached the ground. Leaning her back against the cool stone, she sighed as he watched her. "Well, are you going to waste all your time of demanded rest standing?"

Draevyn moved then and did the same as her, sliding down the wall across from where she sat. The two of them stared at each other silently beneath the dim, teal light.

Her jaw tightened the longer she watched him. She could tell he believed it was only a matter of time until he found a way out of this, until he was back within the comfort of his father's grand castle that loomed over their starving kingdom.

"Is there a particular reason you're glaring at me, Esmyra? Or am I just that difficult to look at?" He smirked.

Esmyra knew why all the women in Lephyrin gawked over the Rowe brothers. It was also why the females of other kingdoms came for Atlas's hand the night she kidnapped Draevyn. Not only were they princes, but they were undeniably handsome.

She took in his dark, reddish-brown hair and the sun-kissed skin of his forearms peeking out from his rolled-up sleeves, a golden bronze from his time at sea. The intensity of his fiery, whiskey-colored eyes made her feel as though she could be consumed by his flames, even with his magic locked away.

No, Draevyn Rowe wasn't *difficult* to look at. If anything, she found it difficult to look away.

"Yes, you're quite vile, if you would like honesty," she lied.

The smirk he wore morphed into a full, feral grin. "Apologies, Esmyra. Hopefully, you won't need to bear the sight of me much longer."

"Unfortunately, I don't believe I'm that lucky." She tried to suppress her smirk, but it formed without her permission as she moved to lay on the stone floor, and he did the same. "Any trickery from you while I sleep, and you'll find your bloodstream full of venom," she threatened, though she knew her tone wasn't nearly as terrifying as she intended.

A soft chuckle escaped him. "Wildfire, indeed."

His voice was barely audible, but Esmyra heard the words perfectly, and her brows furrowed. She wasn't sure what he meant, but perhaps between exhaustion and starvation, he was already losing his mind.

CHAPTER 33

*Draevyn*

D raevyn's eyes fluttered open as the cold, damp air bit into his skin.

The runes carved into the walls were no longer lit. The tiny, subtle glow from Esmyra's arms was their only light.

Draevyn blinked, his heart hammering in his chest. He couldn't see anything, not even his hands in front of him, yet everything inside him screamed in alarm. His fingers brushed over slick stone as he tried to push himself up, but his muscles screamed with exhaustion, his limbs heavy. He cursed the cuffs for bringing his mortality to the surface.

"Esmyra?" he called out, his voice hoarse. The sound echoed, stretching into the surrounding void.

"*Quiet*, you fool," Esmyra snapped in a whisper. "We're not alone."

Draevyn shot up, frantically turning in every direction as if he could see a gods-damn thing in the pitch black. "What is? Who? Why are the runes no longer lit?"

At first, only silence answered him—an eerie, hollow void that made the hairs on the back of his neck stand on end. But then, faintly, Draevyn caught it. A soft, rhythmic sound resembling breathing, but it wasn't their own.

Something grabbed his arm. Alarm raced through him, and he moved on instinct, rearing his arm back to strike. But whoever it was caught his other hand, and he felt the familiar taloned nails brush his skin.

*Esmyra.*

"How long have you been awake?" he whispered.

"Only moments longer than you," she answered, her voice just as soft.

The foreign breathing grew louder, more distinct, and with it came another sound—an unsettling, wet scraping, like claws on stone.

Draevyn's pulse quickened, the blood draining from his face as he realized he was entirely defenseless.

He stiffened, straining to listen more closely. "You hear that?"

The scraping grew louder, closer. Multiple sets of claws, circling. The sound came from all sides, from above, behind, and directly before them.

"We're surrounded," she whispered, her hold tightening on his arm.

Panic gripped him, his pulse thundering in his ears. They were unarmed, in the pitch darkness, and surrounded by something that set his entire body on edge.

"Esmyra," he started.

"Aye?"

Draevyn nearly scoffed at her being so casual in the situation. "I'm without flame. *We* are without weapons...aside from you. Whatever's here with us feels like much more than one person alone can handle."

"You know nothing of me, Draevyn Rowe. You'll remain bound. Nice try, though."

"Are you saying you have the gods-damn key?!"

The breathing turned into a soft, guttural growl, echoing from every direction. It reverberated off the walls, bouncing through the tunnel like a warning.

Draevyn scrambled to his feet, pulling Esmyra up with him. "We need to move."

The growling intensified, and the wet scrape of claws sent a chill down his spine. It was clear they didn't have a choice and would need to fight their way out of this.

"There are too many," Esmyra admitted.

"How many?" His muscles tensed, feeling the presence only feet from him now.

"Many," she whispered, followed by a gulp. "On the count of three, my eyes will shift, and we need to *run*. And fight our way through."

"I have no means to fight," he reminded her.

Silence answered him for several seconds before she spoke again. "Then it appears our time together is over, Phoenix."

"You're fucking kidding me."

Just as they took their first step, something shifted in the dark—a sudden rush of movement, quick and lethal. A low hiss sliced through the air.

Esmyra's eyes shifted, illuminating the tunnel, and *all gods*...he wished she hadn't.

Hundreds of humanoid creatures clung to the walls of the forked tunnels—their bodies pale, gaunt, and grotesque. They filled every inch of the cavern, some crouched low to the ground, others hanging upside down from the jagged rock formations above, their blind, milky eyes glowing faintly in the soft, teal light. Their nearly translucent skin stretched tightly over sharp bones and gnashing teeth.

Esmyra's breath hitched as she took a step back, her eyes wide with horror. "Kaelypso's tits."

The creatures were motionless. Their heads tilted slightly, as if listening to every word they had spoken since awakening, while their lips were pulled back in silent snarls. The stench of their decayed, rotting bodies stuffed itself in Draevyn's nostrils, nearly making him gag.

"Krechuums," Esmyra hissed. "They're...everywhere."

A sudden, low hiss echoed from above, and they slowly turned their heads up. There were somehow *more* of them, hanging like bats with dangling limbs as their claws clicked softly while they shifted.

There was no escape—not forward, not back, not even *up*.

"What do we do? We can't fight them all," he stated.

When Esmyra didn't answer, he glanced down to find her eyes darting in all directions, looking at the krechuums surrounding them, only waiting for a chance to tear them apart.

"You look as if you're weighing our options," he whispered before slowly bending down to her ear. "I'll save you the time. We have *none*."

Suddenly, the creatures shifted. It was subtle at first—just a twitch of a claw, a tightening of their bony limbs. And then the cavern echoed with a sickening series of clicks and hisses.

"Not ours," Esmyra whispered. "Mine."

His nostrils flared. "You can't be serious."

She scanned the creatures before them, her throat bobbing the more her eyes wandered. The veins in her neck strained as her jaw ticked.

"Fine," she growled. "Slowly—and I mean *very* slowly...reach into my pocket and feel for the key. On the count of three, I'm going to run and distract them. Fight off as many as I can so we can get the fuck out of this place."

Draevyn's eyes drifted down to her legs, where the pocket held the key to his freedom. "You're freeing me?"

"For the time being," she whispered. He nearly laughed at her. Over his rotting corpse would he ever be placed in the confines of these cuffs again.

"One." Her voice was soft, snapping him out of his trance.

A creature on the ceiling dropped silently to the floor, landing with a soft thud. It stood before them as if it were mortal, but its face was anything but. The krechuum's head twisted unnaturally, its mouth opening in a silent snarl as it sniffed the air.

More dropped from the walls and ceiling, moving in on them like a slow tide of death. Their guttural hisses filled the cavern, echoing and multiplying in the darkness.

"*Two*." The word left her in a near growl. It was a warning to him that he wasn't moving fast enough, while her eyes shone brighter, revealing endless rows of the beasts.

Draevyn's hand moved too quickly as he plunged it into the confines of her pocket and wrapped his fingers around the key. Esmyra never got the chance to say *three* as the creatures launched themselves to attack.

He ripped the key from her pocket as she reached for the pistol strapped to her side. A creature was directly before them in seconds, and she leveled the weapon at its face, but the gun never sounded as she pulled the trigger.

"Fuck! Wet gunpowder!" Esmyra screeched, followed by endless grunts and hisses.

Krechuums slammed into both of them, lunging out of the darkness. Several leathery, pale bodies hit him like a boulder, slamming him onto his back. And then he dropped the key.

Draevyn grunted in pain, his cuffed wrists unable to defend himself by flame or fist. Sharp claws raked across his chest, tearing through his shirt as warm blood spilled down his side.

Her eyes continued to be the only source of light, and he caught quick glimpses of her between swinging his bound hands. She fought fiercely—all claws and teeth. Her talons shredded any krechuum that lunged or stood too close, earning ear-shattering shrieks of agony, but it wasn't enough.

Why wasn't she summoning water?

He rolled, kicking with all his strength, managing to knock the creature on top of him off balance. It screeched, a bone-chilling sound that echoed through the cave. More of them raced toward him—eyes blind, yet sensing his every movement, mouths filled with rows of jagged teeth clicking hungrily.

"Fucking Irah!" he roared as he continued to kick and smash the monsters' skulls with the metal cuffs when they reached him.

A small reprieve in their attacks came, and he dropped back down to his knees, his fingers brushing over dirt and stone as he frantically searched for the key.

"I didn't free you for *nothing*!" Esmyra screamed through her attacks, a grunt sounding through every other word. "A little flame would be helpful!"

"Working on it!" he yelled back. "I dropped the—"

"You *WHAT*?!" she cut him off.

The creatures swarmed her then, leaping onto her from all sides until they brought her to her knees. She fought relentlessly, but they pinned her to the stone beneath them. The sounds of her struggles and screams sliced through Draevyn's mind. His fear for her held him by the throat.

Draevyn's hand shot out again, brushing over something small, the cool touch of metal biting into his fingertips. *The key.*

His heart leapt as he fumbled to fit it into the lock on his cuffs as he continued to kick and slam the krechuums into the wall behind him.

One of them pounced faster than he could sense, claws slashing for his throat. Draevyn dropped to the floor and rolled, the key slipping from his fingers as he barely dodged the strike.

"*Draevyn!*" Esmyra screamed for him. Her voice cracked, his name ending in a gasp.

Panic surged through him. He kicked the creature off again, this time with more force, sending it crashing into the stone wall so hard that its skull splattered across the space.

But more were already upon him, jaws snapping near his face. He struggled, pushing with his bound arms to create space, but they were too strong.

Draevyn spotted the key again, glittering faintly in the soft light just a few feet away. The krechuums outnumbered them a hundred to one, and Esmyra's continued screeches and grunts of pain rang through the air.

They couldn't die here. Not like this.

With a desperate roar, Draevyn threw himself at the key, slamming his body onto the stone floor, reaching with every ounce of strength.

As his fingers wrapped around it, one of the creatures bit into his shoulder, fangs sinking deep into flesh. Pain exploded through his body, white-hot and searing. Draevyn bellowed in agony but held on, forcing himself to stay focused. He shoved the key into one of the locks, twisting it with a snap.

With one hand free, he swung out relentlessly through the onslaught of attacks, yet he still couldn't summon his flame with one cuff still bound to his wrist. Draevyn swung around with newfound fury. His free arm lashed out, and his fist connected with a creature's face, crushing bone beneath the force of his punch.

A krechuum leapt onto his back, the creature screeching, clicking, and hissing into his ear as it tried to bite him once more. Draevyn stumbled and backed up, slamming the beast into the wall behind them.

He knew this was his only chance.

As he repeatedly smashed the monster's body into the hard stone, he shoved the key into the remaining cuff and twisted the lock.

And then the velsinyte cuffs fell away.

Power surged through him, igniting his entire being. It was as if a dam had broken, the floodgates torn wide, and his magic came roaring back to life with a ferocity that nearly sent him to his knees.

Heat rushed through his veins, spreading from his core to his fingertips as his senses sharpened. Draevyn's body hummed—the magic crackled beneath his skin, barely contained and ready to erupt. A shiver ran down his spine, his heart galloping as he took a deep breath.

His flames were back, fierce and wild—resembling the woman who stood just beyond his reach. The woman who was on her knees before the monsters, fighting for her life.

Draevyn lifted his hand, igniting a ball of fire that crackled in his palm.

The creatures closest to him hissed and took a hesitant step back.

"My turn," he said, his voice cruel and cold.

As the first of the creatures lunged, Draevyn thrust his palm forward, sending a wave of flame roaring down the tunnel. The fire lit up the darkness, illuminating the creatures as they writhed in the blaze.

But still, there were too many—far more than they could burn away, and more kept coming down the two forked tunnels they faced.

He ran for Esmyra, lighting every creature atop her in flames. They all began to shriek and scream as they scrambled, the skin of their backs melting away.

Draevyn pulled her to her feet, her clothes and flesh shredded from the krechuums attacks. "Are you—"

"Shh," she silenced him, her eyes narrowing on the new wave of monsters now charging at them.

Esmyra stepped forward, her hands swirling in intricate movements, summoning torrents of water from the cave's moisture. Ribbons of it revealed themselves from the crevices of the cave, coiling around her body like a serpent. Draevyn's eyes widened as he watched her magic work.

Her boots dug into the ground, as if bracing herself for the power she was conjuring. With a triumphant battle cry, her water shot out toward the creatures, striking them with the force of a crashing wave before knocking them back into his inferno.

The smell of burning, rotting flesh filled the air, and Draevyn's stomach roiled.

But the creatures kept coming.

"These things are fucking relentless!" Esmyra shouted, her voice edged with rage.

Her arms moved faster, summoning more water from their surroundings as she sent it snaking down the closest creatures' throats, drowning them on land. But for every monster they burned or drowned, two more took its place, crawling over the corpses of the fallen.

A sphere of water formed around them, a shimmering and protective barrier. Draevyn craned his neck as he watched the dome form, and he stepped up to Esmyra, his chest brushing against her back. The creatures pounded against her shield, hissing and snarling, but couldn't break through, and Draevyn matched hers with his own, burning the creatures alive.

"Pick a tunnel and we have to run," Draevyn shouted over the roar of the flames, his fire surging brighter and hotter in his veins. Sweat beaded down both of their foreheads from the heat's intensity.

Draevyn focused his energy into a massive column of fire, sending it spiraling out through the water shield. The heat intensified, vaporizing the creatures closest to them. Steam burned his lungs and felt as if it could melt his flesh down to the bone from his fire and her water colliding and forging as one.

"Esmyra!" he roared, grabbing her shoulder. "We can't hold them off forever. Pick. A. *Tunnel*!"

She sucked in a sharp breath at his touch, and then her stare shot up at him. "Left."

"Left it is, then." Draevyn didn't waste a moment as he summoned every lick of flame he had and poured it into the left tunnel, incinerating the creatures in its path. "Move! Now!"

They took off in a desperate run. His flames lit and cleared the path while Esmyra held a shield of water at their backs.

Echoes of distant screeches bounced off the jagged walls, growing louder with each passing second. Draevyn and Esmyra moved in sync as they entered the mouth of the narrow tunnel swarming with hunched, pale-skinned creatures.

"They just keep coming!" Esmyra shouted over the echoing wails.

"Then we keep burning through," Draevyn growled, his palms igniting in a bright, scorching flame. Draevyn hurled a fireball into the mass of writhing bodies ahead of them.

Suddenly, the tunnel widened significantly, no longer feeling like they were in a tunnel at all, but back in some form of a cavern. His flames lit up in a flash of orange and red, the heat searing, as several creatures screamed and thrashed, their skin blistering before turning to ash.

Esmyra thrust her hand forward, and a spear of water shot through the air, slamming into a creature's chest with the force of a rapid river, pinning it against the cave wall before it crumpled, lifeless.

Draevyn's inferno reflected on the water she conjured as it wrapped around them, looking as if it set her ablaze as she fought at his side.

*Wildfire.* Every time he caught a glimpse of her, the word reverberated in his mind, tearing through his soul.

"We're not going to make it at this rate," Esmyra panted as they halted, her voice tight with strain as sweat dripped down her brow.

"I don't intend to die here, Esmyra." Draevyn's hands erupted into a wild inferno, his heart galloping in his chest, feeling the well of his magic draining.

Draevyn stepped around her, standing between her and the krechuums racing for them in that tunnel, and with a mighty bellow, he dropped to his knees and slammed his fists into the ground. A wave of fire surged outward, engulfing the creatures in its path, but more filled the space almost immediately, like water through a broken dam.

Esmyra drew a deep breath. "I'll clear the way." She stepped around him as he shoved to his feet, his throat tightening as he watched her stride toward them. "If you incinerate me, I will be pissed," she called over her shoulder.

Draevyn's brows furrowed, but despite his better judgment, he laughed. *Laughed* while they were about to be swarmed and meet their end together.

Without waiting for an answer, she thrust both hands forward. A torrent of water gathered and surged before her palms, erupting through the tunnel ahead of them, knocking creatures off their feet.

He didn't hesitate. Draevyn followed right behind the water's wake, his hands blazing. "Keep pushing them!"

Together, they moved like a storm of flame and sea. Draevyn incinerated everything in sight, leaving the tunnel glowing with molten heat, while Esmyra's water cooled the stone—steam rose in thick clouds around them as the two forces collided.

The Phoenix and the siren moved as one, their powers creating a deadly dance.

As their magic merged together into an unstoppable force, the hissing and snarling finally ceased. The last of the creatures lay broken all around them as nothing but piles of charred bone and wet ash.

Esmyra's chest heaved as she stepped up to his side. "Is it over?"

He noted they stood just beyond the narrow tunnel's reach. His flames dimmed to a low, cautious glow. "For now."

"Aye," she responded, panting.

Draevyn glanced down at her as the runes atop her flesh lit brightly once more. He shielded his eyes with a hand, watching between the cracks of his fingers in awe—until Esmyra's eyes rolled into the back of her head.

The next thing he knew, she collapsed into him, and he caught her in his arms.

"Esmyra!" He fell to his knees, carefully rotating her body to find her face was still and lifeless, as hard as the stone surrounding them.

A moment later, the markings on her arms returned to their usual hue of a burnt red, and the entire cavern fell once more into darkness.

Hidden beneath a hooded cloak, Atlas strode through the bustling streets of Lephyrin, scanning the array of ships in the harbor. The sun was low, casting a golden sheen on the water, but his heart was heavy with worry.

His brother had been missing since the night he was forced to find a future queen for their kingdom. He settled on one of the elven king's daughters, Elowynne. She was beautiful, and while Atlas was thankful, he found himself hoping a connection would grow between them.

When each king, lord, and family left to retreat back to their own kingdoms after the horrific events of that night, he'd sent word to every port, but no one seemed to know where his brother had vanished.

The scent of the saltwater was thick in the air as Atlas approached Draevyn's new ship, *Valor*, anchored at the edge of the docks. Its sails were furled, and the crew looked sullen and weary. These men were far different from the company he kept with Lephyrin's lords.

"And to what do we owe the pleasure, Your Majesty?" a voice called from the deck.

Atlas looked up at the man who called to him, watching his

brown hair flutter around beneath his hat. He recognized him as Draevyn's first mate.

"Where's my brother, Samwell?" Atlas's voice was firm, but desperation tinged his words.

Samwell glanced at the other crew members, who shifted uneasily. The wind stirred, and for a moment, all the sounds of the busy port faded. "It may be best if you come aboard, Prince."

Atlas nervously sucked on his tooth before letting out a sigh, taking his first step up the gangplank.

As he approached, Samwell's voice was low. "Captain Rowe's been missing for over a week. Since that night. We haven't seen or heard anything of him." He paused, shrugging. "Assumed the king had him on other business, but he's never gone this long without talking to us. We've essentially been waiting around."

Disbelief tightened Atlas's chest. "This is a gods-damn nightmare."

His thoughts were a jumbled mess, spiraling out of control. His brother was a skilled sailor, someone who'd faced every peril the sea could offer and always came out alive. For him to disappear without a trace...something more was at play.

"I assume you've asked your father?"

Atlas's jaw locked beneath the shadow of his hood. "The king's been trying to clean up the mess of that night with Rymelle's other rulers. I believed the same, thinking he had Drae running about. Perhaps to find some leads on who attacked that night." He reached up and scratched the back of his neck. "Yet you stand before me here and now."

"Indeed." Samwell's jaw tightened.

"And there's no other crew he would sail with?" Atlas asked.

A noise erupted from Samwell that was half laugh and half scoff. "The bastard better not have."

A few of the crew members began to laugh along with him, and Atlas pulled his hood back, revealing himself fully to them, but his face showed anything but amusement. The reflection of the sun beaming off the harbor's waves nearly blinded him as they reached his eyes. "He's your prince, just as I am, and you will treat him and his name with respect."

Atlas knew all his brother endured being the second son. He had watched the torments and rude remarks all their lives. He couldn't believe Draevyn even dealt with it from members of his *crew*. And to think the realm believed him to be a monster...Draevyn was anything but, allowing people who disrespected him to breathe the same air he did.

Shadows danced in Atlas's grey-hued eyes as they narrowed on his brother's first mate.

Samwell lifted his hands in a defensive gesture while he took a hesitant step back. "Apologies, Prince. I know you don't know us well, but Draevyn is more than just a captain to us. He's a friend and someone we care for." A moment of silence passed between them. "A brother. It was only a joke."

*A brother.*

Atlas unclenched his fists as they hung at his sides.

They cared for Draevyn? Maybe these men were more brothers to his own flesh and blood than he was. Perhaps Draevyn spent so much time at sea, not because of the cruelty of their father, but because it was where he felt most at home himself.

He sucked in a long breath through his nostrils. "Well, it's no wonder Draevyn prefers your company over mine."

Samwell took a step up to him and clapped Atlas on the shoulder. The gesture was foreign to him from someone who wasn't Draevyn.

"I would hope you know that Captain Rowe's reasoning for keeping his distance has nothing to do with you, Prince." Samwell looked at him with something that resembled pity, and he loathed it.

Atlas's head jerked back, frowning.

"It appears secrets of the crown are no longer such." He pulled his hood back on and tightened its strings. "If you haven't heard anything of him, then it seems my visit here is over."

Atlas turned on his heel to move back towards the gangplank.

"Speak to your king, Prince." Samwell's voice floated to him on the breeze. "If I had to bet coin on where to begin, I would start there."

Atlas clenched his fists, aware of how difficult the king could be when it came to his brother.

The thought of facing his father made his chest tighten, knowing he would see through him—through his feigned bravado. He'd strip him bare with a single glance.

But he wasn't a child anymore and could no longer hide behind jokes and charm if he was to be a worthy king one day.

He could do this.

He had to. For Drae.

Atlas half-turned to the sailor and gave him a subtle dip of his chin before stalking down the plank and making his way back through the busy streets.

Atlas paused briefly at the door to his chambers, his heart heavy with the weight of everything looming over him. He sighed before pushing it open.

Inside, the setting sun filtered in through the balcony's open door, the sheer curtains flowing on the light breeze. And there, standing by the arch, was Lady Elowynne—his newly chosen bride.

She turned when the door creaked, her golden-green eyes soft but searching as they landed on him. Her onyx hair cascaded over the rich, russet brown skin of her shoulders. The elven female was the epitome of alluring beauty. They had spoken only a handful of times since the masquerade, and she was the one he entertained the most that evening.

When his father demanded he choose, he told him he wouldn't without Draevyn's blessing. Only his brother never came back, leaving the arrangement forced upon him by duty rather than love.

"Elowynne," Atlas greeted, his voice low, trying to hide the tension that twisted in his chest. Typically, she was off with the other ladies, taking walks through the gardens or having tea. Seeing her here in his personal chambers unaccompanied caught him off guard.

She inclined her head slightly, offering a small smile, but her gaze never left his. "Your Highness," she replied, her voice calm. She tilted her head. "You look troubled."

And there it was.

Atlas stepped into the room, the door closing behind him. He had hoped to be alone so he could come up with a plan on how to speak with his father, and he certainly didn't plan on having to entertain his soon-to-be bride. But Elowynne was perceptive, and there was no sense in hiding what weighed on his mind.

"I plan to speak to the king once I gather my thoughts the way they're needed," Atlas admitted, moving toward the balcony. The warmth of the setting sun kissed his skin, but it did little to chase away the cold within him. "About my brother."

Elowynne hesitantly stepped closer. "Have you still not heard from him?"

Atlas's jaw tightened. "Draevyn's been missing for a week now." He looked at her and tried to soften his expression, but his frustration made it impossible. "No word. No sign of him. *Nothing*. And I'm supposed to stand there, in front of my father and kingdom, and pretend as if his disappearance means nothing to me."

Elowynne's eyes flickered with understanding, her hands clasped before her. "Your brother's disappearance isn't something to take lightly," she said softly. "But it's not your burden to carry alone. Lephyrin will mourn for their lost prince."

"It *is* my burden, and the kingdom is likely unaware," Atlas snapped, his voice harsher than intended. He closed his eyes and sighed, running a hand through his hair.

Their relationship was still so new, so fragile. He didn't want to scare her away, but he couldn't let her in yet either. "I'm sorry. You don't know the weight of the Lephyrin crown."

Her golden stare raked over him.

"I may not know your brother," she said gently, "and while I don't know the weight of your crown...*yet*, I do know the weight of responsibility. I understand what it feels like to face uncertainty, to bear expectations you never asked for." She took another step closer, her hand touching his arm. "Perhaps I'm here so you don't have to face it alone."

Atlas glanced down at her hand, her touch unexpectedly comforting. He didn't know this female—his bride in name more than in heart—but at this moment, she felt like the only person willing to listen to him.

His eyes lifted to hers, and he looked at her—*really* looked at her, perhaps even for the first time. There was something he couldn't place lingering in her golden eyes, a quiet confidence he hadn't noticed before, or maybe even wisdom.

The gods knew he could use some of that.

If she was to be his queen, he would need to trust her. She was about to marry into the Lephyrin crown, and it was clear she had no idea what she was getting herself into. He saw no reason to shield her from the ugliness that came with the Rowe name.

"I'm Lephyrin's prince and heir," he muttered, "and here I am, unsure of how to even speak to my own gods-damn father."

"Being a prince doesn't mean being faultless." Elowynne gracefully lifted her hands and adjusted the prince's cloak, smoothing out the wrinkles that lined his shoulders. Atlas barely realized he leaned into the warmth of her touch. "It means knowing when to ask for help and when to lean on those around you."

Atlas's shoulders relaxed as her words sank in. She was right. He had been so consumed by the idea of what was expected of him that he hadn't allowed himself to lean on anyone. And until this moment, he felt as if he didn't have anyone at all now that Draevyn was gone.

His father's judgment, the kingdom's expectations, the uncertainty of his brother's fate—it had all felt too heavy to bear alone. He didn't feel like himself, and a coldness had crept into his soul at the weight of it all.

"I've been a fool," he said quietly.

"No. You've been human." Elowynne gave him a subtle grin. "From what I've heard, your kind often make such mistakes."

He let out a soft chuckle at her effortless banter. In any other circumstance, he would've pressed his lips to hers right then, loving a woman with a sharp tongue. "It's not that impressive considering I'm one of only two beings from this kingdom who isn't entirely mortal."

A brief silence stretched between them, the crackle of the fire filling the air. Atlas felt something shift within him, a small spark of relief, no longer feeling quite so alone.

He met his bride's gaze once more. "Thank you."

She nodded. "We'll face whatever comes together, Your Majesty. You don't have to carry this burden alone."

For the first time since his brother's disappearance, he felt a glimmer of hope—a fragile, uncertain thing—but hope, nonetheless. "Please don't call me that. You're to be my wife and queen. Atlas will do."

Lephyrin hadn't had a queen since his mother passed away. That was nearly two decades ago now. Knowing the title would pass on to whoever became his wife had his chest tightening, but the more he spoke with Elowynne, the more deserving she seemed.

Something sparked in her gold and green eyes. "Alright...Atlas. And you, my prince, can call me Wynne."

*Wynne.* He smiled at her nickname.

Atlas reached out his hand and cupped the back of her head, bringing her closer to him, and then pressed his lips gently to her forehead.

"You should know, from what I've heard, the king doesn't expect the Phoenix to return," she said simply.

Every sense of comfort that had just settled into him shattered as he shoved out of her hold, almost sending her stumbling back. "What?!" he barked. Shadows crept in from the corners of the room as his voice rose, all sense of the comfort he just felt now gone.

Her eyes darted in all directions, sensing their presence. She swallowed. "It's just gossip. Servant talk."

A dark haze clouded Atlas's vision. He spun abruptly on his heel. He restrained his fury and stormed out of his chambers, passing the guards stationed at his door as he began searching for his father.

"What in all gods do you mean Drae isn't coming back?!" Atlas shouted at his father as he stood beside the fireplace of his bedchamber. His fists shook at his sides, shadows coiling up his forearms like serpents.

The king cleared his throat, unbothered. "What is it that you aren't understanding, Atlas?"

"He hasn't been seen since the night of the party, when you *forced* me to find a bride and all hell broke loose from you bringing your little prisoner out on display. Nobody has seen him, and now rumors have spread that you're stating you don't believe he'll return. Why is that?"

"You need to learn your place, *boy*," the king spat.

Atlas moved towards him, each step deliberately slow. "My *place* is right where your useless ass sits in the throne room. At least it will be once you croak. Which, if you ask me, can't come soon enough."

The guards stationed throughout went on alert at his threat, hands placed on the pommels of their swords.

King Rowe took a step up to Atlas. "How about I lock you up alongside Blackwood, eh? Teach you something for once in your spoiled, *privileged* life."

Atlas's jaw clenched at the threat. He knew his father had done just that or something far worse to Draevyn when they were just children. While he was the heir, he wasn't entirely willing to call him on his bluff.

He swallowed his original retort. "Where's my brother? I know you know *something*."

King Rowe's jaw locked, his eyes drifting around the room before they shot back to Atlas with a fury-filled intensity. "Leave us," he ordered his guards.

No one moved as they exchanged weary looks.

"Now! Everyone." He lifted his stubby finger and pointed it in Atlas's face, making his heart thud in his chest. "Except you."

The guards rushed from the room, shutting the doors behind them.

"You're afraid of Drae. You always have been," Atlas stated the moment the click of the doors sounded.

He no longer gave a damn if his father lashed out at him. Beat him senseless, cursed his name, revoked his title as heir—Atlas no longer cared. What he cared about was his brother.

His father's face flushed with anger. "You know nothing."

A cackle erupted from deep within Atlas's chest. "You think your sons don't speak to one another because you separated them by duty? Draevyn is the *only* person who understands me."

"Understands you?" The king chuckled as he shook his head.

Shadows swirled between Atlas's fingers. "Understands what it's like to have a father willing to sacrifice his heirs and kingdom for the sake of power."

"Fucking Irah, you're just as dramatic as he is." The king rolled his eyes.

"You stand before me here and now as if you haven't feared him since the day his power revealed itself."

King Rowe stormed up to his son, gripped him by the collar of his shirt, and shook him violently. Atlas's hands balled into fists, but a grin crept up his face at his father's abuse, knowing he finally struck the nerve he intended to.

Atlas's shadows lingered but remained hovering just beyond the king's flesh as a subtle threat.

"Out at sea," the king growled.

"What?" Atlas shoved out of his hold.

"Draevyn. He's out at sea. Searching for the lost kingdom."

Atlas huffed out a laugh. "Why wouldn't you just say that?" He thought about it for a moment and realized none of it made any sense. "Why wouldn't he say goodbye?" He took a step back, anger crawling back into his tone. "And why is his crew clueless down at the docks? Who is he even with?!"

"How dare you go down to the docks unaccompanied! The

people in those streets are violent and nothing but *filth*." The king spat the words with disgust.

Atlas's face twisted in revulsion. "Those are *your* people you're speaking of."

The king scoffed. "As if I give a damn. You're just as reckless and defiant as your brother."

He was gods-damn right about that, and Atlas couldn't have been more proud.

"And do you know who he sails with? *His* ship is still in our own fucking port!" He imagined striking the king then, and it took everything inside of himself to unclench his fists and appear as non-threatening as possible.

"I do not." A malicious grin crept up his father's face, and he knew nothing good would come of it. "But perhaps he ran off with a beautiful woman. Or *perhaps* he had no choice in the matter at all." He shrugged. "Only one person in this castle knows who he sails with for sure, and it's not I, boy."

Atlas's mind spun at the riddles thrown at him as he turned toward the door.

"Give up on him, Atlas," his father called, and his steps faltered.

He straightened his shoulders as shadows hovered around him like a dark mist. "I won't give up on him. I'm not you."

Esmyra stirred as darkness draped over her mind. The first thing she became aware of was the soft crackling of embers, their warmth crawling across her skin. Then came the dull ache that seemed to weigh her whole body down, muscles sore and bruised from the attack she and Draevyn had barely escaped, but she knew her body had likely healed most of her wounds.

Eyes fluttering open, her chest rose and fell in shallow breaths as she tried to make sense of where she was. Esmyra turned her head, and her gaze landed on him. Leaning against a boulder, Draevyn's gaze remained fixed on the fire he conjured. The flames danced and flickered, their warmth and light fueled solely by his magic with nothing beneath it but damp stone. The firelight cast sharp shadows on his face, illuminating the tick in his jaw and the intensity of his whiskey-hued eyes.

He hadn't noticed her wake yet, or maybe he simply didn't care. Either way, the tense silence between them remained unbroken.

The memory of the krechuums they fought came flooding back—nightmarish beasts from the darkest depths of the earth, all claws and teeth.

Everything slammed into her at once. She remembered the ferocity with which they'd fought together, an alliance forged by necessity between two enemies. Now he was freed, his flames roaring between them, yet he didn't move to attack her. She was shocked he didn't kill her to find an escape route for himself. Or perhaps he had and discovered that entering the cave was a death sentence for them both.

"You're awake." His voice echoed through the space between them.

She slowly sat up, her body protesting, but she refused to let herself look any weaker than the collapse already had. That had never happened to her before...not in nearly a thousand years. But she'd never had to work so hard to conjure her power from nothing—pulling every drop of water through each crack and crevice in that gods-forsaken tunnel until it nearly ran dry.

"How long was I out?" she asked warily, loathing that she was at his disposal.

"A few hours, perhaps," he said, watching her with an intensity she couldn't place. "Though it's difficult to tell time when you're miles beneath the realm's soil."

"Aye," she answered softly, her eyes wandering.

Endless questions swarmed her, and she thought her mind would explode. Why did she collapse? Why had she run out of power? And where in all gods were they?

Esmyra's magic ached at the edge of her fingertips, easing some of her panic. Though the sudden loss of it before she'd gone unconscious made her skin crawl. Twice now, in a matter of weeks, she'd come across things that weakened her power and made it cower within her. Centuries she'd lived unscathed, feeling every bit invincible, yet now she felt closer to mortal than ever before.

She knew one thing with certainty in her very bones—she couldn't let Draevyn know these thoughts plagued her.

Quickly glancing down at her sides, she realized she didn't have the velsinyte cuffs on hand, yet they didn't encircle her wrists.

Either they lost the one thing powerful enough to contain their magic, or he was holding them to place on her at the most opportune moment. Was he trying to see if she would attack? Or perhaps he thought she lost her power when she collapsed. The markings on her arms were teal once more, yet she remembered them burning their fiery red right before she fell.

Countless unknowns kept pouring into her mind, and she doubted any answers would present themselves. So, she opted to just blatantly ask. "Where are the cuffs?"

Draevyn barked out a laugh, his head flying back in amusement. "You can't be serious."

Esmyra's lip curled. "Well, they're not on your wrists."

His head cocked to the side, a crease forming in his brow. "What do you remember?"

"Everything," she hissed. "Just wasn't sure if one of us was smart enough to grab the cuffs once I freed you."

Another laugh erupted from him, and annoyance surged within her. "You," he pointed to her, "didn't free me. I freed myself after grabbing the key from your pocket."

"Because I allowed you to do so."

"Because you would've been krechuum food if you hadn't."

Esmyra's eyes narrowed on him. "Aye, but as would you."

She hated that she didn't know if he had them in his possession and was toying with her.

Draevyn sighed, shaking his head. "I don't have the cuffs. I dropped them. And I won't lie...I didn't even think of grabbing them once I was freed. I was too concerned with getting you out."

This time, it was Esmyra's turn to lift a brow. Why would he care about getting *her* out?

He cleared his throat. "I was too concerned with escaping," he corrected himself. "How are you feeling?"

"Fine," she rushed out, averting her gaze from his. "Never been better."

A deep chuckle rumbled from him. "You don't have to lie. You reached your well. Has that never happened to you before?"

Esmyra tilted her head in confusion. "Well?"

"The end of your magic."

"My magic knows no end," she stated with no room for argument. It was the truth...at least, until today.

A smirk played on Draevyn's lips in the firelight. "Everyone's magic has an end. I'm surprised you reached yours so soon."

She blinked, her mind racing with what this could all mean. When she spoke next, her voice was soft. "I cannot conjure water—only manipulate what's already there."

"Interesting," he said.

"Glad you think so." A roll of her eyes earned her another grin. She extended her arm and gestured to him, her talons slipping out with the movement. "It appears your magic doesn't work the same as mine."

"All that's needed for fire is air. Luckily, we haven't run out of that down here." He paused. "Yet."

"And how am I to trust that you won't roast me alive the moment I turn my back?"

Draevyn shrugged. "If I planned to, it would've been much simpler to achieve when you were unconscious." Her jaw locked at his words. "And it appears whatever magic lurks down here reacts to your touch. Each new cavern you unlock seems to reveal a more dangerous threat than the last. You might be my only escape from this nightmare."

After a few minutes of uncomfortable silence, Esmyra huffed out a breath. "So, I would assume you've already explored down here while I lay unconscious. Is this another cavern?"

His back straightened. "For the record, I caught you. You didn't collapse to the ground. I placed you where you sit now." Her eyes scanned their surroundings as he spoke, and Draevyn mimicked her, glancing around the space. "Yes, I think it's a cavern. Only this is significantly different from any other place we've come across so far."

Esmyra's brow furrowed. She lay on cold, uneven ground, propped against what looked like the remains of an ancient stone pillar. The fire cast long shadows across the cavern, but in its glow, she could see they were no longer in any ordinary cave.

"What?" she whispered to herself. Pushing herself to her feet, her neck craned upward, taking in the sight of everything the firelight provided as Draevyn watched her.

They stood in a vast, temple-like space, hidden deep within the earth. The ceiling soared high above, lost in shadow, while the walls were layered with crystallized minerals. They shimmered in the subtle light, mimicking her scales—the opalescent blues and greens blended with the soft whites of calcified shells that had become one with the stone.

Esmyra nearly smiled, feeling an odd warmth in her chest at the sight of it. Her eyes shifted, their glow lighting up the space before them while Draevyn held a ball of flame over his palm.

Scattered about their surroundings, remnants of architecture jutted from the rock, half-buried and ancient pillars encrusted with barnacles, coral-like carvings wound their way up them like underwater vines.

"We found it," Esmyra whispered, her lips parting.

She turned to Draevyn.

"It appears that we did," he answered.

The warmth in her chest started as a subtle caress of comfort and nearly burst into a roaring inferno at his confirmation, feeling a sense of home—similar to how she felt in the sea, yet somehow so much more.

*"You found me in the kingdom of the sea and lied about it my entire life. Why would you even lie?! You stole me. Didn't you?"* The last words she screamed in her father's face aboard their ship roared in her ears.

There was a reason this underwater, forgotten trove had a familiar feeling.

The entire cavern hummed with a quiet magic, as if it were holding its breath, waiting for someone to awaken the kingdom that had been lost to the ocean's depths—now entombed within the realm's heart.

"This place," she muttered, her voice rough, "has been forgotten by most, if not all. I've never seen anything so beautiful."

She turned to him and found his expression unreadable.

"Perhaps it's not so much forgotten as it is lost." Their eyes roamed while he spoke. "Because that's what it is, Esmyra. *Lost.* Just as we are. And we will likely die down here just as they had nine centuries ago."

Her heart thudded painfully at his words, not due to *them* being lost—but the kingdom. What had once been grand was now reduced to echoes in the darkest of depths. She wondered how much history had been buried here—how many stories, lives, and families lost in the collapse.

*Families.* Had hers perished? They must have. And the guilt of it weighed on her.

And now, like the remnants of the once great kingdom around them, she and her enemy were trapped together. Though the more she looked around, the more she didn't feel trapped at all.

Esmyra's gaze fell upon a dry fountain-like basin in the center of the cavern and made her way to it. She halted at its edge, frowning as her fingers grazed a series of those same strange symbols carved into its stone.

"Easy with the *touching* things," Draevyn called as he followed her.

She didn't respond immediately. The deeper they traveled, the more the foreign symbols seemed...familiar. And not because her flesh bore them, but more as a whisper tugging at the edge of her memory.

One specific symbol caught her eye over all others—it lay carved in the center of the fountain's bowl. Several half circles with lines, dots, and symbols resembling arrows protruding from all sides. She knew that mark—it matched the largest of her brands that ran along her spine, appearing as a compass.

*Bring us home*, the voice whispered in her mind.

Without thinking, she pressed her palm into the center of the carvings, answering its call once more—and then her body was no longer hers.

The last thing to reach Esmyra's ears was her name bellowed from the man behind her. It felt as if he were begging—a plea screamed from her enemy's lips. However, she couldn't resist the urge, her body having a mind of its own.

Her breath caught in her lungs, vision bursting into a blinding white light. The ringing in her ears was deafening as a rush of energy pulsed through her hand, pulling her into a vision with a dizzying force. The surrounding air shifted, no longer the stuffy dampness of the cave but the fresh air rolling off the waves of the sea.

Esmyra stood within the once great kingdom of Maerinys—not the empty, ruined place she uncovered, but a city on the brink of collapse.

As her vision cleared, everything around her seemed to shimmer and distort, creating a surreal, mirage-like effect, as if she were standing in a living memory.

A memory of the day Maerinys fell.

The sky was as dark as midnight, heavy with clouds that mirrored the restless sea crashing against the kingdom's walls. The wind screamed through the narrow alleyways, carrying with it the cries of the people. She could feel their terror, a sharp emotion that pierced her like cold steel. Her chest rose and fell rapidly in panicked breaths.

A palace towered above the city, perched on a cliff overlooking that and the bay. It was grand, built of pale stone that was glowing even under the darkened sky. Cracks splintered across the foundation of the buildings surrounding her as creatures she had never seen ran for their lives.

With a boom, the barrier walls of Maerinys collapsed, the waves cascading in torrents over their edges, no longer contained. The ground beneath her feet shifted as water filled her boots, and she realized the entire city was tilting, the foundations of the earth giving way to the relentless force of the ocean.

Esmyra couldn't catch her breath as she turned in circles, frantically looking in all directions as the shadowy, distorted figures ran by her from all sides.

The wind screamed in her ears, and she watched helplessly as buildings collapsed, streets split apart, and the people—mortals, mer, and creatures of all kinds—were swallowed by the sea.

Esmyra turned to face the palace once more and was forced to shield her eyes as a light, bright and blinding, erupted from one of the castle spires.

She was there, in the midst of the chaos, the cold water climbing her legs, waist, and chest.

Just when Esmyra thought she would be lost forever with the kingdom, her vision burst again, and she was abruptly pulled back into her body, greeted by the sight of a deadly spear aimed mere inches from her face.

CHAPTER 36

## *Draevyn*

Draevyn watched in horror as Esmyra placed her hand within the fountain. He ran, reaching for her. The last thing he needed was for her to touch more of those symbols, but he was too late.

When the skin of her palm brushed the stone, he was thrust back by a violent force, his body thrown into a crumbling pillar. The flame he'd kept lit was extinguished.

Draevyn's back ached as he pushed himself to his feet. His eyes widened. Esmyra's midnight hair levitated around her as if she were beneath the surface of the sea, gently swaying in all directions.

He tried running to her again, his chest heaving as he realized she was unreachable. Her eyes were flared wide, radiating their familiar light, yet they were so pale they were almost silver, illuminating the space around them.

The cavern trembled.

"Esmyra!" Draevyn called, his voice echoing through the shuddering temple.

When no response came, he took a step closer, reaching out to her hesitantly. The rune pulsed beneath her fingers, a dim, rhythmic glow that synced with her breath. Her lips moved, whispering words he couldn't hear. A chill crawled along his spine.

Water pooled atop her hand as it remained in the bowl, as if she was conjuring it when she had just told him moments ago she didn't have the ability.

The ground beneath him continued to rumble. Loose stones tumbled down from the ceiling, clattering across the floor. He glanced back at Esmyra and found her expression remained serene, almost peaceful—completely unaware of the growing danger around her.

"Fuck," he muttered under his breath.

A groan resonated from deep within the space, and his heart leapt in his throat. He turned, and before him, at the far end of the temple-like cavern, an archway revealed itself.

The arch shimmered, ancient carvings and symbols taking form, pulling themselves from the rock. The rumbling grew louder, and a palpable sense of raw power emanated from the archway while Esmyra remained in her trance. The solid wall trembled, dust and grit falling as cracks splintered across their surface.

*What the fuck is happening?*

This wasn't like the door or arch she had opened before. He knew in his very bones this was different, and something ancient lay on the opposite side of that wall.

Did she have her powers back? Was the fountain she touched absorbing her power and draining her body dry? Would they be able to fight whatever was about to present itself to them? He didn't know, and his pulse thrashed in his ears as his mind raced.

With a grinding groan, the splintering stone *burst*, sending rock and debris flying in all directions. On instinct, Draevyn leapt in front of her and threw up a wall of flame, protecting both him and Esmyra.

When the cavern went silent, Draevyn dropped his fiery shield. His intuition screamed for him to flee, yet he found himself rooted in place, feeling obligated to stay by her side.

As the dust settled, shapes emerged—first as shadows, then figures that moved with an unnerving grace. Draevyn's breath caught in his throat as they came into view.

"Fucking Irah." His voice was barely above a whisper as his eyes worked to track their movements, but there were too many of them. "Esmyra, if you can hear me, I need you to snap out of it."

Nothing and no one answered him. She remained as she was— silver glowing eyes as her hair levitated, flowing around her in waves.

When he turned back toward the arch, he found himself face-to-face with several humanoid creatures of the depths. One of them aimed for Esmyra, pointing an enormous spear at her face.

Draevyn's jaw locked, a liquid blaze igniting every vein in his body. "Touch her and you'll fucking burn."

He blinked, not having any idea where *that* came from. All he was certain of was that he meant every word.

Draevyn took a step up to the clan as he went to summon flame to his palms, but they were snuffed out before they had the chance to burn when a bolas latched around his wrists. The weapon was whipped at him from the side, barely catching his attention before he was too late to dodge it.

One of their attackers, a tall figure with intricate patterns painted across its chest and arms, stepped forward, the creature's gaze locked on him. It bared its sharp, pointed teeth and let out a guttural hiss, echoed by its companions. Draevyn could see the intelligence in those eyes—a cold, calculating awareness that made his stomach twist.

The bolas, normally crafted with rope and stone, was forged from a seaweed so strong that Draevyn's muscles strained against its strength as he worked to snap them in half. But what the weapon was bound by wasn't what put the fear of all the gods in him.

He realized with sinking dread why his flames winked out when the bolas had latched.

It wasn't made of mere stone.

It was velsinyte.

CHAPTER 37

*Esmyra*

Esmyra gasped at the weapon mere inches from her face. She ripped her hand from the fountain and the once-floating locks of her hair fell past her shoulders. Glancing around, her eyes found Draevyn, bound and gagged, but not of her doing.

They were surrounded by beings who appeared as mortals and something else—beings she had never seen or read of in books.

Their skin tones ranged from the lightest pale to the richest brown, all with an iridescence, resembling a shimmering pearl reflecting beneath the water, with eyes and hair ranging from every color in the sea. Their sleek bodies bore webbed and elongated fingers, their gills trailing up their necks. Esmyra's stare drifted along her assailant's arm, where fin-like ridges traced the contours of its limbs. The last thing she took notice of was their ears, pointed and finned, slightly protruding from the sides of their heads.

They seemed foreign, yet so familiar—some of their traits resembling her while in her siren form.

These creatures weren't anything like the krechuums that attacked them earlier. They were aware, alert, and had forged weapons. Her stare fell to Draevyn once more, whose eyes seemed to plead for her to cooperate.

Why hadn't he summoned his flames? And why wasn't he now?

Suddenly, she felt a faint prick of pain against her sternum, and she slowly turned her head to face her attacker as he lightly pressed his spear to her chest. Esmyra lifted her hands in mock surrender, wiggling her fingers as she allowed her talons to slowly slip out.

The creature pressed the sharpened spear deeper into her chest, this time drawing a small bead of blood. "State your name."

It was a demand. However, Esmyra never took kindly to those. She watched as her blood dripped down the spearhead's edge.

"Name. State it," the creature repeated. Its voice was deep, almost otherworldly.

Her gaze leisurely lifted to his, and a smirk lifted the edge of her lips. "You first."

Everyone around them stiffened, gripping their weapons tighter.

The one who appeared as their leader kept his eyes on hers as he ordered, "Kill the spare."

Draevyn flailed in the arms of his captors, bellowing against his gag, but the words were unintelligible.

Her eyes flared. "What? *No!*" she screamed, but they never halted. "ESMYRA! My name is Esmyra."

Still, they didn't yield.

"You speak when spoken to. And you did not," the male said, making her lip curl back.

A laugh of rage left her before her jaw locked. "I wouldn't do this if I were you."

In unison, those who circled Draevyn lifted their spears, preparing to plunge the sharpened blades into his chest—as if her threat meant nothing.

Not a second later, Esmyra's eyes shifted, and she lifted her hand to summon the water that conjured in the fountain. The movement caught everyone's attention.

Esmyra closed her eyes for a moment, her breath steadying. She could feel the water, sense its flow and rhythm like a pulse waiting to be commanded. Slowly, she raised her hands, her palms facing the fountain now positioned behind her.

"I warned you," she whispered, her voice steady despite the spear's proximity.

The creature's eyes widened, and he glanced back as the water behind her surged, breaking free of the fountain's confines. It twisted through the air, flowing like a serpentine ribbon as it wrapped around Esmyra's arms, coiling up her limbs in spiraling bands.

Her eyes snapped open, and a faint smile touched her lips. With a swift motion, she thrust her arms forward. The water reacted instantly, splitting into two distinct streams that shot out, twisting through the air like living entities.

The liquid formed into several glistening, crystalline daggers—their false blades shimmering like glass as they hovered before her.

The leader took a single step back as his eyes widened in awe, but his soldiers were still ready to kill Draevyn, and he was her only bargaining chip to get her father back.

Plus, she owed him—he saved her, too.

Esmyra spun, the water moving as an extension of her will. She lashed out, the watery blades slicing through the air, and watched as her conjured weapons severed their spears and Draevyn's gag. The next moment, the ancient cavern was filled with the sounds of splashing water, gasps of horror, and the clatter of weapons hitting the stone floor.

Draevyn's wide eyes were fixed on her, jaw hanging open.

The leader stepped up to her once more. "You opened the gate."

"Gate?" She lifted a brow.

She summoned the water that spilled to the ground to lift, instantly forming a spear that resembled their own.

The leader's stare traced up and down the spear. He took a step up to her, but Esmyra didn't falter, just watched him with wary curiosity as he did her. She couldn't shake the feeling that this place, with these people, whatever they may be, was exactly where she was meant to be. And because of this, she allowed him to move closer.

His webbed hand reached for her own, and her body stiffened at his touch. His flesh felt like rough scales brushing against her skin.

"You come from above?" he asked, though each word came out slowly like he was searching for the correct ones to use.

"Yes," she breathed, hoping he couldn't sense her heart racing. She could feel Draevyn's eyes boring into the side of her face, but refused to remove her stare from the creature.

"Forgive me." The pad of his thumb stroked the top of her hand, making her eyes flare, but it was too late.

The moment she moved to tear her wrist from his grasp, the cool touch of stone met her flesh a moment later—only it wasn't binding her wrists, but *cutting* into them.

Esmyra screamed as she felt her power draining, her heart slamming against her ribs as she watched the native leader take a sharpened piece of velsinyte and slice it through her skin.

Her breath hitched, the pain so sharp it momentarily blinded her. She could feel the velsinyte hooking into the very essence of her being, like talons digging into her soul.

It wasn't just pain anymore; it was *loss*. Her knees buckled, and a cry—guttural and wild—tore through her throat.

Multiple males were on her a moment later—wide-eyed with a mixture of confusion and awe spread across their features as they attacked her.

The skin of her wrist burned, as if Draevyn's flames were melting it to the bone, while they pulled her arms tightly behind her back and cuffed her as the prisoner she now was. The next thing she knew, she was blindfolded.

"Get the fuck away from her!" Draevyn bellowed, fighting to get to her.

Esmyra thrashed, kicked, and screamed, but nothing helped. Nothing stopped the creatures from throwing her over one of their shoulders and walking off with her as if she were nothing but a helpless child.

A defiant child kicking and screaming, just as her father had described her. Would she ever see him again? Or was this the fate they both deserved after all they had inflicted on others? She sailed the realm's seas as if she were a god, not caring for the consequences of her actions or believing there was any creature powerful enough to cause such things in the first place.

And now, that very cockiness had cost her everything.

Esmyra's blindfold had turned the world dark, and every sound seemed to come alive, echoing through the silence. Once set back on the ground, she stumbled over uneven stone beneath her feet as the grip of their captors was unyielding, pulling both her and Draevyn along with every step. Her heartbeat pounded in her ears like a distant drum as the burning sensation radiated through her flesh where they cut her.

They moved in silence—the natives giving no clue as to their intentions, making her feel helpless in a world hidden beneath their own.

The air felt damp and cool against her skin, and the scent of salt filled her nose—the unmistakable mark of the sea seemed to cling to everything. A soft whooshing sound reverberated in the distance, reminding her of waves rolling against a shoreline. She wondered if they were still underwater or if this strange labyrinth wound through some secret part of Maerinys that had somehow survived the collapse.

She fought to keep herself calm and sensed Draevyn next to her, his scent of cedarwood and leather mingling with the brine. They were forced to walk for what felt like miles, hearing the murmurs of the folk that had captured them. The sensation of countless twists and turns disoriented her.

"Any idea how to get out of this?" Draevyn mumbled.

"Clearly, I'm walking blindly, just as you are, so I would say you know the answer. And *you're welcome* for saving your life, by the way. Consider us even."

"No speak!" a voice boomed from behind them before someone shoved at her back, making her stumble forward.

The rough cloth of the blindfold scraped against her skin, its tight knot biting into her temples. She couldn't see any looming shadows around them or make sense of the sounds—just echoes and whispers, the clatter of their boots against stone.

Her throat tightened as each second passed. Who were they being brought to? Would they be immediately put to death? Eaten?!

*Gods*, the last thought had her nearly gagging.

They could be walking into anything, and the unknown of it all threatened to suffocate her. Her thoughts churned, a relentless stream of questions and fears, imagining rows of sharp-toothed warriors or monstrous sea creatures lurking in the shadows, just waiting for a chance at a meal.

The sea serpent guarding the trench came to mind, and she audibly swallowed.

"If *you're* scared, I think it's safe to assume we're fucked." Draevyn's words almost forced a nervous laugh out of her, but she couldn't even manage that.

Because he was right.

"Separate them," the leader's voice called.

Esmyra's head whipped in all directions, though she still couldn't see anything through her blindfold.

"Get the fuck off of me." Draevyn's voice carried to her as she sensed him being pulled further away. His words were followed by a grunt and the sudden dragging of feet.

"To the cells with him," someone said.

"Draevyn?!" Esmyra squealed, desperation clear in her voice as she remained blind while her only ally was dragged away from her.

She halted her steps and shoved out of the hold of the creature, lashing out in any direction she could, but then an embrace wrapped around her chest and lifted her from the ground. What at first resembled a hug, quickly grew tighter and tighter until air refused to fill her lungs.

"Release me!" she bellowed, her tone filled with nothing but fury.

"We cannot do that," the voice of her captor struggled to say as he worked to keep her steady.

"Fuck you!" Esmyra screamed as her feet violently kicked and swung through the air. Her legs were captured within another's grasp, forcing her body to go limp. She hung in the air as if she were hanging from a spit roast.

Her body went tight, on edge as she sensed someone's lips directly next to her ear. The warm breath of the leader brushed against her cool, damp skin. "Easy. If he behaves, he will not be put to death."

"Release us immediately," she spat, chest heaving in rapid breaths as she bared her teeth. "And perhaps I will spare your pathetic lives."

The feeling of his proximity lessened and his voice sounded as if he were marching away when he spoke once more. "You'll need to get through *her* first."

"What?!" she rushed out, but her voice was nothing but a confused whisper as she continued to struggle against their hold.

"Don't fight them," Draevyn's voice called a moment later, but he sounded so far away.

Esmyra didn't give a damn about the man aside from his worth, but she knew she would rather have an ally than face this alone, no matter how unlikely that ally might be.

Who in all gods were these people and creatures? Were they even still in the cave?

The natives placed her feet on the ground once more but held her arms in a powerful grip, guiding her forward.

She tried to focus on the surrounding sounds, to piece together where they might be leading her. The air felt thick, almost heavy, and she could hear the distant, muffled roar of water pressing against unseen barriers. Everything felt alive in a strange, otherworldly way, as if the world itself was breathing beneath a crushing weight.

Suddenly, the stone beneath her feet gave way to something

smoother—tiles, perhaps, or a path worn down by countless footsteps.

Voices whispered around her, soft but insistent. She tried to make sense of them, tried to pick up a tone or a phrase that might help her understand, but the words slipped past her.

Her senses heightened in the absence of sight—every sound, every shift in the air, seemed magnified. Somewhere nearby, a strange clicking caught her ears—a rapid sequence that reminded her of crabs scuttling along rocks.

The tugging on her arms guided her upward, feeling stairs with the tip of her boots, and then the sound of heavy doors opening echoed as their metal hinges strained. The temperature changed, the chilly dampness shifting to a more oppressive warmth.

The sounds of their footsteps echoed, mimicking the sound of an empty, grand hall.

How was this beneath the realm? Within a cave at that? It wasn't possible.

*Had Maerinys survived?*

She felt the natives shift around her, their hands loosening but not letting go. There was a pause, a moment of stillness, and the sound of another heavy door creaking open.

They pulled her to a halt, and then there was a tug at the back of her head as the blindfold was untied, and the rope binding her hands was cut, freeing her. The fabric fell away from her face, and she blinked rapidly, her eyes adjusting to the sudden light—light she certainly wasn't expecting so deep within the earth.

Esmyra's lips parted as she stood at the center of an elaborate throne room. Its ceiling seemed impossibly high, covered in aquatic murals that danced with colors of the sea. Light filtered through what appeared to be glass or crystal, casting everything in a shimmering glow. Pillars resembling the ones in the crumbled temple lined the walls, and the floor was made of the same pale, polished stone that reflected the blue light.

She glanced over her shoulder and saw Draevyn being dragged

elsewhere through the open slit of the grand doors, right before they closed.

The natives stood around her, their faces unreadable as their gazes were fixed ahead. When Esmyra's eyes followed theirs, a voice sounded, making her throat go bone dry.

"Welcome home...*Esmyra*."

CHAPTER 39

*Esmyra*

Esmyra's entire body went rigid.

In the center of the grand chamber, a massive dais rose like a pedestal from the floor, carved of shimmering pearl. Upon it sat a woman, her back straight, her posture regal and serene as her crown glinted in the light.

The woman's stare bore into Esmyra's, and it stole the breath from her lungs.

It wasn't just the stranger knowing her name that had her heart nearly stopping.

Her lips parted as she took in the sight of the woman. It was like looking into a mirror, only different. The same sharp markings traced up her arms while matching cheekbones, full lips, and almond-shaped eyes adorned the queen's face. However, everything else appeared inverted.

While Esmyra's skin was tanned from several lifetimes at sea, the woman on the dais was pale, almost luminous in the dim light. Where Esmyra's hair was dark as the abyss, the woman before her was as golden and warm as the sunrise.

Aside from the shape, their eyes, too, were different—while Esmyra's were a piercing, glacial blue, the other's were a fiery amber.

Esmyra felt like she was looking into her own reflection within the sun itself.

A moment of silence passed between them, thick with the weight of something she couldn't place. Perhaps it was recognition, though she knew she'd never seen this woman before in her very long life.

As the woman on the dais smiled, Esmyra was taken aback by the unexpected kindness radiating from her, a stark contrast to the cold sneer she had anticipated.

Suddenly, the woman's eyes narrowed on her arms—something she was used to due to the runes her flesh bore, but she soon realized that wasn't what caught her attention.

"Release her." The words came out as a demand radiating through the throne room, and they immediately removed their grip on Esmyra's arms.

The native soldiers all took a single step away from her in unison —the sounds of their steps and the shifting of weapons echoed with the movement.

A million thoughts were rummaging through Esmyra's mind, though she couldn't find a single word to speak.

The woman, who she could only assume was their queen, stood from her seat and descended the steps of the dais as if she were floating.

Esmyra watched in awe as she moved. The dress she wore was revealing, yet stunning—a style she'd never seen in any other kingdom. The fabric was a cream color with a pearlescent sheen, draping over her shoulders as it crossed in an X pattern over her breast, revealing glimpses of skin before wrapping around her natural curves and flowing to the floor. With each step she took, her lean thighs were exposed as the fabric of the high slits flowed around her.

The queen came to stand before Esmyra, her gaze roaming over her slowly. Then their eyes met. "Why can I not sense your power?" The words left the woman in a near whisper, seeming confused.

Esmyra's brows furrowed before lifting her wrist to reveal the wound from the velsinyte. It didn't appear like any other wound she'd received before or seen on any other. Her body hadn't even begun to heal it. Onyx, spider-like veins cracked atop her skin and crept along her forearm, spreading slowly.

Her eyes flared at the sight, not realizing this was what had been causing such pain. "What in all gods?" she whispered, bringing it closer to her face to get a better look, but the woman's hand reached out and grabbed her wrist, only her touch was gentle as she carefully rotated it to inspect the wound.

"Azarian," she said, facing the one Esmyra assumed was their leader. "Why does she bear this mark?"

Esmyra could sense the rage beneath her false tone of kindness. She recognized that fury, knew it as if it were her own—for that was what it mirrored.

"To be sure it was her," he answered.

*What the fuck?*

The queen dropped Esmyra's arm and cocked her head to the side as she stared her soldier down. "And if it killed her?"

Azarian shrugged. "Then she wasn't who we needed."

Esmyra's lips curled back, revealing her canines. "It could have *killed* me?!"

"Not *you*. But anyone else, perhaps."

Esmyra stomped a foot in his direction as she threw her wrist before her on display. "You will release me and my..." she searched for a word that would make the most sense, "*companion* at once, or I will skin you down to the bone with my teeth."

She looked at the queen, whose face wore a subtle grin. The golden woman lifted her hand and pointed to the wound, her gaze fixated on it. Esmyra's eyes flared as she watched the onyx veins retreat to the site of the wound. And then, a vile, black substance lifted from it, levitating in the air just like when she conjured seawater from Draevyn's lungs.

Her lips parted as she gasped, eyes wide in disbelief, while her power surged within her chest once again. And then her skin began to mend.

"Esmyra, forgive me for the late introduction, but my name is

Syrena. You don't remember me, do you?" The queen's voice was soft, almost tender.

Esmyra's brows furrowed in confusion as she rotated her arm, inspecting it. "I don't know you," she whispered before her stare lifted to meet the woman's.

She was met with a genuine smile. "But you do, sister."

The word hit Esmyra like a wave, knocking the breath from her lungs. She took a hesitant step back, shaking her head in disbelief. "Sister?" she echoed. "That's impossible. I don't...I don't have a sister. I don't have anyone."

Syrena's smile remained as she reached out, gently cupping her face in her hand. There was no malice in the touch, only warmth. Yet, Esmyra pulled back.

"You do," she said softly. "We were born of the same waters, the same magic. Separated long ago, before either of us could remember." Her hand fell to her side as their eyes remained locked. "I am Syrena Aeress. Queen of the Kingdom of Maerinys. And *you*, Esmyra...are my twin sister. Stolen from us long before we had a chance to properly meet."

*Maerinys.*

*Aeress.*

The lost, sunken kingdom and the ancient family name that ruled over it in servitude to Kaelypso and Naerysa.

*How was any of this possible?*

Esmyra's heart raced, her mind spinning. Her memories were hazy, like a mist that clung to the edges of her mind. But there was something deep within her that stirred at the name. Something old.

"I don't...I don't understand." Her eyes widened with confusion, and for one of the first times in her life, she found herself utterly speechless.

Syrena's warm gaze roamed over her. "That's quite alright, I wouldn't expect you to. But we've been waiting for a very long time, hoping you would return home."

*Home.*

Esmyra took a shaky step back, her chest rising and falling in a sense of panic at the queen's words. Conflicting emotions surged through her. She wanted to recoil, to reject everything Syrena was saying, but there was a part of her that longed to believe it—longed for the connection of a family she had never known, of a people who would understand who and what she was without judgment or greed.

She felt the truth in Syrena's words, in her very being, and that terrified her more than anything. Esmyra, however, had never been a trusting woman, and she wasn't about to start now in a strange, lost world.

"Say I believe you, Syrena." She swallowed before squaring her shoulders. "What comes next? And what of my captive your soldiers stole from me?"

"Perhaps," Syrena started, "we should take a walk together in private. I can show you better than I can tell you. And as for the man, he's currently being placed in a holding cell. But if he's your captive, and not a companion as you stated, then I assume he's an enemy. So, I suggest he remain where he is, and we'll retrieve him once our story is told to keep our kingdom's secrets safe."

*Enemy.* Was that what Draevyn still was to her? It certainly didn't feel that way any longer, but she didn't know who she could trust.

Was her enemy the son of a king who held her own father hostage in his need of greed and power? Or was it the ancient, forgotten queen of Maerinys, claiming to be her kin?

The queen offered her arm to her, and Esmyra stared at it through narrowed eyes. A giggle left Syrena as she lowered her arm. "Apologies, Esmyra. I don't want to make you uncomfortable."

"Aye," Esmyra breathed. "Lead the way, Your Majesty." She gestured to the door and allowed the queen to guide her as the soldiers followed at their backs.

The walls of the castle shimmered as Esmyra and Syrena walked side by side through the grand corridor. The soft pads of her sister's steps were a whisper against the floor, while the scraping of Esmyra's boots seemed to reverberate through the fortress.

She glanced down at herself. Her dirty, torn garbs were a stark contrast to the ethereal beauty of the flowing, robe-like dress Syrena wore beside her.

The two were nearly identical, yet couldn't be any more different.

Esmyra couldn't believe this was happening. And how did she have a *twin*?

As they stepped through the towering, ornate doors and out into the streets of Maerinys, her breath caught in her throat. The city stretched out before her, a blend of coral architecture and the living ocean, bathed in a pale blue glow from the light filtering through the water above.

Her stare lifted as she craned her neck toward the sky. A massive crystalline dome arched overhead, cradling Maerinys in protection from the crushing depths of the sea as schools of fish swam freely just beyond its barrier.

She took a step up to the edge of the stairs and her heart thudded at the sight. It was unlike anything she had ever seen. Overwhelming emotions welled up inside her, feeling as if this place, with its pulsating, ancient power, had once belonged to her, patiently waiting for her to return.

Syrena stepped up beside her. "It's beautiful, isn't it?"

"It is," she breathed.

Esmyra felt hundreds of eyes on her as her vision adjusted and settled on the bustling streets below, where several kinds of creatures watched her intently.

Syrena half-turned to her as she took her first step down the stairs. "Maerinys awaits you."

The brush of her sister's fingers slid against her own as she gently grabbed her hand. Esmyra's hand jolted back at the touch but gave Syrena a closed-lip smile, hoping she took it for the apology it was. The queen gave her a dip of her chin before guiding her along to follow her to the streets. The presence of the guards behind them sent a chill down her spine, and she wondered if she even had a choice to stroll through this place.

But Esmyra's curiosity got the best of her, and she went without a fight.

Once they descended the stairs, they passed citizens of the hidden kingdom, Maerinyseans, who glanced curiously at her, their eyes gleaming like pearls in the soft light. Some appeared mortal, while others looked like the creatures who had found her and Draevyn in the caves.

Now that Esmyra wasn't blindfolded and being dragged against her will, she felt uneasy as they gawked and whispered as they passed.

"They're staring at me like I'm an animal behind bars," Esmyra said, her tone a mix of caution and annoyance.

A soft giggle left Syrena, and she gently placed her hand on Esmyra's shoulder. "You must understand, they have been waiting for you for centuries." Esmyra's gaze whipped to her. "As have I," Syrena finished.

*Waiting?* Esmyra wasn't sure if the word even left her lips. How could this have been hidden from her for so long? From the world?

They were nearing towering statues of goddesses that appeared to be dancing atop an open cockle shell, hair flowing around them wildly as if they were within the sea. The sisters came to a halt before them.

"Those are—"

"Kaelypso and Naerysa," Esmyra cut her off as her neck remained craned, staring up at the stone statues. "The sea goddesses who abandoned the realm when their kingdom sank, dooming their people with it." Irritation flared within her, thinking of what the gods had done.

"I wouldn't be so sure about that," Syrena said, earning Esmyra's attention. "Do we appear *doomed* to you?" A smirk curved her lips before she began walking once more.

With a final glance up at the statues, Esmyra let out a huff through her nostrils as her lips pressed into a thin line before following. She didn't know what to think anymore. The impossible was unfolding in front of her as each second passed.

The streets were wide, lined with bioluminescent plants and odd glowing orbs that pulsated softly in the air, casting an almost dream-like atmosphere around the city.

"Merlights."

Esmyra blinked, turning toward Syrena. "What?"

Syrena gestured above to the floating orbs with her chin. "Merlights. It's the most basic magic for our kind. It's the only reason we haven't been left in complete darkness."

*Huh.* She had never seen such a thing. It must've been magic based in this very kingdom, for the elven possessed no light in their magic, nor did the shifters.

They weaved through the narrow streets in silence, and Esmyra wasn't sure if Syrena was just as speechless as she was or if she was allowing her to take it all in on her own terms. The deeper they walked into the heart of Maerinys, the more she felt a pull—a connection, feeling as though the currents themselves were wrapping around her, drawing her in.

"Do you remember any of this?" Syrena asked softly, her voice almost drowned in the gentle hum of their surroundings.

Esmyra shook her head. "No, but it feels familiar. Like a dream I've dreamt countless times throughout my life. It feels like…"

"Home," Syrena finished for her as her eyes softened, a flicker of understanding passing through them. "It's in our blood. This kingdom, this power—it's been waiting for us, for you, to return. You belong here, just as much as I do."

Esmyra wanted to believe that, but doubt gnawed at her. The enormity of it all—the lost history, the forgotten magic that had been hidden from her—was too much to grasp at once. She looked up again, trying to take it all in, to force herself to see this place as home as she watched the merlights flicker off the dome above them.

Their stroll brought them to a large, open square where a small pool of water was filled with children and younglings of all creatures as they played and splashed.

*A sea within the sea.*

"How can you live down here?" she asked, her voice laced with both wonder and shock. "How is any of this possible?"

"Magic is a curious thing, Esmyra," Syrena started. "Its essence cloaked us and our citizens all that time ago, becoming one with the ocean itself." Sadness crept into Syrena's eyes. "You'll understand in time. I don't wish to overwhelm you on your first day here with everything you've missed these past several centuries."

"I'm sorry. I just…I have so many questions that not a single one can even form at the moment." The last few words left Esmyra with a nervous laugh.

"And that's okay." Syrena reached for her hands and they turned to face one another.

Esmyra desperately fought the urge to pull away.

"Now, why don't we get you cleaned up and brought to your chambers before we have the cooks prepare dinner," Syrena suggested.

*Dinner.* Esmyra's stomach growled ferociously. When was the last time they had eaten?

Her eyes flared then, remembering everything it entailed to get to Maerinys in the first place, and her throat tightened.

"And what of the man who accompanied me here?"

Syrena's brows furrowed. "Your captive?"

"Aye," Esmyra answered. "He...there's much to the story, but he doesn't need to be bound and locked behind bars."

"You're sure?" Syrena's tone was worrisome.

Esmyra gave a dip of her chin. "If he does anything to make you believe otherwise, by all means, lock him up once more."

As much as she wanted to trust this person who claimed to be her sister, who looked nearly identical to her, she just couldn't—not yet, anyway. And somehow, in a twisted sense of fate, the only one she *could* trust was Draevyn Rowe.

Syrena nodded, her eyes going distant as if lost in thought. "We shall bring your companion up and give him his own quarters as well, then."

Something inside of Esmyra relaxed at the words, anticipating no longer being alone with these people in this strange, underwater world.

CHAPTER 41

*Atlas*

The air in the dungeons was thick and damp as Atlas silently crept through the shadows. His heart galloped in his chest, his mind racing with worry for his brother and the gnawing frustration of being kept in the dark by their father.

He had to find Draevyn before it was too late. And the only one who *might* have answers was the gods-damn pirate lord they currently held captive.

The guards were half asleep, their attention elsewhere as Atlas easily slipped past them beneath the cover of his shadows. He approached the velsinyte-barred cell at the end of the chamber, his boots barely making a sound on the cold stone.

Inside the cell, Cyrus Blackwood sat with his back against the wall, his shackles clinking faintly as he shifted. His eyes lifted to Atlas as he approached.

A smirk formed, but there was no humor in it—only pure hatred lay in his dark eyes. "Well, well," Cyrus rasped, low and mocking, even through his uneven breaths. "The prince himself. Come to poke the bear in his cage?"

Atlas didn't waste time with pleasantries. "I need information," he said, each word more clipped than the last. "Tell me where Draevyn is."

Cyrus raised a brow, his lips curling into a slow grin. "You've got a lot of nerve, *Prince*. Coming down here, demanding answers from me as if I owe you anything."

"Trust me, you're the last person I wish to speak with," Atlas admitted, his tone growing sharper. "If you ever want your life to be somewhat bearable again, then you will tell me where Draevyn is."

Cyrus chuckled, a rasping sound that echoed like a gurgle beneath water. "Your brother, eh? Rumors claimed you have a soft spot for each other. Is that because your father is a spineless prick who offered your souls to Irah for power?"

Atlas's hand clenched into a fist, his shadows swirling around his fingers as his frustration grew. "You're wasting my time, Blackwood. I need answers. *Now*."

His beady, black eyes gleamed in the dim torchlight. "Ah, there it is. And here they say your brother holds all the fire." He let out a laugh as if the words were actually funny, but it ended in a hacking cough.

Atlas took a step closer to the bars, his patience fraying. "Enough games, Cyrus. Where is my brother?"

"How in all gods would I know when I've been locked down here?" he growled.

Atlas kicked at the cell's door, the reverberations of the bars echoing through the dungeons. "The only information I have is that he's *possibly* with a beautiful woman and *likely* has no choice in the matter at all." The words came out in an angry bellow, and he took a deep breath, trying to reel in his self-control. His lip curled. "Now, I'm assuming it has something to do with the little ambush your crew attempted the night of Lephyrin's ball."

Cyrus let out a wicked chuckle. "I promise you, Atlas, if the beautiful woman I'm thinking of is who holds him, your brother was lost to you before you even realized he was missing."

"Who is this woman?!" Atlas spat, his throat tightening with rage and terror.

A cruel grin crept up Blackwood's face. "Rumors claim your daddy is after the treasure that was left behind in the fall of Maerinys."

"So?" Atlas's brows furrowed.

Cyrus leaned forward, his voice dropping to a low, secretive murmur. "Sail south. That's where you'll find your answers."

"South? That's all you have for me?"

"Aye."

Atlas scoffed. "Pirates and their stupid fucking games."

The pirate lord's smile widened, his gaze cold. "There's more, boy, but you're not ready for it." His eyes went distant. "The realm itself isn't ready for it. Just be prepared for what comes next."

Atlas's frustration flared again, but he reined it in, forcing himself to stay focused. He glared at Cyrus, wanting to rip the answers from his lips, but something in the man's eyes told him he wasn't lying— not about sailing south, at least.

"If you're wasting my time, I will make you regret this," Atlas said, his voice low while shadows coiled up his arms.

Cyrus only smiled, that same cold, mocking grin. "No, you won't. You'll sail south like the doting older brother and future king you are." A click of his tongue sounded. "But don't say I didn't warn you."

Atlas turned on his heel, and the echoes of his footsteps mingled with Blackwood's fading, cruel, hacking laugh as he left the dungeon. His mind was a whirlwind of questions, but at least now he had a heading.

Atlas didn't care what it took. He would sail south to find his brother and kill anyone who tried to get in his way.

Now, all he had to do was convince Draevyn's crew to do the same.

# CHAPTER 42

# Draevyn

The cold, dirt-covered floor pressed against Draevyn's cheek as distant voices roused him from being unconscious. His body ached—muscles sore while his wrists remained bound.

His mind raced, alternating between rage and panic. A persistent, dull throb ached where his magic once flowed freely. Now he and Esmyra, two of the most powerful beings he knew of, were trapped and powerless.

*Esmyra.*

Draevyn glanced side to side, noting she wasn't there with him. It was clear he was in a prison cell—the space was filled with damp, stale air, and the only light was an odd teal glow seeping through the barred window. He had no way of knowing how much time had passed.

*Think. There has to be a way out of this.* They wouldn't have taken him alive unless they needed him for something.

Then voices sounded down the hall once more.

They were faint at first, like a ripple in the silence, but growing steadily as they approached—and they were female.

He slowly sat up, his back resting against the wall as he strained to listen. His pulse quickened as the voices grew clearer, and he knew then he would recognize one of them anywhere.

*Esmyra.* Only she didn't sound distressed or even detained as he was. The last he saw her, she'd been bound and held captive alongside him. Was she...walking about freely? And in casual conversation?

The thought of it had Draevyn nearly rolling his eyes, because, *of course,* she would be.

The clank of keys rattled outside his cell door, followed by the unmistakable groan of rusted hinges being turned. Adrenaline surged through him as the door creaked open, letting the teal light of the hallway spill into his dark prison.

He squinted against the soft light, and then he saw them—two women standing in the doorway. The first was striking, wearing robes that seemed to ripple like the sea itself, her golden hair flowing in soft waves. Behind her, Esmyra lingered, her expression uncertain, but her wild eyes were sharp.

How had she already found an ally to get them out of this hellhole?

"Is this him?" the golden one asked, her voice filled with curiosity, though there was a hint of caution in it.

Esmyra nodded. "Aye. He's the one who accompanied me here, and he's not to be harmed if I'm able to make such requests."

Draevyn's brows shot up his forehead in confusion.

Esmyra stepped closer to him, her eyes locking onto his as if in warning, or perhaps pleading. "And once they remove your bindings, you will prove you're no threat, correct? After all...you're only mortal. And you bear no magic."

It was the wildest lie he'd ever heard, and for it to come out of Esmyra's lips made him even more wary. If Draevyn was one thing, it was dangerous. Esmyra knew that, and she was the other side of the same coin.

She would never have him walking about freely if she didn't need him to have access to his magic. Something was happening, and the unknown of it all was nearly suffocating.

Draevyn glared up at her, biting back a retort. However, if they would free him based on her word alone, he had no choice but to follow along.

The second woman moved forward, stepping into the subtle light, and Draevyn's eyes widened, realizing she looked strikingly similar to Esmyra.

*Good gods, there's two of them.*

Her eyes narrowed slightly as she studied him. "State your name."

"You first," he mocked.

"*Draevyn*," Esmyra warned through clenched teeth, her brow creasing.

"Draevyn," the golden woman echoed. "Interesting name."

"A name of no meaning, I assure you," Esmyra lied. "He hails from Lephyrin."

What in the hells was happening?

The first woman tilted her head, a small smile forming. "Hello, *Draevyn*," she said, emphasizing his name, unaware that it held royal lineage from being trapped down in Maerinys. "My name is Syrena Aeress. As a thank you for helping my sister reach me, we're granting you your own quarters in my home."

"What the fuck?" The words slipped from him, unable to help it. His gaze whipped to Esmyra, the veins in her neck straining beneath the pale teal light. But her stare held no answers.

Guards rushed in from behind them and grabbed Draevyn by his arms, pulling him to his feet before unwrapping the bolas. The moment the bindings left his skin, the surge of his power returning nearly brought him back down to his knees, and it took everything in him to hide it.

"Follow along, would you? If you're to be presentable for dinner, I must insist we get a move on down here." Syrena turned from him and stalked out of the cell, her gown twirling around her ankles before flowing down the hallway after her.

Esmyra rushed to his side and helped him steady himself as he moved to take his first step. "Play along. Please. I can't even fucking *believe* I have to ask."

"What in all gods is happening, Esmyra? Why are you not in a cell?"

"I can't explain right now, but play along and maybe we can find the information we need and escape to the surface somehow."

He scoffed. "You expect me to believe you convinced our new captors to release me *and* my power on some whim? You wouldn't be down here if you didn't need me for something. So let's skip the games, shall we?"

Her eyes narrowed on him, her pupils morphing into slits.

He hit a nerve. Good.

"I will have you know, Draevyn Rowe, that I am once again saving your stupid life when I should leave you down here to rot. However, you are the *only* thing that will release my fa—" she cut herself off, and he raised a brow in confusion. "Release my captain from your father's hold!"

He would never be anything more than a pawn in her game—in anyone's game. Draevyn's jaw ticked at the realization.

"Esmyra," a guard called from beyond the door.

"We're right behind you!" she answered as her eyes remained locked with Draevyn's.

She lifted herself onto her tiptoes and whispered into his ear. "I don't trust them. Not fully. We get their story and we find a way out. Speak nothing of your royal name, and don't use your magic if you can help it. We know they somehow possess velsinyte, so our powers are useless until we think of a plan."

Draevyn suppressed a shiver as the heat of her breath brushed against his skin.

She took a step back from him. "Aye?"

His gaze traced up and down the curves of her body. Her stance was stiff as her eyes seemed to plead.

A feeling of dread settled in his stomach, realizing that even Esmyra was frightened by the position they found themselves in.

"Aye," he echoed.

Before them, the castle's great halls revealed themselves, radiating an elegance he'd never seen in any kingdom above. Draevyn walked in silence a step behind Syrena and Esmyra while the guards remained at their backs. The soft glow of the bioluminescent orbs illuminated their path as they hovered along the coral-carved walls.

The palace was a perfect blend of natural sea formations and intricate designs. Its floors beneath them were smooth stone, polished and veined with luminous silver and gold threads that looked like currents frozen in time. The ceilings soared above, domed and adorned with faded paintings of the sea's waves.

He had to admit, despite his growing suspicion, the place was magnificent.

Draevyn kept his steps steady, his senses alert as he took in the surrounding beauty—only the castle wasn't the only beauty that plagued his thoughts.

The two women walked in silence in front of him. While their features were identical, it appeared their similarities halted there. Where Syrena's movements were graceful and unhurried, Esmyra's were stiff and forced, looking just as tense as he felt.

His stare traced their bodies, the teal markings along their arms mirroring each other. Only Esmyra's no longer glowed, nor did they appear as burns, but as if they were inked into her skin by the sea itself.

Esmyra's steps slowed just enough to walk alongside Draevyn, though she wouldn't meet his stare, her own fixed on Syrena's back.

"What do you know?" he whispered.

She shot him a death glare and pressed a finger to her lips. He forced himself to suppress his smirk as they continued to walk in silence, the only sound coming from the echoes of their footsteps.

They passed through a massive archway leading into a sprawling courtyard, where plants native to the deep sea glowed softly. A fountain flowed in its center, its water overflowing to the ground in small streams that twisted through the garden like veins of life. Beautiful women surrounded the garden, tending to plants and whispering as they passed, though he could tell by the slits of their eyes that something else lurked beneath their skin, much like Esmyra.

Once on the opposite end and back within the castle walls, his thoughts were interrupted as they came to a stop before two grand opposing doors at the end of the corridor.

"These will be your quarters," Syrena said, turning to face them as she gestured to each door. "My wing is close by. I would hate for us to lose track of each other." There was a faint edge of warning in her voice as a feline smile curved her lips.

Two guards stepped out and opened the twin doors in unison before standing at attention on their sides. Draevyn looked between the two doors, his gaze narrowing slightly. He loathed the idea of being kept under watch.

He hadn't realized Syrena was watching him, waiting for a reaction. "A precaution, I'm sure you understand, Draevyn." He hated how she spoke his name so casually. "There's a lot to take in, and this castle can be a maze. I'm sure this is overwhelming, but you'll find it easier to adjust in time."

Draevyn glanced over at Esmyra as her eyes softened at the woman's words—though there was something distant in them, as if she, too, was still coming to terms with all of this.

His stare drifted to the underwater queen once more. "Just a bit odd to have two quarters readily available on such short notice." He shot her a fake, closed-lip smile.

Syrena's smile mimicked his before letting out a soft chuckle. "Well, this is a fortress. There are many wings. Many unoccupied rooms and chambers. If it's this that makes you wary, please allow me to apologize for keeping my home clean and presentable." Her stare raked over him. "Unless you prefer the dungeons. You didn't seem so on edge while down there."

Draevyn's nostrils flared before he cleared his throat. "Was a question, is all. Do forgive me for being...wary." He cocked his head to the side, and he could feel Esmyra's dagger-like glare blazing into the side of his cheek.

"You're forgiven." Syrena gestured to one of the doors. "Esmyra, this is your room. I hope you find it suitable."

Draevyn crossed his arms, studying Esmyra's face for a moment, trying to read the layers of her emotions as she stared into her room.

Her lips were pressed into a thin line, seeming guarded as she always had, but there was something in her eyes he couldn't place. Longing, perhaps.

Syrena spoke again, cutting through the quiet tension. "Both of you will get cleaned up and we'll meet in the great hall for dinner in one hour. I look forward to hearing of your grand adventures then."

With that, she turned and aimed back down the hall, most of the guards following behind her while two remained right at their doors.

He stood there for a moment longer, watching Esmyra, wondering if she would say anything more. She hesitated at her door, her hand resting lightly on the handle. "It seems I will see you in an hour," she said quietly. Her eyes met his with a seriousness that caught him off guard, as if she were begging him to continue to play along.

Before he could respond, she slipped into her quarters. Draevyn stared after her, her warning from in the dungeons echoing in his mind.

Finally, he entered his new chambers, taking in his surroundings once the door shut behind him with a soft click.

His quarters were large, more luxurious than he expected for someone who wasn't royalty, though he supposed he was now considered a royal guest.

Despite the luxury, the room felt like a cage, especially knowing the guard stood just beyond the door. The castle's beauty couldn't disguise the fact that he was still a prisoner, watched carefully. He moved to the window that overlooked the gardens, pressing his hand against the cool glass as he gazed into it.

The silence of the large space pressed in on him. Maerinys and its creatures might be beautiful, but he knew better than to be lulled by appearances.

For beauty could be as lethal as any weapon.

The wildfire across the hall was proof of that.

# CHAPTER 43

# Esmyra

With a soft click, Esmyra closed the bedchamber door, the sound echoing in the silence. She leaned against the painted wood, her eyes squeezed shut as her mind raced.

What were they going to do? She was able to have Draevyn released from the cells, but she also wasn't sure if that would benefit them or not, especially now that they both had guards just beyond their doors. Would she still have a guard if she hadn't convinced Syrena to release him?

She blew out a breath and cracked her eyes open. The moment her vision adjusted, the lavishness of the room enveloped her, a stark contrast to the life she led aboard *The Night Wraith*. It was as if she had walked into a different world—one filled with elegance that felt entirely foreign.

Though she supposed that was exactly what happened.

Her lips parted as she took a step into the room, gazing in awe at everything it had to offer. She had looted and robbed ships and ports of every kingdom—had seen Lephyrin's king's personal bed chamber —but she had never seen something like *this*.

The walls appeared the same as the corridor with its coral carvings, while the ceiling shimmered with iridescent hues, glinting like scales in the light. A magnificent bed stood in the center, draped in fabric that shimmered like liquid silver—its canopy woven with strands of sea silk. Plush pillows in every size imaginable were piled high on the bed, begging for her to leap into them.

On either side, massive windows showcased a breathtaking view of Maerinys, framed by navy curtains with silver stitching.

"Wow," she whispered, eyes wide as she gently placed her fingertips on the windowsill and peered out at the kingdom.

A door suddenly swung open to her left, startling her, before a small entourage of staff glided into the room.

"Kaelypso's tits!" she screeched as she nearly leapt out of her skin.

"Welcome, Your Highness," a woman greeted, her brow slightly raised at her outburst.

*Your Highness.*

Esmyra suppressed her laugh at the title.

In her life as a pirate, she was never one to adhere to nobility or courtly manners; she fought for every scrap she owned, bled for her crew, and lived by the tides. Her life was simple, and what surrounded her now was anything but.

It even represented everything she loathed about Draevyn's lineage. And being surrounded by it now, the possibility of being a *part* of it, made her skin crawl.

"Please don't feel the need to call me that," Esmyra said, trying to make her tone soft.

The woman blinked, confusion flashing across her features, but it was there and gone in only a moment. "We'll prepare a bath for you," she said with a cautious smile as the staff began to move about the room. "The waters are infused with soothing herbs we've grown within Maerinys. It will help you relax after your journey."

Prepare a bath? Gods, she'd mocked the lords and ladies of every kingdom her entire life for luxuries like that.

She nodded, feeling overwhelmed, not having any idea how to accept being pampered as if she were royalty.

They led her toward a beautifully crafted bathing alcove, where an enormous, deep tub carved from onyx stone awaited her, resembling a private lake within her chambers. As she inched closer, she blinked rapidly, half-expecting it to disappear.

Something like this wasn't possible—though she assumed none of the past few days were either.

The indoor lake's water glimmered, swirling gently with floating petals from delicate flowers. The scent of brine mingling with hints of jasmine enveloped her.

"We shall bathe you whenever you're ready, Your Highness," a different handmaiden said.

Esmyra whirled to face them once more. "Please don't call me that." She forced a smile on her face, but she knew it didn't reach her eyes.

The woman averted her gaze to the floor as her hands clasped in front of her. "And what shall we call you then?"

"Esmyra will do," she answered. "After all, it *is* my name." She tried to hide the sass from her tone but knew it was useless.

The three handmaidens dipped their chins in unison. "Forgive us, Esmyra."

Esmyra blinked at them as she pursed her lips. "There's nothing to be forgiven for. Though you should know there isn't a way in any hell that I'll allow you to bathe me. I'm more than capable of doing that myself."

All three of their stares widened, and they glanced back and forth at each other in shock.

"We promise to have a gentle touch. And with all due respect—"

"Once again," Esmyra cut the woman off. "I'm more than capable of doing it myself."

They all remained looking hesitant.

"If you fear you'll be punished for it, by all means, blame me." She winked. "Now, don't make me threaten you."

Wide-eyed, they all scurried out of the room in silence, the only sound the shuffling of their feet.

And then Esmyra was entirely alone.

*Finally.* She turned to face the bath, and gods, if it wasn't the most glorious sight.

She peered into the floor-length mirror tucked away in a corner, and was appalled at the sight staring back at her—filthy and exhausted were a few words that came to mind, but it didn't even scratch the surface.

Esmyra pulled her shirt off, allowing it to fall to the floor before shoving out of her ruined pants. Letting out a huff, she gently swiped her hand across the water, welcoming the warmth it brought to her frigid skin. She sat at the edge of the tub and allowed her body to shift, scales replacing sleek skin in the blink of an eye before she settled into the bath.

The bath was exactly what she assumed when she first stepped into the room, truly replicating a small body of water with stone that slowly dropped off and morphed into a sand-covered floor. She dove beneath the surface and swam a few feet, allowing her eyes to illuminate the tub, finding that it seemed to stretch on an impossible distance.

A genuine smile formed as she took it all in. She missed the sea, missed the feeling of salt and sun on her skin. At least now she had one of those for the time being.

"Once you're ready," a handmaiden called softly through the door, the sound muffled, "we will help you choose an outfit suitable for your dinner with Queen Syrena."

Groaning, she decided it would be best to explore her chambers later. With a single thrust of her tail, she was back at the edge of the pool, finding various jars of soap that she washed herself with, revelling in finally feeling clean for the first time in what felt like weeks.

Esmyra stepped out of the tub and wrapped herself in a towel.

A knock on the door sounded a moment later, and Esmyra cleared her throat. "Come in."

Five maidens walked in—some appearing human, while others resembled the native warriors from when they were first bombarded in the caves, with fins adorning their forearms, cheeks, and spines.

One of them approached her, arms laden with light grey fabrics. "My name is Briar, and I will be your main handmaiden for your stay in the castle, Miss Esmyra. Are you ready to get dressed?"

Esmyra glanced between the fabric in Briar's arms and her eyes before skeptically saying, "Aye."

She warily watched Briar as she moved around her, scenting the girl's fear plain as day as it exuded from her, but one would never be able to tell by her face.

People easily sensed that *something* lurked beneath Esmyra's skin. They were just clueless as to what it was. But Esmyra wasn't even sure if that would matter in the sunken kingdom, or if it was even uncommon.

Briar gently placed her hand atop the small knot tying Esmyra's towel. "I'm going to remove this if that's alright with you."

She swallowed thickly, her jaw locking. "If you must."

Her new handmaiden smiled softly before removing her towel to begin dressing her. Briar wrapped Esmyra in soft, flowing fabrics that felt foreign against her skin before tying them tightly at the small of her back.

Esmyra loathed the feeling of someone else dressing her. However, if she were being honest...she wouldn't know the first step of how to put the damn thing on to begin with.

"Is a fashion like this necessary for dinner?" Esmyra grumbled, already uncomfortable.

"You'll be dining with Syrena's council to discuss your journey here, and this was what she desired you to wear for your first meeting with them."

Esmyra's eyes flared and her neck snapped in Briar's direction. "I'm sorry? Did you say *council*?"

All the maidens looked uncomfortable at her outburst.

"I did. You and Sir Draevyn won't just be having dinner with Queen Syrena, but her council and court as well."

When Esmyra didn't have an answer aside from her jaw locking, Briar continued. "This is how royals and females of higher nobility dress day-to-day. It's very standard." She paused. "Unlike the pants you arrived in."

The other girls snickered across the space—some tidying up the room, while another combed Esmyra's hair.

A soft, wicked chuckle slipped from Esmyra. "Bold of you to insult someone you fear." Her voice was laced with venom, not appreciating their laughter.

Briar visibly froze, her green eyes widening as she met Esmyra's stare. The maid cleared her throat. "Apologies, Miss Esmyra. It wasn't my place." She gestured to the floor-length mirror. "Why don't you take a look for yourself?"

Taking a step up to the mirror, Esmyra's brows shot up at the sight. The garments were beautiful and wrapped in the same manner Syrena wore upon her arrival. It crossed over her breasts, revealing far more skin than she was used to, while the high slits showed glimpses of her tanned, sleek legs with every step she took.

Esmyra didn't recognize the woman staring back at her in the mirror, yet she didn't balk at the sight either. The regal reflection staring back at her felt like a veil—a disguise masking the ruthless pirate beneath it.

"I look..."

"Beautiful," Briar finished for her, though it certainly wasn't the word she was going for. "Now, we really must be going if you're to be on time for dinner," she said before shuffling to the door along with the others.

Esmyra gave herself one more look over in the mirror—her hair already nearly dry and flowing in waves down her back. Her blue eyes seemed to illuminate in contrast to her grey dress.

She turned to the maidens, who stood at the door, waiting. "And what's to be discussed at this dinner?"

"I already told you, Miss," Briar started. "The topic of discussion will be you."

# CHAPTER 44

## Esmyra

Stepping out of her chambers, Esmyra tugged at the strange fabrics of her dress. The gown flowed around her like water, the sea-silk light and cool against her skin, but it felt strange, constricting in a way no leather vest or weathered coat ever had. She took a deep breath, squaring her shoulders.

If she could face down entire fleets without batting an eye, she could handle a dinner with a foreign council. But when her eyes fell on the door across the hall, the sight of Draevyn staring at her made her breath hitch as that wild flame in his gaze flickered and surged.

But irritation quickly followed.

Draevyn stood there, eyes wide, as though time itself had paused. The man who was her captive—no, her ally, now—looked at her like he was seeing her for the first time.

Her skin prickled beneath his gaze. Esmyra suddenly became aware of how the shimmering fabric clung to her curves, and the loose waves of her dark hair as it brushed the small of her back.

For a beat, neither of them spoke.

Draevyn's expression darkened, replaced by something she couldn't quite place—hunger, perhaps. It was the look she envisioned he would have at Anchorage Cove, when she first tried to seduce him.

*Men.* She suppressed rolling her eyes.

"You clean up nice," he said. The smug look on his face nearly had her talons slipping from the tips of her fingers, though she ignored the subtle flutters of her heart at his words.

Her eyes narrowed on him, her tone sharp. "Don't get used to it."

Draevyn's smile only widened, as if her irritation amused him more. "Wouldn't dream of it."

There was a tense pause as the two of them stood there, staring at each other.

"Shall we?" he asked, offering a mocking bow as he gestured toward the awaiting guards. His tone was dripping with sarcasm. His whiskey-hued eyes gleamed with amusement at her discomfort.

Scoffing, she strode past him, ignoring the infuriating smirk on his face. The two guards ahead led the way through the long, ornate hall. She glanced around, trying to take in the surroundings, but it was hard to focus with Draevyn walking beside her—far too close for her liking.

"I'd say you look uncomfortable," he whispered, "but that would be an understatement."

Esmyra clenched her jaw, refusing to give him the satisfaction of a response. *Of course* she was uncomfortable. Every piece of fabric she wore clung to her body. It made her feel exposed, and the unknown of everything occurring was suffocating.

"You're not exactly blending in either," she shot back under her breath, not bothering to look at him.

His smugness radiated off him.

"Oh, I'm blending just fine. I'm quite used to courtly gatherings," he replied smoothly. "You, on the other hand, look like you're ready to jump out a window."

She cast him a sidelong glance, eyes narrowing. "Don't tempt me."

He chuckled softly, the sound low and far too entertained. "If you really hate the sight of me so much, why bother having them release me from the cell? Clearly, they're interested in *you* and would prefer to see my head on a spike. Consider me shocked you didn't let me rot."

"And let your father hurt Cyrus?" she snapped back. "Not a chance."

Draevyn leaned in closer, his voice dropping to a low whisper. "You're really fun when you're angry, you know that?"

Esmyra's fists clenched at her sides, every muscle in her body tense with barely contained frustration. "You're really irritating when you're breathing, you know that?"

His only response was to chuckle quietly.

She blew out a breath. "Well, it's not as if any of this has gone according to plan since the moment we stepped into that cave. I have a duty to my crew and captain."

"I have some news for you, Esmyra..." His tone darkened, all sense of amusement gone. "The king will have Blackwood hang regardless of my return."

A tightness formed in her throat, and she forced herself to look at him. She was surprised to find his eyes were soft, almost pitying. "Your father is no king of mine. What good is a man who cannot keep his word?"

"Finally, something we agree on." Draevyn's words silenced them both, and something in Esmyra's chest strained, remembering that he appeared to loathe his father just as much as she did.

As they approached the grand doors leading to the dining hall, she said something that surprised even herself. "I'm sorry." The words were barely a whisper, but she knew he heard them, judging by the slight flare of his eyes, as if he were shocked to hear the words from her —from *anyone* regarding his father.

The doors swung open before them, revealing the grand dining hall inside. The council members were already seated at the long, decorated table, and the soft glow of merlight candles reflected off the tableware. She took in the scene, her annoyance at Draevyn dissipating entirely, and now focused on finding out as much as she could— about her past and ties to Maerinys.

Within a matter of days, she had gone from taking over *The Night Wraith* to being seated in the heart of a lost kingdom's power.

And Esmyra felt like she was about to be swept into that power, whether she liked it or not.

As she and Draevyn were led into the room, he leaned in toward her and whispered, "We need to make it out of here alive, and we're vastly outnumbered. So do me a favor, Wildfire…" He paused and her heart thudded at the nickname. "And try not to kill anyone tonight."

She shot him a sidelong glare, her lips curling into a smirk. "No promises."

"There's the siren I know. Fear doesn't suit you, love." He winked, and a warmth pooled in her stomach.

"There they are!" Syrena's voice cut through the air, snapping Esmyra from her trance. "Esmyra and Draevyn, please, won't you come take a seat?" Her smile beamed brightly.

Syrena sat at the head of the table with a golden crown atop her head, adorned with seashells, shimmering pearls, and jewels, as she gestured to the two seats at her side.

The council members sat in their places, clad in cream-colored robes. Their faces were impassive as they silently watched Esmyra and Draevyn as if they were unknown creatures within a gilded cage.

Reluctantly, Esmyra slid into the chair on her sister's left, casting a quick glance at Draevyn as he sat on the opposite side. She tore her eyes away from him as she felt the weight of his gaze.

The queen's voice broke the unbearable silence. "Welcome. And now that our guests have arrived, let the feast begin!"

The moment she spoke the words, doors burst open on all sides of the room, with maidens and butlers gliding through the great hall with covered trays in hand. When they placed them scattered around the long table, the intricate covers were removed to reveal food of all kinds—kelp salad, oysters, seagrass risotto, and about ten other things Esmyra had never seen before, making her nose turn up.

Esmyra went to reach for a spoon, and Briar gasped from behind her before reaching for it herself and piling food on her plate, making Esmyra's blood boil.

Glancing over her shoulder, she said, "Briar, this isn't necessary. I'm more than capable."

Yet her handmaiden ignored her, a look in her eye making it appear she was pleading for Esmyra to go along with it all.

She turned back around to face Draevyn, whose brows were

furrowed as he poked at some type of tentacle with his fork. When his stare lifted to hers, both of them had to suppress a laugh. He moved his hand to scratch at his beard, covering his mouth before anyone else could see his smirk.

Esmyra fidgeted in her seat, her knee lightly bouncing under the table.

Syrena turned to her. "Esmyra, we're curious to learn more about how you both found your way to Maerinys. And how it is you survived."

The last part was pointed, the queen's eyes flicking briefly to her before settling on Draevyn. Esmyra could feel the council's attention sharpening, their gazes suddenly more intent. They were interested in more than just pleasantries—they wanted answers.

Draevyn leaned back in his chair, as calm and collected as ever, clearly used to these settings, while Esmyra was anything but. "Our paths crossed under...less than ideal circumstances," he began smoothly, as if telling a casual story.

One of the council members, an older man with salt-and-pepper colored hair, leaned forward. "And what might those circumstances be?"

It was then, in that moment, Esmyra decided to keep anything they could a secret. At least for now. They didn't know these people, and were being held in a strange world, miles beneath the sea. She wanted to get to know the one who called her 'sister,' yet her desire to return to the surface was far greater.

"Well?" another man interjected when neither of them responded quickly enough.

Draevyn was watching her, waiting to answer as if he could tell something wasn't right.

Esmyra bit her bottom lip under his gaze, holding back the urge to say something snarky, but she knew she couldn't afford to be reckless. Instead, she forced herself to meet the council's stares. "A shipwreck," she said flatly. "His ship had sunk not far from a small isle and I saved him from drowning."

There was a murmur of interest around the table, the council exchanging glances. Syrena's expression didn't change, though Esmyra could tell she was weighing her words, and she wondered if she could sense the lie.

Draevyn's eyes were burning a hole in the side of her cheek. They hadn't discussed a plan—hadn't had the time. And now they would be forced to go along with whatever they said here and now.

"And why were you in such southern waters, Draevyn?" Syrena asked.

His eyes never left Esmyra. "Was just a merchant sailor exploring new waters, is all," he answered. "Got caught in the tides."

"And what did you believe you would find in waters uncharted for hundreds of years?" Syrena challenged him.

He tilted his head slightly, feigning nonchalance. "Let's just say I had reason to believe there were forces at play in these waters that could shift the balance of power." His eyes seemed to drink Esmyra in. "And as you might imagine, certain people have an interest in keeping such forces in check."

Syrena snorted softly. "I believe what you mean is you were a pirate, hungry for loot and lost gold."

He flashed her a quick grin, one that said *you're not wrong*, but he didn't correct her. "Power, balance, stability—it's all relative, isn't it?"

Esmyra's lips parted at his words, knowing he may as well have taken them right out of her mouth.

The queen's gaze held him for a moment longer before she turned to Esmyra. "And do you always linger in these southern waters, sister?"

She didn't see a reason to lie this time. "No, I don't actually."

"And why were you near here?" The question caught Esmyra off guard, feeling as if this was becoming more of a trial than a dinner among the royal court.

She placed her fork down. "I'm sorry, but why would that matter? Why are we suddenly being questioned so intensely?"

Syrena's back straightened, her tone softening. "Apologies, Esmyra. We didn't mean to make you feel uncomfortable. Simply trying to get to know you both and understand how you found us is all."

Esmyra cleared her throat. "Someone very dear to me was taken, and I was sent here in search of any sign of Maerinys in exchange for his return."

Draevyn's brows furrowed as he listened, taking a sip of something resembling wine. Syrena and the council members all leaned in closer to her.

"However, once I reached the southern waters...I felt a...*pull*," she admitted after a few seconds of silence. "It was like I was being called here. To Maerinys."

The queen offered a closed-lip smile. "Now *that* pleases me greatly."

The council all began whispering among themselves.

"And why is that?" Draevyn asked before bringing his glass to his lips once more. Esmyra kicked him under the table and he didn't even try to hide his grunt.

"That will come." Syrena pursed her lips. "I'm so very sorry someone special was taken from you. Was it a lover?"

"No," Esmyra rushed out. Her stare drifted to Draevyn's, and for some reason, she once again opted for the truth. A truth she still hadn't yet admitted to him. "My father."

Draevyn's face paled the moment the words left her lips, staring at her wide-eyed. Yet, he didn't utter a word, and she was thankful for it.

"Who would kidnap your father, Esmyra?" Syrena asked.

She couldn't help her snarl. "The king of men."

Draevyn swallowed, averting his stare down to his plate.

Syrena studied her for a moment. "And you believe him to be your true sire?"

"No, I don't," she admitted. "He found me a very long time ago and saved me."

Murmurs broke out once more among the council, their expressions turning furious.

"I will have silence," Syrena demanded. She placed her hand gently atop Esmyra's, and it took everything inside of her not to pull away from the caring touch. "Forgive me for what I'm about to say, but your father is a *liar*."

Esmyra's heart twisted painfully as she squared her shoulders. "I know."

She could feel Draevyn's eyes on her, knowing they hadn't so much as blinked since she spoke the word *father*.

"And your father was captured so easily, unable to break free?" Syrena questioned. "Interesting he's survived so long."

Esmyra shook her head. "It was my fault. I left him defenseless and our ship was attacked in my absence." She met Draevyn's unyielding stare. "He was cursed by forces long ago to be tortured if he sets foot on land, but he's immortal."

Syrena's head quickly drew back as her eyes bulged. "Well, we have much to discuss, but it doesn't need to be right now."

Esmyra was taken aback by how dismissive the queen was at the mention of Cyrus's curse.

She glanced around, realizing she was being questioned about her father, yet no other family had presented themselves. "Your par—" Esmyra cut herself off and cleared her throat. "*Our* parents...where are they? Are they here?" Her heart raced, her throat tightening at the thought of meeting them. Of having a mother, and maybe even seeing where her features hailed from.

The queen averted her gaze to her plate. "They perished in the fall."

"Oh," Esmyra whispered, pushing down the ache in her chest as the dream she just imagined shattered within seconds. "I'm so sorry."

"It happened a very long time ago." Syrena took a bite of her kelp salad before blotting her lips with a threaded cloth. "So this alliance formed due to you rescuing him? What of you mentioning him being your captive?" Syrena gestured between her and Draevyn, changing the subject.

*Fuck*, she forgot about that.

"Just a bit of a minor dispute along the way," she muttered under her breath.

Draevyn cleared his throat, sitting up straighter. "Our interests weren't aligned at first, with her wanting to explore the cave due to the pull she felt, and me wanting to search for any passing ships that may allow refuge."

Esmyra's jaw almost fell open at his effortless lies.

"And we may have irritated one another a few times…" He glanced at her again, his grin barely contained as she glared at him.

*Irritated* didn't even do it justice.

"But circumstances have a way of forcing unlikely partnerships," he finished.

"Circumstances being the dangerous creatures guarding your kingdom," Esmyra added, her voice firm.

She wasn't about to let him spin their story however *he* wanted— she intended to remain in control.

Syrena's expression finally shifted, a flicker of seriousness crossing her otherwise composed face. Her golden hair fell atop the table as she leaned in closer to Esmyra. "There's a reason you felt a pull to Maerinys."

"I've assumed as much since the moment we met," she answered, nearly tasting the answers she had craved her entire life. "Being mirrors and all." Esmyra gestured to the teal tattoos adorning their arms before fluttering her fingers toward her face.

Syrena gave her a dip of her chin before her attention turned to her court, who watched them all in silence. "Our guests have had a long day. We should reconvene in the morning."

With those words, the council members all rose as one, chairs scraping against the floor as they silently filed from the room.

It was eerie—they were all essentially onlookers during the entire dinner, and yet still, none of Esmyra's questions were answered. Heat rushed to her cheeks as aggravation crept in, realizing she'd given up information, but Syrena hadn't.

"And what of our questions for you?" Draevyn's voice cut through the tense air like a blade.

The queen turned to him, her eyes narrowing. "Tomorrow is another day. I think this day has been shocking enough for us all. And now that my council has seen that you're truly our lost princess, no one will question your return to us."

Esmyra and Draevyn exchanged a quick glance.

"Briar, will you please escort them back to their chambers so they can get settled?" Syrena asked. "We have much to go over tomorrow. Sleep well, the both of you. I'm eager to see what magic you possess."

Esmyra's eyes roamed over the queen. "Aye. Goodnight, Syrena." She gave her a dip of her chin before following Briar out the door, while Draevyn walked silently at her side.

# CHAPTER 45

# Draevyn

Draevyn lay in bed, staring up at the carved ceiling, the dim merlights from the city beyond glowing through the windows' curtains. The castle felt too quiet, too still. Beneath the surface of the water, everything seemed muted, as if the world had been swallowed whole by the silence of the deep.

But his thoughts were loud, chaotic even.

Lies. All they had given the council were lies, carefully spun to conceal the truth of why they were here. But the truth gnawed at him now—Esmyra had been lying to *him* the entire time.

Cyrus Blackwood wasn't just merely her captain. He was her *father*.

No wonder she was so intent on rescuing him, willing to risk her life for it and refusing to back down even an inch whenever someone challenged her on it. And the curse she spoke of? His mind reeled with everything that could mean.

However, now with even more lies spun in their web with their captors, he couldn't shake the feeling that they were walking on a tightrope, teetering dangerously close to a fall that could be their undoing.

Where they were was impossible—or should've been. How had this kingdom survived, and what was the dome surrounding it?

They weren't here by accident. He was certain of it. Esmyra had mentioned a pull bringing them here, and he witnessed it as it glowed atop her flesh.

She'd nearly killed him when they first crossed paths, and frankly, he had thought about returning the favor more than once. But now... now they were stuck in this uneasy alliance, playing a game neither of them fully understood. And nothing would benefit them if they continued lying not only to their captors, but to each other as well.

Draevyn shifted in the bed, unable to find comfort.

Every fiber of his being screamed not to trust her. She was a pirate, after all—cunning, ruthless, and unpredictable. And she was the worst of them, living by no one's rules but her own. The thought of relying on her, of counting on her to not betray him *again*, was a risk that gnawed at his gut.

And yet...

Draevyn groaned, rubbing a hand over his face. He *wanted* to trust her. Some part of him, buried deep under layers of mistrust, wanted to believe she wouldn't turn on him the second she got what she needed.

Esmyra was fierce, independent, and unwilling to play nice. He respected all of it, even if it made her dangerous.

But it was more than that.

He couldn't ignore the way she looked tonight. The moment she stepped out of her chambers, dressed in flowing robes that he knew made her uncomfortable, but somehow made her look even more untouchable. She wasn't meant for silks and gowns, for the trappings of court life. *That,* he knew. But she had worn it with that same defiant edge that she carried everywhere, like a challenge to anyone who dared underestimate her, playing the part she needed to.

And she was beautiful. The kind of beauty that was wild and raw —nothing like the poised, delicate women of the court he had grown accustomed to.

There was fire in Esmyra—a dangerous allure that made him want to get too close, knowing it would burn.

*Wildfire,* he thought.

Draevyn cursed under his breath. She was too sharp, too dangerous, and he couldn't let the allure of her get to him. Esmyra was nothing but trouble. She was a pirate, and a godsdamn siren on top of that.

But the truth was, she was already under his skin, her talons sinking and clawing at his flesh. Every word she said, every time she shot him one of those scathing glares, it dug a little deeper. She challenged him in ways no one else ever had, and he didn't know how to handle it.

It made him uneasy, restless, and absolutely *craving* her in every way imaginable.

And now, lying in the dark, the quiet pressed in on him, and he could feel it all slipping out of control. The lies, the danger, the woman he desperately wanted to trust, even if he didn't know why.

Perhaps it was because they were both trapped, forced to rely on each other to survive when they were both the most dangerous beings known to all kinds above the surface. Or perhaps it was because, beneath all that fire and defiance, he could see a glimmer of something more to her—something that made him wonder if they weren't so different after all.

"Fucking Irah," he huffed before rolling onto his side.

Every time he closed his eyes, he saw her standing across from him in that damned hall, her eyes blazing and mouth set in a hard line. The sight drove him to near insanity.

Once Draevyn was finally on the edge of sleep, a soft, faint *click* sounded from across the room. His instincts flared instantly, flames rushing to the tips of his fingers as adrenaline surged through his veins. He shot up in bed, eyes wide and alert as he scanned his chambers.

The room was still, bathed in the dim glow of the watery light outside, aside from the tiny ball of fire he held above his palm. But something was wrong, and he sensed he wasn't alone. His pulse quickened as he threw off the covers and silently slid to his feet.

The door to his chambers was still closed, but he knew that sound hadn't been his imagination. He crept forward, his muscles tense as every sense remained heightened.

He didn't give a damn that Esmyra warned him against using his flames while in Maerinys. It was the only means he had to protect himself—and her—against those here.

Then Draevyn saw it—a faint glimmer in the shadows of the window. It was almost impossible to spot, like a ripple in the air. He squinted, his breath catching as he froze while he watched the shimmer shift and take form.

Someone was there, *blending* into the wall like a phantom, its figure barely distinguishable against the stone.

The fireball held above his palm surged as he took a step closer and pulled aside the curtain. His eyes fell to cream-colored clothing that almost blended with the stone wall, shaping to a curvaceous body hidden beneath. The hair on his arms stood sentinel at the threat lurking before him—a dress clinging to a phantom form.

Draevyn's jaw locked as his gaze traced up the camouflaged bodice until his eyes met the vertical slits of ones glacial blue.

"Esmyra." He exhaled sharply, anger flaring.

The siren stepped out from the wall, allowing her skin to shift back into its usual hue. A sharp, almost evil giggle left her, and he extinguished the flame in his hand.

"What the hell are you doing here?" he growled, his voice low but heated.

Draevyn tried to hide his awe at her ability to blend with her surroundings by glaring at her. He'd never seen or heard of anything like it before.

But she just stood there with a wicked grin.

Esmyra's eyes glinted in the low light. "Just wanted to make sure you weren't plotting any betrayal while I was defenseless in my slumber." She placed her hands on her hips.

His jaw clenched. "Funny. Considering you're the one sneaking around in *my* chambers while I was trying to sleep." He took another step toward her. "*Defenseless* is also laughable. Couldn't mind your own business even for one night?"

She narrowed her eyes, her posture still casual but tense. "Mind my own business? You *are* my business. Whether we like it or not, we're stuck in this mess together." She paused, tilting her head, her voice dripping with sarcasm. "Or did you forget that part in between all the lying we did today?"

Draevyn glared at her, the heat flaring in his chest. "Oh, I've forgotten nothing. I'm just curious as to why you're silently prowling through my room in the middle of the night." He pointed toward the door. "Or do you make it a habit of sneaking up on people who are supposed to be your allies?"

Her lips curled into a smirk as he gave her shit right back to her, but there was no humor in it. "You think I trust you just because we made some unspoken truce in front of her court? You're a lot of things, Draevyn Rowe, but trustworthy isn't one of them."

He scoffed. "*Me*? You think I'm the problem here? You're the one who's been keeping secrets since the moment we met. I don't trust you any more than I do your supposedly cursed father, Esmyra *Blackwood*."

Esmyra's eyes flashed with fury, and she took a step closer, her voice dropping dangerously low. "Perhaps I'm here so we can come up with some sort of *actual* plan, yet you're proving useless once more."

"Useless," he echoed with a sharp laugh.

"You don't have to trust me, and frankly, I don't give a damn if you do."

"You've been lying since the moment we met, Esmyra," he snapped, his voice rising. "You want to work together in this? It's clear you're working so hard for my survival to get your father back. It all makes sense now—why fight so hard for your captain back when you were promoted to the title and equally respected by your crew."

She crossed her arms again, her gaze unyielding. "It wasn't your business who Cyrus is to me."

"Does my father know?" he asked.

"Know what?" she spat.

"That Cyrus is your father. Or adoptive father, whatever you consider him."

"Aye." Her stare fell to the floor, her jaw locking. "Though beyond that, nobody knows outside of the crew of *The Night Wraith*."

"So Jak knows then?" The words poured out before he could stop them, and he cursed himself for it. He refused to acknowledge how much her relationship with her first mate bothered him.

She lifted an onyx brow. "Jealousy doesn't suit you, Prince."

A breathy laugh left him. "Jealous? Hardly," he said through his teeth. "The dynamic of your crew is one I've been trying to decipher since I woke up on your ship."

Esmyra shrugged as she moved past him and strode toward his bed, glancing over her shoulder with that infuriatingly seductive smirk. "What is it that you want, Draevyn Rowe?"

Draevyn opened his mouth to respond, but the words caught in his throat. His stare followed her. *You*, he was desperate to say. His pulse quickened at the shock of her being the first thing that came to mind. The word was at the edge of his tongue and he swallowed it before it slipped past his lips.

*Why does she always do this to me?* Every time she walked away like that—so slow, so damn confident—it had become the bane of his existence. The sway of her hips was damn near hypnotic, like she had a direct line to his pulse, and she knew it. Gods, she had to know it.

The way her midnight hair fell loose, brushing her bare shoulders —looking effortlessly lethal. And that dress...clinging to her curves like it was molded to her skin. He could barely breathe as his eyes followed the dip of her waist, the long lines of her tanned legs peeking out through the slits.

Every inch of her was designed to destroy his self-control.

He shouldn't want her, shouldn't even be thinking about her like this. But here she was, walking towards his bed, like it was all a game to her—knowing damn well she was winning.

His hands clenched at his sides. *She's going to be the death of me.*

"What I want is to survive this mess we've found ourselves in. The rest we can figure out later," he finally answered.

Esmyra's gaze fixed on him, as if trying to decipher his words. "Aye."

Draevyn let out a frustrated breath, raking a hand through his hair. "We need to start this over with honesty. If we're going to find our way out of here and help each other, we can't have any more lies and secrets between us, Esmyra."

Her eyes softened, but only for a moment before the hardened edge returned. "Then maybe stop looking at me like I'm your enemy."

*Enemy.* He had to choke back his laugh—this *certainly* wasn't how he looked at enemies.

"Then perhaps you should stop acting like one," he challenged. "I've spent every second since we got here trying to figure out whether you're going to turn on me the second it benefits you."

Her jaw ticked. "Silly me for thinking that bargaining for your release from the dungeons didn't already prove that I have no intention of leaving you to die."

Draevyn stared at her for a long moment, the tension between them crackling like sparking embers. He could see the storm of emotion in her eyes—frustration, fear, something deeper she wasn't ready to show. He didn't trust her, not fully, but he understood that she had even more shocking truths revealed to her in the last day than he had.

"Do you believe all that Syrena said? About your relation to her and this place?" he asked.

Her expression told him that she was rummaging through her brain for an answer, and he wondered if she would feel compelled to lie.

"To be determined," she eventually said. "I'm hoping to learn more tomorrow."

Draevyn let out a huff. "Look, we're both in this deeper than we want to be. But if we're going to survive this, we have to stop treating each other like enemies and start to actually work together. Like true allies."

Her eyes locked onto his, searching for something—maybe truth, maybe some sign that she could lower her guard. But then she squared her shoulders, her hard expression slipping back into place. "Tell me one thing before we make this truce, Draevyn."

He took note of her not including his last name, like she typically did when she was mocking him or trying to get under his skin.

"I need to know the true feelings you have for your father."

He huffed out a bitter laugh. "I believe you already know your answer."

Esmyra took a few steps toward him, until the top of her head was mere inches below his chin. "Aye, but it must be spoken aloud."

Draevyn cleared his throat as he gazed into her sharp, glacial eyes, his mind a whirling mess. He'd never spoken the absolute truth of it before—not even to Atlas, though he knew his brother was aware, along with his crew. But with her, for some reason, speaking the words was almost the easiest decision he ever had to make. This was likely because he knew with every fiber of his being she felt the same way.

"King Rowe is a tyrant, and father or not, Lephyrin and all of Rymelle would be better off without him atop a throne," he admitted. Even though it was considered treason, there was something freeing in the words, as if they unlocked the gilded cage of his princely title.

"The enemy of my enemy is my friend," she whispered, and his eyes flared.

They stood there for a beat longer, staring each other down, neither willing to fully surrender to the uneasy truce between them. However, something in the air had shifted.

Finally, she turned toward the door, her hair swaying behind her. "Next time, lock your door," she teased over her shoulder.

Draevyn put his hands in his pockets as he watched her walk away. "Forgive me for believing locks are unnecessary when there was a guard at the door when I came to bed."

Esmyra pulled the door open and turned to face him, the dim merlights in the hall filtering in and casting her in a subtle glow. "Do forgive them for their inability to perform their duties, Draevyn Rowe... They got caught in a song." She winked. "Goodnight."

Draevyn's eyes fell to the floor—to the two bodies of the guards that were now unconscious on the ground at her feet.

As the door clicked shut behind her, he stood in the middle of the room, heart still racing in his chest. Yet, he couldn't help the smirk that twitched on the edge of his lips as he stared after her.

"Goodnight, Wildfire," he whispered.

CHAPTER 46
*Atlas*

Atlas stood in front of his chamber's mirror, staring at his reflection in the dim candlelight. His royal garb lay discarded on the floor, replaced by the plain, rough-spun tunic and trousers of a commoner among men. Nausea crept in as he slipped on a dark cloak, pulling the hood low over his face.

Tonight, he was no longer the prince and heir to Lephyrin. He was simply a brother—one determined to defy his king's orders.

He had pleaded with his father for days, demanding they send ships to find Draevyn. But the king had been adamant, warning that the act of abandoning his kingdom would be considered treason under his rule. His other son was gone, and he wouldn't allow his heir to chase after him and risk his life.

Atlas didn't give a fuck. He would never believe Draevyn was truly lost. Not without proof. His brother was still out there, somewhere, possibly sitting at the edge of an enemy's blade. And if no one else would go, he would lead the search himself. Atlas had always felt the need to protect Draevyn ever since the day their mother died. He wouldn't let the fact that he had rarely left Lephyrin stop him.

He turned toward his bed, silently looking at his sleeping bride-to-be, her chest rising and falling beneath the covers. Elowynne was

313

unaware of his plans, and she may get angry with him enough to break off their engagement, but it was a risk he was willing to take.

Atlas quietly tiptoed to the edge of their bed before gently pressing his lips to her forehead, brushing her hair away from her face. "Forgive me," he whispered.

And a moment later, he was beyond his chamber's door.

Atlas moved swiftly through the shadowed corridors of the castle, his heart pounding with each step. Moonlight slanted through the windows, pooling silver across the stone corridors, but he kept to the edges of the walls where the torches burned low. His breath was shallow, his pulse quickening as he glanced over his shoulder, half-expecting to see guards rushing after him.

He darted through the narrow halls, avoiding the main passages where the sentries would be posted. Just a few more turns, and he'd be free of the royal quarters.

As he rounded a corner, his footfalls suddenly stilled, a flicker of movement catching his eye.

"Going somewhere, Your Highness?"

The voice had a slight stutter, giving away the man's nerves. Atlas turned to find two guards stepping from a side hall, hands already on the hilts of their swords.

*Flaming balls of Irah.* "You've got to be fucking kidding me," he said under his breath.

"Out for a stroll," he said easily. "The air gets quite stuffy in here, don't you think?"

The taller guard frowned. "At this hour?"

"Have you seen the moon?" He gestured to one of the windows, where its silvery light was pouring through. "It's quite lovely tonight."

The shorter guard sighed, exchanging a look with his companion. "We have orders, Prince. You know you can't leave."

Adrenaline surged through Atlas, and he grinned. "Oh? And what exactly do you plan to do about it?"

They both shifted on their feet. "If you resist, we'll have to—"

Atlas didn't let him finish.

The torches flickered, their light dying out.

Darkness surged, and the shadows at his feet exploded outward, swallowing the corridor whole. The guards barely had time to react before the black tendrils reached for them.

One of them gasped as a shadow coiled around his arms, twisting tight, yanking him back. The other swore, drawing his sword, but it was useless. The shadows curled up the blade, devouring it, climbing to his wrists like living ink.

Their breathing came sharp and erratic as they both began to panic.

Atlas stepped forward, his darkness pressing against his skin, bending to his will. "If you know what's good for you, you never saw me. I was never here."

The guards struggled, and the tendrils curled around their necks, not tight enough to choke—just enough to make them hold still until he was out of sight.

Atlas's stomach twisted, but he forced it down. It wasn't like he was hurting them. He could have done much worse.

Besides, what choice did he have? He had to get to Draevyn, and these men were only in his way by the order of his father.

"Remember who you'll serve as Lephyrin's next crown," he warned, and their eyes widened at the subtle threat.

Would they obey their current king, or would their loyalty move onto the man who would one day wear the crown?

Atlas took off in a run, his magic cloaking him like a wraith in the night as he slipped through the remainder of the castle unseen.

It had been years since he wandered menacingly about the castle in the dead of night, sneaking around as a mischievous boy. He watched as more guards stationed throughout went on alert, sensing something, or someone, was among them, but he easily evaded their gazes and snuck out a window in the staff's kitchen.

The night was quiet, and he moved swiftly through the darkened streets, past the rowdy taverns and merchant stalls, until the familiar scent of saltwater filled his lungs.

The docks stretched out before him, ghostly in the pale moonlight as the fog crept in, rolling off the waves.

As he approached his brother's ship docked in the harbor, he spotted a small group of figures gathered near the gangplank. The crew turned to face him, murmurs of confusion and concern spreading among them.

Once he came to a stop before them, Samwell spoke up. "What's this about, Prince? We're just minding our business."

Atlas's gaze raked over the men. "Still nothing from your captain, I presume?"

"You would assume correctly," he answered. "To what do we owe the pleasure at such an odd hour in the evening?"

Atlas sucked on his tooth, unsure of how to even begin to convince them to defy their king and sail on his orders. "Who is your loyalty to?" he asked.

Samwell and the rest of the crew exchanged wary glances.

"Lephyrin, Prince. Our loyalty is to the Lephyrin crown."

Atlas's eyes darkened as he took a single step closer to the crew. "To who in Lephyrin?"

Samwell's hardened gaze softened. "You're not here on the king's orders, are you, Prince Atlas?" he asked, squaring his shoulders.

"I am not," he admitted.

"And what brings you down to *Valor*, Your Highness?"

Atlas glanced up at the ship, watching as the sails fluttered lightly in the breeze. "I have reason to believe that Draevyn may be in danger, and you and I are the only ones who give a damn about it." He took another step forward, now only standing mere inches from Samwell, towering over him as shadows swirled around his wrists. "So, I will ask you one more time. *Who* in Lephyrin holds your loyalty?"

"My captain," Samwell answered without hesitation, his voice strong. "My loyalty and sword will always be to Captain and Prince Draevyn Rowe."

Atlas grinned. "As is mine." He took a step back, allowing his shadows to retreat into the palms of his hands.

"Now, if you're all to get involved, you should know what you're about to get yourselves into," he started, addressing them all. "The king has declared that searching for Draevyn will be considered a treasonous act, assuming he's lost at sea and the efforts wasted resources. Now, personally, I don't give a damn what the king has said."

Atlas's heart raced as the words left him, but he knew in his soul they were the truth. "My brother is still out there, and I'm going after him. With or without you."

The crew exchanged uneasy glances, but none of them spoke. They had been loyal to Draevyn, but defying their king? It was treason—dangerous ground, even for a crew who didn't necessarily always abide by the law.

Samwell flashed him a toothy grin, not even bothering to take a vote among his men. "As I stated, our loyalty lies with your brother." He looked Atlas up and down. "And our *future* king."

Atlas's eyes widened. Not necessarily because they clearly loathed the king, but that their loyalty was undoubtedly to Draevyn. He was thankful his brother had these men at his side.

"King Rowe is hiding something, and I believe he knows what's happened to Draevyn, and that's why he's trying to hide everything regarding it. The realm will eventually realize a prince is missing, second son or no. I intend to find my brother and bring him back to Lephyrin alive."

A man stepped forward, older by many years. "And if the king finds out we defied his direct orders, we'll be branded traitors. Though I doubt the same goes for you."

"Easy, Tommy," Samwell muttered.

Atlas looked at the crew, his eyes hard as steel. "I'll take full responsibility if it comes to that. But ask yourselves—if Draevyn were here, and one of you were lost, would he just give up? Would he let the king's orders stop him from searching?"

Chuckles rang out among them.

"No, he wouldn't," the man—Tommy—admitted, shaking his head. "Draevyn never left a man behind."

There was a long silence, the sound of the waves lapping against the docks filling the void. Samwell turned to the horizon, where dawn would shortly rise. "When do we leave, Prince?"

Atlas nodded, relief flooding him. "As soon as the ship is ready."

A breathy laugh slipped from Samwell. "Well, we best get going then, shall we?" Without even a glance toward Atlas, Samwell and the crew began walking up the gangplank to board the ship.

"I don't understand…" Atlas called up to them. "*Valor* is ready to sail?"

"She's always ready," was the only answer he received before the sun began its ascent on the horizon.

Once aboard the ship, Atlas looked back toward his kingdom as the wind tousled his dark hair around his face. His eyes fell to the castle, to the highest spire, where he knew the king's chambers were. He grimaced, repulsed by the man he called *Father*.

"We're coming, Drae." The words left him in a whisper as he left Lephyrin for the first time on his own terms, defying the orders of his king.

The next morning, Esmyra woke to the soft glow of merlights filtering through her window, imitating the transition from night to day. Her mind was still clouded, groggy from a restless night, but as she blinked the sleep from her eyes, the memory of everything came flooding back.

Arriving in Maerinys. The dinner. Her and Draevyn's argument.

She groaned and sat up, rubbing her temples. The conversation had been tense, as it typically was, and the frustration still gnawed at her, knowing she would likely have to answer more of his endless questions.

But what stuck with her even more than their exchange was the way his stare had lingered on her. Beneath all the anger and the mistrust, there was something she couldn't quite place in his flame-fueled whiskey eyes—something that unsettled her more than she cared to admit.

She didn't want to think about it, and couldn't afford to. He was still a liability, a reluctant ally at best. The last thing she needed was to be distracted by whatever the hells was going on between them.

Esmyra was more than aware that men noticed her. Though it was rare, she had taken lovers to her bed over the centuries. However, all it took for that to end was one man who made it known he wanted her for nothing more than a position aboard *The Night Wraith*. She never allowed herself to get close to anyone after that—always keeping them a talon's width away.

But she wasn't used to anyone looking at her the way Draevyn had, and she sure as hells wasn't prepared for whatever feelings it stirred.

No. She couldn't let herself go down that path.

*Focus*, she told herself. There were bigger things at stake. They had to find a way out, to escape with the proof they needed before they were tangled up in whatever power struggle was brewing beneath the surface in this sunken kingdom. The lies they'd fed the council were a temporary shield, but they couldn't keep spinning those forever.

They needed a plan, and they needed one fast.

Esmyra knew the next step would be gathering information, seeing how the magic allowed everyone to survive this long. And then there were the matters of the queen—her *twin*—and everything she entailed. Something inside of Esmyra was desperate for the queen to be telling the truth, and all signs pointed to the fact that she was.

Before she could spiral deeper into her thoughts, a soft knock on the door pulled her back to the present. She cursed under her breath, knowing she would never know peace as long as these godsdamn maids were strutting about constantly.

"Come in," she called, her voice still groggy.

The door swung open, and Briar appeared, a smile beaming ear-to-ear. "Good morning, Esmyra. I hope you slept well."

Briar moved to her wardrobe, pulling out an intricate gown that made her cringe inwardly. She'd never get used to this. The silk, the jewels, the soft fabrics—it was all so far removed from her world of leather and salt.

The maiden set the dress down before waltzing into the bathing chambers and began preparing a bath. Esmyra reluctantly stood from her bed and stretched, her muscles still tense from fighting the krechuums, the natives, and the hold of the velsinyte the day before.

Gods, how had all of that only been a day ago?

"Queen Syrena is requesting you at breakfast shortly," Briar announced as she stood in the bathing chamber's doorway.

"Aye," Esmyra sighed, before following her into the room.

Briar worked quickly, guiding her into the bath, and she tolerated it in silence, her thoughts elsewhere.

What would today entail with Syrena? She had so many questions and wasn't even sure if they would be appropriate to ask. How did Maerinys sink? How had they survived? How and why were they separated at birth? The questions and unknowns were endless.

And then her mind flickered back to Draevyn, and the heat of his stare. Warmth pooled in her belly, and she shook the thought from her mind, shuddering as goosebumps prickled her skin.

"Is the water too cold, Esmyra?" Briar asked, startling her.

"No," she rushed out. "It's fine. My mind just...drifted."

She nearly rolled her eyes at herself.

Once Esmyra was bathed and dressed in another robe-like gown, Briar said, "The queen awaits you, my lady. Azarian already accompanies Her Majesty, but if you don't remember the walk to the great hall, I can accompany you and Sir Draevyn."

They were allowing them to roam around together? *Alone?* Thank the gods.

"That won't be necessary. I remember the way," she announced while moving to leave the room.

With every step she took toward her bedchamber door, her mind was a raging storm. Esmyra knew the part she would have to play today—smile when needed, lie when necessary. But as she stepped into the hallway and met Draevyn's gaze as he leaned against the doorframe, she couldn't shake the feeling that everything was about to get significantly more complicated.

Especially with him.

He pushed off the wall, his footsteps falling into sync with hers as they began their walk down the corridor. The silence between them was thick, strained, and she sensed his eyes on her. She ignored it at first, refusing to give him the satisfaction of a reaction. But, of course, he couldn't keep his mouth shut for long.

"I see they've made you their own personal doll once more," he muttered, just loud enough for her to hear. His tone was casual, but there was an edge to it.

Her voice dripped with sarcasm as she said, "Apologies if my skin is distracting to you, Draevyn."

He smirked. "It's just a little strange seeing you dressed like that."

"Trust me, this isn't by choice," she admitted, pulling at the sage fabric of the gown with obvious distaste. "But since we're playing this little game, might as well look the part."

Draevyn was silent for a moment. "Though I suppose you've always been a bit of a chameleon, blending in where you wouldn't otherwise. A whore in a tavern. A lady of nobility at a ball. A pirate..." His words trailed off. "A fucking *wall*."

Esmyra couldn't help the sharp laugh that left her. "Perhaps I just prefer to keep people on their toes."

Draevyn let out a low hum, almost as if in agreement, but there was an underlying tension to his words when he spoke again. "You should be careful, though. People are watching. Especially Syrena." He glanced at her, his voice lowering. "Don't let them see you as something you're not."

Her steps faltered as annoyance shot through her veins. "And what's that supposed to mean?"

His eyes flicked down the hall, then back to her, his expression turning serious. "I'm saying...we've got enough to deal with without them thinking you're some perfect little princess they're clearly trying to paint you as. They'll use it against you. And I don't trust any of them. Especially not your sister." The way he said *sister* made it clear he didn't believe it for a second.

The weight of his words settled over Esmyra, and for a moment, she considered them. But before she could respond, his gaze lingered on her a bit too long, something almost possessive flickering behind his eyes.

It wasn't the first time she'd noticed it—how he watched her, or how he tensed whenever she met his stare.

"Don't get too comfortable. I don't want you to see this as something it's not," he added, his voice a bit gruffer, as if he was warning himself as much as her.

She let out a sigh as her eyes narrowed on him, earning a small grin. "Aye."

They continued walking, the tension between them palpable, until they reached the grand doors of the dining hall. Two guards, clad in shimmering, scale-like armor, opened the doors without a word, revealing the grand breakfast spread laid out before them.

The room was even more elaborate than she remembered from the night prior, the table long and set with enough food to feed her entire crew—fruits she had never seen before, platters of seafood arranged in beautiful displays, and cups filled with something that sparkled like liquid gold.

Syrena sat at the head of the table. Her eyes gleamed as they entered, a soft smile on her lips. "Ah, you're here. Good morning," she greeted, her voice smooth. "Please, sit. We have much to discuss."

Esmyra and Draevyn took their seats without saying a word, and the queen's attendants began serving them immediately. Esmyra halted her scoff, remembering she had to play the part.

Syrena clasped her hands together, her gaze flicking between them. "I trust you slept well?"

"I've had better nights," Draevyn muttered under his breath, earning a sudden snort from Esmyra. She kicked him under the table as she tried to reel in her amusement.

Syrena's smile didn't falter, though there was a subtle tightening around her eyes. "I apologize for my palace not being what you're accustomed to aboard your ship, Sir Draevyn." Her words trailed off as her doe eyes looked him up and down from across the table. "Perhaps you can take a nap while I take Esmyra."

A low sound, almost growl-like, brewed in Draevyn's chest. "And where will you be taking her?"

Esmyra's head subtly tilted to the side at his sudden overbearing protectiveness—acting as if she wasn't just as powerful as he was.

Syrena took a sip of the bubbling, golden liquid in her glass before saying, "I don't think that's necessary for a common sailor to know. However, I assure you, she's in safe hands."

Esmyra didn't appreciate the way either of them were speaking of plans regarding her. Her lip curled back. "And what exactly do these plans entail?"

Syrena turned her full attention to her. "We'll be delving into your magic today and you will learn more of Maerinys. That is, of course, if you desire."

Esmyra blinked. "What does that mean?"

The queen leaned back in her chair. "You and I share a bond, a unique connection to this kingdom and its magic. But there is much we still don't know about your potential. I have...ways of exploring that, of helping you tap into what lies dormant within you. I've been one with Maerinys since our birth, while you've been beyond the surface. I would like to see what kind of power you hold."

"You believe she has *more* power within her?" Draevyn asked with a raised brow as he met Esmyra's stare, who assumed her face appeared just as confused as his.

"What do you mean, you have ways to explore that?" she asked.

"Nothing to fear," Syrena said lightly, though her tone was anything but reassuring. "With time, we'll discover just how powerful you truly are. But that requires trust."

*Time.* That was something she certainly didn't have.

Esmyra exchanged a quick glance with Draevyn once more, feeling his unease radiating beside her. They both knew *trust* was a word that carried weight between the two of them, and neither gave it freely.

Syrena must've sensed where her mind wandered. "You have nothing to fear. We're bound by the same blood. I have no reason to harm you. In fact, I want nothing more than to see you grow into your true potential."

Her words were sweet, but they left a bitter taste in Esmyra's mouth. Everything in this life was a game—politics, power, manipulation—and she had always been someone's pawn. But, for now, she had no choice but to play along, to keep her cards close, and wait for the right moment.

Esmyra took a bite of the odd-looking fruit atop her plate and leaned back in her chair as she stared at her twin. "Well, if there is more to the powers within me, I assume it would be best to delve into them where they originated," she said carefully between bites, refusing to break eye contact.

"I'm so glad we agree, Esmyra," Syrena replied as she gracefully stood from her seat. "Maerinys has always thrived on unity. Divided, we fall, after all."

*Divided we fall.* Those words settled into her, and she couldn't help but think they had a deeper meaning.

Draevyn's hand brushed Esmyra's knee, and she froze at the sudden heat of his touch. She turned and met his stare, and found flames thrashed behind his irises—a silent acknowledgment of their shared suspicion.

"Esmyra, let's take a walk and I'll show you more of Maerinys and answer any questions you still have." She turned to Draevyn. "As for you, do try to stay out of trouble. I would hate to have to waste resources and have guards on you at all times." A smile tilted her lips, but it didn't meet her eyes.

"That won't be necessary," Esmyra interrupted, a bit of challenge in her voice that earned her sister's curiosity. "He's trustworthy."

She swallowed thickly, knowing the weight of the words she spoke.

"Excellent," was all Syrena said before she guided Esmyra out of the room, leaving Draevyn behind in the empty, great hall of the castle.

Their footsteps echoed through the castle halls as Syrena led Esmyra through the winding passages. The tension from breakfast still lingered, and she followed a step behind in silence. Esmyra scanned the endless stream of delicate carvings and murals along the walls, trying to piece together the history of Maerinys.

"You can ask me questions, you know," Syrena broke the charged silence. She turned to face Esmyra, her golden waves flowing around her shoulders. "I apologize if I wasn't as kind to your companion as I should have been. It's just that..."

"He's a stranger," Esmyra finished for her, still watching the walls as they passed.

Syrena cleared her throat. "Indeed. We just...we've been down here for so long on our own, and trusting strangers isn't exactly easy. We don't even *know* any strangers aside from him. It's just been those down here since the sinking."

"And what of me, then?" Esmyra's steps halted, forcing Syrena to do the same. "You don't know me any more than you know him."

Syrena's eyes softened. "But I do. You're my sister."

"Aye, but blood doesn't mean you know who I am." And it was true—Esmyra recognized that she didn't know a godsdamn thing about Syrena. Not her motives, who she was behind closed doors, or anything outside of the queen she'd seen over the last day.

Syrena smirked before continuing their walk, forcing her to follow.

Esmyra was taken aback by the sudden dismissal, and irritation swirled in her chest. "Perhaps I'm a horrible being who has done many wretched things."

It wasn't a lie—in fact, it may have been the most truthful thing she'd said since they met.

"Whatever you've done, you were forgiven upon your arrival in Maerinys."

A crease formed in Esmyra's brow. "With all due respect, Syrena, you don't know what I've done. And unfortunately, I'm quite confident that much of it is considered unforgivable."

"We all do things in order to survive," Syrena admitted without turning back to face her.

And with those words, silence fell upon them once more.

As they ascended a spiral staircase, the walls seemed to shift. The light grew dimmer, and the air felt cooler against her skin. They climbed higher and higher until the queen pushed open a set of intricately carved doors, revealing a vast, circular room that made Esmyra pause.

The first thing that caught her eye was the brickwork—the walls of the tower were made of a dark grey stone that shimmered faintly in the low merlights. Massive windows stretched from floor to ceiling, showing an unbroken view of Maerinys, and the ocean beyond the dome—the endless blue stretching out in every direction.

It was both breathtaking and unnerving.

A basin unlike any she'd ever seen stood in the center of the room. Even from where Esmyra stood in the doorway, she could see that the water was perfectly still. It mimicked liquid glass, reflecting the room like a flawless mirror.

"This," Syrena began as she walked in, "is one of the oldest rooms in the kingdom. It's sacred to our family." She moved slowly toward it, her fingers trailing lightly over the surface of the water. "I can see this has already caught your eye."

Esmyra finally took a step into the room, her neck craning as her gaze traced up the walls, before finally falling back to the enchanted basin in its center. "I can feel the magic here. It's pulsating, pressing against my skin." She pointed to the pool of still water her sister stood next to. "Is it because of that?"

A subtle hum resonated through every vein in her body.

"We call it the Veil of Visions. It shows truths when you need them, lies when you crave them, and everything in between."

*Lies.* The word seeped into Esmyra, and her gut twisted into painful knots, not knowing if Syrena had already used this on her the moment she and Draevyn were escorted back to their chambers last night.

Syrena's gaze remained fixed on the water as she continued. "Our kingdom once thrived above the surface, a prosperous land full of life and power. But as with all powerful empires, we were not without enemies."

Esmyra couldn't find the words to speak, too indulged in the history she could sense her sister was about to unveil to her. The story she craved more than anything. The history of *herself* and where her blood stemmed from.

The queen's eyes lifted to meet hers. "The gods turned against us. Our power was seen as too great, too dangerous. And so, we were cast down, drowned by the very forces that brought the realm and its four territories to be. Our kingdom was lost beneath the sea, buried in silence and darkness."

An icy chill ran along Esmyra's spine. "And that's why Kaelypso and Naerysa abandoned their children? They believed us to be too powerful?"

The warmth vanished from Syrena's eyes, suddenly turning cold. "Did I say it was our own goddesses who betrayed us?" Her head tilted to the side in challenge, and the resemblance to Esmyra herself was so striking that it took her aback, as if she were staring at her reflection.

"Are you saying the other gods betrayed our own, and, in turn, destroyed Maerinys?" Esmyra asked.

Syrena stepped up to her and twirled a lock of Esmyra's midnight hair around her finger. "I knew you would catch on quickly."

Esmyra's lips curled back, and in her anger, her fangs slipped out, but Syrena's eyes only lit with satisfaction. "Why would they do that? The realm was balanced," Esmyra said.

She couldn't think of a reason for gods to betray one another. If they sought more power, why hadn't the rest of them turned on each other? And why did they all hide behind a veil now? Only coming to their people's aid if offerings were brought to their temples.

The realm believed the gods were to remain hidden—unseen and untouched—to avoid another tragedy like Kaelypso's and Naerysa's disappearance, but she now questioned everything the realm's history stated.

"Power rivals power. However, the gods' betrayal wasn't enough to destroy us. We adapted and survived. Our magic—*your* magic— runs deeper than anything in all of Rymelle, for it is the sea itself." She paused, watching Esmyra. "We found our place here, beneath the waves, where no enemy could ever reach us again."

Esmyra swallowed, desperately trying to absorb everything the queen of this underwater world revealed to her. "And this is where you wish to remain? Where you wish for *me* to remain with you?"

She dreaded the answer, having a feeling she knew what it would be. Esmyra would never be able to stay down here, *live* down here, while her father rotted in a cell for all eternity. She couldn't do that to him, would never—no matter how badly she may want to see what this world could be to her.

Syrena glanced back at the fountain. "Survival came with a price. We've been cut off from the surface for generations. The mortals among us morphed, their skin turning to scales as years passed, their lives preserved by the dome of magic."

That must've been why she didn't recognize the native creatures. They weren't known to the realm above, created by the depths they were condemned to.

"Those who were native to Maerinys survived as they always were, accustomed to the abyss that's now become our home," Syrena continued, snapping Esmyra from her thoughts. "Our power may be great, but it's confined down here. And we no longer wish to remain in the depths. That's where *you* come in."

Esmyra blinked, the queen's words settling over her like a net closing in. "What do you mean, where *I* come in?"

Syrena's eyes gleamed, clasping her hands behind her back before taking a step up to Esmyra. "You're a crucial piece of this kingdom's legacy, a piece of the puzzle we have been missing. Your powers, unshackled, could set us free."

Esmyra stood frozen, her heart pounding a frantic rhythm.

Her sister grabbed her hands and held them gently in her own before she continued. "*You* are the key to breaking our chains."

Esmyra's gaze hardened, her brows furrowing as she ripped her hands from Syrena's grasp. "I'm sorry, but this isn't possible."

"And why do you think that?" Syrena's head cocked to the side in curiosity.

"My powers, while different from those above the surface, only coincide with the sea."

"That's not true. There are no others here in Maerinys whose powers match your own, aside from myself. And even then, we may be different."

Esmyra's eyes flickered nervously, unable to focus as her thoughts spiraled. "How is any of this possible?" The words were barely above a whisper.

Syrena smiled, though it was cold, almost calculating. "Oh, dear sister. *Anything* is possible. Maerinys should be proof enough for that. We'll explore your abilities, and in doing so, we may find a hope for the survival of our people."

Unease, curiosity, and even a flicker of hope warred within Esmyra, though an inner voice warned her, screaming this wasn't right.

"Survival?" she asked, her voice quiet. "Why does the kingdom's survival rely on my powers if you possess the same?"

Syrena's smile faded, her eyes sharpening fiercely. "Our kingdom has always been one with the sea, but we've been condemned to it in a way that no longer allows us to thrive, but to suffocate, cut off from the rest of the world. Food is scarce and emotions have run high for many years. What was once our home has now become our prison. I believe, sister, that with our combined powers, we may finally have the strength to bring it back to the surface. To raise Maerinys from the depths, free from the gods' curse."

*Food is scarce.* They were starving down here, just as those were in the streets of Lephyrin—only their leader cared. *Syrena* cared for her people, unlike King Rowe.

Esmyra swallowed thickly, her throat tightening as she took it all in. "Would this not defy the gods who placed you here?"

Syrena's brow rose. "You fear hidden gods?"

"Kaelypso and Naerysa have been lost just as long as Maerinys has been. If it was the other gods who—"

"Kaelypso and Naerysa are not lost," Syrena cut her off. "They are simply bound to this curse, just as we are."

Esmyra's jaw fell open. "They're alive?"

"They are," she answered, her gaze softening. "There's so much you don't know, Esmyra. So many lies have been spoken regarding our kingdom. Truth lost in destroyed texts while lies were whispered above the tides. But now that we're finally reunited, we can bring our truth to light."

"Our truth," Esmyra echoed, though it was more a question than a statement.

Syrena reached for Esmyra's hand once more. The warmth of her sister's palm against her own sent a strange sensation through her, unable to deny the sudden surge of power that came with their intertwined fingers. It was akin to a bolt of lightning coursing over her skin.

"You may feel like an outsider here, as though you've been cast into a world that isn't yours. But our power was meant to be united," Syrena said. "Alone, neither of us could raise Maerinys from the depths. It would take an extraordinary amount of power that no one being can bear. But together...together, we may finally break the hold that binds us."

The siren within her purred, startling her.

Esmyra always believed there was a monster lingering beneath her flesh, but she had told herself it was because of what the realm had made her out to be—what her father had turned her into and used her as. But to learn she could be something *more* had a flicker of hope flaring in her chest, as if this stranger's words had lifted a weight she hadn't realized she bore for centuries.

The queen stepped closer, her golden blonde waves bouncing with the movement. "Together, we can end our exile. We will learn to wield our magic. And with that power, Maerinys will rise again. And the realm's balance will be restored."

*Together.* The word was foreign to her. Amidst a lifetime of isolation, she finally met someone who understood her—understood that dark loneliness.

Syrena walked around the Veil of Visions fountain and met Esmyra's gaze, mirroring smirks adorning both of their faces. The queen reached out her hand and held it above the pool of water. "What say you, Esmyra Aeress..." The use of the royal name attached to her sent a jolt through her body, as if replacing *Blackwood* erased everything she had done in several lifetimes. All her wicked deeds and sins. "Will you help me save our people?"

Esmyra's stare lingered on Syrena, feeling as though the moment she agreed, nothing would ever be the same again.

What first started as a rescue mission for her father had suddenly turned into so much more—a hunt for her identity and the answers to all she ever sought.

She reached her hand out, levitating it alongside her sister's above the pool. "Aye," Esmyra answered in a whisper.

Her eyes flared the moment their hands met. A surge of energy ignited between them once more, powerful and unyielding. Lightning crackled in the air, and sparks of energy shot through the room, lacing through the walls, the floor, and into the very stones.

The basin in the center swirled violently, its glassy surface breaking apart, creating a whirlpool. Tendrils of light rose from it like streams of water, curling and twisting in the air, wrapping itself around their locked arms.

Esmyra was speechless, her eyes wide, as a rush of magic coursed through her veins, electrifying her with a surging power that left her breathless.

And then suddenly, everything halted when she pulled her hand back into her chest with a small gasp. The tendrils of light went out, the rattling ceased, and the energy dimmed, leaving Esmyra's body exhausted.

Chest heaving, she locked eyes with Syrena once more. "What in all gods was that?!"

A feline smile curled Syrena's lips. "That, dear sister, is proof that this is only the beginning."

Draevyn watched as Esmyra left with Syrena willingly, but even he knew she didn't have a choice in the matter. She likely felt just as much a prisoner down here as he did. Draevyn couldn't shake the feeling that the queen of the depths wanted Esmyra for something. He didn't entirely buy the "lost sister" nonsense she fed them, and he hoped to find an answer somewhere in the castle.

Once he noticed he was alone, curiosity and suspicion drove him to wander about the castle, searching for anything that might help him find an escape. Each corridor of the fortress led to another twist, another turn, until he finally faced a pair of elaborate double doors.

Draevyn glanced down both ends of the hall, realizing he hadn't seen a single guard. He found it odd, but he wasn't accustomed to the life down here. It was likely normal considering Maerinys was so small, doubting anyone ever dared defy their queen.

The doors were heavy, reinforced with gilded coral and seashells, and with a hard push, they creaked open. His eyes widened as he stepped into an enormous library that could rival that of any other kingdom—even his own.

The room stretched endlessly, shelves climbing high along the walls in perfectly organized rows, filled with scrolls, leather-bound books, and strange artifacts that shimmered in the low merlight filtering in from stained glass windows.

"Holy Irah," Draevyn breathed, his steps echoing in the vast chamber.

A strange stillness filled the room, and it seemed as if no one had set foot in it for years—centuries even. He wondered how much information was hidden down here, lost to the kingdoms above.

Trailing a finger along a dusty shelf, his eyes caught on a book placed on a podium beneath a far window. His brows furrowed as he made his way to it. The book was thick and ancient-looking—its binding as smooth as polished stone. The title was written in a language he didn't recognize, and yet he felt an eerie familiarity with it.

*Runes*, he realized. Everything down here led back to the markings on her flesh.

Draevyn picked up the book and walked to the nearest table, taking a seat at its head before carefully flipping through the pages. The parchment was delicate, covered in diagrams and script detailing rituals, ancient stories, and the history of a place lost long ago.

*Maerinys*. He traced his fingers over an intricate drawing of the kingdom as it had been, standing proudly above the water, just south of Lephyrin.

There were pages with ink so faded he couldn't make out the words, though the drawings accompanying them appeared to picture the kingdom's descent into the sea. The further he flipped through the book, the darker the ink became, as if it were new. As he skimmed, he realized the pages described the gradual transformation of its people—mortals who now had fins protruding from their flesh.

Turning the page, he came across a section devoted to ancient rulers—kings and queens of Maerinys' past. And there, sketched with careful detail, was the unmistakable face of the woman who haunted both his sleeping and waking dreams.

She looked ageless, her piercing gaze haunting even on paper— and on the next page was one to match.

*Esmyra and Syrena.*

His jaw tightened, suspicion deepening. She hadn't told him everything. How would they have a portrait of her in a library long forgotten? Esmyra had been here—she *must've* been. Though her lies were very convincing. However, this book was essentially useless to him if he couldn't fucking read it, and he didn't trust anyone enough to ask to translate.

Draevyn slammed the book shut in frustration.

A faint tremor ran through the floor, making the library's silence feel suddenly ominous. His head snapped up, glancing around the room. At first, he thought it might be his imagination, but then the shelves began to rattle, scrolls slipping off in waves, tumbling onto the floor. The chandeliers overhead swayed, their jewels chiming together as they collided.

*What in all gods?!* His neck craned as he glanced in all directions, watching the room come undone by forces unseen.

The tremor grew stronger, rolling through the walls and floors as if something vast and ancient were stirring awake. He stood, steadying himself against a nearby shelf, but his instincts screamed this was no simple earthquake.

His eyes flew to the doors, where the symbols etched into its wood seemed to glow faintly, reacting to the pulse of energy that filled the air.

An uneasy feeling clawed at his mind. "Fuck. Esmyra!"

He didn't know where she was, but he knew something had to have happened to her. This felt similar to what happened in the cave, and he knew how helpless she had been when the power took over her body—she was nothing but a vessel to the magic she held.

Draevyn ran toward the doors to find her. Then, just as suddenly as it began, the tremor slowed, fading until the library returned to its eerie stillness, making his steps falter. Dust floated in the air, and scattered books lay strewn about the floor. He stayed tense, his hand still gripping the book he had pulled off the podium, heart racing as he glanced around.

Voices sounded in the hall, snapping his attention back to the door he was mere feet from now. He ran to the nearest aisle of shelves and hid, sweat slicking down his back at the undeniable sensation that he was in a place they wouldn't want him to be.

The door creaked open, and Draevyn peered around the shelves to get a better look. He watched as Azarian and another guard stormed through the doors. They were looking for something—or someone.

"He doesn't seem to be in here," the guard said. "The tremors caused a mess, though."

Azarian let out a huff. "Find him. Now that we know everything will work, I don't want him wandering about unsupervised. He vanished from the great hall before we could watch where he went. He's to believe he has free rein to go wherever he pleases, so we must be discreet. We don't need anything getting in Syrena's way. This is vital."

A low growl brewed in Draevyn's chest as he listened. He *knew* the queen lied, and now he had the proof. What he needed to figure out next was whether or not Esmyra was in on it with her.

Azarian scanned the room once more. "And get someone in here to clean this up once you find him. I want every tome and book accounted for."

And with those words, he turned on his heel and stormed out of the library, the guard following behind.

Draevyn glanced down at the book in his arms, thinking the knowledge he'd stumbled upon was dangerous, perhaps even deadly. He stalked back across the room and placed the book back on the podium, praying it was still there once he returned with Esmyra.

He slipped from the library into the corridor, keeping his steps light as he listened for anyone near. But just as he rounded a corner, the two guards appeared, blocking his path.

"Ah, there you are," Azarian said, his voice edged with a false cheeriness. "You must return to your quarters at once."

Feigning surprise, Draevyn raised a brow, the heat of his flames dancing at the edge of his fingertips, begging to be used. "Is there an issue?"

The second guard's face tightened, but he forced a polite nod. "It's for your safety. We've experienced...structural tremors in this part of the castle. They've happened from time to time since the sinking. We're investigating to make sure the halls are secure."

He held their gazes, keeping his sense of confusion and casual interest. "So it wasn't my imagination then."

The first guard's eyes flickered, and he gave a stiff, guarded smile. "I assure you everything is under control, but for your safety, it would be best to return to your chambers until the events have ceased."

"Events?" Draevyn echoed, letting just the faintest hint of curiosity slip into his voice.

"Nothing you need to worry about." Azarian's face remained impassive. "As he said, it's for your safety."

The unnamed guard aggressively grabbed Draevyn by the arm and pulled, working to guide him back to his quarters.

*Absolutely fucking not.* Draevyn shoved out of his hold, but a small flame burst to life in his palm the moment it touched the man's flesh.

"Fuck!" the guard bellowed in pain.

Draevyn squeezed his eyes shut, cursing himself as his heart raced rapidly. When he opened his eyes, his stare fell to the bubbling, burned skin on the male's forearm—an imprint of Draevyn's hand.

*Fuck* was right.

The two guards drew their weapons instantaneously, their eyes darting back and forth between Draevyn and the burn.

"Show me your hands!" Azarian barked. "Now!"

Draevyn held his palms out before him. He was the only known fire-wielder in all of Rymelle, so he prayed to Irah himself that the males would disregard his burning touch as something else.

Azarian grabbed Draevyn's wrist, turning it over and inspecting it, running the pads of his fingers along his palm. "It's not hot." Their stares met, and he took a step back, pointing to his soldier's arm. "Why did that just happen?!"

"I don't know," Draevyn lied through clenched teeth, fists shaking at his sides as his temper continued to slip.

"You possess magic!" the guard yelled.

"I do *not*," Draevyn snapped, lip curling back as he considered turning them both to ash.

But then he would need to run. And he didn't know where Esmyra was or if she would be punished for his actions.

"I'm not going anywhere until you tell me where she is."

"Our queens' whereabouts are not your business," Azarian snapped as he pressed the tip of his spear to Draevyn's chest.

Draevyn lifted his arms in a mock surrender. "I don't give a damn where Syrena is. I want to make sure the woman I arrived with is safe. Where is *Esmyra*?"

A cruel grin formed on Azarian's face as he lowered his spear. "As I stated, Sir Draevyn...our *queens'* whereabouts are not your concern."

It was then Draevyn realized he meant plural. They considered Esmyra a lost queen.

"Fucking Irah." The curse left him in a growl.

"You will not speak that name here!" Azarian snapped, an odd aura seeming to exude from him that had Draevyn's brows creasing. "Now you can accompany us back to your chambers, or it's back to the dungeons you go. Especially after *that* little incident." He pointed to the other male's sizzling flesh.

Draevyn could tell Azarian was practically begging for him to slip up again, wanting nothing more than to throw his ass back behind bars, but he refused to give the male that satisfaction. No matter how badly his fingers ached to set him on fire and watch him burn.

Draevyn gestured down the hall. "After you." Forcing a false smile on his face, he allowed himself to be led, but his mind was turning over every word the guards had said.

They were hiding something—*all* of them—and it seemed that the tremors were only the beginning.

Hours later, Draevyn's mind was churning over everything he'd seen and heard.

Syrena's motives, the guards' lies, the tremors—he knew there was more to this place than the glimmering facade they'd been shown in the last two days. He also didn't know if he should tell Esmyra about burning the male's arm. They didn't throw him back in the dungeons, seeming to still believe he didn't possess magic. Surely something would've happened by now if they knew he was lying.

Suddenly, his door burst open with a crash. Draevyn's heart leapt in his throat as he saw Esmyra standing there, breathless and wide-eyed. Her hair was a mess of midnight waves, face flushed as if she'd run the entire way there.

Every muscle in Draevyn's body tensed. "What's happening? Is everything alright?!"

Ignoring his words, she shut the door behind her, a swirling storm in her eyes. "We need to talk. You won't believe what just happened, or where I've been."

He studied her, trying to read the emotion flickering in her gaze. "Well, spit it out, Blackwood," he said, carefully neutral, though a knot formed in his gut.

She lifted a brow at the use of her last name as she stormed toward him, her gown flowing behind her. "Did you feel it?! I don't know how you couldn't have."

"The tremors?"

"Yes!" she nearly gasped, an odd look of excitement on her face he had never seen. She no longer appeared the guarded, tense woman he had come to know, but now as someone else entirely—someone lighter.

"We did it," she said, voice almost reverent, as if she didn't believe her own words. "Those tremors—that *power*—it was us. Syrena and myself."

Draevyn watched her intently. "As in, a combined power?"

"Yes!" she said on a breath as she walked around him and fell back onto his bed, her hair sprawled out in all directions.

He warily approached her. "Where were you? What happened?"

If she was this excited, he didn't know if it would be wise to tell her of what happened in the library or not.

"Syrena and I...we're going to bring Maerinys back to the surface. I think—no, I *know* we can do it."

"Wait, what the fuck are you talking about?" His jaw fell open, brows furrowed in utter confusion. "What do you mean raise Maerinys? That's impossible."

Esmyra sat up quickly. The scorned look that typically graced her face returning. "They're starving down here, Draevyn."

"What exactly did she tell you?"

Esmyra stood and began to pace, her hands moving animatedly as she spoke. "Syrena brought me to this tower. It must've been the tallest spire of the castle…" She began rambling, and Draevyn's head turned with every movement she made, trying to follow her story. "The energy was everywhere, like nothing I've felt before. She said if we could unlock our power's full potential together, Maerinys would rise again."

He struggled to ignore the thrill in her voice, the excitement that seemed to bubble over in every gesture. She looked at him, waiting for some reaction, but his thoughts were racing in the opposite direction. Esmyra was convinced, maybe even *enchanted* by Syrena's words regarding this kingdom and the history of the gods, but every instinct he had screamed that something was wrong.

Draevyn took a step up to her, his eyes never leaving hers. "You think she's telling you everything?" he asked quietly. "That this isn't just a ploy?"

Esmyra stopped pacing, her brows knitting together. "A ploy for what? She's the queen of a lost people, and they won't survive down here much longer. They're suffocating—starving! She needs my help." She pointed to her chest on the last few words, eyes pleading. "This is my chance to prove I'm not the monster everyone believes me to be. This is my chance to do something good."

*Something good.* He knew the need for that all too well.

Draevyn ran a hand over his jaw, shaking his head. "Do you really believe that?"

"I do," she answered without hesitation. "If she could do it on her own, then why wait for me? Knowing there was a possibility I could never find my way back home."

"Home," he echoed in a whisper, ignoring the bitter taste the word brought to his tongue. It was then he knew that Syrena had already sunk her talons deep into Esmyra. All it took was a false show of familial love and an understanding of who she was.

What Draevyn hadn't told her was that, with each passing moment, *he* understood who she was.

"Yes," she said, a snarl working its way across her lips. "Maerinys was always supposed to be my home."

"Esmyra, this place, these people—they're hiding something from us. Haven't you noticed how the guards are watching us, how no one seems willing to let us out of their sight? Even when they state we're alone...we aren't."

He purposefully used Azarian's words.

Esmyra took a step toward him, folding her arms stubbornly. "Aye. A bit paranoid, aren't we, Draevyn Rowe? I understand you're used to being the one in charge, since you're of royal lineage, and if that makes you uneasy—"

"Uneasy?" he interrupted, his voice sharper than intended. "This has nothing to do with that, and if it hasn't been made clear to you before, let it be laid before us here and now. I am *not* royalty in the eyes of Lephyrin's crown."

Her head reared back. Understanding flashed across her face, but it was there and gone in only a moment.

"This place is flooded with secrets they won't share, no matter how much she plays the devoted sister," he began again. "How can you trust her so easily? It's barely been two fucking days!"

Esmyra bit her bottom lip, averting her gaze from his. The veins in her neck strained, and he was thankful it seemed he had reached some part of her. Though seeing the light in her eyes dim once more caused a sharp ache in his chest he couldn't ignore.

"Syrena understands me," she whispered. "I wouldn't expect you to know what it feels like to be so isolated...so..."

"Alone," he finished for her. Another feeling he knew all too well.

It was at that moment that he realized Esmyra wasn't the one lying—it was all Syrena. Esmyra didn't understand her powers, and regardless of the fact there was somehow a portrait of her in the castle, he believed her—her desperation to learn everything of her past.

Her chest rose and fell in quick breaths as she watched him curiously. "Syrena possesses the same powers as me, and if she knows a way to understand it further, then I have to trust it."

Draevyn stepped into her, lifting his hand to brush his knuckles across her cheek. The gesture was intimate, and he didn't know what possessed him to do it. Her lips parted at his touch, and to his surprise, she didn't scoff or pull away from him.

"If what she's said so far is the truth, it took *gods* to sink Maerinys," he started. She opened her mouth to speak, but he pressed on. "You don't know what you're agreeing to." His voice softened.

The spark of defiance in her eyes faded slightly, replaced by a flicker of uncertainty, but it didn't last long. She lifted her chin. "I know what I felt and the potential of what we can do. And if you're too afraid to believe that, then stay here. But I've made my choice. She will teach me to further understand my powers and what we can do together, and if you can't accept that, then you are *once again* in my way."

A thought crossed his mind then. He didn't know how long they would be trapped in Maerinys, but what he was certain of was the more time Esmyra spent with her sister, the further she would be pulled away from him. He also knew the more he pressed her now, the less he would likely ever know.

Their relationship was fragile—too fragile for him to risk pushing her to the edge.

She spun on her heel, already heading for the door, but he reached out and caught her wrist. "If you train with her, then also train with me," he breathed, his eyes searching hers as she turned to face him. "You may think you're making a choice, but this place...it's choosing for you. Don't let it."

Esmyra ripped her wrist from his grasp and took a threatening step toward him. "What do you mean, *train* with you? Our magic is polar opposites, and you can't use yours down here. They believe you to be mortal, remember?"

He shrugged a shoulder. "Who said anything about magic? We wouldn't be training with that at all. As time has shown, you rely on yours *far* too much. They have velsinyte down here, which we still don't understand how or why. If you wish to roam about with a long-lost sister, I would feel better if you knew how to defend yourself."

"I wasn't aware my well-being was any concern of yours."

The sass in her tone had him grinning. *There's that wildfire.*

"It would help if my one ally in this place were useful in times of danger." He winked.

For a moment, they held each other's gaze, unspoken words hanging between them.

Esmyra's spine straightened. "Well, it appears everyone around here wishes to exhaust me in any way they can."

Draevyn could certainly find ways to exhaust her further, but he wouldn't dare voice those thoughts. Heat rushed to his cheeks, his cock hardening as it pressed against his pants.

He cleared his throat. "When do you plan to train with her again?"

She shrugged. "Daily, perhaps? I would assume sometime after breakfast, just as we had today."

"Then we start tomorrow at dawn," he announced. "Meet me in that pretty little courtyard we walked through our first day."

Esmyra rolled her eyes in response.

"Unless you're afraid," he added.

A wicked giggle slipped from her. "Oh, I fear nothing." She turned on her heel and slipped out the door, poking her head in one last time before saying, "I'll see you at dawn, Draevyn Rowe."

CHAPTER 50

*Draevyn*

L ater that night, Draevyn's mind reeled with everything that happened earlier in the day. From what he discovered in the library, accidentally burning the guard's arm, to everything Esmyra had said.

And now they would be training together every morning.

Draevyn desperately tried to shove down the thoughts of what that would entail. Of having her body pressed against his as they sparred, teaching her how to move and strike swiftly.

This wouldn't be any opponent or trainee working up through his ranks. It would be entirely different with Esmyra. He'd noticed for a while now—the way his pulse reacted when she was near, and the way his cock would harden when she so much as smirked in his direction.

Draevyn's throat went dry. He wasn't sure he wanted to know what she'd do if she ever gained the knowledge of how he'd started to feel.

*She'd probably threaten to cut my favorite part off.* He chuckled at his thoughts, already imagining the threat slipping past those lush lips of hers.

Draevyn scrubbed a hand down his face as these thoughts spiraled, muttering a curse to the darkness.

This was pointless. It was clear he wouldn't be able to sleep tonight. At least, not with his mind tangled in thoughts of her and the godsdamn mess they found themselves in.

So, if his mind wouldn't let him rest, he'd at least put it to use.

He'd been searching the library for answers, chasing half-truths hidden between ancient pages, but maybe if he kept digging, he'd find *something* useful. Something to shift his focus away from the way his fire-fueled blood would damn near boil at the thought of her.

The halls were silent as Draevyn snuck out of his room, the castle draped in dark teal shadow. And yet, something was off. He could sense it in his bones as the air grew heavier. The castle felt awake and alive in a way it shouldn't, especially at this hour.

Draevyn frowned, scanning his surroundings as he pressed himself into the shadows. He was mid-step when he heard it—a low, breathy sound drifting from the corridor ahead. Several of them.

He froze.

For a moment, he thought he'd imagined it, that maybe exhaustion and the pressure beneath the sea were playing tricks on his mind. But then it came again, softer this time—a hushed gasp, followed by several more.

His brows lifted. What the fuck?

Draevyn's soft steps turned into a near sprint down the corridor, the moans and gasps growing with each step he took. Before he knew it, he was just beyond the throne room. One more turn was all it would take.

His breathing picked up as he started to panic, his curiosity driving him further. As Draevyn neared the slightly ajar doors, another muffled sound reached his ears. A voice—one that turned his blood cold, followed by a sudden rush of rage surging through his soul.

It...it sounded like *Esmyra*.

As he edged closer, the moans grew louder. His fingertips ached as flames burst from them, and he balled his hands into fists as he tried to put them out.

His stomach twisted, breath catching in his throat. It *couldn't* be.

He swallowed hard, suddenly too aware of the sharp pounding of his heart.

What in all gods was happening behind that wall?

Draevyn's mind was a storm of unwanted thoughts, crashing into him all at once. Was Esmyra being fucked in her sister's throne room? Was she tangled in someone's arms, breathless and wild? Was someone else's hands all over the very body Draevyn had been trying to force out of his mind?

His jaw clenched, nails biting into his palms as he forced himself to breathe.

*Think.* He didn't know if it was her. Truthfully, he didn't even have the right to be as horrified as he was. But something inside of him was thrashing, waiting to be set loose at the thought of another man's hands on her.

Draevyn carefully pressed himself to the edge of the doorframe and peered inside, his breath stalling at the sight.

Sprawled across the throne room floor and leading up the steps of the dais was a mess of tangled limbs and discarded clothing. Several figures were wrapped around each other in a haze of pearlescent skin, silks, and pleasure. However, the moans that had sent his blood into a frenzy still lingered in the air, forcing his gaze up to the throne.

Draevyn's stomach clenched as he took in the woman perched at the center of it all, her lean body half-draped in sheer silk, a lazy smirk curling her mouth as her teeth sank into her bottom lip. Golden waves of hair tumbled over her bare shoulders as a crown glinted atop her head.

Her doe eyes gleamed with mischief as she stared down at the male whose face was buried between her thighs, feasting for all in the room to see. Two maidens stood behind her on each side, one reaching over her shoulder and kneading one of her breasts, while the other's tongue traced up the side of her neck.

A slow exhale left his lips as he finally allowed himself to breathe. Relief crashed into Draevyn, seeing now that it wasn't Esmyra's moans echoing throughout the corridors in the dead of night.

It was her twin's. It was *the queen's.*

Draevyn tore his eyes away from the display Syrena was putting on, but anywhere his stare fell provided a similar view.

There were...so many bodies. Draevyn knew his brother loved to participate in escapades like this, often hearing him speak of his nights spent down at Lephyrin's finest brothels. However, to actually witness it was something entirely different.

They all lay entwined, hands roaming lazily, skin gleaming with sweat and...gods knew what else in the flickering merlights. He turned to the left and saw two guards he recognized as they each plunged into a woman beneath them, filling her...*entirely*. And when his eyes drifted to the right, he found a few others on their knees, each taking turns sucking off Azarian.

Throaty laughter hummed through the air, mixing with half-formed moans. A few bystanders, both male and female, sat propped against the pillars, dazed as they watched him with hooded eyes.

Draevyn couldn't tell if they were tired out or eyeing him as if they would take him next.

This was a display of indulgence like he'd never seen.

He took a step backward to try and slip away, but when his eyes drifted back up the dais, his heart stopped in his chest.

Because Syrena wasn't looking at the lovers draped around her anymore.

She was looking at *him*.

Syrena stood from her throne, pulling away from the tangled bodies. The sheer silk draped over her did little to conceal her bare curves, and she let it slip tantalizingly down one shoulder as she descended the dais, her eyes locked on his. She wore a grin that sent a violent chill along Draevyn's spine.

*Fuck.*

What would she do if he ran? Would she chase after him? Have her guards pull their cocks from the womans' mouths and seize him for snooping about the castle at night?

"You don't have to hide in the shadows," Syrena purred as she reached him. Her voice was smooth as honey, warm like the sunrise on the sea. "Unless, of course, you prefer to watch."

Draevyn's jaw clenched, muscles tightening. "Apologies, Your Majesty. I was just leaving." He moved to turn to the door, but Syrena reached out and grabbed his arm.

"Oh, but we're just having a bit of fun." Her brown eyes were heavy, her tongue lazily licking her bottom lip as she stared at him. "Don't you want to have fun, Draevyn?"

*No.* No, he certainly didn't. Not with her, anyway. It took everything in him to keep his flames at bay as he tried to steady his breathing.

Soft giggles echoed through the room as two naked women peeled themselves from the mass of lovers and glided to Syrena's side before their attention flickered to him.

Draevyn's brows furrowed as he noticed their pupils were vertical, like a serpent's. Esmyra's were only like that when she allowed them to shift, but theirs appeared to be that way permanently.

He suppressed the urge to take a step back.

"He seems tense," one of them murmured, stepping close.

The other hummed in agreement, reaching out until her fingers grazed the collar of his shirt. "Poor thing," she whispered, tracing the fabric.

Before he could stop them, deft hands worked at the buttons before peeling back his shirt. Syrena's talons slipped from the tips of her fingers and walked them along his chest—a slow, teasing touch that would unravel a lesser man. The other two women pressed closer, their hands trailing over his arms, his shoulders, their breath warm against his skin. The sheer intimacy of their touch made his skin crawl.

Draevyn sucked in a sharp breath and his hand shot out, catching Syrena's wrist. Her eyes narrowed beneath furrowed brows.

"I'm not here for *this*," he growled. "I couldn't sleep and tried to walk it off. I heard...noises." He gave her a knowing look. "I wasn't sure what I was going to walk into, but it certainly wasn't this."

Syrena tilted her head, her smirk deepening. "Then what kept you here so long?" she countered, taking a step toward him, her face barely an inch below his chin. "Curiosity? *Jealousy*?" She tsked, eyes gleaming.

Draevyn released her wrist, his teeth clenching as he matched her step back.

Her eyes were heavy with seduction. "Join us." His nostrils flared as she observed him. "Or perhaps you and I can go somewhere private, if you'd rather not share."

Draevyn certainly wasn't like his brother in that regard. When he had a woman, she would be his and his alone. But he didn't give a damn about Syrena.

"Enough," he said, his voice edged with warning. "I'm not interested."

The room suddenly felt colder, an icy chill creeping in.

The amusement behind Syrena's eyes darkened, something sharp slipping beneath the surface. "Not interested," she repeated, tasting the words like they were foreign to her.

A wicked chuckle slipped from her and Draevyn's pulse began to race. The two women flanking her sides glanced at one another, as if taking the false laugh as a warning, before rushing back to join the writhing bodies on the floor.

Syrena took a slow step forward, her silk slipping further down her arm, exposing her bare breast. "You wound me," she purred, a dangerous edge to her tone. Her lips curled, the warmth in her brown gaze vanishing as something far colder crept in. "Tell me, then," she murmured, tilting her chin, "is it because of someone else? Is it because of my sister?"

Draevyn stiffened, and he cursed himself, knowing that she witnessed it.

He cleared his throat, leaning in slightly. "You're not my type," he admitted, giving her a wink.

A flicker of rage passed through her expression, quick as lightning.

"You have plenty of things to play with here, Your Majesty," he said flatly. "You certainly don't need me."

Then, with a final, pointed look at the debauchery surrounding them, he turned from her and strode back through the throne room doors without giving her a backward glance.

The first merlights indicating dawn barely crept through her curtains when Esmyra slipped out of her chambers, the castle still quiet and dark. She moved silently, her bare feet padding across the cool stone floors as she snuck out to meet Draevyn in the gardens.

Draevyn wanted to ensure she was protected in the case of falling victim to velsinyte once more. And while she could've argued the same for him, she wasn't blind—she had heard the whispered rumors of how skilled he was, had seen how he moved with that practiced, predatory grace.

But Esmyra wasn't naïve, either. Draevyn didn't trust Syrena, or anyone down here, for that matter, and he made no attempt to hide it.

His words from earlier echoed in her mind, a prickle of doubt seeping into her excitement. *You may think you're making a choice, but this place...it's choosing for you.*

She frowned, hating that a part of her couldn't shake his words.

Esmyra just didn't understand why he suddenly cared. Her mind drifted back to the day they met—when Draevyn instantly moved to aid her and come to her rescue in Anchorage Cove. So, perhaps, the concern wasn't sudden at all, and had always been there, lingering behind his fire-lit stare.

*You don't need his protection,* she reminded herself as she moved through the halls. She'd made her choice. Syrena had offered a connection to something far greater than anything she ever fathomed before.

For once, Esmyra wasn't some pawn or piece to be pushed across the board. This kingdom could be as much hers as Syrena's.

But beneath Esmyra's defiance, a sliver of uncertainty pulsated. What if she was being swept along by forces she couldn't control? What if Syrena wasn't the person Esmyra desperately wanted her to be?

And then there was Draevyn, who seemed to want to make sure whichever path she chose was the right one, instead of trying to move her in whatever direction he wished.

*Ugh. He's only a temporary ally.*

The sooner she understood her power and brought the kingdom up to the surface, the better. Esmyra would free the people of Maerinys. She would save her father from an eternity of suffering. And she would finally have a purpose in this endless life, aside from destruction.

But as she rounded the final corridor, Draevyn's face lingered stubbornly in her mind—his intense, whiskey-hued gaze burning through her like flames.

Esmyra wasn't afraid to play with a little fire, but what would happen if she allowed herself to be burned?

She finally reached the inner gardens they had walked through that first day. The tall sea grasses and wildflowers filled the air with a briny sweetness, while pale blue light filtered through the delicate coral framing the pathways.

Truthfully, she had never dealt with hand-to-hand combat—never had to. Draevyn was right. She had always relied on her magic and would occasionally shoot a pistol for fun. So, as much as she was irritated, she needed *practice* with something; some part deep inside her was thankful, excited, even, to learn something new.

When she spotted Draevyn leaning against a weathered stone pillar, arms crossed, she couldn't help the little flutter in her chest. His expression was as unreadable as ever, fiery eyes locked on her as she made her way to him.

"You're early," he remarked, pushing off from the stone.

"I could say the same," she replied, trying to sound as unbothered as he did. "I was half expecting to be stood up."

"Couldn't sleep." A haunted look passed across his face, but it was there and gone in only a moment. "Besides, I'm the one who requested your presence. That would be a bit counterproductive, don't you think?" Draevyn gave a short laugh, though his eyes never softened. He gestured to a clearing just past the flowers and grasses, where the ground was flat and open enough to spar. "Shall we?"

Esmyra nodded, but her palms became slick with sweat, unsure of what to expect or how to spar. She squared her shoulders, stepping into the clearing before turning to face him. The early morning light cast a sharp glow over his features, shadowing his jawline and making him seem somehow more intense, more lethal.

They circled each other, the silence stretching as they sized each other up. "We're fighting with fists?" She cocked a brow. "And here I thought you don't hit women." She winked.

"Was a bit difficult to find weapons. We'll need to make do for now."

He struck then, his movement swift. She parried, but was significantly slower than him, barely blocking the initial blow.

"Well to start...your stance is shit," Draevyn taunted.

Esmyra's lip curled. "You didn't even touch me!"

Another barely dodged swing came from him, and his grin was infuriating.

"You're all over the place. Find your balance," he demanded. Draevyn reached around her, placing his large hand at the small of her back, and her spine straightened at the contact. "Good girl." He winked, and heat rushed to her cheeks.

Draevyn struck again before she could recover, and she was forced to quickly adapt to his rhythm during their intense back-and-forth of punches, kicks, and strikes. Esmyra's body began to warm up, her muscles loosening, and she allowed it to distract her from her heart fluttering at his touch.

"Keep your feet shoulder-width apart!" he bellowed between hits. "Stay light on the balls of your feet."

Esmyra loathed being told what to do, but she listened, taking his advice. She soon found herself with a smile beaming across her face as she got the hang of it.

Her fist collided with Draevyn's cheek, and his eyes flared. Their stares met, and she didn't miss the lilt in the corner of his lips. "Perfect. Just like that," he praised, and her smirk turned wicked.

Their sparring continued a moment later, both of them not bothering to hide their grins.

Was she...having *fun*?

Though she wasn't skilled in physical combat, her muscular build gave her an advantage in the fight. Swimming beneath the waves for centuries had sculpted her body, giving her unparalleled strength—especially in her legs.

"Perhaps you're not a lost cause after all," Draevyn admitted, his voice low and mocking as he sidestepped one of her punches, catching her wrist before she could strike again. "Though I wonder if that'll mean much when you're not up against someone going easy on you."

Breath heaving, she pulled her wrist from his grasp, her eyes glaring. "And here I thought we were just warming up." She tsked. "Or are you just trying to get inside my head and discredit me?"

They slowly circled each other again in a dance.

His gaze darkened. "It's not about credit. It's about reality. And you're putting your faith in people you don't know every second we're down here."

"While I may not know Syrena yet, I felt the power we had together. You weren't there," she snapped, frustration flaring as she threw herself back into the spar, kicking him in the center of his chest.

Draevyn grunted as he stumbled back, hands flying to his sternum. Pride flared through her.

His gaze fell to where she struck him, a knowing grin on his face. "Maybe not," he countered, "but I'm here now. The only thing that holds true is that you don't know her. And all I see is someone charging into a story she doesn't even know the ending to, trusting that strangers to our entire world above will bring her peace."

*Peace.*

She bared her teeth as they fell silent, their sparring growing fiercer. A mixture of strength and pent-up tension surged through each of her strikes, the heat of her fury rising within her.

Esmyra moved to trip him, but when he side-stepped her, she leapt onto his back, her legs wrapping around his torso with a crushing strength against his ribs. He stumbled forward a few steps before regaining his balance. She kept his neck in a headlock as a single talon slipped from her finger and pricked the edge of his throat.

She brought her lips to the edge of his ear and whispered, "You fear I'm putting my trust into strangers, but is that not what we are, Draevyn Rowe?" Her voice dripped with sweetened venom.

A throaty chuckle left him, and her vicious smile dropped. He pivoted his head as much as he was able to in her grasp. One fiery eye boring into hers. "Is that what we are, Esmyra? Strangers?"

Her breath hitched. *No*, she thought. The more days that passed, the less Draevyn felt like a stranger at all.

"Oh, you're making this too easy," he said with a laugh.

*Fuck.*

He reached back, calloused hands sliding up the back of her thighs as he secured his grip on her legs. The tips of his fingers dug into her skin, making her pulse quicken. The touch was steady, but it lingered just a moment too long, sending a shiver down her spine.

Esmyra tried to ignore the way his hands felt on her, her mind desperate to stay focused on the fight rather than the heat of his touch.

Without warning, Draevyn shifted his stance and, with a swift move, flipped her over his shoulder. She tumbled forward, bringing him down with her before landing on her back in the grass. Esmyra was breathless as he loomed above her, his hands still resting on her thighs from the flip.

For a moment, neither of them moved. He was close—entirely

too close. The weight of him pressed down on her, his face only inches from hers, his gaze intense, dark, and searching. His stare flickered down to her mouth for only a moment before returning to her eyes. That, combined with the heat of his body, had her cheeks flushing.

"You cheated," he said, his breath hot against her ear. His voice was rougher now, but playful.

Esmyra couldn't bring herself to look away, her words catching in her throat. "You pissed me off," she managed, her voice coming out softer than she intended as her chest rose and fell.

Draevyn smirked, his infuriating dimple on display, before leaning back just enough to release her from his hold. "The point of this is to act *powerless*," he said, offering a hand, though the glint in his eyes suggested he knew the effect he'd had on her.

She reached for it, her fingers brushing against his calluses. The steady beat of his pulse beneath his skin fell in line with her own as he pulled her to her feet.

For a moment, they just stood there, the tension thick, an unspoken charge lingering between them.

"There you are!" Briar's voice echoed from across the garden.

"Shit," Esmyra muttered.

Briar walked up to them hesitantly. "Is...is everything alright?" She glanced back and forth between the two of them before her eyes landed on Esmyra once more. Her next words were a whisper. "Do you need me to call the guards?"

Esmyra barked a laugh, but Draevyn grumbled some retort she didn't care to decipher. "That won't be necessary. We were just sparring," she admitted.

Briar raised a brow. "Like the soldiers?"

"Yes. Like the soldiers," Esmyra answered, merely guessing.

"Is this normal in the world above?"

Esmyra was about to say *no*, but Draevyn cut her off. "It is. It's how we start our days."

She turned to face him and saw no kindness in his eyes when he spoke to Briar, and it rekindled a bit of her irritation toward him.

"Do you need something, Briar?" Esmyra asked as she tucked her hair behind her ear and crossed her arms, changing the subject.

"Queen Syrena won't be able to join you for breakfast this morning, but it's ready in the great hall. She wishes for you to meet her in the tower when you're done."

"Aye," Esmyra answered with a sigh. "Thank you."

With those words, Briar reluctantly turned away and left the garden.

Esmyra whirled on Draevyn the second she was out of view, smacking him in the stomach and earning a grunt as he barrelled over. "Really? I know you don't trust the people down here, but Briar is nice enough. The girl is skittish, for fuck's sake."

Draevyn straightened himself and shot her a glare. "I don't trust *any* of them. And she thought I was abusing you for everyone to godsdamn see. Last night, I—"

"She just doesn't know you," Esmyra cut him off.

His jaw ticked. "She doesn't know you either."

"Ugh." She took her first step to follow Briar's steps. "You're infuriating sometimes."

"Well, that's a relief," he said. "Two days ago, it was all the time."

Esmyra had to turn away from him to hide the laugh that nearly slipped from her.

Draevyn stepped up to her and offered her his arm. "Shall we? You mustn't keep *Her Majesty* waiting," he mocked.

"And what of this?" She gestured to the empty garden.

He shrugged. "We'll pick back up where we left off tomorrow."

Esmyra's eyes narrowed before they fell to his arm, still extended toward her. She let out a huff before sliding her own through and allowed him to lead the way back through the corridors and to the great hall.

Atlas leaned against the ship's rail, gazing out at the dark, churning sea. The endless blue stretched around them, offering no sign of his brother. And with every mile of an empty horizon, his frustration gnawed at him.

He cursed under his breath, recalling the vagueness of Blackwood's instructions: *Southern waters,* he'd said, as if that alone was guidance enough. No map, no stars to follow, no landmarks—just the word of the realm's most dangerous man.

Fighting his rising impatience, he stalked up to the ship's wheel, where Samwell gripped the helm. "Anything in sight?"

Samwell sighed, glancing from Atlas to the empty waters. "Not yet, Prince. And if I might speak freely—it would be helpful if your source had given us anything more to go off of."

"I figured as much," Atlas admitted, running a hand through his disheveled hair. "I don't know the first thing about sailing or the sea. How are we supposed to find him when all we have for a lead is the vague notion to go south?"

"Are you certain your source is trustworthy?" Samwell asked, casting him a skeptical look.

Atlas nearly barked a laugh. "Not trustworthy in the slightest. But it's the only lead we have. And I can't see any reason for the man to lie."

Samwell's brow knitted. "Who's your source, Prince? We're risking a great deal on this."

Atlas's gaze hardened as he looked past Samwell, out toward the endless waters. "That's none of your concern."

"Respectfully, Your Highness, I'd argue it's every bit my concern. We're sailing south against our king's orders, risking treason. If we're acting on the word of a liar, it's my neck in the noose as much as yours. Perhaps even more."

Atlas let out a slow breath. Shadows swirled around his hands, twisting in response to his emotions, and he forced them to still. "Cyrus Blackwood."

Samwell's eyes widened, and he choked on a sharp breath. "Blackwood?! Why in all the gods would you ever speak to the man? Let alone take his word on anything?"

Atlas clenched his jaw. He knew the reaction was warranted, but his gut told him Blackwood hadn't lied. "Because it's the only lead we have. My father hinted that Blackwood might know something about who took Draevyn, so I went to the dungeons and spoke with him myself. He told me to sail south, and that we'd find answers there."

Samwell exhaled sharply, letting out a low whistle. "Did he say anything else? Anything specific?"

Atlas's mouth tightened. "Only that if we don't find him before... whatever they're searching for is complete, may the gods help us all."

Samwell let out a bitter chuckle. "Dramatic words from a dying man."

"So it would seem," Atlas agreed as a small smirk formed, but there was a dreaded feeling in his gut telling him that Cyrus's warning was warranted.

Clapping Samwell on the back, he said, "Keep an eye out. Surely we'll spot something useful within the next day or two." He turned, descending the stairs toward the lower deck, his thoughts reeling.

As he made his way across the deck, a thin figure by the mainmast caught his eye—a young sailor with cropped brown hair coiling rope in silence. When Atlas met the man's gaze, the sailor's face paled, and he quickly turned away, shoulders hunched.

"Oi," Atlas called, stepping closer. The sailor tensed, keeping his back to him as he approached. "What's your name?"

The man stiffened but still wouldn't turn, and Atlas's irritation flared. He moved to face him head-on, stopping a few paces away. "Your prince asked you a question. I've ordered all hands below deck for supper, aside from myself and the acting captain. Answer me."

The sailor's head ducked slightly before he finally muttered, "It's Owen, Your Highness."

Atlas frowned, studying him. "Owen?" His voice grew sharper. "And you hail from Lephyrin?"

"Yes," Owen said smoothly, his voice now low, his face wearing a half smile.

Atlas felt a strange, almost unnatural urge to let the matter drop. But then a glimmer caught his eye as the man continued to coil the rope, a small golden ring with a ruby in its center twinkled on the sailor's finger.

*His* ring—the one he had made for his betrothed.

"Owen..." Atlas's voice was taut as his fury surged, shadows building at his feet. "Where did you get that ring?"

The sailor half turned to face him, mouth breaking into a sly grin in the dim moonlight. In the blink of an eye, Owen's form shimmered, a faint gleam surrounding him as his cropped hair softened and lengthened into dark curls. His slender form shifted into the familiar curves of the woman he'd left in his bed back at Castle Lephyrin.

Atlas's heart raced painfully, his throat tight as he watched.

"Elowynne," he hissed, grabbing her arm and tugging her into the shadows beneath the mast. His own swirled around them to shield them from prying eyes. "Are you out of your mind? Sneaking aboard in disguise? How did you even manage this?"

She lifted her chin, her golden eyes gleaming in the moonlight. "Someone had to be here with you," she replied, her voice fierce. "You're out here defying the king's orders, risking your life in search of Draevyn—and I wasn't going to let you do it alone when I could help."

Atlas's anger lessened as he looked into her stubborn gaze, though worry still twisted his gut. "The sea is no place for you, Wynne, and I don't need the added burden of keeping you safe on top of finding Draevyn."

She scoffed. "Burden. You men…"

Atlas's lips pressed in a tight line. "Apologies. Burden wasn't the right word. I just want to keep you safe."

"Which is precisely why I didn't tell you," she said calmly. "You would've fought me and won. But you know it as well as I do—my powers could be the difference between finding him and returning empty-handed."

He sighed, pressing a hand to his brow. "How? How could you possibly help?"

She folded her arms, her eyes narrowing. "You forget that I'm not human, Atlas. I have magic beyond what you've seen. I can manipulate minds, control what others see and feel. I made you believe I was someone else without ever changing my form."

His eyes flared. "You didn't shift?"

Elowynne's brows furrowed. "Do they teach you nothing in Lephyrin? Elven can't shift. Our magic is that of the mind. We can break into them, make them see what we want them to. Their dreams —or nightmares. Even make them see things that aren't there."

He stared at her, dumbfounded. "That is…terrifying."

"And useful."

He hesitated, his heart torn between his worry for her safety and the hope her abilities offered. "So that's why you disguised yourself? To sneak aboard and offer your aid?"

"Well, yes. And I wasn't about to be left behind and bored out of my mind in a kingdom foreign to me," she answered. "Also, it was working beautifully, if I do say so myself. I would have fooled you, too, if you hadn't seen the ring."

Atlas couldn't help his smile that formed at that. "You're infuriatingly clever, you know."

She laughed softly, her fingers intertwining with his. "Let me stay, and I swear I'll follow your every order."

After a long moment, he sighed as his gaze raked over her. "Fine. But stay close to me. And if anything feels wrong, you come straight to me."

Elowynne grinned, her eyes filled with excitement. "Wouldn't dream of doing otherwise, Your Highness."

Atlas took a step into her, their chests brushing against one another. "What exactly did you have in mind for your...*use*?" A sly grin formed on his mouth.

"While my powers may not help you find him, they will come in use if we run into anyone who becomes an...issue. Any threat, or anyone who dares challenge you or gets in your way of finding Draevyn. I can break into their minds." She gently pressed her palm against his cheek. "Make them surrender to you. Make them see their fears."

Atlas's breath hitched as Elowynne's words sank in. The intensity in her golden gaze, the promise threaded through her voice—it ignited something primal within him. Her beauty had always been magnetic to him, but this...this was something else.

The idea of her wielding her magic in his favor, bending others to their will, stirred a dark thrill inside him. He found himself drawn closer to Elowynne, caught between admiration and a fierce desire for her he never thought would come.

After all, she was chosen by his father.

*His father.*

Had the king known she was like this all along? Hoping she would give him the push his father always thought he needed? To give him the courage to rule with an iron fist.

The way she looked at him now, her lips curved in that knowing, mischievous smile, made him ache to press her against the rough wood of the mast, to run his hands through the dark waves of her hair and claim her lips with his own. But even through the haze of want, he knew he needed to keep his head clear.

Gritting his teeth, he forced himself to take a step back, his gaze never leaving hers. "You're beautiful, and insane, and the best possible choice I could've made that night."

Her laughter was low and soft, like the promise of something wicked, and it took all his self-control not to pull her closer again.

"We need to talk to the crew," he said, a trace of reluctance in his tone. "They'll need to be made aware of the change of plans. And now, if danger finds us, we'll have a weapon no one would expect from a ship that hails from the kingdom of men."

Elowynne's fingers traced lightly down his arm, leaving a trail of warmth. The only answer she gave was a slight curve of her lip.

Back in the tower, the morning merlights filtered through the tall arched windows. The room felt charged, like the sea air before a deadly storm. Syrena stood beside Esmyra, next to the Veil of Visions, while the water swirled and shimmered, but she refused to look her in the eye.

Esmyra cleared her throat. "Is something wrong, Syrena?"

Her sister lifted her stare then. "Have you lied to me, sister? I ask of you nothing but the truth."

Esmyra's eyes flared as she bit the sides of her cheeks, trying to keep her face as neutral as possible, but she knew it was useless. Her throat tightened, her palms instantly slick with sweat, because...what *hadn't* she and Draevyn lied about?

"What do you mean?" was all she could manage to ask.

Syrena pursed her lips, her eyes narrowing. "You told me your companion doesn't possess magic."

Esmyra was certain her heart stopped. Had Draevyn fucked up? Why wouldn't he tell her? And why was he using magic in the gods-damn first place?

"I—" she cut herself off, her eyes darting back and forth.

"Esmyra, do you even know why I asked this of you?"

She swallowed. "To keep your people safe."

"To. Keep. *Our*. People. Safe," Syrena echoed, tone borderline furious. The way she corrected Esmyra made her spine straighten. "Now, please, answer this question truthfully. Does Draevyn possess magic?"

"Yes," Esmyra answered. "He does."

"And where does he hail from?"

"Lephyrin."

Syrena's brows creased. "Mere mortals don't possess magic. So are you lying to me again, sister?"

"I am not." Esmyra worked to keep her tone as even as possible, desperately trying not to let her own aggravation surge. "Draevyn was gifted magic by Irah himself."

Syrena's head drew back quickly, eyes flaring at the mention of Irah. "That makes little sense."

"I don't know the full story," Esmyra admitted. "But he wields the power of flame."

Syrena's lips parted. "So it must be true. Fire-wielders didn't exist a thousand years ago. They would be too destructive. Only Irah held flame in his blood."

"Aye," Esmyra answered, holding her stare. "I'm unsure of the details, but the god placed a piece of his magic into Draevyn."

Syrena crossed her arms, hurt flashing across her features. "So not only did you lie about his possession of magic, but of how destructive he is. Why?"

Esmyra's chest ached, feeling nothing but guilt. She licked her lips. "I don't know. We know you possess velsinyte. It was a way to... protect ourselves in a strange world." She paused. "For what it's worth... I'm so sorry."

Syrena's eyes drifted over her, and she had never felt more bare. "I understand why you did it. But as the protector of Maerinys, something will need to be done."

Esmyra moved to step around the fountain, shaking her head in denial. "Draevyn won't hurt anyone."

Syrena straightened her gown. "He already has."

Esmyra stopped in her tracks, her eyes going wide as they darted back and forth, refusing to land on anything. "What? Who?!"

"One of my guards was left with burns."

*That fucking bastard.* May the gods help him if he didn't have a justified reason for this.

Her lips parted. "Syrena, I'm so sorry."

Syrena held up a hand. "What's done is done. He won't be thrown into the dungeons, but I would like to meet with both of you after this."

Esmyra averted her gaze to the floor. "Aye."

She was horrified. Absolutely mortified that Draevyn had attacked someone but never told her. What else was he hiding? Her talons slipped from the edges of her fingers, imagining sinking their venom into his flesh for lying to her.

"But enough of that," Syrena started, clasping her hands before her. "Now, explain to me what you're able to do with your power."

The sudden change of subject was a bit alarming, but Esmyra was also grateful for it. "I can manipulate water any way I desire, so long as it's there," she started.

Syrena's brows knitted, and she cocked her head to the side. "Meaning what, exactly?"

"I can bend the water to any shape, mimicking any form. Even a monster of the deep." She thought of her kraken she used to bring down enemy ships within minutes.

"So you cannot conjure water from thin air, is what you're saying?"

Esmyra hated the way her sister was looking at her—almost judgingly. "Aye," she answered, a bit of a sharpness in her tone. "If there's moisture in the air, I can. But otherwise no."

Syrena sucked on her tongue and took a step toward her. "Close your eyes," she instructed, her voice steady, coaxing. "Feel the pull of the sea that surrounds our kingdom. You see, Esmyra, the water isn't something you control; it's something you tune into. Let it speak to you. Let it *guide* you."

Esmyra thought it was a waste of time, but decided to play along anyway. She inhaled deeply and closed her eyes, imagining herself, not in this dome, but floating below the surface.

Her skin prickled with energy—the same electric sensation she'd felt yesterday when they'd combined their powers—only now she was reaching for it internally. A tingling spread through her fingers as she focused. Her talons extended without summoning them, while imagining her hands as extensions of the water's current, moving and merging with it.

"Good," her sister murmured, her voice softer now. "Now call it to you. Gently, as if drawing it out from within you."

Esmyra exhaled, lifting her hands and feeling the water respond as it was summoned, a delicate current weaving around and between her fingers. It was exhilarating, feeling it answer her, as if an ancient part of herself was finally being awakened. She opened her eyes just a sliver and saw the water hovering in silent command just above her outstretched palm.

The siren within hummed in approval.

Syrena mirrored her movements, bringing her hand alongside Esmyra's until they intertwined in midair, both streams of water twisting and turning in intricate spirals between them.

"There," Syrena whispered, smiling as she watched the water rise and fall, weaving between their hands like living threads. "Can you feel the connection? The balance?"

She nodded, feeling a rush of pride mixed with wonder. The water seemed to hum, alive with a power that coursed between them. But something gnawed at her—a small kernel of doubt lingering in her chest, seeded by her and Draevyn's conversation that morning.

*Is this truly my power?* Or was she just a conduit for something much older, something that could just as easily consume her?

"What's wrong?" Syrena's gaze sharpened as she observed the shift in her.

"It's just..." Esmyra hesitated, glancing at the swirling water. "I've never been able to summon water on my own. I've tried for centuries, but to no avail. How can I conjure it so easily once I'm here?"

Syrena's doe eyes softened. "That's why we're here. Together, we can awaken our full strength. But it requires surrender to the magic that lingers within us."

Hearing those words, she tried to shake off the lingering doubt.

The tendrils of water answered her unspoken commands, bending and moving in sync with her sister's. For a moment, she lost herself in the feeling, letting go of the nerves that seemed to grip her every so often since she arrived there, and focusing only on the energy thrumming between them.

"Together, we're stronger than any force in this world," Syrena continued. "And when we raise Maerinys, it won't just be one of the four great kingdoms—it will be the greatest. And it will be *ours*, bound to our very souls and essence."

The water pulsed faster, responding to her sister's words, shimmering like liquid silver in the merlight. The ancient magic beckoned to Esmyra, its alluring promise of power impossible to resist.

"And nobody will be able to take you away from it this time," Syrena added.

Esmyra wanted to trust it, to trust *Syrena*, and with each passing moment, she found herself doing just that even more effortlessly.

This was where she was meant to be. *Who* she was meant to be.

But her father had taken her away, and the man wasn't even her true sire.

He had stolen her.

Stolen *this* from her.

With one last gesture, she lowered her hands, guiding the water to fall gently into the fountain. Syrena's eyes beamed with pride as she did the same.

"This may be possible sooner than expected," her sister said, wrapping her arms around Esmyra in an embrace that caught her off guard. Her body stiffened on instinct.

She pulled away from Syrena. "Our first night here, at dinner with your council, you said my father was a liar." If the queen was shocked at the sudden change of subject, her face never showed it. "All I said to you was that he found me. Saved me. Yet you said this isn't necessarily the truth."

Syrena's gaze darkened, shadows passing over her eyes. "He was *never* your father," she replied, her voice steady but cold. "The man stole you from us—from me, from your family and kingdom. He was no savior; he was a *thief*."

A chill traced along Esmyra's spine, and she took an unsteady breath. "A thief to his core, that man." Her stare lifted to Syrena's. "I recently became aware that the false narrative I was told all my life wasn't necessarily the truth."

"He likely twisted the truth to make you feel safe with him," Syrena snarled. "He wasn't protecting you; he was hiding you from your birthright."

Esmyra shook her head. The weight of her memories with him pressed against her like a storm, memories now fractured and tainted by the lies he told. "Why would he steal me? How was the man anywhere near a royal heir? None of this makes sense."

"Power, I would assume. Has he not harnessed your magic? Controlled it, and you, to make it his own?" Syrena's words cut through the fog in her mind, sharp and relentless.

The reminder was like a dagger to the heart.

"Aye." Esmyra's nostrils flared as she let out a hate-filled, breathy laugh. "That's exactly what he's done."

"As a result of the gods' actions, and Maerinys' heir lost, our home sank into the sea."

A hollow feeling spread in Esmyra's chest, sinking to the depths of her stomach. "All of this," she gestured to their surroundings, "was caused by the hands of my father?"

Syrena gave a stiff nod, her expression solemn. "We still stood a chance when the gods betrayed us, but when you were ripped away, he doomed us all." Syrena reached out and gently tucked a stray lock of Esmyra's midnight hair behind her ear. "I'm willing to bet that's all he ever saw you as. Not a daughter. A vessel for unmatched power."

The weight of the truth pressed down on Esmyra, her breaths shallow as she processed the betrayal, the lies that had bound her whole life.

She knew Cyrus was a liar, but to hear it confirmed by the very person she was stolen from felt like an entirely new betrayal. A betrayal of her trust and unrelenting love. Esmyra would have given her father the world if he demanded it of her. She had already given him the seas.

Finally, Esmyra looked at her sister, the anger smoldering in her chest. "I want to learn everything. Everything I lost, everything I am. I want to know the truth—my *real* truth."

Syrena took her hand, a fire flickering in her golden-brown eyes as ribbons of conjured water appeared, coiling around their wrists like serpents. "And learn you shall."

CHAPTER 54

## *Draevyn*

The library was dim and silent, save for the rustling of old parchment as Draevyn pulled book after book from the shelves, spreading them across one of the vast tables. Each tome was thicker and dustier than the last, their spines cracked and worn by time and the briny air. He already lost hours in the endless sea of faded texts, yet he pressed on, his fingers brushing across centuries-old ink, eyes tracing the names of long-forgotten bloodlines and history.

He was desperate to find more information on how Esmyra had been in Maerinys before—the painted portrait of her in a long-forgotten book plaguing his mind. The way she spoke of this place, he knew she fully believed she had never been here before, or in the least, didn't remember.

Draevyn was thankful at least some of the books were written in Rymelle's language, and not the rune-like symbols he had found in several books and throughout Maerinys.

The history of Maerinys was richer than he'd expected, even darker than the whispers he'd heard throughout his life—though everything was hearsay centuries after the kingdom sank.

He opened a worn, leather-bound book, its cover embossed with a symbol that looked strangely like a serpent coiled around a trident.

The first page detailed the origins of the sea goddesses, their descent from the ocean itself, each imbued with powers that ran as deep and dark as its trenches. It spoke of how they governed over the seas, kept balance, and offered their blessings to Maerinys and its people—until they vanished alongside their kingdom.

Only, the kingdom *hadn't* vanished. So where were the goddesses?

There once was a time the gods walked among Rymelle's soil, but they retreated to their own world after the fall of Kaelypso and Naerysa. They only remained accessible from their temples to pray to and leave offerings.

Irah remained with Lephyrin in more ways than he cared to admit—Draevyn was the proof of that. And from what he knew, Vydenne and Villaem were the same with their followers in Sumnae and Terrana, the continents they hailed from.

However, Kaelypso and Naerysa were lost to their people below the tides, just as much as they were above. It was how Blackwood was able to gain control of the seas so easily centuries ago. The balance, once in place, had ceased.

*We're going to raise Maerinys to the surface*, Esmyra had said to him.

It had taken gods to sink it to the depths, yet someone as ordinary as an heir had the power to raise it? Something wasn't right—the pieces of the puzzle not fitting together entirely. And he knew it was because Syrena was lying to them. Or at least, telling half-truths.

After the stunt she pulled the night prior, trying to bring him into her little fuck-fest, every alarm in his mind was flaring. He wanted to tell Esmyra, but would she even care? Truthfully, what the queen of Maerinys did was no business of his. And, regardless, he hadn't partaken in it.

Draevyn rubbed his hands over his face, the weight of it all settling on his shoulders.

His and Esmyra's alliance was still so new—so breakable. And even then, it was only based on survival. Nothing more...at least for her.

If he said the wrong thing, he knew she would retreat into herself again, start keeping secrets from him, and leave him in the dark.

Syrena claimed there was no way to escape Maerinys, but was that still the truth? They had found it after all. Esmyra managed to open doors and break barriers that had otherwise been sealed.

Who's to say those weren't still open?

Now that he thought of it, he realized nothing was stopping them from walking right back into that cave and following the way they came. The only thing that stood in their way was the initial drop from when Esmyra had fallen through the archway.

Draevyn didn't know where the cave was, considering they had been blindfolded as they were dragged from it. However, he was determined to find it and see for himself.

Maybe then he could convince Esmyra to leave.

He glanced around the vast library, a sinking feeling in his gut that his hunch regarding everything was more than true. With a cautious glance over his shoulder, he closed the book, brushing a thumb over the emblem on its cover before slipping it into his coat.

Draevyn moved quickly, tidying the rest of the books into neat stacks, pushing the larger tomes back onto their shelves. He took one last look around to ensure he'd left no sign of his search and turned toward the towering doors.

What would happen if he were caught with this? Would they assume he was stealing? Would Esmyra even believe him if he tried to deny it?

*Was just looking for a bit of light reading*, he practiced the lie in his mind, and let out a huff of a laugh.

Pushing the feeling down, he slipped out into the corridor and strode toward his chambers. He kept his pace calm, casual, even though his mind raced with the secrets hidden beneath his shirt.

As he entered his bedchamber, his pulse slowed, but his thoughts spun faster. Still, he couldn't shake the feeling that the book he just uncovered was leading him down a path of no return.

Walking up to the side of his bed, he reached for the book, the intricate symbol of the trident gleaming faintly from the room's merlights. Draevyn dropped to his knees and lifted the skirt of his bed, placing the book in the far back corner.

Draevyn had barely stood back up when a knock sounded at his door. He stilled as his pulse spiked, wondering if the missing text had already been discovered.

But then Esmyra's voice filtered through the door. "Are you coming to dinner?"

He closed his eyes, swallowing his nerves as he smoothed his coat.

When he didn't answer her, she spoke again. "I don't have all night, Draevyn. And frankly, a day of sparring and magic-wielding has made me hungry."

He snorted before straightening his shirt and approaching the door. When he opened it, Draevyn found her leaning casually against the wall with a wry smile.

"Do you always take this long to get dressed?" she teased, eyeing him with an arched brow. "I'm forcefully wrapped in endless fabric, and I'm quicker than you."

"Ever heard of a nap? You tired me out earlier," he answered with a wink. But his heart still raced as his mind remained with the book under his bed.

"Since when are you one for flattery?" Her eyes lingered on him, sharp and assessing. "And since when are we back to *lying*, Draevyn Rowe?"

His heart leapt in his throat. Was it the book he just hid? What he discovered in the throne room last night? Technically, he wasn't lying about those if they hadn't been mentioned. "What do you mean?"

Esmyra stormed past him, barging into the room before slamming the door behind her. She spun back to face him, her lip curling back. "Who the fuck did you burn, *Phoenix*?!"

"All gods," he whispered, rubbing his brow between his thumb and forefinger. "It's not what it sounds like."

"Really? Are you serious? Because to me, it sounds like not only did you use your magic, but you assaulted somebody. We had a deal,

Draevyn. No magic. No lies." Her chest was heaving, both fury and hurt etched into her features, and he hated that he was the one who put it on her otherwise perfect face.

"I didn't lie. I simply omitted something." He'd omitted quite a few things, and nausea rolled through him the more he thought of it.

She scoffed, a wicked cackle slipping from her as she shook her head. "You're despicable."

Draevyn's eyes narrowed, taking a step closer. "Listen to me. I didn't think they realized I caused it. Azarian had some other male put his hands on me and I shoved out of his hold. My magic burst, trying to protect me. It wasn't on purpose, and they never saw the flames. I was convinced they thought it was just some strange occurrence because they dropped the subject." His jaw locked, his next words a growl. "But it appears they instead just ran to their queen."

"Why would they put their hands on you? Surely you were doing something you shouldn't have been."

A breathy laugh left him. "If inquiring about your safety is something I shouldn't be doing, then forgive me for having a very different opinion, Esmyra."

Her pouty lips parted, and his eyes fell to them with the movement. "I—"

"I was worried after the tremors," he interrupted. "And they tried to physically drag me back to my chambers without answering questions. I apologize that my magic slipped, but I have no regrets regarding my concern for you."

She went completely still, her gaze locked on his. Her tongue swiped across her bottom lip, and Draevyn imagined pressing his own to them, wondering what they would taste like.

"Syrena wishes to see you in the throne room for punishment." Her voice shattered his trance.

*Punishment in the throne room.* Draevyn would be lying if he said he wasn't used to it.

A humorless chuckle escaped him, all thoughts of his sudden arousal fleeing his mind. His eyes lifted to the door as he shook his head. "Well, let's get this over with then."

And then he stalked out of the room, Esmyra following behind him in silence.

Syrena sat regally on her high-backed throne as the council lined the walls of the room. The usual warmth in her doe eyes now gleamed with nothing but a bone-chilling iciness as she stared down at Esmyra and Draevyn just beyond the dais.

Draevyn glared at the two guards flanking him, their hands tightening on their spears. He couldn't help but think of how different this room looked the night prior. It seemed, however, that Syrena's cold gaze remained in place since he'd denied an invitation to her bed.

Esmyra stood on the opposite side of Azarian on his left, making it impossible for him to look at her without blatantly peering around the guard.

"You swore to me," Syrena began, her voice cutting through the heavy silence, "that you were powerless. A common man of Lephyrin. Yet now you stand before me in a private trial, caught wielding the power of *flame* and striking my guards."

Draevyn's jaw ticked. "It was a mistake, Your Majesty. They tried to—"

"I will have silence, Draevyn," the queen interrupted as she stood. "You lied to me and this court. You betrayed the trust extended to you when all we've given you is a roof over your head. We asked if you possessed magic and you lied." A look to Esmyra. "*Both* of you lied."

*To protect ourselves.* He ached to voice the words as Esmyra flinched out of the corner of his eye.

"Syrena," Esmyra said carefully, "the male who was burned cornered Draevyn and put his hands on him. His magic worked to protect him, just as our own would. I would like to know why that happened. He's not a threat. He—"

"No threat?" Syrena raised a brow. "The restraint he shattered, the flame he conjured to scorch my guard's arm—do those sound harmless to you?"

Draevyn's heart hammered in his chest as Esmyra defended him. He wasn't aware of the customs of Maerinys or what a punishment for this would entail. He knew if he were anyone else back in Lephyrin, he would face the noose for something far less.

The silence hung heavy in the room, the air thick with unspoken consequences. He knew Esmyra's hands would be tied.

Draevyn took a step forward, and the sound of shifting spears echoed as the guards watched his every movement. "I sincerely apologize and take full responsibility for the act and the lie. Don't punish Esmyra. I'm the one to blame."

Syrena crossed her arms. "You think I would punish my sister for your incident?"

"With all due respect, I know nothing of you or your kingdom. So yes, I feel the need to protect her. If the dungeons are what awaits me, then take me to them. If it's a noose around my neck, then let me hang. I will accept the consequences for my actions, so long as she goes free."

Draevyn's life hadn't been filled with many good deeds—his nickname, the Phoenix, was proof of that—but if his final act involved saving the woman who had repeatedly done the same for him, he'd embrace death as it came for him.

"Are you out of your mind?!" Esmyra whisper-shouted at his back, her voice cracking.

The skin around Syrena's eyes tightened as she glanced back and forth between him and Esmyra. "We are not savages and brutes, as the kingdom you hail from, Draevyn," she finally said. "I'm not without mercy, unlike your *god*." She spat the last word.

Draevyn's brows furrowed as she spoke ill of Irah, as if she held something personal against the god of rage and war.

The queen stepped down from the dais, her golden waves bouncing with the slow movements. She held out her hand, and Azarian stepped up to her, placing some strange cuff in her palm. "Now, I don't know or understand how a common man can wield

Irah's flames, but what I do know is the destruction they can cause…"

Draevyn bit the inside of his cheek, the veins in his neck straining as he sensed what was to come.

"Syrena?" Esmyra's voice cut through the silence, but the queen's eyes remained on Draevyn, assessing him.

"If you prove you can be trusted, this shall come off. But for my safety and that of my people, if you wish to roam as a free man during your time in Maerinys, you will wear this cuff." Syrena held a bracelet up before him as she took a step toward him, mere feet in front of him now.

Draevyn tilted his head, hoping to mask the challenge in his stare with feigned curiosity. "Velsinyte, I would assume?" How they came into possession of it still gnawed at him.

"You would assume correctly." A cruel gleam filled her eyes, the glint like polished obsidian. It left Draevyn wondering if he was being punished for his magic or for his refusal of the queen.

Before he could say another word, the cuff snapped onto his wrist, and the flame in his chest winked out. A shiver ran along his spine, and he gritted his teeth as an invisible weight pressed down on him, as if the depths were trying to crush him.

Esmyra stepped up to them then, trying to stand between them. "I swear to you, it will never happen again."

Syrena looked toward her twin, and Draevyn never got used to how eerily similar they were. "I know. This will make sure of it. He will wear it until I deem him fit to be trusted again. Should he remove it without my consent, the consequences will be far graver." She looked to Draevyn and gave him a bone-chilling smile.

His jaw locked, clenching his teeth to keep his retort in.

"Consider yourself lucky, for if Esmyra didn't vouch so greatly for you, you wouldn't stand before me here and now," Syrena continued.

Draevyn looked to Esmyra, and she averted her gaze to the floor, her jaw ticking.

"Now, if you wouldn't mind," Syrena continued, "I have other matters to attend to." That kind smile fell into place once more in the center of her golden features, but Draevyn saw right through it as her eyes bore into him.

"Thank you, Your Majesty." He bowed, playing the part. "Your kindness will not be forgotten, nor taken for granted."

And when he turned away from the dais and stalked out of the throne room, Esmyra didn't follow.

CHAPTER 55

*Esmyra*

A spear rested in Esmyra's hand, its wooden shaft unfamiliar in her grasp as she faced down Draevyn on the opposite side of the garden.

He spun his own spear in one hand, a practiced, almost lazy movement that only made her grip her weapon tighter.

They hadn't talked about the prior evening—truthfully, she didn't know what to say. It seemed to all be laid bare before them, but now the cuff encircling his wrist could complicate things if they ever found a way out.

"Where did you even find these?" he asked with an amused lilt to his voice. "I'm surprised they offered to hand over weapons. Especially after yesterday."

"Oh, they didn't. I followed Azarian and took them from a weaponry room on the third floor." Esmyra shrugged. "I doubt they'll mind."

"Such a little thief you are, Wildfire."

*That name.*

"Old habits and all." She winked as the corner of her lip lifted. "Although, I'm not the one with fire in my veins, Son of Irah."

His eyes traced over her body, and her skin prickled beneath his gaze. "I wouldn't be so sure."

381

Esmyra turned her face away as heat rose to her cheeks.

Staring at the spear in her hand, she twirled it between her fingers. "Think you're ready for a real fight?" she taunted, her stance lowering as she shifted her weight, watching his every move.

Draevyn's smirk morphed into a devilish grin. "You might want to worry about yourself," he said, settling into a stance. "But feel free to prove me wrong."

Without another word, she lunged, closing the gap between them with a swift strike aimed at his chest. He sidestepped as his spear met hers in a sharp clash. The impact reverberated up her arms as he pushed back, forcing her to plant her feet more firmly. The force in his strikes made it clear he was going easy on her, and it only aggravated her all the more.

The faint grin on his face was just begging her to wipe it away.

"Is that all you've got?" he taunted.

Esmyra glared and pulled her spear back, this time aiming a swipe at his legs. He blocked her with a downward swing, lifting his arm against her to hold her back.

And then, with a twist, Draevyn broke their hold and thrust his spear toward her side. She dodged, feeling the faint whisper of the blade brush past her.

Her heart pounded, but she grinned as her body kept up with his.

Their spears clashed again, a fierce ringing sound that reverberated in the quiet garden. She pushed forward, testing his defenses, but he was faster than anticipated—*always* faster than her without the use of her magic.

With a quick twist of his spear, he knocked her weapon from her grasp and lunged. Draevyn's arm wrapped around her waist, pulling her body flush against his chest, and lifted her feet from the ground.

The moment their bodies pressed against each other, her mind scattered. Draevyn's spear was held to her throat, cool against her skin, but all she could focus on was him—the strength of his arm pinning her to him, the steady heat radiating from his chest against hers. The weight of his gaze made her breath hitch, her pulse racing far beyond what was caused by the act of sparring.

*Kaelypso's tits, Esmi,* she cursed herself, but it was impossible to ignore the way his eyes locked onto hers.

Draevyn's breath was warm against her cheek, his scent of cedar and leather clouding her thoughts.

Esmyra was *supposed* to shove him back and throw out some witty retort, but her voice failed her, trapped somewhere in her throat. With his hand at her waist, his fingers pressing into her skin like he had no intention of letting go, she found herself frozen.

His closeness left her disoriented. She didn't want to admit to herself that seeing that spark in his eyes—for *her*—had a warmth pooling between her thighs.

It was inappropriate.

It was infuriating.

It was *possessive*.

And it thrilled her like nothing else ever had.

When he leaned in, his words were a whisper against her ear, his voice soft but threaded with something darker. "Maybe next time, you'll be faster."

Her whole body tensed before he finally let her go and placed her on the ground.

Draevyn's eyes were dark and fixed on her. "Give up?" he murmured, his voice a low rumble with a grin stretching ear-to-ear.

Esmyra swallowed, defiant despite the thrill sparking down her spine. "Only in your dreams, Phoenix."

The playful taunts faded, replaced by a tension that felt more dangerous than anything she had found herself up against before.

The quiet of the garden shattered as the staff flooded in, tending to the surrounding greenery. Esmyra straightened, instinctively stepping back from him as he lowered his spear.

"Well," he drawled, running a hand through his hair as he glanced around at the bustling servants, "looks like our session is done for the day." His gaze flicked back to her, halting just long enough to make her heart race again.

She jutted her hip to the side. "Next time, I won't go easy on you."

"Good," he said, his voice dropping slightly. "Would hate to think I intimidated you."

She rolled her eyes but couldn't help the smirk tugging at her lips. As she turned to walk away, she felt his gaze follow her, the weight of it sending a chill through her.

Just as she reached the garden's edge, Draevyn called after her, "Don't get too worn out with her. I don't want you to come here with more excuses tomorrow."

She glanced over her shoulder. "Not a chance!"

With that, she found herself counting down until the following morning, when they would continue this dangerous dance—a dance she found herself craving.

Esmyra was surprised to find today's meeting with Syrena wasn't back in the tower they had been held up in the last several days, but instead, was out on the edges of their city. She was thankful Syrena's anger from the prior night didn't seem to continue into the following day.

A secluded lagoon stretched before them, the soft waves lapping at the shore, and the air fragrant with the scent of salt and wildflowers. Bright merlights danced across the water's surface, shimmering like scattered diamonds.

"Esmyra," Syrena said as she took a step up to her side, "did you know you were born with gifts that extend far beyond the manipulation of water?"

Esmyra already knew that, and it was how she found out she wasn't a typical siren shifter as mentioned in any of the texts she had pried through over the years. It only made her believe she may be mixed with some other race—perhaps elven.

Syrena gestured toward the lagoon. "First, you must connect with the creatures of our world." Esmyra took a few steps toward the water as her sister continued. "You see, our people aren't only that of our kingdom, but all creatures of the sea. They're under our protection.

They trust us, and they work with us as needed. But first, you must learn to understand them."

Kneeling at the lagoon's edge, Esmyra placed her hands in the cool, clear water, feeling the pulse of it beneath her palms.

"Drown out the world and all of our surroundings and listen," Syrena instructed.

Esmyra closed her eyes, inhaling deeply, trying to tune out the world around her. At first, there was only the sound of the waves and the gentle breeze rustling through the tall grasses along the shore.

But soon, she sensed it—a faint whisper coming from beneath the surface.

She opened her eyes, focusing on a school of vibrant fish darting playfully in the shallows. They paused as if sensing her presence, their tiny forms shimmering from their scales.

A wave of unfamiliar excitement washed over her as she whispered, "They don't fear me."

"Of course they don't," Syrena said, a bit of confusion in her tone.

Syrena kneeled in the sand alongside her. "Now, reach out to them. Speak to them as they speak to you."

Focusing again, Esmyra concentrated on the fish, allowing her mind to blend with theirs. Images of the ocean's depths flooded her thoughts—coral reefs, open water, and the rhythm of the tides beyond their dome.

It was exhilarating, feeling their trust and connection. Though an undeniable sadness came with it, feeling for herself how much they longed to be beyond the prison Maerinys had fallen into.

"Now, for something a little more challenging," Syrena started. "Have you ever shifted into something that is *not* your siren form?"

A smirk formed on Esmyra's lips. "Aye."

She lowered the tips of her fingers to the ground, and the skin of her hand immediately morphed, blending in effortlessly with the grains of sand.

Syrena's eyes flared. "Well, then," she started as she began a slow clap. "It appears you're already several steps ahead."

Esmyra couldn't help her prideful smile as she allowed her skin to take its normal hue. "It's a fun little trick I enjoy using on shore. Though, it is a bit of a pain if clothing is involved."

Syrena chuckled as she stood. "Well, what if I were to tell you that, in time, that may no longer be the case?"

Esmyra's brows furrowed as she rose to stand at her side. "What? How?"

"Anything is possible." Syrena winked.

Esmyra's lips parted—the question she'd been yearning to ask for days settling on the edge of her tongue. "And you believe that includes raising Maerinys?"

No matter how desperately she wanted to help, she still wasn't entirely convinced it was possible—nor that she would be the key to doing it.

Syrena took her hands and looked into her eyes as she said, "I believe it with every fiber of my being, Esmyra. But in order to summon the power it would take to raise Maerinys...it has to be *wanted*. It will take both of us. I cannot do it myself. Believe me when I say I've tried to unlock the power. You and I are two halves of the same whole."

"Wanted?" Esmyra nearly gasped on a half-laugh. "Of course I want it. Why wouldn't I? Why would I even be here trying, if not?"

Syrena shook her head. "No, sister. It will take a massive eruption of energy. You must want nothing else more. It will burst within you. Within both of us, when the time comes. It will take all of our focus. All of our strength. Distractions will do us no good."

Esmyra's gaze moved over her sister—a mirror to herself if it held warmth. Her golden waves fell to her waist, her eyes as welcoming as the sun hovering above the horizon.

It was then that she knew Syrena was the missing piece in her life —in her heart. The other half of her, separated and torn away at birth.

But they had found one another.

Esmyra had found her home. And she would be damned if she let anyone or anything else take this away from her again.

"Distractions?" Esmyra's head cocked to the side.

Syrena studied her, pursing her lips. "You know, I've noticed how you look at him," she began, her tone light yet probing. "It was a bit impossible to ignore last night."

Esmyra's heart raced at the implication. "Who? Draevyn?" She waved her hand dismissively, feigning indifference, but she could tell Syrena wasn't fooled.

"In your own words... *Aye*," the queen replied with a wink. "Do you have feelings for the man you rescued?"

Her brows furrowed at the question, her stomach twisting in knots. "Absolutely not. It's not like that at all."

"Isn't it?" Syrena pressed, crossing her arms. "You're spending a lot of time together, training in the garden. And I've seen the way you look at him when you think no one's watching. Both of you, actually. He even offered his life to ensure you wouldn't be punished for his actions..." Her words trailed off, her eyes going distant. "No man does that, Esmyra."

Esmyra's inner turmoil was palpable. "Draevyn is just the only familiar thing down here, even if we barely knew each other before we found ourselves trapped." She forced a dismissive laugh. "Consider it...bonding through trauma. And he seems to be one for heroic dramatics."

Syrena raised a brow, a knowing smile forming. "Are you sure? Because if you don't want him—"

"I don't," Esmyra interrupted, her voice sharper than intended. The sudden edge of her tone made her cheeks flush with embarrassment.

*What am I even saying?*

Her sister continued, unfazed by her outburst. "Well, he's handsome. Strikingly so." Syrena's gaze roamed over her.

"You think Draevyn is handsome?" Esmyra forced the words to come out as if they repulsed her, playing it off as if Syrena declaring her interest didn't feel like a dagger to the chest. Her brows furrowed. "You just bound the man in a velsinyte cuff." She suppressed the snarl that threatened to slip through the words.

"I ran into Draevyn two nights ago. He said he couldn't sleep and was roaming the halls of the palace. It...it seemed like he was trying to seduce me, but perhaps I misread his intentions." Syrena shrugged. "It's been a while since I've had anything new to play with, but it didn't feel right to accept without speaking to you first."

*Draevyn did...what?!* Her chest ached as the vision of it crept into her mind.

She hadn't even seen them speak to one another, and the last she knew, Draevyn didn't trust Syrena—*loathed* her even, especially after last night. But perhaps it was all a lie.

Esmyra cleared her throat. "And the cuff?"

"I just needed to make an example of him for his lies," she admitted. "Well, and assaulting my guard...but if he proves himself a model citizen, then the cuff will come off."

Syrena let out a low giggle as she guided Esmyra back to the path, beginning the trek back to the castle. "I would be lying if I said his power didn't intrigue me. You must admit, it could be beneficial for our kingdom once it's raised. We would complement one another."

Esmyra bit on her tongue until blood spilled down her throat. "Oh?" was all she could manage to say.

"I'm the light of the sea, all things serene and life-giving, just as the sun. And he's the rays of it, the very flames that fuel our world. Together, we would be the features of both sun and sea. Together, we could be a force, him and I."

*Together. Him and I.*

Panic clawed at Esmyra's chest as those words repeated themselves in her head—Draevyn's fire to Syrena's golden warmth. Everything about them would make sense.

While Syrena had proven herself to be just as she described, serene and life-giving, Esmyra was the opposite. She was the storm, the sea's dark abyss.

She didn't know light—didn't deserve his fire after all she had done.

But Syrena? Perhaps she did. Her twin had been stuck down here, locked with their people. All she knew was giving. All she knew was kindness.

Esmyra had the world at her fingertips, and all she had ever caused was death and destruction.

*And he showed interest in Syrena.* He tried to *seduce* her. While Esmyra assumed he'd been playfully flirting with her these last few days, or maybe even since the moment they met, she couldn't deny the fact that he'd never seemed interested otherwise. Certainly not while wandering about in the middle of the night.

The fairytale she'd been imagining these past few days turned to ash as the vision cleared, realizing it was never herself alongside Draevyn, laughing and falling in love.

It was her mirror.

It was her sister.

Not her.

*Never* her.

Syrena's words reverberated in her mind, blending what was once hope with fear and rage.

"I think it would be best for both of us to keep our minds away from that of men," Esmyra finally said. A lump formed in her throat that she desperately tried to ignore, but the thought of them together had her forcing herself to make her eyes not shift in fury.

It wasn't just that it was Syrena speaking of Draevyn this way. She would be this way with anyone, she realized. And that scared her more than anything.

Esmyra wasn't the jealous type, had never been. Men were a mere tool to her. So why was this happening now?

Syrena laced her fingers through Esmyra's, and their stares found each other as her sister let out a soft giggle. "Forget I said anything. You're right, and that's probably for the best. I'm clearly getting ahead of myself after being so lonely all of these years. Okay, Esmi. No men."

Esmyra's lips parted at the use of her nickname.

Was it easy to guess? Had she let it slip since they arrived and never realized it?

Relief flooded her that Syrena didn't press any further, and Esmyra answered her with a smile as they continued their walk back to the castle in silence.

However, the pit of dread in Esmyra's gut grew. A nauseating feeling squeezed the air from her lungs at the thought of Draevyn looking at Syrena the way she thought he once looked at her.

Esmyra swung her fist with a snarl, aiming for Draevyn's face. He caught it, stumbling with the impact. The force behind it was impressive, he had to admit. But there was something charged behind it that hadn't been there before.

She put a wall up, and he didn't know why.

It had been a week since they arrived in Maerinys. Seven long days of being trapped beneath the waves of Rymelle's seas. Draevyn was out of his mind with theories and pieces of the puzzle he was putting together regarding this kingdom's past. But he still wasn't anywhere closer to discovering a way for them to escape.

Her leg swung in a roundhouse kick, a blur of motion through the air. He barely caught her ankle before it struck his face. Flashing her a grin, she ripped it from his grasp with a snarl.

One thing, however, was certain from the last three days since their heated moment in the garden—Esmyra was different. Their nights had grown quiet, separate, and more distant than they'd been even since they met in Anchorage Cove.

When they'd first arrived, she'd been so fierce—untamed and fiery in everything she said or did, but now…she was a shell of that. Anger was visible in her features, no matter the angle.

And, all gods above, he couldn't figure out why. Had she found out about what Syrena tried to get him to do?

When he thought about it more, he realized everything had changed after the day he held her close to him as they trained. Perhaps he overstepped, but she never shoved him away. And he knew her well enough to know that if she was against what he did, she would've made it known.

Likely violently.

Draevyn hardly recognized her. Standing across from him, spear in hand, Esmyra wore that same steely expression she typically did. Only her eyes were cold. She hadn't looked at him with anything resembling amusement or warmth in days. It was as though she'd closed a door, and he hadn't been quick enough to catch it before it slammed shut in his face.

Esmyra threw herself into their spar and held nothing back, each of her thrusts more forceful than the last. It was like she was pouring everything into keeping her focus there, on the fight. Anywhere, it seemed, but on him.

Draevyn replayed the last few days in his head as he continued to block her attacks. He went over their interactions, trying to pick apart each conversation, each sparring session. He recalled making a few stray comments about her stubbornness, or the way her eyes seemed to flash when she was defiant, but he assumed she knew he was joking.

Well, perhaps he wasn't. But it was all in good fun.

He thought she liked it—that bit of banter that made everything feel less serious, less suffocating down here. Even if only for a moment.

But then it all came to an abrupt halt.

The glances she used to send his way, the barely hidden grins when she'd get a hit in or even when she missed on purpose—those were gone, faded into something distant and cold.

Esmyra swung her spear again, and he barely had time to deflect it. He tightened his grip on his weapon, unable to shake the feeling that she was fighting more than just him.

Perhaps she was just exhausted. However, he noticed she didn't seem nearly as eager to leave anymore, not having brought up Blackwood or their crew in days.

They were supposed to be allies, but as more days passed, the more he felt that she had been keeping something from him again. Esmyra had barely said anything to him outside of what was strictly necessary. He didn't mind silence—but this was different. She was pulling herself away, and he didn't know how to bring it up without her retreating even more.

Another blow came hard and fast, her spear aimed just shy of his shoulder. He managed to duck, twisting his weapon to disarm her, but she countered with alarming speed.

"No cheating," he said, trying to break the ice. "No magic."

She'd gotten better. Focused. Somehow even more deadly, but that was the point.

Esmyra didn't say a word as she struck again, and Draevyn barely parried it as his grip tightened on the shaft of his spear to push her back.

"You're holding nothing back today, are you?" he said, attempting a grin, though he could feel the strain behind it.

Draevyn was beginning to see through her walls. See her for who she was—who Jak had said she was.

So, what happened to that fire? He missed that raging blaze, full of life and defiance, loathing this cold flickering flame she'd become.

Again, Esmyra didn't respond, just met his gaze with sharp, narrowed eyes.

His frustration burned hotter, clenching his jaw so tightly he thought his teeth would shatter. If it weren't for the wretched bracelet encircling his wrist, flames would likely dance at the edge of his fingertips.

With an aggravated exhale, he threw his spear down to the ground, the clang echoing across the garden as it fell to the stones beneath their feet. Esmyra halted, brows furrowing as she looked at him.

Crossing his arms, he held her gaze, letting every ounce of his irritation bleed through his stance. "What in all fucking gods is with you?"

"Absolutely nothing," she snapped, her jaw tense.

"Nothing?" he challenged. "You're going to stand there and lie, telling me nothing's wrong when you've barely looked at me in days? You've been acting like a stranger."

A breathy, irritated chuckle left her, but her stare never left his. "I have some news for you, Draevyn. That's *exactly* what we are."

His nostrils flared, jaw ticking. He knew it was only a matter of time before the garden was flooded with staff, just as it was every morning, and he wanted this addressed here and now.

"I don't believe that for a second. Like it or not, we're far from strangers."

Esmyra threw her spear down to the ground next to his and placed her hands on her hips. "Oh? And what makes you think that?"

Draevyn snorted. "We've held each other captive one too many times to be considered as such."

Together, they had harnessed their magic and merged it into a single, unstoppable force in the caves. They had saved each other's lives. Desperately screamed each other's names when danger found them.

But he couldn't bring himself to say any of those things.

"Aye. Well, perhaps stranger isn't the right word then. So acquaintances will do, I suppose."

"Did something happen, Esmyra?" He ran his fingers through his hair. "Fucking Irah, I can't even tell if you still want to find a way out of here anymore."

Her lips pressed into a thin line. "Of course I do!" She threw her hands out to the side. "I've done my part, haven't I? Syrena thinks we're getting closer. That's our *only* way out, Draevyn. We're as stuck down here as the rest of them now. My father fucking *rots* because of yours, and there's nothing I can do about it until I do the impossible and find a way to raise this kingdom!"

"Then what is all of this about?!" he bellowed. The tension

between them tightened, the sharp sting of her words ringing in his ears. "You're different. At least with me."

She averted her gaze to the ground. "No, I'm not," she said quietly, but he didn't miss the small crack in her voice.

A growl brewed deep within his chest at her stubbornness. "I don't think you believe your own lies, Esmyra."

Something flickered in her stare that he couldn't quite grasp. But it was there, and he saw it. Perhaps he had reached her.

Draevyn swallowed. "If this is about the other day...when I held you."

Her blue eyes flared wide. "What? No! Of course not. Why would you even think that?"

"Well, considering it's the last time you were acting normal toward me."

She scoffed. "You don't know me well enough to know what's *normal*, Draevyn Rowe."

Draevyn stepped up to her, their chests brushing against one another. "I know wildfire when I see it. And she's gone. Far from anywhere near me, that's for damn sure."

Esmyra's breath hitched. "Well, I'm sorry you thought you saw something in me that wasn't there." She paused for a moment, and he could've sworn he saw hurt flash in her eyes. "It wouldn't be the first time."

Before he could respond, she slammed her shoulder into his and stormed past him. Draevyn watched as she walked out of the gardens and beyond his sight, leaving him there, speechless.

# CHAPTER 57

# *Esmyra*

The water of Esmyra's walk-in bath formed gently against her skin as she floated, letting her siren form drift just beneath the surface. Teal scales shimmered like stars in the night sky as her hair floated around her in dark tendrils. It should have been soothing, the way the water cradled her—the way it dulled the edges of everything pressing down on her. But tonight, it offered no comfort.

She lost control today, of both her temper and thoughts. And she lied straight to his face repeatedly. Esmyra sighed, sinking deeper as the water curled around her.

Draevyn was right—she had been pulling back. Her heart ached with the knowledge that the warmth he brought her was a dangerous illusion, a tempting mirage she couldn't afford to chase. It wasn't even an option.

Not for a monster like her.

Esmyra's fingers traced through the water absentmindedly, as if the motion might help her piece through the tangle of thoughts. And yet, she couldn't deny that she missed whatever had been sparking between them. The way Draevyn had looked at her, a hunger in his eyes that typically only held fire.

He'd looked so disappointed today as they fought, almost betrayed, and it stung in a way she couldn't comprehend.

But Syrena's words played over again in her mind: *He tried to seduce me.* Even though Syrena said she could've been wrong about his intentions, Esmyra needed to pull herself back. Perhaps Draevyn acted like he loathed her sister *because* she denied his advances.

Esmyra was here to help bring the kingdom back from the depths, not for Draevyn Rowe. Not for the son of the king she loathed so intensely that it fueled the very reason they were even there.

She had to keep her focus. For the sister and kingdom she'd lost. For her father, who rotted in a cell beneath Castle Lephyrin, regardless of the fact he was the reason they were in this mess to begin with. She would never let him perish there, withering away in a miserable existence, even if she knew he likely deserved it for all he had done.

But what surprised Esmyra even more was that she needed to do this for herself. And getting distracted by a man wasn't an option.

Still, Draevyn's face drifted back into her mind. His frustration, his intensity when he'd stepped closer, demanding she be honest with him. Maybe he really did care about her. Maybe he saw something worth saving in her, something she thought had died a long time ago.

Her heart squeezed at the thought. She clenched her fists, letting her talons bite into her palms as her gills breathed for her beneath the surface.

What if she let herself believe that? What if she let him in, only to have him turn on her or leave?

These swarming thoughts overwhelmed her, and Esmyra let out a scream; the sound pouring out of her in a rush of bubbles. It was fierce and silent, swallowed entirely by the surrounding water, as all her anger and confusion spilled out in a voiceless fury. She watched the bubbles rise, dissipating before they even reached the surface. It was raw, yet strangely freeing, though the silence in its wake felt hollow.

Breaking the surface, she drew in a shaky breath as she crawled up the slanted incline of the pool, her body weighed down by exhaustion that went beyond the day's training. She shifted back into her mortal form and brought her knees to her chest, hugging them tightly as she sat there, entirely bare.

Just as she started to gather herself, the door creaked open, and soft footsteps approached.

"Ms. Esmyra?" Briar's voice made her go still. She turned to face her, watching as she carried fresh towels and a robe. "Are you ready to get dressed, milady?"

With a small nod, she stood from the water, mentally preparing herself to see Draevyn and Syrena together at dinner.

The great hall was quiet that evening, the only sound between them the clink of silverware and the soft murmur of the council as they spoke among themselves.

Esmyra kept her gaze on her plate. Draevyn sat across from her, and every time she snuck a peek, she found his expression distant, a slight crease between his brows that hadn't left since their earlier argument. Every now and then, she felt his gaze flicker in her direction, but she pressed down the urge to meet it with her own.

Syrena watched them with a curious eye as she sipped from her goblet of gold, seeming to pick up on the tension that neither of them addressed.

She leaned forward and broke the silence. "Tomorrow evening, we'll be holding a grand celebration in the heart of Maerinys. A long-overdue gathering for the kingdom. Our people have waited centuries for such a night, and they deserve to rejoice. After all, I think we're rather close to breaking free of our bindings." She smiled, a glint of excitement in her eyes. "It will be a night of music and dancing, with you two as our honored guests."

The announcement caught Esmyra off guard. She looked up from her plate, her heart skipping at the idea of the kingdom's people all gathered in one place—for her. Draevyn looked equally surprised, his arms resting on the table while the rest of his body looked taut.

Syrena continued. "I know this is short notice, but we'll need to cancel our meeting tomorrow, Esmi. There's much to prepare."

Draevyn shifted the moment the nickname slipped past Syrena's lips.

Esmyra wondered what he was thinking. Perhaps that she'd asked Syrena to call her that, while she threatened to cut his tongue out for it.

"Does all of this sound good to you? Will you fancy a night of dancing in the streets of Maerinys?" Syrena added, directed at him.

Draevyn gave a slight, restrained nod as his foot bounced beneath the table, rattling it subtly. "Of course."

Esmyra felt the weight of the unspoken words between them, as if he wanted to say something more but didn't.

Dinner resumed, filled with chatter between Syrena, the council, and the staff as they moved about the room. While they discussed the celebration's finer details, Esmyra and Draevyn shared quiet glances across the table, each look a conversation of its own.

When her gaze fell back to her plate, she felt his linger on her like a steady heat. Her cheeks flushed beneath the weight of those fiery eyes.

*Why does he do this to me?* It was driving her to near madness. And she needed to get to the bottom of it.

A soft knock sounded at the door of Draevyn's chambers, pulling him from his spiraling thoughts of Esmyra.

He couldn't help but wonder if maybe she was right earlier that morning—perhaps he didn't know her the way he thought he did. It was like she was slipping further out of reach each day, and the thought unsettled him more than he wanted to admit.

*It shouldn't matter. She doesn't matter.* Even as he thought it, he tasted the bitter sting of the lie.

Draevyn scoffed at his own thoughts, pressing the heel of his palms into his eyes. "Gods, what the fuck is she doing to me?"

Another knock sounded, a little more rushed and impatient than the first. "Who is it?" he called, nervously glancing at the stolen book on his bedside table.

When silence answered him, he frowned and stood to cross the room. The moment he opened the door, his head jolted back at the sight. He wasn't sure who he expected it to be, but he certainly hadn't anticipated Esmyra to be the one standing in his doorway.

She looked up at him, her eyes softer than he'd ever seen, yet there was something tense in her stance.

Draevyn blinked, caught off guard, before stepping back to let her in. "Couldn't sleep?" he asked, trying to keep his tone light, though his heart slammed against his ribs.

She hesitated before shaking her head. "I just came here to apologize."

*That* also certainly wasn't something he expected.

"Um, come again?" A smirk crept up his face at the sight of her nervously standing before him.

Her eyes narrowed. "Don't make me repeat myself."

"Oh, I absolutely will." He stuck a pinky in his ear and twisted it. "Perhaps being down here has damaged my hearing. So, what was that, Esmyra?"

"Kaelypso's tits, you're insufferable," she growled, rolling her eyes.

He crossed his arms, grinning as he looked down at her. "And what would you be sorry for?"

She shrugged as she lifted her talons to her face, pretending to inspect them. "For just being...awful to deal with, I guess."

"Irah himself must've frozen in hell, because I can't be hearing what I think I am."

"Gods, you're irritating. If you're going to be this way, I will show myself out." Esmyra went to move past him, but he caught her shoulder and spun her back to face him.

"I don't think so, Wildfire," he said, voice low.

Esmyra pursed her lips as her brows knitted together. "Why do you call me that?"

"It's what you are." Draevyn couldn't help his smirk.

Her cheeks flushed a shade of pink, and his cock pressed against his pants at the sight.

"Well, what am I to call you? What the rest of the world does, *Phoenix*?"

A sinking feeling fell in his chest. "Anything but that."

Esmyra frowned. "Well, am I to just continue calling you Draevyn Rowe? Or Prince? I refuse to call you *Captain*. That title is taken by yours truly." She gestured to herself, the amusement creeping back into her features.

Her rambling caused his smirk to slowly transform into a wide, beaming smile. "How about Drae?"

She lifted a brow. "Drae?"

He nodded.

"Hmph," she let out as she pushed past him again, only this time it was to walk further into the room. "I like it. Simple. Easy to remember."

Draevyn let out a snort at that, which made her *giggle*.

He didn't even know the woman was capable of giggling.

"So, what's your angle, Wildfire?" he asked as he took a few steps toward her while she roamed about his chambers. "Trying to tire me out to get an easy win in sparring tomorrow morning?"

Draevyn watched as she approached the bed, her fingertips gliding gently over his sheets as she glanced back at him over her shoulder. Her sultry eyes gleamed in the room's darkness. "Oh, I'll tire you out, alright."

His eyes nearly bulged out of his head at her words.

She winked, but then nodded to his bedside table. "What's that?"

*Fuck.*

"Reading is the only thing to do when you're off frolicking with your *long-lost twin*." The last few words were accompanied by mocking air quotations with his fingers.

"Oh yes, the one you supposedly *loathe*?" Esmyra raised a brow. "Tell me, do you also happen to loathe her in the middle of the night?"

Her words were clipped, pointed.

Draevyn's throat went dry, his eyes widening. "Even more so, I've come to find."

"Interesting," she said, her voice soft but calculating.

Had Syrena told Esmyra about him denying her in the throne room that night?

Their eyes locked, that challenge creeping back into her stare. "Have you heard otherwise?"

She shrugged. "Just wondering about your intentions with my sister."

"I'm not sure where this is coming from, but I assure you, I have absolutely none." A heat burned in his chest at the implication. "If your sister were the one I wanted in my bed, I wouldn't try to hide it."

Esmyra's eyes flared, her cheeks flushing a shade of pink as she sat on the very bed he just spoke of. His eyes followed the movement—how his sheets and the mattress formed to her curves.

Was that why she'd been so distant? She thought he wanted *Syrena*? He needed to fix this.

She cleared her throat and crossed one leg over the other as she lifted the giant book from the table and placed it in her lap. "Well, now that *that's* out of the way, let's see what kind of reading you're into, shall we?" She blinked and illuminated the room with her eyes.

When she glanced back down at the book, he leapt across the distance between them.

"Wait!" he shouted as he reached for it, but the moment his hand fell to the book, a sharp pain radiated through it.

Looking down, he realized she had sunk her talons into the top of it, and they were sitting right between each of the bones.

His eyes lifted to hers, and found nothing but grim annoyance on her face. "Um. Ow? What the fuck, Esmyra!"

She let out a soft, vicious cackle. "Well, so much for Wildfire." Her talons retreated into the tips of her fingers, leaving tiny pools of blood in their wake. "Next time I'll use the venom."

He ripped his hand from the book and started to inspect it, but she was already off the bed, pacing in a small circle as she began to flip through the pages. His breathing quickened, nerves taking over him as she turned through the information he hadn't yet told her about.

"Draevyn, what is this?" As she looked at him, she slowly shook her head, as if not believing the words on the page before her.

"I can explain," he rushed out. "It's something I've been wanting to talk to you about, but haven't had time."

"Haven't had time? We're together every morning... How long have you had this? Where did you even get it?" Esmyra closed the book and her fingertips traced over the emblem of the trident and its coiling sea-serpent.

"The library," he answered honestly.

"They have a library? Why haven't I been there?"

Draevyn let out a huff. "Well, as we've stated…you've been off doing other things." He reached out his hand toward her. "Come sit. I'll explain everything I've seen and what I think I know. I wasn't hiding this from you."

"Everything you know about what?"

"Just come here, Wildfire." Draevyn's voice was soft, offering her a closed-lip smile as his hand remained held out to her.

She waved a finger in the air toward him, a single talon slipping out. "Now don't go and think your little nickname holds any power over me, Drae."

The way she said *Drae* sent his pulse racing.

He sat on the bed. "Yeah, yeah. Now get your ass over here before I make you."

Her eyes sparked, and he anticipated her rebuttal, expecting her fire to erupt full force, yet it never came.

Rolling her eyes, she approached the bed wordlessly and sat at his side, sinking into the mattress' edge.

"Good girl." Draevyn winked.

She was close enough that he felt the warmth radiating from her, close enough to catch the faintest scent of aquatic florals and drift-wood. The intimacy of their proximity was suddenly unmistakable, and he forced himself to focus.

But Esmyra was an irresistible distraction. She always had been.

"I've been spending nearly every free hour in that library…" He rubbed a hand over the stubble along his jaw before carefully prying the book from her hands and placing it on his lap. "The shelves are from floor to ceiling and hold thousands of books, likely ones lost to the kingdoms above." He watched the way her gaze flickered with something uncertain, wary. "I think they've been keeping secrets from us."

She didn't break his gaze, her expression tightening as she leaned forward, carefully opening the book's cover and turning its first page.

"What could they possibly be hiding? She needs help to raise the kingdom since Kaelypso and Naerysa have been lost."

His jaw tightened as he sorted through the chaos in his mind. "I'm not entirely sure yet, but some of the books account for the kingdom's history before its sinking. It mentions two beings of immense power —sisters, bound to each other and the sea."

She shrugged a shoulder, her eyes lifting to his. "Aye. Kaelypso and Naerysa, I would assume."

"I'm not entirely convinced," he said, refusing to break her stare.

Esmyra's face paled, and he knew in that moment she had pieced together what he was trying to say. She pulled her knees up onto the bed, wrapping her arms around them before leaning into him. It took every ounce of effort to keep his composure as her skin brushed against his.

"And you think the texts are referring to Syrena and myself?" she finally asked.

Draevyn took a deep breath, casting a wary glance at the closed door of his chambers before he spoke. "Listen...I just don't think Syrena is telling you everything, and I'm not sure her intentions are as pure as she's made them seem."

She searched his face. "You're saying you still don't trust her?"

"It's more than that." He paused, weighing his words. "I've been watching, paying attention to how she talks about this kingdom, about you. There's this...edge to her. Something just doesn't add up."

Her brows drew together, but he pressed on. "What if she's more powerful than she wants you to believe? How would she have access to the powers she does, knowing you would have the same and teach you so easily? While I don't know what happens when the two of you are alone, I'm worried she's hiding what you're truly capable of. Or worse—she's trying to control it."

Esmyra's jaw ticked, and turmoil swirled like a raging storm behind her glacial eyes. "Everyone has an outside agenda to you," she whispered, hurt evident.

His heart raced, but his gaze remained unwavering. "I can't shake the feeling she's only told you what she wants you to believe."

She turned her attention back to the book, and he could see the strain in her face, the weight of everything pressing on her. "So, while I've been off with her learning more of my powers...you've been unearthing all this?"

He nodded, watching her carefully.

"Why didn't you tell me sooner?"

Tension eased around Draevyn's eyes as his gaze softened. "I wanted to make sure there was evidence behind how I felt first. I didn't want to bring this to you without proof of something being off about Maerinys and Syrena. That combined with how you pulled away from me..."

Her lips pressed into a thin line at those words.

"However, after combing through this for days, there's still something I just can't shake." His hand lingered near hers on the bed, fingers only inches away. "I needed to be sure before I threw you into the middle of this."

Esmyra's hand shifted, fingertips brushing his, and for a moment, the charged silence filled the space between them. She was quiet, and he could feel her pulse thrumming in that one subtle touch.

The moment stretched—too close and vulnerable. Yet, he couldn't bring himself to pull away.

"So you trust me now?" she whispered, her voice barely audible.

His eyes held hers, and his chest tightened with all the unspoken things he felt, the things he'd tried so hard to deny. "More than anyone here," he murmured. "More than I probably should." A subtle smirk curved the corner of his mouth.

She carefully closed the book, brushing her thumb along its emblem.

"If you still don't trust me fully, that's fine," he added when the silence from her ate away at him. "However, tomorrow, I say we skip our sparring sessions and sneak into the library so you can see for yourself and make your own decisions. Does that sound like a deal to you?"

Draevyn held his hand out to her, his smirk remaining in place.

The edge of Esmyra's lips tilted before placing her hand in his, shaking it in agreement. "Aye." She grinned. "Only, I say we go *now*."

"Now?" he gasped out with a laugh.

She leapt off the bed and placed a hand on her hips as she gazed down at him. "Unless you're afraid of getting caught."

Draevyn stood, letting out a breathy laugh. "Allow me to lead the way, Wildfire."

The castle was steeped in shadows as they slipped from Draevyn's room and moved silently down the dimly lit corridors. The air was cool, and every step they took seemed to echo louder than they should in the empty halls.

Esmyra's mind spun with the weight of all he revealed. She could still hear the intensity in his voice, his suspicions sharp as blades.

*Could he be right?* The thought twisted uncomfortably in her chest.

It was almost easier not to believe him, to convince herself that his warnings were born of misplaced fear or jealousy. But he had the book, and it contained history lost to their world above, so detailed it was difficult to dismiss. Draevyn had looked at her with such raw concern, and she didn't know how to take it.

*Your sister's intentions aren't pure.* The phrase lingered, seeping in deeper with each silent step they took through the darkened halls.

A part of her resisted. She'd dreamed of finding what she had down here—of a family and a place where she belonged. The idea that Syrena might see her only as a means to power wasn't something she had even considered. Esmyra hated herself for being so naïve to not believe such things to begin with, blinded by finally finding somewhere that felt like home.

Everyone in her life had seen her as nothing but a weapon, so why would Syrena be any different? Likely because Esmyra believed the two of them to be one—one being split into two souls.

Because that was exactly how Syrena spun it.

These thoughts unsettled her as they raced down the halls on silent feet. A strange sense of gratitude settled within her that Draevyn was here beside her—that he cared enough to uncover these truths and share them with her without an ulterior motive.

For the first time in her long life, she wasn't sure where her loyalties should lie.

When they reached the library doors, they both paused, checking for any lingering guards. After a moment, she gave him a nod. He responded by nudging the door open, and they slipped inside, the heavy wooden doors creaking shut behind them.

They were encased in pure darkness, only the light of her eyes casting a small path. With a wave of her hand, Esmyra cast merlights into all the unlit sconces lining the library walls—the small, teal orbs drifted from her fingertips until they fell into place.

The flicker of the lights barely reached the towering shelves and dark corners, but at least they had a subtle view of their surroundings.

Draevyn turned around to face her with a raised brow. "Neat trick."

She winked. "One of the things I've learned since being down here."

He motioned her over to a shelf in the far corner. "It's all here. Everything I've been piecing together so far."

His fingers traced the spines of ancient books, pulling tomes down one by one to spread out across the nearest table in an organized chaos. Draevyn began looking over the notes and half-deciphered texts as if their lives depended on it.

Perhaps they did.

Esmyra pulled out a chair and began to do the same, uncovering ancient family trees of the Aeress family dating all the way back to the dawn of Rymelle, all leading up to where it abruptly ended—with the births of her and Syrena.

A chill ran up her spine at some of the illustrations, appearing as rituals performed in the past. Some were disturbing, seeming as if they ended in gruesome death.

Draevyn sat across from her, relentlessly scanning over pages she had no doubt he already had read several times.

Her gaze lifted over his shoulder, catching on an older, rolled-up piece of parchment tucked beneath a stack of papers shoved into a shelf. "What's that?"

Draevyn cocked his head to the side, but his eyes followed her as she stood and walked toward it, grabbing the parchment before sitting beside him at the table.

He unfurled the ancient, crinkled paper before them. His eyes widened. "I haven't seen this one yet," he admitted, leaning closer.

It revealed an intricately drawn map of Maerinys, depicting the kingdom with details they hadn't seen before—the castle, gardens, winding streets, and hidden alcoves all laid out on the outskirts of the kingdom.

Esmyra's eyes fell to a faintly marked tunnel network reaching out to the very edges of the map. She traced a finger along the tiny inked passageways. "Caves," she murmured, excitement and something resembling dread pooling in her gut.

Dread that Syrena had *lied*.

He leaned in, his eyes tracing over the marked lines before lifting his stare to hers. "This could be our way out," he said, though there was a light growl in his voice.

Esmyra huffed through her nostrils, her jaw tightening in irritation. Not toward Draevyn, but her sister.

Was he right about her? Was she truly hiding a way out of Maerinys from them? From her people?

"Then let's find out where they lead," she whispered.

They exchanged a look, a silent understanding passing between them. "Are you alright?" His whiskey eyes roamed over her with concern.

"Fine. Why wouldn't I be?" The words were more clipped than

she meant for them to be as she rolled up the map and slipped it inside a fold of her dress.

"It just seems like a lot to take in, is all," he answered, studying her every move.

They both stood from the table, and with a wave of her hand, she extinguished the merlights. The room fell into total darkness once more.

"All my life, all I've ever wanted was the truth. And it seems to be the only thing I never fucking get." Esmyra paused, and even in the pitch-black, she could feel the weight of his stare, the warmth exuding from his chest as he stood mere inches from hers. She ached to lean into it—lean into *him*. "And after countless false claims of allegiance and love, it finally seems as if it's within reach."

"And how does it feel? To finally get the truth?" His voice was rough, almost pained.

"Terrible," she answered.

Without another word, she made her way to the door, feeling Draevyn's presence close behind her.

They slipped out of the library, moving back through the darkened, winding hallways.

He leaned closer, his voice low in her ear. "We should leave at dawn to look. You know they'll be wondering where you are the later it gets. Especially with this sudden celebration Syrena mentioned."

*Kaelypso's tits.* She had forgotten about that.

Esmyra nodded, her hand resting on the map beneath the folds of her gown.

Suddenly, Draevyn's gaze shifted ahead as a shadow moved across the corridor.

A guard rounded the corner, his eyes sharp as they locked onto the two of them. He straightened, taking a step closer. Esmyra took note of his grip tightening on the spear he held as his eyes fell to Draevyn.

"What are you doing here?" the guard called, his tone wary as he looked between them. "It's the middle of the night."

"Fuck." Draevyn stiffened.

Power exuded from him, and she sensed his flames aching to burst to life, but they were blocked by the velsinyte bracelet.

Esmyra stepped forward before he did something idiotic, meeting the guard's eyes as she whispered, "Leave this to me, Drae."

"What in all gods are you up to?" he growled.

She took a deep breath as she stalked toward the guard. "Oh, don't mind us." She waved a hand casually through the air. "We just couldn't sleep."

The guard's stance went rigid as she approached, and she knew he had direct orders to never attack her. However, she didn't know if they had a secret protocol regarding Draevyn, and she wasn't willing to take the risk.

"Apologies, Esmyra. It's just an odd hour to be wandering about at night. It may not always be safe."

Esmyra cocked her head to the side as she halted a few feet before him. "And why wouldn't it be safe? Is there something we should fear?"

Before the guard could get another word out, she lunged forward, wrapping her hand around his throat before shoving him against the wall. His eyes flared, but he didn't have time to react before she captured his gaze with her own as they shifted with her power.

The sound of Draevyn's footsteps filled the corridor as he rushed to her side.

"Stop struggling," she hissed, her voice laced with her compulsion. The guard thrashed, his instincts resisting, but she didn't relent. She brought her lips to his ear, her fingers pressing into his windpipe. "And I have news for you, little soldier. The only thing worth fearing here...is *me*."

The guard bucked against her hold. "Tell me about the tunnels surrounding the kingdom," she demanded, her power weaving through the guard's mind like a blade.

He grunted, his face twisting in pain as his pupils dilated from her power surging through him.

"Esmyra," Draevyn warned, but she ignored him.

"Tell. Me." Her arm shook as she held him beneath her strength, desperately clinging to any form of self-control she could muster before she accidentally killed the male.

"Tunnels. They lead to the caves."

Esmyra hissed at his words. "And where do these caves lead?"

"Many places."

Her nostrils flared, her fingers tightening their grip around his throat as he danced around the answers.

Draevyn's hand fell to her shoulder, the warmth of it causing goosebumps to line her neck. "Easy, Wildfire. We don't need to start piling bodies."

"But that's half the fun." A wicked smile curved the edges of her lips as her attention returned to the guard. "Is Syrena aware of any paths that could lead us out of Maerinys?"

"Yes," was all he could say, his eyes swirling still beneath her compulsion.

"Which tunnel does?" she demanded, a sharp pain of betrayal erupting through her.

"I'm not sure, Your Highness."

Esmyra was clenching her teeth so hard she thought they would shatter in her mouth, but she knew he wouldn't be able to resist her demands. She realized Syrena likely never shared this with anyone.

"You never saw us," she growled, her voice cold. "You walked these halls alone, and no one was here. *Say it.*"

"I...walked...alone," he stuttered, his voice broken as he fought her influence.

She pushed harder, watching as his face slackened, his memories dissolving under her command.

"And now, you'll forget," she demanded. "You will go to your quarters, you will close your eyes, and when you wake, you will never recall this interaction."

The guard's resistance faded entirely, and he gasped for air as she released him.

Her chest heaved with fury as they watched the male silently walk back down the hall he had come from.

Draevyn stepped up to her, eyeing the guard, then her, with something between awe and unease. "Remind me never to piss you off again," he muttered.

Esmyra brushed her hands off, giving him a fierce smile. "Would be wise." With one last glance at the guard, she motioned for them to continue back to their chambers. "We're not getting caught tonight. And I wanted to be sure we wouldn't be wasting our time tomorrow. I still wasn't sure what to believe."

"Well, I'm glad you have your answer," he said calmly as his eyes found hers. "And what is it you believe now?"

Their gazes remained locked as she said, "That the only person I can trust, likely in this entire godsdamn realm...is *you*." She let out a huff of a laugh. "My enemy's son."

A mixture of shock and relief flashed across his features before he gave her a subtle nod in response.

They spent the remainder of their walk back in silence as she began counting down the minutes until dawn.

CHAPTER 60

*Esmyra*

As dawn approached, Esmyra and Draevyn silently slipped from the castle, the stone pathways of Maerinys gleaming under a heavy mist.

They kept their hoods up and heads down, navigating the unfamiliar roads as quietly as possible. They passed several carts in the streets; the merchants laughing amongst each other as they set up their stands for the day—some displaying an array of food, while others hung bolts of fabric and jewels.

The further they wandered from the castle, the more people emerged from their homes to start their day. Children darted around, chasing each other, and their laughter echoed as they raced by.

It was strange to think she belonged here, to this kingdom beneath the waves. It called to her—her blood and name. Yet she was a stranger here, surrounded by nothing but secrets and lies, aside from the man accompanying her.

As much as she didn't want to entertain the doubts he voiced about Syrena, the guard last night had all but confirmed that, at the least, her twin was hiding *something*.

Whether that was knowing a way out of Maerinys and secretly keeping her as a hostage, or something entirely more sinister, Esmyra wasn't sure. All she knew now was that Draevyn's instincts were right, and he had rooted them deep inside her, twisting with her own.

As they ducked beneath a darkened archway, she thought of how Syrena had seemed so genuine in her lessons, guiding her with ease as she found herself. But it had all come so easily, as if she were being shaped into something she didn't fully understand.

Just as her father had shaped her before.

Esmyra noticed guards and staff she recognized from the castle out among everyone, hanging decorations for the celebration that was to come in the evening.

A sinking feeling crept into her gut, realizing she wanted no part in it.

Every minute down in Maerinys now felt more suffocating than the last. Only a day ago, she was excited to be there and learn more of herself and people. Now she was counting down the seconds until she could escape.

Before she made any decisions, she had to find out the truth—whatever it was.

Draevyn stretched his arm out to halt her as he peered around the corner. "Fucking Irah," he huffed as he pressed her body against a building with his own. The warmth of his chest against hers, even through their cloaks, sent her heart fluttering.

Only a second later, several armed guards marched by.

"There's so many of them. Why?" he whispered. "They're fucking *everywhere*."

"Keeping tabs on everyone, it seems," she muttered back, catching sight of a guard stationed near a group of music performers. She bit her bottom lip. "Or maybe they're looking for us?"

He let out a low, humorless chuckle. "Of course they are. You're not in your room or the gardens, and Syrena stated she would be occupied. That's likely exactly what's happening."

They hid in a narrow alley between two buildings as she pulled the map from her cloak and rolled it open. "We only have about another mile before we're on the outskirts of the city."

"Well, we best be quick then, before they send more of her goons out looking for you."

"Aye," she answered, while giving a sharp nod. The thought of Syrena sending people to spy on either of them irritated her.

Draevyn signaled all was clear, and they raced from the alley, stepping through narrow side streets to avoid the more crowded paths. As they ventured deeper, the sounds of the bustling marketplace faded, and the streets became quieter, less inhabited. Buildings became replaced by hints of ancient architecture before the sinking, as it jutted out from the sea floor—half-shattered columns wrapped in algae and partially reclaimed by coral.

"There," he murmured, nodding to an archway half sunken into the earth. It was hidden beneath overgrown kelp several yards from them.

As they approached, Esmyra noticed a faint etching of a trident with a coiling serpent carved above it, surrounded by the familiar runes.

It was the same symbol that marked the book Draevyn stole from the library.

She unrolled the map once more. Looking back and forth from the parchment to the arch looming before them, she said, "This has to be one of the entrances to the caves."

The path beyond the arch was dark, disappearing into shadows as its steps sloped downward, looking entirely uninviting.

"This is it. I know it is," she whispered, looking at him.

His eyes were assessing her, and she would've given anything to know what he was thinking. "If this is our way out, there's no going back," he said.

The arch seemed to pull at her, drawing her toward the remaining mystery of Macrinys—a mystery that felt painfully entwined with her existence. Syrena had told her so many things, so many half-truths and lies. Esmyra realized the only way she would uncover the truth of her past was by taking matters into her own hands.

She nodded firmly, and without another word, they descended into the shadows, leaving the stone paths of Maerinys behind them.

The moment they were a few feet beyond the arch, total darkness enveloped them.

"What in all gods is this magic?" Draevyn growled.

They both turned to face the path they came from, finding the merlights indicating day still shone brightly behind them.

"It's definitely odd," she whispered, brows furrowing. Esmyra blinked, her eyes illuminating where they stood. Craning her head, she looked in all directions. "Perhaps this is what's keeping everyone in Maerinys trapped down here."

Draevyn turned to her, only his face visible in her dim light. "Then how would they have come to grab us in the cave to begin with when we arrived?"

Esmyra blew out a breath and shrugged. "We should keep moving."

She took a few steps down the set of stairs before she halted abruptly, and Draevyn accidentally slammed into her back. His arms wrapped around her waist to steady her, making her eyes flare. Remaining in his grip, she pivoted to face him, his hand resting on the small of her back.

"Is there a reason you stopped?" he asked.

A smirk crept up her face. "I was going to suggest you light the way for us." She walked her fingers teasingly over the velsinyte bracelet encircling his wrist.

He glared at her, though there was a hint of amusement in his voice when he said, "Very funny." Draevyn released her, and with a wave of her hand, she conjured several floating orbs of merlights.

"Show off," Draevyn huffed with a soft chuckle, earning a grin from her.

They moved cautiously down the stairs, their footsteps muffled by the damp ground beneath them. Her pulse raced, the silence pressing in more intensely the deeper they wandered.

"Maybe this isn't the right tunnel. There seemed to be several markings on the map. Should we turn back and search elsewhere?" Draevyn asked.

Her jaw locked, knowing they didn't have much time. Only suddenly, the tunnel widened, and she felt a slight shift in the darkness.

"No," she whispered, turning to gaze up at him. "We're exactly where we need to be."

Esmyra could feel the pull again. The pull that had guided her here to her home and people. It was radiating in her very bones—only, not to the kingdom at their backs...but *forward*.

Her steps quickened, and his matched. It didn't take long before they stepped into an open cavern and her jaw fell open the moment she took in the sight.

The crystallized walls that mimicked scales. The ancient pillars encrusted with barnacles jutting from the ground. The giant, empty temple-like space they had entered after defeating the monsters guarding Maerinys. And finally...her eyes fell to the small basin—the one that had shown her the kingdom's demise when she pressed her hand to the rune in its center.

"Oh, my gods," she whispered as she took off into a run, her merlights floating alongside her.

"Esmyra, wait!" Draevyn yelled, but she refused to halt.

The basin once again called to her, and she finally realized why the one in Syrena's tower seemed so familiar.

She stopped before it, running her fingers along its edge. What shocked her next was that the bowl wasn't empty and dry as it had been when they first arrived—it was full, its water completely still, reflecting as a mirror.

Esmyra gazed into her reflection, hoping to see something more, just as she had the last time...only all she was met with was her own haunting stare. A moment later, Draevyn's reflection appeared directly beside her.

He placed his hands atop her fingers as she gripped the bowl's edge, carefully prying them from the stone. "Now, what did I say about touching things, Wildfire?" His voice was soft, gentle, even. But all she could do was continue to stare into their reflections.

After a few moments of silence, her stare met his in the pool. "I never told you what this showed me that day, did I?"

His brows furrowed, and he shook his head. "What do you mean?"

Esmyra swallowed. "It showed me everything. The fall of Maerinys."

Draevyn's eyes slowly widened as she turned to face him. His hands fell to the stone, caging her between himself and the fountain-like structure. "You *saw* it?"

She sucked in a long breath. "It was as if I were there. Standing in the middle of it all. I felt everything, heard *everything*. The panic. The screams. The children crying for their mothers." She paused for a moment, and when she spoke again, her voice was a whisper. "The roar of the waves as they swallowed the streets."

Draevyn placed his hand gently on her shoulder. "This wasn't your fault. You can't bear the weight of what happened. You were an infant. You had no control over what Cyrus did that day."

Pain stung the back of her eyes, and a tear slid from her lower lashes. A sinking feeling fell in her gut as she was overcome with endless emotions—heartache, regret, fury, a deep sadness she never knew was possible.

Esmyra turned her attention to the still water. "I know my father is a terrible man." She swallowed. "He molded me into who I am now, and it's equally horrifying. A greater monster than he ever was..."

"Esmyra," Draevyn started, his gaze piercing through her reflection. "You're not a monster."

She whirled on him, nostrils flaring as she tried to choke back the emotions threatening to suffocate her. "You don't know me, Draevyn Rowe."

His stare never faltered, never left hers while she raised her voice.

"You can keep telling yourself that, Wildfire. But you know it's not the truth."

Esmyra's heart nearly broke open and poured itself onto the floor at his feet, knowing in her soul he was right.

The longing looks he had snuck since the moment they met at the tavern, the kindness he had repeatedly shown since that day, even when she didn't deserve it. Draevyn was the only one who tried to save her as they entered the cave, dooming himself with her as they tumbled over the cliff's edge while the cave collapsed around them. And every moment since, all he ever seemed concerned about... was *her*.

But she couldn't admit she recognized this. Esmyra was barely ready to admit it to herself, never mind say it aloud. She had a kingdom to raise and a father to save from a cursed damnation.

Draevyn, though her only anchor to her sanity, had become a distraction from all that mattered. A distraction she couldn't afford, no matter how intensely she craved it.

"Aye, well..." Esmyra began. "Cyrus is a terrible man. Truthfully, he is many things. As we all are, I suppose. Was he a good father? No." She let out a chuckle that had Draevyn lifting a brow, but there was a glint of amusement in his eyes.

"But, to his core, he was a leader. And while he did terrible things, he always took care of those he cared for. His crew and me." She let out a shuddering breath. "He does know love. He just doesn't know how to show it."

Draevyn lifted a hand and wiped away her tears with the edge of his thumb. "Are you sure we're speaking of your father, Wildfire?"

Esmyra's lips parted. "I am my father's daughter, I suppose."

He let out a huff of a laugh through his nostrils, but let her continue.

"What I'm trying to say is...if taking me is what caused the kingdom to sink...I don't think he knew that would be the consequence. Perhaps it really was because he knew I would be powerful and wanted the magic for himself. After all, he's a pirate, and the best of them. And maybe I'll never know the truth of it, but—"

"But you still love him," Draevyn finished for her. "He's your father. Has been for centuries, and regardless of how he raised you, he's shown you love."

Her lips parted at how easily he knew the words she was trying to say, knowing they felt wrong to even be thought. "And do you think you'll ever have it in you to find love for your father?"

If Esmyra loved her father, who shaped her into a weapon, perhaps he felt the same way for his own.

Draevyn's gaze darkened. "I wish I could say I felt the same way you do. His priority has been, and always will be, power. He proved that the day he offered our souls to Irah as infants. Atlas, his heir, is second to that."

*The king offered his sons' souls in exchange for power?* She wanted to ask more, to find the truth within the legends of Lephyrin's heirs and how they received their powers, but the pain in his voice had her halting.

"I understand that Atlas is his heir, but you're his son too," she said, anger flooding her veins to think of the man disposing of one of his own children because he was the second-born.

Draevyn let out a lifeless laugh as he scratched the back of his neck. "It's complicated." He was silent for a long moment, his expression unreadable. But then his voice hardened. "Some fathers don't care about the cost of their cruelty—only about the end result. Mine wouldn't so much as blink if my power consumed me and I turned myself to ash. The only part he would mourn is losing Lephyrin's feared Phoenix."

Esmyra averted her gaze from his, empathy twisting her stomach.

She wanted to reach out, to find some words that might ease the pain behind his hardened stare, but nothing seemed enough. All this time, she assumed she knew how he felt, how it was likely only a minor hatred or defiance against his father, but this was something more.

While Cyrus had been brutal, she knew at the end of every day that he cared about her and her well-being. The last time she had seen him aboard *The Night Wraith*, they were arguing about just that.

Draevyn's father sent him out to sea, never caring if he would return. Even though she knew she was missing significant details regarding their relationship, she now understood why it was so easy for King Rowe to give up his son when she kidnapped him.

He truly never gave a damn about Draevyn. And Esmyra imagined setting the king on fire herself, reveling in watching him burn.

Before she could ask anything more, Draevyn turned abruptly, his gaze moving to the walls. "But enough about all of that," he muttered, his voice flat. "It's possible that I missed something while you were unconscious and I was checking things out. After all, I was afraid to leave you defenseless on the ground."

*I was afraid to leave you.* Her chest felt odd, like her heart was fluttering.

Draevyn moved away from her, his eyes scanning the carvings within the walls on the cavern's edge. She watched him, her heart still heavy with everything he had revealed in such few words.

Draevyn was just as lost as she was. Just as alone.

Esmyra couldn't help but feel a strange closeness growing between them—a bond forged in shared scars and different paths that had somehow led them to the same place.

Half of her conjured merlights followed him as he drifted to the farthest edge of the cavern. She examined the walls and floor for any signs of a hidden path, anything they might've missed when they arrived here before chaos broke loose.

Esmyra sighed, running a hand through her hair and twirling a lock around her finger as she felt the weight of Maerinys' dome pressing down on her.

And that was when she realized what they were truly standing in.

Her eyes flared before narrowing on certain carvings and pillars, and then her gaze darted in all directions.

This wasn't a cavern at all.

It was a temple.

Each kingdom had a temple dedicated to their ruling god—and this, what they were standing in the center of, was the temple dedicated to the goddesses of the sea.

"All gods," she whispered, jaw hanging open as her neck craned up toward the domed ceiling.

And then her gaze found the once grand stone depictions of Kaelypso and Naerysa. Their figures were seated on enormous thrones, half crumbled with veined cracks, encrusted with barnacles and sea moss.

Draevyn's voice cut through the silence a moment later. "Come here. I think I've found something."

Her pulse quickened as she ran to him, making her way around the jagged rocks and broken pillars. The darkness thickened as she raced around the ancient statues, and then she halted at his side.

"It's a door," he said, almost to himself, brushing aside a thick layer of moss and revealing more rune symbols hidden beneath. Esmyra took a step closer, her gaze falling to the center of the stone door, where all the runes encircled that same trident and serpent emblem from his book. They seemed to be guarding it, *protecting* it.

"Drae," she started and she could've sworn his body stiffened at the nickname. "I think this symbol is a crest—the Aeress family crest."

He blew out a breath. "That would make the most sense. But why isn't it shown all throughout Maerinys? Normally, there are banners... markings atop their weapons. They have nothing. The only places we've seen this so far are—"

"The book and the arch that led us in here," she finished. "Why wouldn't Syrena have our family crest displayed?"

"I find myself questioning just about everything when it comes to her," he admitted.

Returning her focus to the door, she reached out, her fingers slightly grazing the stone. The carvings twinkled faintly at her touch, just as the others had when they stumbled upon the cave.

Esmyra couldn't deny the magnetic pull that seemed to beckon her behind the wall.

"I know I've had a habit of telling you not to touch things..." Draevyn began, and a grin crept up her face. "But this one, I think you should." He stepped aside as he nodded slowly, his dimple on full display.

"Something's behind there," she said. "I can feel it."

His gaze found hers. "Then maybe that pull you've felt this whole time wasn't to the kingdom itself...but to whatever is locked behind here."

"Aye," she whispered.

With a steadying breath, Esmyra pressed her hand to the center of the trident symbol, feeling the stone's chill seep through her skin.

The emblem's glow grew blinding, stretching to all the runes surrounding it. The door shuddered, a deep rumble echoing around them, and then, suddenly, it fell through the ground, as if sliding into a secret pocket in the earth.

Esmyra jumped back, yelping at the sudden shift of stone, but was steadied by Draevyn's hands as they found her hips. She found herself yearning to lean into his touch.

Endless clouds of dust erupted before her, followed by the overwhelming scent of stale, briny air.

Once the dust settled, it revealed a dark chamber.

They exchanged a look, and with a wave of her hand, the merlight orbs floated into the space, illuminating it for them as they followed.

At the center of the space, on a raised stone platform, were two massive stone slabs with runes carved along their sides. And then on the wall directly behind them, the blades of two daggers glinted in the merlight.

"It's a crypt," she murmured, her voice barely above a whisper.

The walls of the chamber were lined with deep, rectangular alcoves carved into the stone, resembling gaping mouths. Dust clung to their edges, and cobwebs draped like veils over the sealed tombs.

Draevyn stepped closer to the platform in its center, his eyes lingering on the carved symbols. "This must be where the Aeress family is put to rest."

A strange sensation washed over her, a feeling that seemed to root itself in the very marrow of her being. Without thinking, Esmyra walked up the platform as Draevyn remained standing just before it, watching her.

Atop the rune-covered slabs, fully intact skeletons were laid to rest. But that wasn't all that caught her eye—on the remains were those same markings her flesh bore, carved into the bones of the deceased.

Standing before them, an odd sensation ignited in her chest— something raw, almost intimate, as if an invisible thread bound her to the remains scattered across the stones.

"Wildfire?"

She knew Draevyn was near, but his voice couldn't have sounded farther away.

A shiver ran along her spine, not from the cold, damp air, but from the ancient magic whispering through her veins and calling out to her.

The beckoning began as a gentle pull, a lightness in the chest that suddenly erupted into a deep ache.

"*Touch it*," the siren whispered from within.

Esmyra's hand stretched toward the bones, and the last sound she heard was Draevyn as he screamed for her. His voice was pained, it was *desperate*. But by the time she realized he said the word *no*, it was already too late.

## Esmyra

Immense power surged through Esmyra. It was stronger than anything imaginable, roaring more violently than the tides, akin to lightning burning her from the inside out. A scream tore from her throat until the surge finally settled, the rush of magic skittering over her flesh.

She worked to catch her breath, and when she finally gathered the courage to open her eyes, they flared wide as she glanced down at her shaking hands.

The runes. They were *gone*.

Her heart raced to the point where she thought it would burst as she frantically took in her surroundings. No longer was she standing in the hidden crypt, but in the castle's tower.

When her stare fell on the Veil of Visions, she ran toward it, stumbling over her own feet. Panting, she gripped the stone edge and peered into the water. Shock struck her like a dagger once she saw her reflection.

The woman gazing back at her possessed such raw beauty that it nearly brought her to her knees. Her skin shimmered with a pearlescent sheen, as though kissed by moonlight on waves. Her hair no longer matched the midnight sky, but was a hue of blue-rooted silver, adorned with glistening pearls and shells, hovering around her as if she were within water. Her talons and webbed fingers were on display, making her guess they were a permanent feature rather than something she could shift into.

All she recognized of herself was her eyes. Those haunting, glacial blues.

A sharp pain ignited in her skull, and in flashes, visions rapidly spun through her mind. Esmyra saw herself in this new form and someone who appeared to be its twin, standing tall, effortlessly commanding the seas—she could only assume the other was Syrena. With the flick of their wrists, waves crashed down, storms erupted, and whirlpools spun at their will.

She realized then that they weren't visions at all—they were *memories*.

Esmyra and Syrena were *goddesses*.

*Twin* goddesses.

The ones who had been lost to the realm for centuries...

The visions darkened, colors bleeding into one another as the memory shifted. A surge of dread turned her blood cold, a tremor formed in the core of her being as the scene before her drastically changed.

Back in the highest tower of the castle, a scene played before her. She and her sister—at least she *thought* it was them, in these new, unfamiliar forms—were backed into a wall, bound by velsinyte cuffs, vines, and flame as blood seeped from their eyes.

The room was crowded; other beings, exuding endless power, stood around the twins as they were secured to the wall. Esmyra stepped closer to get a look at who these beings were.

The first was a man. His frame was massive, every muscle forged as if sculpted by centuries of violence, while crimson light pulsed beneath his rich brown skin like veins of living fire. Another man stood at his side. He was tall and lithe, his hair a wild, tangled mane of red with vines braided within it. And flanking them both was a woman of flawless beauty. Her hair was a flowing river of raven-black that shimmered with both silver and gold with every subtle move-ment, while her fair skin had a subtle luminous glow.

Cool, sickly horror crawled through Esmyra as recognition slammed into her. She'd seen depictions of them throughout her long life across the realm— in statues carved of stone, ancient texts, and stories passed down.

They were Irah, Villaem, and Vydenne. The other gods of Rymelle.

And they were all using their powers against the twins to hold them in place.

Esmyra's gaze fell to the floor, only feet away from where they held the goddesses. She gasped at the sight of two bloodied bodies sprawled out before them, crowns entangled in their hair.

And then, in the corner, with terror etched into every feature of his face, Cyrus Blackwood stood.

"What have you done to the Aeress family?!" he bellowed.

She took a hesitant step closer, eyes focusing on the corpses.

*Aeress.* Those must be her...her *parents.*

And they were dead, discarded as nothing in a bloody pile on the floor.

Esmyra's jaw fell open in horror while the gods ignored Cyrus's outburst.

Something caught her eye, and she found Irah standing before the sisters with two daggers in hand—the blades glistened like liquid starlight that swirled with velsinyte. The weapon itself radiated a power, as if it were forged from the essence of the gods themselves.

Esmyra watched, horrified, as Irah's gaze met her other form—her *goddess* form—strapped to the wall. She raced to stand next to them, to stop whatever was about to happen.

When she looked at the god of rage and war, all she saw was an endless conflict in his eyes. It was then Esmyra realized she *knew* those eyes.

Her favorite pair of whiskey eyes that held thrashing flames.

They were Draevyn's eyes.

Only now, they flickered with fury and anguish, and she couldn't figure out why.

Why were they doing this? How could this have happened? And why in all gods did Irah care, if he was the one who held the blades?

Then her twin spoke, voice trembling with rage. "They mean to end us, Kae."

*Kaelypso.*

Esmyra's jaw dropped. Eyes widening in disbelief, she watched as her other form spoke to Irah. Kaelypso's voice was filled with desperation as she said, "Do you truly mean to kill me?"

For a heartbeat, Irah's face softened, his lips parting as if longing to speak. But the glint of his blade caught the merlights, and he took a step forward. "It's too late to go back now," he whispered, as if speaking to himself as much as her. "This isn't my choice."

Esmyra's heart shattered into endless pieces, as if it mimicked what was happening inside of Kaelypso's chest.

The two other gods stepped forward, and her sister's power surged through the tower, pressing against the velsinyte bindings until they emitted a glowing heat. The eruption of magic was so great it had Esmyra clutching her chest.

But the surge of power still wasn't enough to break free, and there was nothing to be done.

And then Irah moved.

Esmyra could see it in his eyes, in the way his grip on his weapon faltered.

"You don't have to do this," Kaelypso said, her voice soft, almost pleading.

Naerysa, or Syrena, let out a bone-chilling cackle from beside her. "You know what they fear—they cannot control us, and so they wish to destroy us."

Esmyra turned to her father, who was watching the scene unfold, gazing right through her, as if she weren't even there. Though she supposed she wasn't.

"DO SOMETHING!" Esmyra screamed at him, begging, as tears slipped from her eyes.

But all Cyrus could do was watch.

Irah exhaled sharply. His jaw clenched as his gaze hardened. "This is the only way to protect the realms," he murmured, as if trying to convince himself.

"Liar!" Naerysa hissed.

"You shut your mouth! If I don't do it, they will," he barked at her, gesturing to Vydenne and Villaem, who looked as if they would rip the blade from his hands and finish the goddesses themselves.

But then Irah turned to Kaelypso, and when he spoke again, his voice was soft. "And I can make it quick."

"Get on with it, Irah! It needs to be left in their hearts!" Villaem hissed, and Vydenne nodded alongside him.

"I will find you again," Irah whispered, his voice sounding broken.

Esmyra's hand clamped over her mouth as bile burned the back of her throat.

Before Kaelypso could respond, Irah's hand moved, and in one brutal motion, he thrust the velsinyte dagger into her chest—into her heart.

An agony greater than Esmyra had ever known seared through her, stealing her breath. She felt as if she were drowning in flame and ice. She screamed as her body writhed, matching the movements of Kaelypso against the wall, her strength crumbling with each heartbeat.

Through Esmyra's blurred vision, she watched Irah move toward Naerysa. Her sister screamed as she violently thrashed, but with one ruthless strike, he plunged the second dagger into her.

The twin goddesses crumpled together, their once-divine forms weakening. The hue of their skin became ashy under the velsinyte curse as the daggers remained in their chests.

Esmyra fell to her knees, feeling as if her soul was ripped from her body. Her gaze slowly lifted to her lifeless goddess form as Irah gently brushed his fingers against her cheek.

She felt everything as Kaelypso had. His touch burned as the darkness claimed her—her essence tearing free from her body, drifting like smoke billowing on a wind.

The tower began to tremble, the kingdom itself shuddering in protest, as the waves beyond the kingdom rose in wrath.

The gods began bickering, fighting over what to do as the castle shook and screams erupted from the far edges of the city.

"Asyris needs their souls for it to be complete!" Vydenne screeched.

"Surely something would've indicated what would need to happen once they were stabbed!" Villaem countered.

*Asyris? What in all gods was an Asyris?*

"They forged the daggers, and that was all the instructions they gave. You were there, so you're aware of just as much as I am," Irah snapped, his eyes a storm of raging flames.

Vydenne stepped up to him, pointing a finger in the god of rage's face. "You better have stabbed their hearts, or so help me, *you* will be the next to find a dagger in your chest."

Movement caught Esmyra's attention, and she watched as two orbs, resembling lightning-fueled merlights, emerged from the goddesses' bodies, gliding from the room while the gods bickered among themselves.

Cyrus followed them, running after the orbs as if his life depended on it.

And then her anguish faded, along with her spirit. She felt herself being pulled, her essence scattering, seeking something new. As her vision swirled and shifted, the cries of two newborns echoed, and then she stood inside a royal bedchamber, two elaborate cradles in its center.

Esmyra's gaze drifted to the door, where the two glowing orbs, one teal and one golden, floated through and drifted towards the infants. Cyrus ran through the door a moment later, and they both watched, jaws hanging in disbelief, as the orbs slipped into the fragile bodies in the cradles.

The infants' skin immediately cast an otherworldly glow, each matching the orbs that claimed them.

The castle continued to tremble as the fall of Maerinys raged on just beyond the walls—chandeliers shook, shelves rattled, and screams erupted from the halls.

Cyrus's gaze lingered on one of the baby girls—with hair dark as night and eyes blue as the sea—before he reached in and took her from the cradle.

"Don't you dare, you bastard," Esmyra whispered as she watched.

And a second later, he ran from the room, leaving the other baby behind.

Esmyra reached for her sister's infant body, but her hands passed right through her, as if she were a ghost.

"Fuck!" she bellowed, but the castle trembled again, and water began to seep into the room from beneath the doors. "I'm so sorry," she said, tears bursting from her eyes as she turned away from Syrena and sprinted out the door.

She raced through the halls, trying to get back to the tower, back to her body—*Kaelypso's* body.

Once she was halfway up the spiral staircase, sharp, piercing pains erupted down her arms and spine. She fell to her knees as a scream erupted from her throat.

Esmyra laid sprawled across the stairs in agony when she found the runes marked her flesh once more, racing up her arms.

"Oh, my gods." She lifted her shaking hands to her face, twisting her wrists to view the red-hued markings.

A strange sensation swept through her, like an invisible force trying to drag her back to the world she came from, as her vision's edges blurred and frayed.

"No," she gasped, her fingers scraping over the ancient stone steps she remained on.

She needed more, needed to understand. In that memory, Esmyra had been powerful, untouchable—a *goddess*.

Esmyra was Kaelypso, one of the lost sea goddesses of Rymelle. Only Syrena had been right—they were never lost. They were *betrayed*.

She strained against the pull dragging her back, her heart thundering in her ears. But the force was relentless as the vision continued to slip away, her grip on the memory fading like water slipping through her fingers.

The last of the vision dissolved like mist, and when she opened her eyes, she was back in the crypt.

CHAPTER 63

*Draevyn*

"Wait, no!" Draevyn bellowed as Esmyra reached for the bones, but he knew before the second word left his lips, it was already too late.

He watched helplessly as her body shuddered, her skin growing pale the instant her fingers brushed against the remains, as if they had sucked the life force from her. The runes marking her arms surged so brightly it nearly blinded him as he dove for her. And when they winked out, they were a dull crimson with a similar ashy hue to her flesh—no longer teal, as they had been since they arrived.

The power she always exuded no longer pulsated from her body, but now from the bones.

Draevyn lunged forward, catching her just as her knees buckled, forcing him to fall to his own on the ground. Her form sagged against him, lifeless and limp, as he lowered her carefully to the floor. Esmyra's pulse fluttered weakly as he pressed his fingers to her neck, but her breaths had ceased to rise and fall with any rhythm.

Panic seized him, and he found himself barely able to catch his breath as he stared down at her in his arms.

This wasn't like how she collapsed when they fought against the krechuums. She still had a heartbeat then, and her chest rose and fell. And now, he feared she'd vanished entirely—lost to whatever magic

435

had taken hold of her the moment she touched those remains. He'd never seen her so vulnerable, and he tightened his hold around her, refusing to let go.

"Wildfire." He gently shook her, his voice a hushed murmur, desperate and pleading. "I need you to wake up. Come back to me..."

Draevyn's jaw clenched, feeling as if he were pleading with a corpse, but he refused to believe it. His heart hammered painfully at the thought. He wasn't prepared for the panic that clawed up his spine, or the gnawing helplessness that made him want to rage against whatever just took her from him.

"*Esmyra!*" He couldn't help the crack in his voice. His fingers dug into her arms as if his touch alone could anchor her back to him—to the world.

Draevyn studied her face, taking in every detail as if he hadn't already memorized every feature of her. Esmyra no longer held the defiant gaze he looked forward to seeing every morning.

Now, she lay in his arms as if on the edge of life and death, seeming so fragile...so *human*.

It was then he realized, somewhere in the chaos of their reluctant truce, she had clawed her way into his heart. Esmyra was a force of nature, a tempest barely contained, and he wanted her back—here, with him.

With his heart racing, he brought his lips to her ear. "Wherever you are, fight your way back." The words were barely louder than a breath. "Find your way back...*to me*."

Seconds passed like hours, and just as his grip wavered, as the icy thread of dread wrapped tighter around his heart, the runes atop her arms began to glow once more.

The bones on the altar rattled with matching glowing runes, and then, with a sudden burst of light, Esmyra's eyes flew open with a desperate gasp.

Her chest heaved, and she blinked, her eyes flooding with panic. Her gaze snapped up to meet his, wild and searching, as if she'd surfaced from the darkest depths of hell itself.

"Esmyra! You're okay!" Draevyn steadied her, brushing strands of hair from her face. "You're safe," he repeated over and over, as if he were more so trying to convince himself.

A shudder rippled through her, and her hands shot out, gripping his arms as her eyes grew feral and unfocused. Talons slipped from her fingers and dug into his skin, but he barely felt the pain of it over his concern. He pressed one hand firmly to her shoulder, the other gently cradling her face as he searched her sea-blue gaze.

"Wildfire," he whispered, the word heavy with relief. "You're back. You're here. You're here with me."

Draevyn watched her, taking in the haunted look in her eyes, like she'd just seen the horrors of a lifetime and was struggling to find her way out of them.

She blinked, a wave of exhaustion settling over her features, and took a deep, steadying breath. But her talons still clung to him as if afraid he might vanish if she let go.

"What happened?" His thumb traced the line of her cheek. "Where did you go?"

Esmyra stared at him, her breath still uneven, and he noticed a faint tremor in her hands. It took her a few moments, but finally, her voice broke through, rough and laced with shock. "We're in the cave. In Maerinys."

He nodded rapidly. "Yes."

"We're alive." She sounded as if she didn't believe it, and her once dull pulse now thrummed beneath his fingertips.

His brows furrowed for a moment, unable to imagine what she must've just gone through for her to believe otherwise. "We are."

Esmyra swallowed hard and moved to stand, but Draevyn's grip on her arm remained in case she faltered. Once she straightened, her stare fell to the rune-marked remains. Her hand drifted to the bones she'd touched but stopped short, a flicker of fear crossing her face.

"What happened?" Draevyn asked again. Fury seeped into his veins, and his flames lashed against the hold of the velsinyte bracelet, waiting to burn anything that may have harmed her. He had never seen her so rattled—never thought it was even possible.

"I was here and then I wasn't," she said at last, her voice raw. "Like

I was transported through time itself and placed inside a memory." She paused for a moment as her stare remained on the bones, unyielding.

His eyes flared. "What do you mean?"

"Draevyn..." Esmyra's voice cracked as she turned to face him. Her eyes searched his as her expression became overcome with grief. "Naerysa and Kaelypso."

"The lost goddesses," he finished for her.

"They...they never left the realm. Never abandoned their people." She swallowed as rage warped her perfect face.

Draevyn's mind reeled as his eyes darted back and forth from her to the bones. A sinking feeling fell into the pit of his stomach, his throat tightening. "Esmyra, whose remains are these?"

A single tear slid from her rage-filled eyes. "Mine," she whispered.

His world spun, grappling with the single word spoken so confidently. It tangled itself around his mind, tearing through his memories of her. How she was never like any woman he had ever met, exuding power unlike any being he had ever crossed. Power like...like a *goddess*. Esmyra herself said she never understood how she possessed such magic, only assuming she had ties to the lost kingdom. She had been desperate for answers. Desperate to find someone like her.

And then she finally had—in a *twin*.

Could it be possible? Were Esmyra and Syrena the lost goddesses of Rymelle?

Draevyn studied her, expecting to find uncertainty or perhaps even fear in her eyes, but instead, he found nothing but a calm fury. When he couldn't find words, she spoke again, meeting his stare. "The moment I touched the bones, I was transported to the day of the betrayal. The day Maerinys sank to the depths."

In that moment, Draevyn felt the walls of his doubt crack, questioning everything he thought he knew. He reached out and took her chin between his fingers, bringing her stare back to his. "Tell me everything."

And she did.

Esmyra spoke of being in another form—of watching her death at the hands of Rymelle's remaining gods and their betrayal of her and her sister, without any explanation as to why. She told him how she felt Kaelypso's pain, as lethal and agonizing as if it were her own. How she looked into those same teal eyes and knew in her soul they were one and the same.

When he asked who had plunged the dagger into their hearts, she hesitated for only a moment, her eyes lifting to those very daggers that now hung on the wall behind their remains. Her gaze held something he didn't quite understand, but when the word *Irah* left her lips, he could've sworn his heart stopped.

Draevyn's power stemmed from the very god who had betrayed her in another life. No wonder she had hated him so intensely. Perhaps she still did, maybe even more so now.

Esmyra swallowed. "I know how it sounds...but the memories, the feelings—they were real. It was me, but not *this* me." She gestured to herself.

"I believe you," he stated.

Her eyes darted back and forth between his. "Thank you," she breathed. "There was...one other thing. One detail I still can't grasp."

"What is it?"

She bit her bottom lip. "Have you ever heard of an Asyris?"

Draevyn scratched at the stubble lining his jaw. "I don't believe so. Why?"

Esmyra looked to the daggers on the wall. "I think whatever Asyris is, or whoever it is, they had something to do with the creation of velsinyte." Her gaze found his. "Asyris is the reason they discovered how to kill a god."

Draevyn blew out a breath. "It's something we'll need to look into, but after seeing the archives down here, I can't even begin to imagine how much history has been lost to Rymelle."

She nodded along with his words before asking, "Do you think Syrena knows about what happened to us in another life? Do you think she kept this from me this entire time?"

"It's impossible to say," he answered, but the second he spoke those words, he knew. He knew Syrena must've known. All the talks of them finding a way to raise the kingdom—only they had to be together to do it. She must've known all along.

Draevyn pulled Esmyra into his chest, her body going stiff at the sudden contact before allowing herself to melt into him. "But let's find out," he whispered, determined. She looked up at him, and he could've sworn he saw hope in her eyes. "We'll get to the truth, no matter what it takes."

"Aye," she whispered.

The moment Esmyra and Draevyn arrived back at the palace, she was swept away by Briar and other handmaidens. Everyone fussed over her appearance—her hair, the kohl lining her lashes, and the rouge on her cheeks—before placing her in the most elaborate gown she had ever seen for the celebration that evening.

The soft, cerulean fabric clung to her form in all the right places, somehow even more so than the ones she had grown used to wearing. Its top layer possessed an iridescent shimmer that moved with her body as if from the light of the moon. Intricate silver, coral-like embellishments adorned the bodice, framing her collarbones and emphasizing her waist and hips.

Sheer, flowing sleeves draped down her arms like tendrils of mist, while the high-slit skirt flowed to the floor, pooling at her feet. The gown billowed softly with every movement she made.

When Esmyra looked at herself in the mirror, she knew it was the goddess lingering within her flesh who stared back at her. She now realized that the subtle voice she'd been hearing since she entered the cave...that *monster* lingering within her was never her siren at all.

It was Kaelypso. And it terrified her more than anything.

She never thought the day would come where she would long for the life she knew back on *The Night Wraith*—of long coats, pistols, and brawls.

But now, seated upon a throne amidst a celebration in her honor, she realized her former life was fading away, rapidly slipping through her fingertips.

The city square pulsed with life, lit by orbs of blue, while stretching wide and grand. The area of the city was bordered by massive coral structures with intricate carvings and archways, strings of pearls and seashell garlands looping from post to post. Musicians played their melodies as the air was filled with laughter and people cheering from all around.

Sitting next to her, Syrena looked every bit the role of a queen, gazing over her people with a calm, almost detached expression.

But then Esmyra's attention strayed to the edge of the dais, where Draevyn lingered in the shadows. Arms crossed, his gaze scanned the crowd as if he were looking for something. And just as she allowed herself a small smile at his brooding, he looked up, meeting her stare.

Heat rose to her cheeks. For a moment, the crowd faded, and it was only the two of them.

Syrena shifted beside her, and Esmyra found that her sister was *also* staring at Draevyn.

A sudden, unwelcome flicker of jealousy twisted sharply in her chest. Esmyra tried to push it away, to brush it off as absurd. But the feeling lingered, pricking at her, and she suddenly became aware of the weight of her insecurities. The connection she felt to Draevyn grew fiercer as every second passed, even as she fought it.

Or had she made it all up?

The longing glances. The flirty sparring. The...the way he held her in that crypt.

They had just discovered the hidden truth of Maerinys and the gods of Rymelle. Draevyn now knew she was a goddess, but...so was her sister.

*Together. Him and I.* The words Syrena had spoken at the lagoon rang in her ears.

Clenching her jaw, Esmyra forced herself to focus on the celebration before her. She would play her part, at least for tonight. But as she glanced once more in his direction, her heart beat a little quicker, and she wished they were anywhere but here.

The urge to lean over and ask Syrena what she knew regarding their past was relentless, but she held back, her gut telling her it wasn't time. Not yet, anyway. Instead, she forced herself to relax, her hands smoothing over the front of her gown.

Suddenly, the cool touch of a hand wrapped around her own as it fell back to the throne's armrest. "Are you ready to be presented to Maerinys?" Syrena asked softly.

Esmyra met her golden-brown stare, quickly taking in the features of her face.

These were never their true forms, though they had always been the same.

The same as each other—identical, yet opposite.

The dark and the light.

The abyss and the surface.

"Well?" Syrena pulled her from her spiraling thoughts.

Esmyra blinked. "Aye. Apologies." She squared her shoulders and gave a subtle nod. "I'm ready."

"Excellent," her sister purred, and they both stood and walked to the center of the stage.

The music subtly drifted to a halt as guards moved through the crowd, their voices cutting through the laughter and conversation. Slowly, a hush fell over the city square as all eyes turned toward the dais where they stood.

Syrena took a step to the edge of the platform, her silken gown that matched Esmyra's shimmering in the floating merlights as she commanded the crowd's attention. She raised her hands, and an expectant silence settled over everyone, each face fixed on their queen.

"Tonight, we honor the legacy of Maerinys, as our missing piece has finally been returned to us," the queen began, her voice carrying across the square.

Esmyra felt the weight of Syrena's stare as it bored into her cheek.

"*My* missing piece," she finished, only loud enough for Esmyra to hear.

A soft smile tugged at her lips.

Murmurs moved through the crowd, curiosity flickering in their eyes as they watched the two sisters on the dais.

"You see, my sister wasn't returned to us by faith, or by the work of the gods," the queen continued. "For Maerinys called to her, and she answered our pleas. For this kingdom, our home, will not be raised by blood alone, but by strength, unity, and sacrifice."

*Sacrifice?* Esmyra's pulse quickened at the word, confusion rapidly creeping in.

Syrena held out a hand, and with a slight nod toward Draevyn, called, "Come forward."

He hesitated, a flicker of wariness evident in his stare as his eyes locked on Esmyra. Then he squared his shoulders and made his way up the steps of the dais, taking his place at her side. She couldn't deny that his presence instantly put her at ease.

The crowd watched his every move, their curiosity erupting into hushed whispers.

Syrena circled them both as she introduced him. "By now, you all know that my sister, Esmyra Aeress, has returned to us after many centuries. Right when we had nearly lost all hope, this man aided her in returning to us. And for that...we owe him our very lives. For that, along with his continued cooperation during his stay with us, he's earned my trust and sincerest gratitude."

Esmyra's head reared back—not expecting her to be speaking of Draevyn so highly, and to her entire kingdom at that. It was only days ago she said the opposite, placing his wrist in a velsinyte cuff.

"It's my honor to reintroduce this man, no longer viewed as a danger to us, but as a friend and a worthy ally after keeping our Esmyra safe."

Esmyra felt a strange, twisting pang at the words as her brows furrowed in confusion. She glanced at him while he silently watched Syrena through narrowed eyes, seeming just as lost.

Or was that what they wanted her to believe?

*If it was your sister I wanted in my bed, I wouldn't try to hide it,* Draevyn's words echoed in her mind.

But why would Syrena suddenly trust Draevyn if they hadn't at least spoken more than she knew of? However, there were several days where Esmyra had put distance between them—and he could've been anywhere, with anyone, all that time. Including the queen, who was the reason for that distance in the first place.

Maybe Syrena wasn't the only one lying or keeping secrets from her.

Perhaps, once again, Draevyn was too.

When Esmyra and Draevyn were alone, she felt the spark between them in her very soul. But when Syrena was around, it was as if everything they built evaporated in seconds. Esmyra had never cared for anyone before. Nothing like this. Was this normal? This overprotective need to claim him as hers.

Only he *wasn't* hers.

Draevyn was a man of his own will, and it left her with a painful uncertainty resembling a blade twisting in her chest.

Syrena turned toward him and reached for his wrist, holding his gaze as her fingers found the velsinyte bracelet fastened there. However, Esmyra didn't miss the way her sister's thumb caressed the top of his hand. "You will now be allowed to once again walk freely among us, Sir Draevyn," the queen announced.

Esmyra and the crowd collectively held their breath as Syrena inserted a small key inside the cuff, unlocking it with a gentle twist.

The stone-like metal slipped free, Syrena pulling it from his wrist as he blinked in stunned silence.

Draevyn's body shuddered, his knees buckling, and the fire in his gaze ignited brighter than she had ever seen. Even his skin seemed to have an intense warmth return to it—she hadn't realized how much the velsinyte had repressed.

Draevyn's surprise was mirrored by the crowd, who exchanged wide-eyed glances, whispering among themselves.

Esmyra's lips parted as she watched in awe, perhaps even horror. "Drae," his name left her in a breath.

His gaze whipped to hers, and molten fire danced in his irises as their eyes locked.

But Syrena's voice cut through their trance. "Tonight is a celebration of the start of a new dawn. A new beginning for us as we prepare to burst beyond the surface and reclaim our place in the world and Rymelle."

Esmyra swallowed thickly. Millions of questions were ready to erupt from her lips, but then Briar came out from the side of the dais with three glasses of that golden wine, handing one to each of them.

They all took one as the queen turned to face Esmyra and Draevyn, lifting a glass toward them. "To our saviors." She winked.

The masses echoed her toast, and music erupted from the musicians, thrusting the celebration back into motion.

Syrena guided them both down the dais' steps, and the people surged forward. They reached out toward the three of them, eager to pull them into the celebration that already overtook the city square.

Drums beat in a lively rhythm that seemed to vibrate through the stones beneath her feet. Esmyra's heart pounded as she glanced in all directions, overwhelmed by how many surrounded them.

She barely had a moment to catch her breath before a group of young women took her by the hands and pulled her from where she was rooted at the bottom of the dais.

Esmyra followed, laughing in spite of herself, spinning and dancing among the people she was desperate to know. Their laughter became her own, and for a moment, she was swept up in it all, almost forgetting the dread she felt for what she knew she would need to ask Syrena.

Glancing across the square, she spotted Draevyn surrounded by a growing crowd of men, women, and children of all kinds, watching him in awe. They gestured at him with eager excitement, calling for him to show his powers now that the restraining cuff was gone. He seemed reluctant, but under their prodding, a flicker of fire sparked in his palm, earning gasps and excited cries from onlookers.

It was then she remembered they had never seen his kind of magic before. Even above the surface in Rymelle, it was rare to see his magic and live to tell the tale. The Phoenix was feared, and for good reason, but as she watched him from across the space, smile beaming, she knew then that he was never deserving of the name *monster*—not like she was.

It was likely the first time he had his power on display with people cheering for him, instead of running in terror or screaming.

The flames danced in his hands, playful and fierce, illuminating his features as he wielded the blaze into different shapes and scenes. Esmyra watched as his smile beamed brighter than she realized was possible. An unexpected warmth flooded her at seeing him this way, freed from constraint and finally admired for the person he was, instead of the villain he was rumored to be.

Draevyn must've felt her stare, because a moment later, his gaze met hers. She raised the glass in her hand in toast, and was answered with a wink before he was thrust back in providing their entertainment.

Hours passed in a haze of music and celebration, and Esmyra found herself forgetting her worries, losing herself to the laughter and joy around her—something she certainly wasn't used to.

For the first time since arriving here, she wasn't thinking of her bargain with the king, her father, or even what she had found in the crypt earlier that day. She simply existed, savoring the feeling of the moment.

But as the night wore on, her social energy waned, and she suddenly felt overwhelmed by her surroundings.

Her fingertips rested at the base of her neck as she stood on her toes and searched through the crowd, realizing she hadn't seen Syrena since her speech. It was as if she vanished the moment the celebration began.

Esmyra stepped off to the outskirts of the square, and when she turned back to face the crowd, she found Draevyn standing nearby, his gaze searching until it landed on her. As their eyes met, a hint of relief flickered across his face, and he made his way toward her, side-stepping clusters of dancers.

"There she is," he said as he halted in front of her, an amused grin on his face. "I got something for you."

Her head reared back slightly as a nervous laugh escaped her. "What do you mean?"

Draevyn lifted a finger before reaching into his pocket, and when he pulled out his hand, he held a necklace bearing a sparkling turquoise crystal.

Her lips parted. "Drae, what is—"

"It reminded me of you," he admitted as he stepped behind her, draping it around her neck. The coolness of the metal chain bit into her skin, sending a shiver through her.

Esmyra glanced down at her chest to look at the jewel before turning to face him. "You got me a gift?"

No one had ever done that before.

Draevyn's nod was accompanied by a wink. "It's beautiful and blue." A smirk formed. "With sharp edges."

Esmyra let out a laugh, her heart fluttering, but a pain twisted in her chest. It was proof that he saw her—the *real her*—and instead of balking away in fear, he only embraced her more. She felt seen, cherished, cared for. And she didn't feel worthy of any of it.

"Are you okay?" he asked, a bit of nerves flashing across his face as he searched her own. "If it's not—"

"No, no. It's perfect." Her fingertips brushed against the crystal as she nodded, chuckling softly. "Thank you so much, Drae."

His smile may have been the most beautiful thing she had ever seen.

Draevyn offered her his arm. "It's getting late. Would you like me to escort you back to the palace?"

"I would be lying if I said I didn't want to get out of this madness." Esmyra gestured to their surroundings. "But I don't think I want to go back there either."

His head tilted to the side, and as he moved to drop his arm, she laced hers through.

"Come with me," she said, a lilt in her voice she didn't recognize.

"I know a place. It might be nice to unwind a little...away from all of this."

Draevyn's brow arched as he studied her. But then a slow and genuine smile spread across his handsome face, and something flickered in his eyes—not his usual roaring flames, but subtle glowing embers.

"Lead the way," he said. "I'd be honored."

CHAPTER 65

*Esmyra*

The music and laughter faded behind them as Esmyra and
Draevyn walked along a quiet path that wove along the
outskirts of the city.

The silence between them was filled with an unspoken tension.
Her cheeks warmed with every casual brush of his arm against hers.
The necklace, along with the simple, unassuming touches, was
enough to send her thoughts spiraling.

Esmyra glanced his way, finding him already looking at her.
Draevyn wasn't speaking, yet somehow his stare said everything.

Lust. Longing. *Desire.*

A smirk flitted across her lips, which only seemed to amuse him.
"What's that look for?" she finally managed, trying to sound casual,
but the nervous giggle in her voice betrayed her.

Draevyn tilted his head to the side, a drunken lust in his eyes. "Just
making sure you don't lead me into a trap. You know, pirates and all."
He leaned closer, his voice dropping lower.

"Oh, really? Don't you think if I were planning to do such a
thing, it would've happened in the cave?" She laughed, though her
voice sounded breathless. "Or perhaps when I snuck into your
bedchambers?"

The fire in Draevyn's eyes burned the moment she mentioned his room. He was practically devouring her with his gaze, and an intense heat rushed between her thighs. Only this time, when it happened, she didn't try to ignore the sensation. She welcomed it.

Something between them had shifted significantly, and she couldn't pinpoint when it happened, or even why. All Esmyra knew was she could drown in this feeling—this feeling of him beside her, looking at her like she was the only person to ever exist.

When he said nothing, she continued. "And besides, if you truly feared me, I doubt you'd still be following me."

"Can't help myself," he murmured, and it made her face flush. She'd never felt so off-balance with anyone before.

Esmyra led him to the secluded lagoon Syrena had shown her a few days prior. The water shimmered in the late merlight as quiet waves lapped against the shore and rocks.

The view was vast and calm, somehow even more striking under the cover of night, and for a moment, they both simply stood there, gazing out at the surface. The air felt cool, tinged with the scent of salt and lilies. She removed her shoes and walked until the water reached her ankles, enjoying the chill it brought to her skin.

"So," Draevyn started, breaking the silence, "how'd you find this place?"

Esmyra turned back to him, smiling as the edges of her gown twirled around her, floating in the lagoon. "Syrena brought me here. It's one of the few places I know of without watching eyes." She gestured to the water behind her. "And, well, it's certainly beautiful."

Draevyn put his hands in his pockets, his eyes never leaving hers as he said, "Beautiful indeed."

Her lips parted, warmth returning to her cheeks.

He moved to take a seat on a smooth rock near the water's edge, and she joined him, feeling the heat of his shoulder just beside hers. The silence was heavy with tension, and she was suddenly hyper-aware of the mere inches between their bodies. Every breath, every little movement, felt magnified.

They sat there for a long moment, listening to the gentle ripple of water.

"Have you...thought about what happened in the crypt?" he asked warily.

"Every second since we left." Esmyra swallowed, her gaze fixed on the water. "It was...overwhelming, to say the least. But I'm sure of what I saw. And it's like a part of me woke up, remembering something I was never supposed to forget."

Draevyn shifted beside her, his hand inching closer to hers. "Are you going to tell Syrena what we found?"

She took a deep breath. "I have to." Her voice softened, almost a whisper. "I need to know why she hid it, why she's been telling half-truths since the moment we arrived."

"Esmyra, what you saw..." he began, searching her face, "no one could take something like that lightly. But you—" He stopped, his gaze lingering.

A lick of ice ran along her spine beneath his stare, unable to look away. "I don't know what I am anymore," she admitted. "And that scares me. A woman, a siren, a criminal...a mere vessel for something else entirely. Who's to say I'm Kaelypso or Esmyra Aeress? Who's to say that I'm not some vessel of power that the goddess can bend at her will?"

The more she thought about it, the more her past began to make sense—the final piece of the puzzle put in place. It was never a siren beneath her skin, coiling around her spine and thrashing within. Esmyra *was* the siren, and the monster pushing itself to the surface all her life had been Kaelypso.

Draevyn reached out and gently tucked a strand of hair behind her ear, his fingers grazing her cheek. "You're not alone in this."

Esmyra's throat tightened at his words, grateful for them, but an icy rage crept through her veins as everything came slamming into her.

Her talons extended as her fury built. "It was all hidden from me. Everything I am, my whole life—it's built on a lie. I...I don't even know who I really am. *What* I am...or who I could've been."

Draevyn took her hand in his and laced their fingers together. "You're Esmyra. Whether you choose to be a Blackwood or an Aeress is entirely up to you. But you are who you are. Nothing will change that. You're fierce and loyal, and more stubborn than anyone I've ever met," he said with a wink. "Don't let this make you question yourself."

She swallowed, and suddenly the rage she felt melted away beneath his heated gaze. "Drae..."

Her thoughts were interrupted as the sound of footsteps and drifting voices approached. Both of their gazes snapped to the two drunken guards wandering up the path.

"Shit," she muttered.

Draevyn chuckled. "Should we not be here?"

A grin formed on her lips. "Not sure, but also not willing to deal with them." She reached her hand out for his. "Come with me."

He raised a brow. "To where?"

"The water."

His eyes flared. "You're serious?"

"Very," she whispered, already slipping quietly into the lagoon, the cool water enveloping her with a soft ripple. Her gown floated up around her before slowly sinking beneath the surface.

She motioned for him to follow, holding a finger to her lips. Draevyn's grin was damn near wicked as he moved after her, sliding into the water with a barely audible splash.

They floated quietly through the lagoon, skimming past rocks and low-hanging vines from surrounding trees, until she motioned toward a patch of lily pads and tall cattails. They drifted behind the cover of the thick green stems, shielding them from sight.

The soft glow of merlights in the false sky filtered through the lilies, casting shadows across the water and their faces. They were barely breathing, and Esmyra was desperately trying to hold in her laugh as every little movement of water sent gentle ripples. Their hands grazed as she readjusted her grip on a stem, feeling a thrill run through her that had nothing to do with the approaching guards.

Esmyra looked up, catching his eye as they hid. He gave her an amused look, his lips quirking to the side, and she realized their hiding spot behind the flowers made everything feel strangely intimate.

Draevyn put a finger to his lips and submerged himself further, leaving only his head above the water, and she mimicked the movement.

Esmyra hadn't shifted yet, finding it more fun to play along in her human form, just as he was forced to. But then her gills slid out from the sides of her neck in a show, earning her an eye roll.

"Cheater," he said in a hushed whisper.

She barely suppressed her cackle.

Above them, voices laughed and chatted along the path, followed by footsteps scuffing the shore. "Do you think they're still out here?" someone slurred.

"They could be anywhere at this point," another voice chimed, laughing.

Draevyn leisurely sank beneath the surface entirely, and she followed his lead. Esmyra found herself holding her breath, even with her gills, as his gaze remained locked on her beneath the water.

They waited in silence as she strained to listen, their bodies pressed close together as the guards lingered near the lagoon's edge. Finally, the footsteps retreated, the voices fading back down the path.

Esmyra surfaced first, pushing her hair back and breathing out a quiet laugh as she whispered, "Gods, I wonder why they were even looking for us." A surge of rage rushed through her at the thought. The thought of Syrena having them followed.

But then Draevyn came up beside her, shaking the water from his face. "Are you always this much trouble?" he asked, grinning as he ran a hand through his soaked hair.

"Maybe." She grinned back. "But you don't seem to mind."

He chuckled softly, the sound blending with the night air as he moved just a bit closer. And for a moment, it felt like they were the only two people in the world.

The cool water lapped against her skin as she drifted there beside him, but the heat building between them seemed to drown out the chill of the lagoon. His gaze softened as he watched her, that playful smile fading as he searched her face.

Every glance felt heavier, closer—*too close*, she thought. Her pulse quickened, her mind scrambling to remind herself why she shouldn't let this go any further.

But as Draevyn leaned in, her thoughts grew softer, dissolving like the surrounding ripples in the water.

"You're not like any man I've ever met, Draevyn Rowe," she whispered.

His head tilted. "And what do you mean by that?"

Her breath hitched as he lifted his hand, his fingers brushing a damp strand of hair away from her face. "I don't believe many men would willingly follow along with his enemy's plans, and then work to protect said enemy after she kidnapped him and tried to murder him." She paused. "Many times, I might add."

Draevyn shrugged a shoulder as if it were nothing. "Seemed like a good idea at the time," he murmured, his touch lingering, knuckles resting against her cheek.

Every nerve in Esmyra's body lit up, and she wondered if he could feel her heart pounding as he leaned even closer. Her mind warned her to pull back, to remind herself of everything at stake—but the feeling of his hand sliding to the back of her neck had every sensible thought melting away.

"In fact, it still does," he added softly, his eyes falling to her lips.

She held her breath, her heart beating wildly as she leaned into him.

Draevyn caught her waist, pulling her closer until their bodies were pressed together in the water, the warmth of him making her feel dizzy as the world around them blurred.

Then his lips met hers, and everything evaporated.

The gentle pressure of his mouth sent a thrill through her that she couldn't control, couldn't temper. Her hands reached up instinctively, fingers tracing the line of his jaw. The roughness of his stubble was foreign to her fingertips as she tried to ground herself in the reality of this—being in his arms as he held her like she was everything he'd ever wanted, and everything he'd ever need.

Esmyra's hands slid to his shoulders, pulling him closer instead of pushing him away.

And then her mind emptied entirely. She forgot the secrets they had uncovered, the visions of memories, and the dome trapping them in Maerinys.

Draevyn consumed her—the sensation of being held by him, of letting herself sink into his warmth.

As they slowly pulled away, their breaths mingling, she found the fire within his eyes blazing. A rush of panic flickered through her, the first time in her life feeling out of control.

"Bad idea?" he whispered, a breathless grin hinting at his lips, still only inches from hers.

Esmyra let out a shaky laugh, still catching her breath, feeling as though she were caught in a free fall. "Terrible," she answered softly, but her fingers traced down his arms, unwilling to let go.

Beads of water slipped from his slicked back hair, falling along his throat and down his chest—she imagined herself tracing the droplet with her tongue.

Draevyn shifted closer, his hands slipping beneath the surface to grip her thighs. Her breath caught as he lifted her, pulling her legs around his waist, holding her to him as he waded further into the lagoon.

Every nerve in her body felt alive, hypersensitive to the feel of his hands on her and the steady strength of his hold. Her fingers clung to his shoulders, and every heartbeat echoing between them felt as if they merged as one.

Esmyra's mind raced, consumed by a whirlwind of confusion and need. She barely registered their surroundings as he led them around the curve of a rocky alcove. The merlights mimicking the moon slanted down in soft beams, filtering through the overhanging vines, making the area feel somehow more secluded.

Draevyn reached a flat stone that jutted from the water's edge and placed her on it just above the waterline.

Esmyra's heart thundered as he stood between her legs, her hands sliding down to meet his as his grip held her waist. She was breathless beneath his gaze as he brushed his thumbs over her hip bones.

Neither of them spoke, and for a moment, she didn't dare breathe, the weight of the silence threatening to suffocate her.

She leaned down, her fingers threading into his hair, and as their faces drew close again, she whispered, "What is it that you want, Drae?" Esmyra could have sworn a shiver ravaged his body as his name left her lips.

"Something entirely forbidden in all sense of the word," he murmured, his hands tracing along her spine, settling her fully against him.

Her lips grazed his like a phantom, and a raging inferno ignited behind his irises. "And what might that be?"

"You," he breathed. "It appears that hasn't been obvious since the moment we met."

Esmyra refused to believe the words as they reached her ears. It had to have been a lie, a trick. She had never used her power on him. Never once compelled him into lust for her. She just never felt the need to, even back at Anchorage Cove.

Was it because deep down, she always knew it was there beneath his heated stares? Or was it because this cursed attraction toward him was something else entirely?

She never pursued men, aside from having them fall into her tricks when needed. But from the beginning, she'd never had the desire to use that on Draevyn.

The world sharpened as her eyes shifted, not by choice or from rage, but from the unbearable amount of emotions that crashed into her like a raging storm. Draevyn was the only card she had to play in order to get her father back, and suddenly the thought of letting him go became unbearable.

"Why?" Her eyes searched his as the word left her in a breath.

"Consider me under your spell, Wildfire. Those talons of yours sank into me the moment we met, and by all the gods, they refuse to let me go." The note of vulnerability in his voice caught her off guard, as if the truth had slipped from him before he'd had the chance to contain it.

Her breath hitched, the weight of his words sinking in. "I've never used it on you. Not in that way. I swear to you."

Draevyn subtly shook his head, the softest smile forming as he watched her. "It was a poor choice of words. What I should've said was the spell of...well, *you*."

Esmyra wasn't supposed to let herself care for anyone—not like this, not with so much at stake. And yet here she was, tangled up with him, pulled in by the raw honesty in his eyes and words. She wanted to resist it, to pull back and remind herself of everything that could go wrong, of the danger and thousands of unknowns they were both wrapped up in.

But instead, she slid her hands down his shoulders, welcoming the heat radiating off his skin as she leaned into him.

When Draevyn brought his lips to hers again, the world fell away once more. It was just him, here, holding her in this hidden alcove. The sensation of his mouth on hers, the way he pressed her body to his in an undeniable sense of need, was more than she'd ever let herself consider with someone before. Her hands fell to his waist, her fingers digging in, as if to ground herself from the dizziness his touch brought to her.

Their kiss deepened, and she lost herself in the feeling—of his flesh against hers, and the strength in his arms as he held her close. His hands traced her skin as though memorizing every inch, every detail.

Draevyn suddenly broke the kiss, his hands balling into fists next to her hips, resting on the rock.

"Is something wrong?" she asked, her pulse quickening.

"Gods, no." There was a growl in his voice, as if he was holding himself back. "I just don't want to take this too far. I don't want to force this on you." He let out a breathy laugh. "It's not as if we haven't had our fair share of trying to kill one another."

Esmyra brushed her nose against his before nibbling on his bottom lip, earning a groan from him. "Do you really believe I would tolerate your touch if it wasn't wanted?"

The blaze in his eyes surged. "Perhaps not."

The soft murmur of laughter and voices filtered through the quiet of their alcove, pulling her back into the present with a jolt. They stiffened, her gaze darting toward the sound echoing along the path beyond the lagoon.

They barely dared to breathe as the voices grew louder—clearly people wandering home from the celebration.

She quickly sat up on the stone, her cheeks flushed from the intimacy they just shared and the abrupt interruption.

Draevyn shifted, glancing back towards the path as he listened. "Looks like we've got company. Again," he grumbled.

"Aye," she said on a breath, still looking in the direction of the noise. "It appears the lagoon isn't as secluded as I thought."

Esmyra sank back into the water next to him before they moved to hide behind the cattails and lily pads once more.

And then a splash sounded from across the lagoon—several mertails lifting from them as people dove into the lake. Both of them whirled in its direction, and Esmyra's eyes narrowed suspiciously as she considered diving beneath the water to see what was occurring.

But then Draevyn's touch halted her.

He ran his hand gently down her arm. "Perhaps I should get you back to the palace before people notice."

Esmyra huffed as she rolled her eyes. "So noble."

Draevyn stepped around her in the water and flashed a teasing grin as he held out his hand for her. "Allow me to escort you, Wildfire."

She couldn't help her smile as she placed her hand in his.

Esmyra and Draevyn moved in silence through the castle's dimly lit corridors, their footsteps soft, but the tension between them lingered. Every glance, every small brush of his hand against hers as they walked, sent a spark through her.

They halted as they reached their opposing doors, both unwilling to break the silence that had grown thick as they left the lagoon. She hesitated, her hand on the door's knob, looking back at him.

Draevyn leaned into her. "It appears this is 'goodnight,' Esmyra." His voice was low, laced with a hint of mischief.

Esmyra didn't answer right away, just met his gaze, searching his face. There was no mistaking the look in his eyes—the burning desire, the restrained intensity that mirrored her rush of emotions.

Biting her bottom lip, she turned and pressed her back against her chamber's door, pushing it open. She pointed beyond the door with her chin, the gesture an invitation, as she walked through.

Draevyn followed her without a word.

Inside, her room was quiet, only the faint rustle of curtains as a gentle breeze filtered in through the open window. He shut the door behind them, and as he turned back to her, the weight of what they were feeling pressed down heavily.

Esmyra moved toward him, feeling her walls slip further. Her guard dropped as he reached out, his fingers brushing against hers before moving up to cradle her face. She closed the distance, her breath mingling with his, just as it had at the lagoon, as the unspoken tension spilled into something undeniably real.

Their noses brushed. "We shouldn't do this," she whispered, hating the words the moment they slipped past her lips.

"You're right. We shouldn't." His answer may as well have been a dagger through her heart.

Esmyra lifted her stare to his, feeling entirely bare beneath his gaze as he drank her in.

"Fuck it." Draevyn's voice was raw as he leaned in, capturing her mouth with his.

The world outside faded to nothing as she melted into him, losing herself to the certainty that, in this moment, neither of them were willing to let go.

His mouth never left hers as his knees bent, and he quickly wrapped his arms around her thighs, heaving her body up into his hold. He held her there as their kiss deepened.

Draevyn carried her to the bed and gently placed her down atop the sheets. "Are you sure?" he asked, his eyes searching hers in the low light.

Esmyra answered by leaning back on her elbows, gazing up at him. A talon slid from her finger, and he watched as she brought it to her chest and sliced down the front of her still-soaked gown, exposing her bare breasts as the fabric fell to the sides. Her nipples tightened under his ravenous stare, but he didn't move, looking as if every ounce of his self-control was being held by a thread.

Esmyra stood, their chests separated by mere inches, and brought her lips to his ear, watching goosebumps form along the skin of his neck. "Take me, Drae," she breathed, and that was all the permission he needed.

His hands raced to the front of her gown that clung to her, and he tore the remaining fabric all the way down the front of its skirt. And then her entire body was bare before him, her pussy growing slick beneath his blazing stare.

With a savage grin, her remaining talons extended. She placed her hand on his shoulder before slowly slicing through his shirt, leaving only tattered shreds in their wake.

Draevyn gently pushed her back down to the bed, and as her back hit the mattress, he pulled himself onto her. The feel of his bare chest against hers had a subtle moan escaping her as he claimed her mouth with his.

His calloused hands traveled down her body, halting at her sensitive nipples before taking one between his thumb and forefinger, taunting her with his caress.

Draevyn's muscular arms caged her against the bed, and his hardened length pressed against her as he ravaged her body. His tongue ran across her lower lip, begging for access, and she immediately opened for him, their tongues colliding in a dance.

Esmyra's clit throbbed to the beat of her racing pulse as Draevyn's cock settled against her, bulging through his pants.

A breathy moan left her, and Draevyn groaned. He pulled himself away, and she instantly missed the weight of him on her, nearly letting out a hiss as he left—until she realized the reason.

Draevyn lowered himself onto his knees, sliding his hands beneath her thighs as he pulled her closer to him, guiding her body down the bed.

"Drae, what are you doing?"

His mouth was on her a second later in answer. Draevyn's tongue ran from her opening to her clit, swirling around it in a tease that had a gasp erupt from her.

Esmyra glanced down, and all she could see was his fire-fueled whiskey eyes, watching her. Heat flooded her body, feeling as if she would burst into flames—*his* flames even, and the thought only aroused her more. Her moans came in desperate, panting gasps as he sucked and licked her pussy as if savoring his last meal.

Draevyn moaned against her sensitive flesh, as if her pleasure was his own, and her hips bucked in answer, her body feeling like it was about to burst. Then, without warning, he slid a single finger into her entrance—sliding it in and out three times before adding a second one, curling them slightly with each pump as he held his tongue against her clit. With each movement of his fingers, little whimpers escaped her, and the pressure of release ached to consume her with every subtle movement.

Draevyn withdrew his fingers from her and crawled halfway up her body. "Too much, Wildfire?"

The nickname made her ravenous.

She reached out, talons lightly digging into the skin of his shoulder as she pushed him backward, wearing a wicked grin. Esmyra fell to her knees beside the bed as she slowly unbuttoned Draevyn's pants.

"Esmyra..." Her name was a whisper, a plea. "You don't have t—"

"Shh," she cut him off, glaring. She reached in and wrapped her hand around his thick length before pulling it out on display before her. His cock twitched in her hand, and it was so thick that her fingers barely met around his girth.

Draevyn groaned, and she reveled in watching him come undone by her.

While she stroked his cock, she placed her tongue on the underside of his tip, earning yet another growl of pleasure from him.

Suddenly, the torches lining the walls of the room erupted—his flames consuming the soft merlights.

"Fuck," he growled, but Esmyra was too entranced by how intensely her touch affected him.

Her tongue swirled over the head of his cock, and his thighs shook as she wrapped her hands around them, holding him in place as she took him to the back of her throat.

Esmyra's pussy grew more soaked with each passing second, dripping down her inner thighs as she licked and kissed every inch of his shaft.

His hand reached for her hair, coiling the midnight waves around his wrist to get it out of her way as she sucked his cock.

She took his entire length in her mouth a final time. It jerked at the tightness of her throat, before slowly releasing her hold, wrapping her tongue around the head before lapping at the moisture that built there over her teasing.

"All gods," he groaned.

Esmyra looked up at him through her lashes and imagined herself being consumed by the blaze in his stare. "Do you wish for me to stop?" She couldn't even help her grin before licking her lips.

She kissed the tip of his cock, and it was as if it unleashed him—the beast he'd been holding back.

The *Phoenix.*

Draevyn leaned down and picked her up, throwing her effortlessly over his shoulder. "You're so naughty, Wildfire."

The gesture was so simple, so *possessive,* and it had her salivating as she wondered what he planned to do next.

Esmyra yelped as he gave her ass a hard smack, before throwing her back down onto the bed.

Her body bounced as it hit the mattress, but Draevyn was on top of her a moment later. His mouth was on her, their tongues colliding through their panting breaths. She groaned into his mouth as she felt the head of his cock resting against her entrance, just begging for her to move her hips slightly to sink on to it.

Draevyn pulled back from their kiss, brushing his nose against hers. "Tell me you want it. Tell me here and now that you want this." His gaze left her breathless, her body vibrating as if surging with lightning. He brought his lips to her ear and whispered, "Tell me you want to be fucked, Wildfire."

When Draevyn pulled back to meet Esmyra's stare, her lips parted. Chest heaving, she answered, "I want you to fuck me, Drae."

A grin twitched the corner of his lips as he pushed his cock into her inch by inch, his size stretching her pussy, and making her gasp out beneath him.

It was an overwhelming ache that set her whole body aflame.

Draevyn worked slowly, carefully moving his cock in and out as she adjusted to him. They both watched as he moved in her, his shaft glistening with her wetness beneath the torchlight.

Esmyra's eyes rolled back as she lifted her hips slightly, a moan slipping from her. His hands moved to cup her breasts, teasing her nipples as he watched her writhe beneath him.

"Does my cock feel good inside of you, Esmyra?" She whimpered as her name left his lips. "Or is this too much for you?" he asked, and she didn't have to look at him to know his grin was downright devilish.

Her eyes opened to find him staring down at her as his hips thrusted into her. "More," she taunted. "I need more."

With a groan, Draevyn shoved his cock inside of her before leaning down and taking her mouth again—the heat of his chest against hers made it feel like their bodies were tangled in an insatiable inferno. His constant, perfect rhythm had her back arching off the bed.

Esmyra's talons traced along his back, sinking in just enough to cause a bit of pleasurable pain as he moved in her. She bit his shoulder, her pussy tightening around his length, and a sound escaped him that was equal parts moan and growl.

He stood and lifted her from the bed, all in the same motion, and her legs instinctively wrapped around his waist in tandem. Their rhythm never faltered as he stood, lifting her by her thighs so her pussy slid up and down on his cock while he held her in the air.

His mouth was on the nape of her neck, and her head fell backward, her long hair brushing the small of her back as she moaned from the pleasure of him.

"You feel so fucking good, Wildfire." Hearing him speak those words while he fucked her mid-air had her nearly finding release.

He must've sensed it, because suddenly, he slowed. Her head snapped back to face him as he leisurely slid his cock in torturous movements while he held her.

"Drae..." His name left her in a breathy moan.

"What's that, baby?"

Esmyra's eyes shifted repeatedly, talons extending and retracting without her being able to help it as her body became overwhelmed with pleasure. They dug into his shoulders, and he hissed.

He was walking then, toward the door.

Her eyes flared. "Draevyn, what are y—"

Esmyra's words were cut off as he slammed her back against the door, pressing his body against hers as he laced their fingers together and pinned her hands to the wall—still thrusting into her.

She shivered at the warmth of his breath on her ear. "I don't care if the entire godsdamn castle hears you screaming for me, Wildfire." Esmyra shuddered in his grasp. "Do you know how they all look at you? Every male and female here? The desire in their eyes comes close to rivaling my own..."

His confession had her release building and building until she thought she may do just that—scream.

"Let this be an announcement to the realm that their chance has come and gone, and they will *never* receive one again." A moan burst from her lips as he continued to fuck her against the door. His next words were a whisper against her flesh. "And if they try, I will burn them alive."

Esmyra couldn't help the bellowing scream of pleasure as it burst from her—the sound erupting from somewhere deep in her soul.

Suddenly, every lit torch in the room burst—their flames licking at the high ceiling as Draevyn followed her over the edge. His cock spilled into her as he reclaimed her mouth in a desperate need.

It was like nothing she ever felt.

It was primal.

It was feral.

It was *soul-consuming*.

And when he pulled away, his gaze locked on hers.

Holding her captive between himself and the door, his eyes burned with an adoration that felt both dangerous and intoxicating, consuming her completely.

Silence fell as they stared at each other while Esmyra trembled in his arms. They both smirked, chests heaving as what they just did settled into them.

"Holy gods," she said, trying to catch her breath.

Draevyn's eyes swept over her. "And you're the most beautiful of them all."

Heat rushed to her cheeks, and he pulled her away from the wall, carrying her back to the bed as he remained inside her. Once he placed her down, he reached for his pants, and Esmyra watched as he put himself back together while she lay there bare.

His cheeks reddened, averting his gaze from hers as he scratched the back of his neck. "I...I don't know what came over me."

Esmyra stood from the bed, noting the hunger flooding his eyes again as they fell to her breasts with the movement. She took a step into him as he finished zipping his pants.

Standing on her tiptoes, she whispered teasingly in his ear, "I'm sure that's what you say to all your lovers."

Draevyn scoffed, as if what she said was the most absurd thing he'd ever heard.

"What?" she said with a laugh.

He shook his head as he stared down at her, reaching to tuck a strand of hair behind her ear. The gesture was obnoxiously sweet, and she hated how much it affected her.

"I swear to you. I don't know what came over me. I just..." His words trailed off.

"Well," she started, "it's not as if that's not believable for a prince and Lephyrin's infamous Phoenix."

Sadness settled into his expression, but it was there and gone in only a moment. "I've never been one to take lovers, Wildfire."

Esmyra's lips parted as her eyes darted back and forth between his. "Then what do you consider me?"

Draevyn took her chin between his fingers, his eyes boring into hers. "My damnation."

Before she could say anything, he pressed his lips softly to hers. It was the most gentle kiss—nothing like how they had just ravaged each other.

A feeling she'd never known before bloomed in her chest, a warm flutter of hope, realizing that the man before her desired her for who she was—knowing *all* that she was.

Only the desire felt different, and all-consuming. She sensed no lies in his words, and that should've terrified her, but all she felt was exhilaration.

When Draevyn broke the kiss, he smiled before reaching for his half-shredded shirt that was hanging off the edge of the bed. She stiffened as he moved to wrap it around her, covering her body as she stood naked in the center of the room.

"Keep this warm for me, would you?" He winked. "I'll see you in the morning, Your Majesty."

Esmyra's cheeks flushed. She watched him as he turned from her and left, closing her chamber's door quietly behind him.

And for the first time in her very long life, Esmyra allowed her walls to crumble, trusting that Draevyn wouldn't let her fall.

Deep within the island's cave, torches bobbed like fireflies as Jak, Ren, Riven, and the rest of *The Night Wraith's* crew repeatedly tried to break the barrier beneath the arch.

They had attacked it tirelessly with fists, blades, gunpowder, and magic—all to no avail. The shield remained an impenetrable veil between them and the cliff that fell further into the cave, where Esmyra had fallen over a week ago, trapped with their enemy.

The cavern was quiet except for the muted, rhythmic hum of the barrier—and everyone's godsdamn bickering. The arch never lost its subtle glow. In the cave's darkness, it cast strange shadows and lit the hollowed faces of the crew lingering before it, defeated.

Jak stood alone at the edge, his eyes fixed on the shimmering surface. He knew in his bones she had survived. And yet, he had no proof—only his gut and an aching in his chest that wouldn't let him turn away, no matter how badly he knew the crew wanted to.

The thought of it made him sick.

Around him, the crew had slumped into silence—the fire of hope that had once been in their stares was long since snuffed out.

At first, they tried everything they could think of to reach her. Hours turned to days, and days had become nearly two weeks. The barrier was here for a reason, blocking something from the outside world—perhaps even Maerinys, as Esmyra had believed. But why had it reacted to her touch?

Jak barely ate, barely slept, hollowed out by the guilt of letting her fall. He was her first mate—the one who was supposed to protect her, to stand by her no matter what, just as she had with Cyrus. He should've been able to find a way through—should've known what to do, but he didn't. He was a fucking failure.

Perhaps that was exactly how Esmyra felt when she came back to *The Night Wraith* to find half her crew was slain and her father captured.

And he never should've let that bastard Draevyn Rowe get so close to her that he damned her to the same fate he chose for himself.

The weight of a steady hand fell on Jak's shoulder. "Esmyra's gone, mate," Ren said, a sadness lingering in his voice.

"She's gone, and we've got to get on with it," Riven chimed in. "There's nothing we can do. If we remain here, we'll starve. We've run out of food."

"And rum," Ren interjected, which had Jak spinning on his heel to face them.

"We *can't* give up," he snapped.

Ren and Riven briefly glanced at each other.

"And what would you have us do?" Riven asked. "Doom ourselves in her honor? We're fucking *pirates*." He nodded to the arch. "As much as it kills me, Esmyra fell behind. She's *gone*, and we ain't nothing but sitting ducks here."

"We can always make port in the nearest city and see if we can find any information about this. Something she might have missed," Ren added.

Jak's nostrils flared, but deep down, he knew they were right. *Gods*, he fucking hated that they were right. He nodded as he scratched the back of his neck, refusing to meet their stares. "Aye."

The rest of the crew filed out of the chamber in twos and threes.

The thought of her being gone twisted in Jak's gut. He had called on every bit of magic he had, every storming force or wind he could conjure, and nothing worked. Whatever that barrier was, its magic was stronger than that of his entire crew.

His fingers traced the cool surface of the arch, his jaw clenched tight. Jak whispered under his breath, "We'll come back for you, Captain." He could almost see her face in the swirling light of the shield, rolling her eyes as she told him to stop being so godsdamn dramatic.

He nearly let out a laugh at his hallucination. She would never give up on him, and he knew that with a certainty that cut deeper than any blade.

Esmyra was fierce and brutal, but above all, she was loyal once her trust was gained.

With a deep breath, he unsheathed the dagger hidden in his boot and pressed its tip against the surface of the barrier, trying again, just one more time. The blade sparked as it touched the shield, but nothing more.

Sighing, he turned back to face Ren and Riven. "Alright, let's head out. We'll see if we can find anything."

As they pressed forward, nearing the cave's entrance, a chill swept through the tunnel, dampening the air and extinguishing half their torches.

"What was that?" Ren whispered.

"*Quiet*," Jak hissed. But the silence only grew more oppressive. And then it began—a slow, creeping darkness that slithered along the edges of their vision, turning the walls into shifting shadows that felt alive, closing in. "What in all gods?"

Riven unsheathed his sword. "Fuck, we're not alone here!"

Suddenly, Ren froze, his eyes fixed on something Jak couldn't see. His face paled, his torch shaking in his hand until it fell to the ground at his feet, its flames winking out. He stumbled backward. "No...no, *NO!*" The last word ended in a scream as he backed into the nearest wall, his breath hitching as he gazed at something just beyond the shadows.

A few paces to his left, Riven's eyes went wide and haunted. "Fuck!" He turned to face Jak. "It's elven magic."

"Elven?!" Jak echoed. He bared his teeth as he grabbed both of them by their sleeves, pulling them toward the cave's mouth.

With every step he took, intense heat licked up his back, and suddenly, his clothing was on fire.

There was no torch—nothing to light the spark. Not even Draevyn Rowe was there to be the culprit.

That was the one thing Jak never told a soul—he feared the kiss of flame.

"Kaelypso's fucking tits!" he screamed, as his arms burned.

They raced out of the cave to find the rest of the crew in utter chaos.

Jak dropped to the ground and flailed in the sand, desperate to put the blaze out, but no matter what he did, they remained. He watched the fire settle on his skin, but his flesh was fully intact. It didn't blister from the heat or melt from his bones.

Alec screamed a few feet from him, swinging his sword wildly at the empty air. His voice cracked as he sank to his knees.

To the side, another mortal from their crew, Torin, spun in frantic circles, his hands clawing at his face as if swatting away invisible creatures. "Spiders," he gasped, his face contorting in terror. "They're everywhere! Crawling...under my skin...I can *feel* them."

The madness spread like wildfire, each man screaming or muttering, trapped in his own personal nightmare. Some swung wildly at illusions only they could see, while others crumbled to the ground, hands over their faces, weeping or shouting for mercy.

Jak called on his magic, summoning a vortex of wind that would put out any blaze, but it only spun around him in a relentless tornado, and the flames danced to its rhythm atop his flesh.

He let out a bellowing cry into the sky, his voice echoing through the clouds like an owl's screech.

Then male voices sounded above the chaotic screams of his crew, barking orders and attacks. Jak lifted his stare to where the rocks narrowed into shadowed alcoves, and found their attackers crouched behind the stone ledges, waiting.

CHAPTER 68

*Atlas*

A tlas's jaw clenched as he took in the scene below. Elowynne was beside him, her golden eyes gleaming in the sun's light as she concentrated, her fingers delicately weaving through the air, amplifying the fears of *The Night Wraith's* crew.

Her power held each pirate in a grip of horror, and he would be lying if he said it wasn't difficult to watch. He glanced around, taking in the pale, horrified faces of his own sailors as they observed her alongside him.

But these pirates deserved it—they had taken his brother.

They deserved far worse.

"Now?" Samwell asked, his eyes wide with fear as he watched the men writhe and scream below.

Atlas nodded and lifted his hand to give the signal. "Now."

On command, Draevyn's crew withdrew their swords and marched toward the crew of pirates, surrounding them as they barely registered their presence through the haze of their terrors.

Atlas gave a nod to Elowynne, and they both followed their men, descending the hill.

"Surrender, and perhaps your fears will leave you," she announced.

Atlas stepped forward, his voice dark and calm. "Yield, or the nightmares will follow you to the depths of hell where you belong."

"Fuck you!"

Atlas's eyes fell to the man who screamed the words as he twisted in terror on the ground, squirming as he shrieked. Elowynne's eyes were now focused on that man.

Still, *The Night Wraith's* crew wouldn't yield to them. Some clung to their weapons with a desperate grip, resisting even as terror clawed at their minds. Elowynne let out a grunt at his side as she pushed her magic further into them, showing no mercy.

Yet, they staggered to their feet, weapons raised, half-screaming, half-snarling.

"This is forbidden!" a man bellowed, his voice a fractured roar that hid barely-contained panic.

Everyone's attention snapped to him, and Atlas noted his pointed ears—he was interested in how a single crew held members of all kingdoms. He had never seen or heard of such a thing. "It's forbidden to cast your mind upon elven!"

A cruel smile graced Elowynne's lips. "Then perhaps you shouldn't have taken my betrothed's kin. Now, where is he?" she snarled. "Where is Prince Draevyn Rowe?"

A sense of pride came over Atlas as she relentlessly fought alongside him to find his brother, even if her tactics were terrifying. "Tell us where he is before your lives are forfeited."

The writhing man stood defiantly. "You're fools to think we wouldn't welcome such. We have fought off worse than the darkness that awaits us. And if you kill us, you'll never find your precious *Phoenix.*"

He spat Draevyn's dreaded nickname as if it held venom, sending Atlas further into his rage.

Atlas's lips curled into a grim smile, his shadowy tendrils curling around his arms as his crew readied themselves. "You haven't met *my* darkness, woodland *cunt.*"

With a silent command, he released his shadows, allowing them to spill across the isle's floor like a black mist. It curled around the pirates' legs, lifting their bodies and restraining their movements. The men staggered, slashing at the shadows, but their weapons merely passed through the inky tendrils, leaving them tangled and helpless as Elowynne continued to attack their minds.

Samwell advanced on the mouthy man he assumed was the captain, his gaze icy and unwavering as he dodged a wild swing from the male's cutlass. In one swift motion, Samwell grabbed the pirate's wrist, twisting it back until he dropped the weapon with a pained gasp. Tommy lunged forward and forced the man to his knees, tying his wrists behind his back.

Atlas then forced the shadows around their mouths, acting as gags and silencing their screams and retorts.

One by one, *The Night Wraith's* crew were bound and gagged, lined up along the outskirts of the cave they came from. They struggled and cursed, but the shadows only tightened, holding them firm as his crew finished cuffing the rest of them.

"That's enough, my love," Atlas said, his voice low.

Elowynne lowered her hand and lifted her illusions, leaving the pirates gasping through their gags as they blinked and squinted, trying to shake the visions. But their eyes quickly refocused on Atlas and his crew, their faces riddled with fury.

Atlas's shadowy hold loosened enough for the pirates to catch their breath. "You came here with someone. Yet he isn't here with you. Now, unless you'd like to be dragged back in chains to face Lephyrin's gallows, I suggest you cooperate." He paused, his fists shaking at his sides. "Where. Is. Draevyn?! Where is my brother?"

The writhing male met his stare, a cold fury in his eyes. "He's no longer with us."

Atlas's heart stopped in his chest, unknowing of whether the man meant they murdered him, or if he escaped. He unsheathed his sword and placed the tip on the male's chest. "And why might that be, you dirty *brute*?" His lip curled in disgust.

The pirate winked. "Easy there, Prince. If you're going to flirt with me, you should at least acquire my name. Which is Jak, by the way. It's lovely to meet you and your little mind manipulating bitch."

Atlas struck him at his outburst, and a satisfied cackle escaped Elowynne from a few paces behind him. "I don't give a damn what your name is. Now, you're clearly the acting captain, since Cyrus rots in one of my cells. Tell me where my brother is, or I will gut you here and now. I was told he was lured out by a woman. I don't see her among you either."

The crew erupted into vicious chuckles, as if anything he had just said was funny.

Atlas took a step closer, his voice low and dangerous. "You kidnapped a son of the king in the dead of night, and you think I'll accept your words claiming he just vanished? You think I will accept the word of a *pirate*?"

"Aye, well, it's the only word you've got, mate," Jak taunted.

Atlas pressed the tip of his blade further into his flesh. Jak's jaw ticked, his nose scrunching as a bead of blood rolled down his chest, staining his shirt.

"Gods, stop!" the elven male from before bellowed. All eyes moved to him down the line. "Something happened in that cave— something none of us were prepared for. They were both lost."

"Riven!" Jak growled at his crewmate.

"What do you mean something happened?!" Atlas's face twisted with horror. Elowynne ran up to his side and laced her fingers with his.

The pirates shifted, each one looking at the cave's mouth as if it might swallow them whole. Jak spoke then, irritation evident in his voice at Riven's outburst. "Your brother was taken as a tool for negotiation with your father."

Atlas's mind emptied as he took in the words. His father knew about this? *Negotiated* this?

"Our captain, Esmyra Blackwood, kidnapped your precious, fire-wielding prick of a brother, planning to barter an exchange for Cyrus," Jak continued.

Samwell spoke up then. "You expect us to believe that our king handed the life of his son, and second heir, to the most feared pirates in all of Rymelle?"

Jak snickered. "We weren't exactly expecting that either." He returned his attention to Atlas. "When she bartered for the life of our captain against the life of your brother, your king proposed another thing entirely. He wanted proof of Maerinys and its wealth that rests at the bottom of the ocean."

The moment he said *Maerinys*, Atlas knew he was speaking the truth. How would the pirates know his father had been after it for years? Sending Draevyn out on endless quests for months looking for it.

"To prove he was trustworthy and that Cyrus wouldn't be harmed, he told us to take Draevyn. If either were harmed, the deal was forfeited. Esmyra was to bring back both Draevyn and evidence of Maerinys in exchange for Cyrus."

Atlas swallowed, his nostrils flaring in disgust toward his sire for once again betraying his own flesh and blood. "So, how were they both lost?"

"They just vanished," Riven answered for him, and Jak rolled his eyes.

Atlas's anger flickered into a scowl. "Vanished?"

"There was a cave-in, and they fell," Jak said, voice pained as if grieving the loss himself, which Atlas found odd. Pirates didn't give a damn about anyone but themselves.

"There are workings of magic in that cave," Jak continued, "and as the ceiling tumbled down on us, the Phoenix shoved Esmyra off a cliff, but she took him with her. One moment, they were there, and the next they were swallowed by shadows."

*A cave-in.* There was a chance Draevyn had perished.

Atlas imagined himself beheading the man before him right then and there, but Elowynne placed her hand on his shoulder. "Listen to what he has to say," she whispered. "I sense no lies."

And neither did he, which made it that much more unbearable to hear.

"A veil of some kind now acts as a barrier between us and where they fell," Jak continued. "We've tried everything to get through it, but it acts as its own entity. Unbreakable by blade, gunpowder, or any force of magic. It holds *power*—a significant amount, if I may add."

Atlas's eyes narrowed, suspicion darkening his expression. "And I'm supposed to believe you? Take the word of the realm's most notorious criminals."

All of their faces hardened, and Jak spoke once more. "Believe what you will, *Prince*. But we didn't want him gone—he's more useful to us alive than dead. Whatever magic binds that cave, it's beyond anything we've ever seen."

Atlas's jaw clenched. "Well, who's to say you tried hard enough?"

Jak chuckled, but it was devoid of warmth as his eyes narrowed on him. "Aye, trust me when I say...no one wants to get through it more than myself. I have quite a few words for your wretched brother for *damning* her alongside him."

"Looks like I'll have to go see this veil for myself," Atlas spat, his shadows curling around his fists. "And then, you'll sail with us to Lephyrin and live the rest of your days waiting for the gallows' noose."

Without waiting for a response, Atlas nodded to his men. They hauled the pirates to their feet before dragging them away from the cave and down the rocky path toward the ship as they bucked and cursed at them.

Samwell was guiding Jak to follow the rest of the crew, but Atlas stepped in, halting them.

"Not so fast." Atlas looked Jak up and down beneath furrowed brows. "You'll be showing me this veil."

CHAPTER 69

*Draevyn*

Draevyn lay awake in bed after a night of restless sleep. He didn't know what had come over him to act out the way he had, and he couldn't get Esmyra out of his mind.

As he lay there, the night replayed in his mind like a vivid dream, one that felt impossible to shake. He knew, logically, that this was the worst mistake either of them could've made. There was so much at stake, and they were possibly stranded down here in Maerinys while his father held hers captive.

Not only that, but also everything they had uncovered the day prior—her past life and the true reason for Maerinys' fall. He knew she had an entire kingdom on her shoulders, all while trying to process who she truly was.

And yet, even knowing that, Draevyn had no intention of turning back. He was too far gone, and she...well, she had a hold on him that he didn't want to escape, anchoring him to her.

He let out a long breath, recalling the way she'd looked at him— the soft vulnerability she was desperate to hide behind her walls he'd come to know so well.

They were mirrors in many ways, each carrying burdens placed on them by others, each wearing armor they had been forced to build to protect themselves.

But last night, Draevyn felt those walls between them fall away, and with that, he wondered if perhaps she needed him as much as he desperately needed her.

Esmyra was everything any man would be lucky to have—she was breathtakingly beautiful, powerful, humorous, and absolutely fucking lethal. Perhaps he was the only man who would enjoy the last one, but the thought of her being someone else's set his blood boiling.

As these thoughts swirled, he accidentally set a small section of his sheets on fire where his hands rested as flames burst at his fingertips. "Godsdammit," he huffed as he patted out the dying embers.

Across the room, the door creaked open and closed with a gentle click. A smile tugged at his lips, assuming Esmyra was sneaking in before anyone else was awake. He sat still for a moment, listening for her footsteps.

"Sneaking in again?" Draevyn called softly, an easy grin spreading over his face as he looked around for a shadow.

There was no answer, but he sensed her presence in the room. He stood from the bed, stretching as he padded across the floor. "Hiding, are we? And to think I thought we were past these games, Wildfire," he murmured, a teasing lilt in his voice. "If it's a hunt you want, you know I'll find you."

He always found her—in every room, every thought, and dream.

Draevyn moved quietly through the dimly lit room, running his hand along the edge of a curtain where he thought she might be lurking. He pulled it back, expecting to catch her there with that familiar spark in her eye, but the space was empty.

Thinking she was hiding with camouflaged skin, he reached out, but all he was met with was the window's glass. He frowned, but then the sound of scattering feet echoed across the room, making him move towards the alcove by the wardrobe.

"There you are." He moved toward it, smirking as he crept closer. "Alright, I know you're hiding in here," he whispered, reaching to push aside the loose fabric of the wardrobe.

But then, his gaze caught on a figure blending seamlessly into the shadowy textures of the wall. For a split second, he hesitated, a shiver of anticipation racing along his spine as he felt her presence.

Then, in a subtle, almost eerie shimmer, the figure shifted. The edges of her silhouette sharpened, her skin lightening. Draevyn's pulse quickened as the shadowed, seamless surface peeled back to reveal the familiar features he'd been falling in love with—until he was met with golden hair.

His heart leapt in his throat at the sight.

Syrena tilted her head, a smirk forming as she crossed her arms, stepping out of the shadows. "Expecting someone else?" she purred, her gaze sweeping over him.

Draevyn matched her step backwards, his thoughts reeling, heart racing. "Where is she?" he demanded. Every nerve was on high alert, his pulse a deafening roar in his ears, knowing Syrena would never set foot in his room without a motive.

"Oh, I'm sure she's still sleeping off last night's...*escapades*." She licked her lips and stepped closer. Her movements were confident, each one calculated to unsettle him. "But don't worry, Draevyn. She doesn't have to know you're here. With me."

His jaw tightened, every instinct telling him to roast the bitch alive, but he couldn't do that to Esmyra. And he would be killed without knowing a way out of the prison Maerinys had become.

But as Syrena drew nearer, her hand brushed his arm, and his heart hammered in a different rhythm—not from her touch, but from the danger exuding from her, having every cell in his body on edge.

"You look surprised," she said softly. "Did you think I wouldn't find out about you and my sister?"

"What are you doing here?" he growled, trying to hide the fury in his tone, but it was useless.

She didn't answer immediately, only took another step forward, closing the space he'd put between them. Her smile turned teasing as she leaned closer, her voice barely above a whisper. "Why should she be the only one to know you this way? We're twins after all." Syrena winked. "We can share."

The implications in her voice had an overwhelming dread

creeping in. "You need to leave," he said firmly, trying to put more distance between them. But she only followed his movements, her gaze unwavering as she watched his reactions.

"What's wrong?" she asked, feigning innocence. "Surely, you wouldn't turn away a queen. *Again*." The last word came out cold and cruel.

Syrena backed him into a corner on the far side of his room, his back hitting the wall as she draped her arm over one of his shoulders, pressing her chest to his as she looked into his eyes.

Draevyn was repulsed, desperately trying to keep his flames at ease.

*Was this a test?* Was this why she released him from the velsinyte bracelet? To edge him on and get him to lash out at her to prove to Esmyra he wasn't to be trusted? He'd made it clear to Syrena before he wasn't interested.

Draevyn shook his head, his jaw locking. "I refuse to play your little game, Syrena," he said, his voice hardening. "Where. Is. She?"

Her eyes flashed, her smile fading as she finally halted her advance. "Has it never occurred to you that I'm exactly who you should be with instead?" Syrena's words dripped with disdain, and he could see the bitterness, the resentment simmering beneath her polished exterior.

She pressed a soft kiss to the nape of his neck as she held him against the wall. His magic was thrashing within him, and every ounce of his restraint not to ignite her in flames was ready to snap.

Syrena gazed up at him, her golden-amber eyes boring into his, and he knew she could see the raging blaze lashing out in them. She brought her lips to his ear, and he was clenching his teeth so hard he could've sworn one cracked. "After all...shouldn't a queen find her king? And who better than the son of one, Draevyn *Rowe*?"

Draevyn's eyes flared, his jaw dropping in horror as she spoke his last name—his lineage they kept secret since arriving.

"How?" he demanded. Draevyn hadn't realized all the torches in the room burst into his flames as they had the night before in Esmyra's room—only this time it was from rage.

"Patience," she whispered, savoring his reaction. "I know every-thing, darling. Your father's kingdom. His tragic ambitions." Her eyes darkened. "And how he offered his infant sons on a platter to the God of Rage and War."

*How would she know that being trapped down here?*

Draevyn's expression hardened. "And what else do you think you know?"

He couldn't risk giving away anything he knew, not about Esmyra and what she meant to him, or the tomb they found in the cave, revealing Maerinys' secrets.

"Oh, I know far more than you'd ever want me to," she cooed, glancing toward the door as if she could see right into Esmyra's room across the hall. "I know the kingdom's history, the truth of my sister and I—of what we really are. The truth you thought you discovered *before* me."

*Fuck.*

His chest rose and fell rapidly, his nostrils flaring as he held himself back, knowing there was a threat in her words. "We were looking for a way out."

"I know. And it's back down the path from which you came."

"Then why the fuck haven't you been leading your people out of here?!" he bellowed.

Syrena rolled her eyes. "So dramatic." She huffed out a breath. "Nobody can leave, aside from the two of you. Esmyra unlocked the gates with her runes when you found the tunnel. My men can go as far as the lake, but when they climbed the wall to get to the arch that awakened the passage, they couldn't step through. We're cursed to remain down here without both of our blood and power to unbind Maerinys from the depths."

"Climb?" The word left him on a breath.

She gave him a malicious smile. "*Very* small crevices in the rock act as a ladder." Her tone was mocking as she shrugged. "I understand how you missed it. It's a bit dark down here."

A growl brewed from deep within his chest, but Syrena's eyes lit in satisfaction as if it was exactly what she wanted.

But he could play her game.

"Tell me what else you know." He cocked his head to the side in a predatory manner. "Just want to be sure we're on the same page and all."

Syrena laughed softly, and Draevyn ignored the chill that ached to seep into his bones from it. "Oh, do you mean like the page you found of Esmyra and myself within the Book of Aeress?"

Draevyn thought his heart stopped as the words left her. How could she have known that?

"Honestly, you men are so predictable. Do you really think that book was placed on a podium without reason? Gods, truthfully, I was expecting a bit more of a challenge from you."

"You put the book there," he hissed, and she winked. "And what *else* do you know?"

"The real question, Prince, is what *don't* I know?" She tilted her head, eyes narrowing. "The Veil of Visions. I already know Esmyra has spoken of it to you."

"That basin in the tower?"

"Indeed," she answered, her body still pressed to his. "It does more than conjure reflections of memory. It's a looking glass, revealing more than just *this* world. It also shows what lies beyond the sea— above its surface."

As her words sank in, his pulse quickened. Syrena had been watching them—more than that, she'd been watching the *realm*.

"So tell me, Prince," she purred, a mocking edge to her voice, "do you still think you're one step ahead? Or are you finally starting to realize you're exactly where I wanted you all along?"

"You vindictive bitch," he growled, lip curling.

Her smile grew more malicious as she leaned in closer, her voice a taunting whisper. "Oh, you're so quick to anger. *So* much like your maker, who felt the same for her. For Kaelypso," she said, watching the fury blaze in his eyes. "You should've listened to your first instincts about me, Draevyn Rowe. I *am* what you would consider evil. And so is Esmyra. Why do you think they tried to kill us in the first place?"

His fists clenched, knuckles whitening as he held himself back. "You don't know the first thing about her, or me."

Syrena's laugh was light, mocking. "Oh, but I do, handsome. I've watched everything. For hundreds of years, I've sat and waited for my vengeance. And now, I know you'll understand how I plan to raise the kingdom once more—by unlocking the bones of our true forms from the crypt. Bones that *you* so conveniently led her to." She shrugged a shoulder. "So, thanks for making that part easy."

Draevyn's face hardened with realization, rage breaking past his restraint. "I will die before I let you harm her. I will melt the flesh from your fucking bones." He meant every word as he spat them at her.

"Ah, yes. I assumed it would come to that, hence the velsinyte bracelet."

"That you removed," he reminded her, grinning as embers sparked at his fingertips. "You think she'll just stand by while you take whatever twisted revenge you have planned?"

An evil, bone-chilling cackle erupted from her before she tsked. "The removal was necessary for my plans." Her voice was like silk. "And 'stand by?' Oh, darling, she'll be exactly where I need her to be. And here's why."

As their stare down continued, her amber eyes shifted, the pupils morphing into slits, mimicking that of his favorite pair of icy blues.

And suddenly, all of his thoughts went quiet—the devastating fear that gripped him by the throat from Syrena's threats loosened their hold, and was replaced by a blissful calm. Gazing into her eyes, he felt an irresistible tug toward her, his reality becoming a haze.

The danger radiating from the predator standing beneath him slipped away, and all he could feel was her seductive allure, dragging him to her like the force of the raging tide.

"Kiss me, Draevyn Rowe."

*Draevyn Rowe.* That was how Esmyra always said his name—a flirtatious threat. His eyes roamed over the face directly beneath his chin, her body pressed against his, and all he saw was her.

As he drew closer, her face became clearer in the soft merlight peering through the windows. Esmyra's perfect face, begging for him to press his lips to hers, and by all gods, did he want to. He craved it more than anything, every second of every day.

Draevyn obeyed and kissed the goddess before him. It felt just as it had the night prior, bringing warmth to his entire being, mimicking the moment one steps into a quiet lake under the sun.

Her kiss was soft, yet filled with need, sending a thrill through him all the way through his fingertips. He couldn't think, didn't want to. Everything faded—the taste of salt on her lips, the softness of her touch. It all threatened to consume him, just as she always had.

There was a strange tug at the back of his mind, a faint instinct telling him that something wasn't right. But her hands slid up to his face, her fingers tangled in his hair, and all doubts evaporated in an instant.

Draevyn became lost in her, in that kiss that felt endless, like falling without fear, like drowning but never needing air.

That was how it always felt when he was with Esmyra.

His Wildfire was his warmth—she was *his*.

Suddenly, a soft creak sounded, and then the door to his chambers slowly swung open.

"Drae?" Esmyra's voice echoed through the room.

The kiss broke, and the trance shattered like glass.

Draevyn blinked, dazed and disoriented. His mind spun as he pulled away, shoving out of Syrena's hold.

His throat tightened, heart thundering in his chest as his gaze lifted to the doorway.

And there she stood.

His Wildfire.

Esmyra's expression was thunderous, her lips set in a tight, furious line. Her eyes mimicked storm clouds—dark and brooding with betrayal.

She didn't move. Didn't say a word, but the weight of her gaze was enough to make him feel as though his entire world had just crumbled in seconds.

A chill ran through Draevyn, and the room suddenly felt unbearably small—the air heavier, suffocating.

"Esmyra, no—" He took a step toward her, but she raised a hand, halting him.

"Don't." Esmyra's voice cracked, and she looked away for a moment, blinking as if to hold back the flood of tears he knew both of them felt.

And then she said the words that shattered his heart, feeling the crack splintering between them. "I trusted you."

The silence that stretched between them was deafening. And it was in that silence that Draevyn realized he may have just lost everything before he even fully had it in his grasp.

Esmyra's eyes lost their fire, now staring at him, dead and cold, before she slammed the door to his chambers shut, leaving his sight.

"I'm so sorry," he whispered, but the only person the words reached was Syrena, who watched him with wicked amusement.

Draevyn's head snapped toward the queen, fury flaring in his chest. "*You—*"

Syrena still wore that mocking, self-satisfied smirk on her face. "Ahhh, young love," she said in a cheery voice, but her next words echoed with pure venom. "It's what fucking cost us everything in the first place."

A raging ball of flame erupted in his palms, and just as he was about to throw it in her face, her eyes shifted once more, and he became paralyzed—locked under her compulsion again, only this time he had all of his senses. It was as if she compelled him to just remain frozen in time.

"Not so fast. I've been burned by your flames before, Draevyn Rowe, and I have no intention of it happening again." The bitterness in her voice seeped through each word. "You see, the power Esmyra and I will wield together is what will break the chains, for I don't possess the magic to do it myself. And once the kingdom is restored above, I'll have no use for her. With her powers under my command, the seas will bend to my will, and Kaelypso will be nothing but a memory."

Her gaze roamed over him as the door opened once more.

Relief flooded him, thinking Esmyra had returned, but when his stare lifted, his heart stopped.

Azarian, the queen's head guard, stood in the archway, along with five others, weapons in hand.

Draevyn writhed against the siren queen's hold, his body vibrating with rage and worry for Esmyra, but all he could feel was his will cracking beneath her grasp.

"Don't feel bad, Draevyn. It was inevitable. Irah couldn't save Kaelypso before, and you can't save Esmyra now." She tsked. "We would've been great together, you and I. But now I fear you will only continue to be a thorn in my side, making an already difficult task damn near impossible."

He was screaming. Draevyn was screaming and raging at the top of his lungs in her face, igniting her in flames over and over and watching her body burn in his mind—only that was where the vision remained. In his mind.

Trapped under her hold, he could do nothing as her guards stalked toward him, grabbed him by his arms, and held their spears to his throat.

"Tell Cyrus I said hello," Syrena taunted, and before Draevyn could blink, she swiped her talons across his eye—three of her claws slicing through his brow and flesh.

"Consider yourself lucky I didn't use venom," she finished.

As he went to roar in pain, an unbearable agony erupted through the back of his skull.

And then Draevyn's world went dark.

CHAPTER 70

*Esmyra*

Esmyra stormed through the castle corridors, her vision blurred with rage and betrayal. Her chest felt like it was splitting open, her mind reeling with what she'd just seen.

The image of Draevyn's lips on Syrena's—her *sister's*—was burned into her memory, replaying again and again until she thought she might scream from the torment of it.

Every breath felt heavy, searing her throat as she stumbled forward. She didn't know where she was going; she just needed to be *anywhere* but there—standing in the doorway of his bedchamber as her heart shattered.

That very heart had remained unyielding to all her entire life—until *him*. Until the son of her godsdamn enemy clawed his way through it and melted the ice it was encased in with his flame.

Her feet carried her through shadowed passageways, out through a narrow door, and then she found herself in the inner gardens—*their* garden. The place they met in the mornings, where they sparred, laughed, and stole glances when no other eyes were there to watch. The place where her walls began to crumble—where she thought he'd only seen *her*.

But he hadn't.

*If your sister was the one I wanted in my bed, I wouldn't try to hide it.*

Liar. Draevyn Rowe was nothing but a fucking liar.

She looked around at the familiar ground, bathed in the pale merlights acting as the morning sun, and felt a sharp pang of fury she couldn't contain. Her hands clenched at her sides, talons extending and digging into her palms until they drew blood.

Esmyra spotted the spears they'd used, propped neatly against a nearby stone, and strode toward them.

Her fingers wrapped around the handle of one, and with a cry that ripped from the depths of her chest, she raised the spear and brought it down, snapping it over her knee. The jagged ends splintered in her hands, but it wasn't enough. She tossed the pieces aside and grabbed another, slamming it against the stone until it, too, broke into useless fragments—a reflection of her own shattered heart.

She didn't stop. She couldn't. One by one, Esmyra tore through every weapon they had collected over their time there. The sound of shattering wood and clattering metal echoed through the empty garden. Her arms ached, her breath coming in shallow gasps, but she kept going, as if each snap and break could somehow mend what splintered in her chest.

Visions of the prior night flooded her mind—Draevyn holding her in his arms, kissing her, claiming her to only be *his*. For the first time in her life, she saw a glimpse of love and what she'd imagined it felt like. But it was all a lie.

A scream clawed up her throat and tore from her lips, raw and furious, reverberating into the air. The force of it left her breathless, dizzy, and she could've sworn the palace shook in her fury.

How could Draevyn have done this to her? *Why*?! She'd let herself trust him—allowed herself to care for him. And despite all her caution, she'd given him her heart, only to have him betray her with the one other person she thought understood her.

And she couldn't let Syrena hold blame—Esmyra had lied to her face, claiming she felt nothing for Draevyn.

*Stupid.* She had been so fucking reckless and stupid in so many ways.

The sharp edges of the broken wood bit into her palms, and she welcomed the sting, the pain grounding her as her emotions swirled in uncontrollable waves.

She stood there, feeling entirely hollow, as if everything she'd fought for, everything she'd hoped for, had been snatched away in a heartbeat by the man who had given her the hope to begin with.

Tears pricked her eyes, but she blinked them away, refusing to let them fall. Draevyn didn't deserve her tears—no man *ever* fucking deserved a woman's tears. She wouldn't give him the satisfaction of seeing her break.

Esmyra squared her shoulders, squeezing her eyes shut, forcing herself to hold on to the anger, to let it harden and shield her from the pain that lingered just beneath. Her fury flooded her veins, igniting every part of her like molten metal and pouring over the wounds he'd left raw.

The anger was different from any she'd felt before—not a sharp, impulsive flash, but a slow, burning flame that took root in her heart, consuming every tender feeling she once had for him.

Esmyra showed him pieces of herself she'd never shown anyone, yet he'd thrown it away as if it meant nothing, when he *knew* it meant everything.

The Rowes had taken everything from her—her father, her crew, and now her heart, leaving it as she once claimed it to be.

*Black*—hollow and devoid of guilt. The heart of a Blackwood.

The world labeled her a monster, but every time she tried to prove she was anything but, it only coerced her into falling more into the title's grasp.

The rune-carved bones in the crypt flashed across her mind, and she felt that pull to them once more. It was as if they were calling to her, beckoning her home.

She knew the crypt held the answers she needed.

If the realm believed Esmyra Blackwood was a wretched, raging beast, then may the gods help them if they ever met Kaelypso Aeress.

Esmyra felt that power in those remains—could practically feel it sparking at her fingertips in her rage, and she vowed that with it, she would become as unyielding as the sea.

Ruthless. Dangerous. And *lethal*.

She stood tall, straightening her spine and holding her head high as she walked back through the gardens and headed toward the great hall as she did every morning. Acting as if nothing had even happened at all as she prepared to face him.

Esmyra lifted a ripe, glistening piece of fruit to her lips, savoring its sweetness with each slow bite. The light cast through the great hall's tall windows, and everything seemed almost peaceful as she sat alone, taking her time. Each chew, each swallow, felt like an act of rebellion. She refused to let anyone see a crack in her composure.

The heavy doors swung open, and Syrena stumbled in, breathless, eyes scanning frantically until they landed on her. She crossed the room in a hurry, looking flustered, her usually poised expression replaced by worry mixed with guilt.

"There you are!" Her sister's voice was full of relief. "I've been looking everywhere for you. I...I'm so sorry, Esmyra. He invited me into his room and I didn't realize..." She hesitated, glancing down at her feet, struggling for the words. "I thought you held no feelings for him."

Of course she thought that. And it was Esmyra's fault.

Esmyra held her gaze steady, reaching for another piece of fruit as if Syrena's words were nothing more than idle chatter. She tilted her head slightly, a feigned look of confusion masking the blaze inside. "What are you talking about?" She gave a light, dismissive smile and took a slow bite. "Please, don't assume such things. I feel nothing for that man."

Syrena blinked. "But...your eyes. The way you...you *ran* from the room, Esmi." Her tone softened, nearly pleading. "I didn't know. I swear this to you."

Instead of lashing out, she let out a soft, almost dismissive laugh. "Really, Syrena, you're reading far too much into things. I don't concern myself with him," she stated, crossing her arms. "Perhaps it's you who sees him that way. After all..." A click of her tongue sounded. "He's repeatedly tried to seduce you."

"No, I..." Her sister's voice trembled slightly, a glimpse of vulnerability that she hadn't seen in her before. "I only meant that if I'd known, I would've stayed away."

*Too late for that,* she thought bitterly, though she forced a soft smile. "Please. Do what you like with him." Esmyra chose each word carefully to mask her anger. "It's not my business, and I've no desire to make it so."

Her sister blinked, her cheeks coloring as she nodded hesitantly. "I...I would never want to hurt you."

"Of course not," Esmyra said, lifting her hand to brush a nonexistent crumb from her dress. "But as I said, there's nothing to hurt. He and I mean nothing to each other. Just two strangers stranded."

Syrena looked uncertain, glancing down as if weighing her next words, but finally, she nodded. "Would you mind if I join you, then?"

"Aye, by all means." Esmyra gestured to the table.

Syrena came to sit beside her. "I ran after you," she said quietly. "He decided to stay behind, but I needed to find you."

For a fleeting moment, her sister's words softened her walls, and an ache stung her chest. *He didn't even care to explain himself,* she thought. Instead, Draevyn had stayed behind in his chambers, hiding in the very place he shattered her trust.

Her eyes met Syrena's, and she knew then that the only person she could trust was her own true flesh and blood. Draevyn wasn't her mirror, as she believed him to be. No, her mirror was who it was always meant to be—her twin and equal.

"Well, good." Esmyra said. "I've been looking forward to spending time with my sister, anyway."

Syrena shifted in her seat, her fingers tracing circles around the rim of her glass as she drew in a slow breath. Her golden waves rose and fell with the movement.

"There's something I need to tell you," she began, her voice quiet, almost hesitant. "Something...about our past. I haven't found the right moment to tell you. I planned to after the celebration last night, but I couldn't find you."

Esmyra's pulse quickened, her mind instantly going to the tomb and who was hidden there.

"Now may certainly not be the right time, but I just can't keep it from you any longer. You deserve to know, and I would hate for you to think I keep secrets from you."

Esmyra placed her hand atop Syrena's on the table. "What is it?"

Having discovered the truth about Maerinys in her visions, she discreetly tested Syrena to see if she would speak the truth of their kingdom's past.

Syrena's thumb grazed along the top of Esmyra's hand. "I was young when they told me—those who survived the fall. The people of Maerinys raised me since I was just a babe. They protected me as I grew up, and slowly—when they felt I was ready—they began to reveal bits of our past. And the true reasons as to why Maerinys fell. Azarian took over from there, revealing truths that weren't public knowledge and showing me what it would take to reclaim what's rightfully ours."

Esmyra stayed silent, keeping her expression steady, though her mind raced.

"Azarian told me of a power we both share," Syrena continued. "A legacy we come from, tied to both the sea and the strength of the gods."

Esmyra took a deep breath as the memories of the vision overwhelmed her.

"I didn't understand it all, not at first," Syrena admitted. "But this isn't our first life lived, Esmyra."

"And what do you mean by that?" Esmyra's words were barely a whisper.

Syrena swallowed. "Do you remember when you spoke of the sea goddesses having abandoned our world?"

Esmyra nodded.

"They're not lost," she admitted. Her sister stood from her chair, offering her hand, and coaxed Esmyra from her seat. "I found a way to find the truth for myself, and there's something I want to show you. Will you come with me?"

She gave a silent dip of her chin in answer.

E smyra trailed Syrena up the tower's stairs, her mind whirling as she contemplated why she wasn't being led to the crypt.

As she ascended the steps, all she could picture was racing up them in her ghostly form as she tried to run back to Kaelypso's body as Maerinys sank, and then falling to her knees as the runes burned themselves into her flesh.

When she opened the door, the faint glow of merlight orbs hovered through the tower's room, reflecting on the surface of the basin's water.

Esmyra's stare instantly lifted to the wall their goddess bodies had been chained and bound to by velsinyte, and found the restraints had been ripped from the stone.

*That must be where they got Draevyn's cuff.*

Syrena stood before the Veil of Visions, the water swirling like a mini whirlpool as her hands lightly brushed the stone rim. The silence between them stretched, heavy with unspoken words, and Esmyra's anticipation threatened to tear her apart from the inside out.

"I didn't want to burden you with this before," Syrena began, her eyes fixed on the gently rippling surface. "But you need to understand why I've kept this from you until now...why I've hidden the truth."

Syrena met Esmyra's gaze. "The Veil of Visions...it allows me to see things. Not just the present, but the past. I can look deep into the past and see all that transpired, even things that were concealed." She paused as she watched Esmyra, but she made sure her face showed no emotion as she listened. "And I saw it, the truth about us. About what we were...and what we are now."

She stepped closer to Esmyra, her fingers skimming the water's surface, as though trying to stir something from within it. "I saw *us*. Goddesses of the sea, together, bound by power."

"Goddesses." Esmyra swallowed. "You knew this, and yet you've kept it from me."

Syrena huffed through her nostrils, not in irritation, but as if she were thinking of how to choose her next words. "Not keeping it from you. More so, just waiting for the opportune moment. Yet, I must say, you're not as shocked as I was anticipating." She gave her a knowing look.

"Because I saw it too," Esmyra admitted as she walked up to the Veil of Visions, standing on the opposite side.

"And what did you see?"

Esmyra sucked in a breath and glanced down into the swirling pool. "When we first arrived here from that tunnel, there was a rune-marked bowl of stone that matched this one. When I touched it..."

"It showed you something, didn't it?" Syrena tilted her head to the side.

"The fall," she answered. "I was standing in the center of it, feeling as if I was truly there."

Syrena's lips curved. "We *were* there, Esmyra."

"There was something else," she started. "A crypt."

Syrena's eyes widened, her lips parting. "The crypt," she echoed.

"Aye, so you do know of it." Esmyra's eyes narrowed on her.

"We were the strongest, you know," she stated, not confirming or denying her question. "*You* were stronger than any of the other gods, and they were afraid of you. They feared what we could become. Together."

A calm fury washed over Syrena, emanating from her. "The people of Maerinys were adamant that our remains had to be hidden

—that our power was fragile and sacred, tied to the kingdom itself." Her sister's gaze shifted, wary and weighted. "The bones in that crypt…"

"They're ours," Esmyra finished for her.

Something mimicking pride flashed across Syrena's face. Her chin lifted high, accompanied by a closed-lip smile. "Yes. They hid them away in case the gods who betrayed us returned for them. But at that time, we were unaware that the gods above no longer walked the soil of Rymelle among their subjects, and it's because of the betrayal of us that they *hide*—their shame of it."

"But why? Why would the other gods betray them?" Esmyra swallowed. "Betray *us*. What did we do?"

"We did *nothing*," Syrena hissed. "They killed our goddess forms in a fit of jealous rage."

"But why would they be jealous? All the gods have their own lands—their own people to rule over and worship them."

Syrena pursed her lips. "They believed it to be unfair that they each only possessed a single kingdom while we ruled over the entirety of the realm's seas, which is a world of its own."

"Unfair," Esmyra echoed, the veins in her neck straining. "We were held down and *murdered* in cold blood out of envy."

*Power. Jealousy. Greed.* It was at the forefront of all beings in their world, and it was at that moment Esmyra vowed to herself she would put an end to it, no matter the cost.

Syrena placed her hand atop Esmyra's as it rested on the edge. "The magic of what remains in our goddess forms is what keeps Maerinys safe in the depths. They cannot access us, and we cannot leave. They damned our people that day. An entire civilization— wiped from the map in their greed, claiming the greed was our own. You see, Esmyra, the power held within them, within *us*, is what's needed to bring our people back to the surface—to lift our kingdom from its watery grave."

"So, you plan to break our curse," Esmyra guessed. "And with that…"

"Our godly powers would return to us. We could raise our kingdom and take our revenge."

*Revenge.*

Esmyra thought of all the wretched people above who deserved the wrath of her vengeance. How they did nothing but take and take and *take*. She had been one of them—learned it from her father. And, unbeknownst to her, *she* had been stolen.

Syrena's expression was unreadable, her eyes distant. "They tried to *erase us*." Her voice broke, fists shaking at her sides. "Every element and kingdom had a ruling god, yet the sea had two. And they believed it not to be fair, for two is more powerful than one."

As she listened, Esmyra couldn't shake how Irah had looked at her with regret and agony in his eyes—*Draevyn's* eyes—as he stabbed her in the heart. It seemed that very act was destined to repeat itself in a cruel twist of fate.

The Veil of Visions rippled again, as if responding to Syrena's words. "You and I were gods. And now, we're still bound by that power in these mortal forms. It's the only reason these vessels have survived this long."

A chill ran along Esmyra's spine as the word 'vessel' was used to describe her body.

Esmyra's gaze swept over her twin. "And what kills a god?"

Syrena clenched her jaw. "*Velsinyte,*" she spat, as if it tasted wretched on her tongue. "In the heart."

"And they made Irah commit it," Esmyra said.

"Now you're following." Syrena gave a bone-chilling smile. "From what I've been able to piece together, it was ordered to be this way by Asyris themself."

*Asyris.* That was the word she didn't understand as she stood in the memory. "And what exactly is that?"

Syrena tilted her head. "The world no longer recalls Asyris?" When Esmyra subtly shook her head, she continued. "Asyris is the divine being of both life and death. The creator and destroyer of all things. Including us, their first creations."

Esmyra's lips parted. So much history had been lost over the last millennia, which included that of *another* god. But not just any god—the divine. Of both life and death.

"You see, Esmyra," she started again, "Gods couldn't be killed until they convinced Asyris we were too dangerous for our world. And it was then velsinyte was born, bearing the blood of our primal. Our end-all be-all. Our maker and monarch ordered Irah to stab us in the hearts with those forged daggers and to collect our souls." She gestured between the two of them. "Clearly, he never completed the second part."

Esmyra licked her lips, her eyes darting back and forth as she took in the words. "And why would they make *him* do it?" She feared she already knew the answer.

Syrena leaned across the Veil of Visions, the swirling water coming to a halt. "*Love*, if rumors are to be believed."

Esmyra blinked. "And you believe these rumors and legends?"

Syrena crossed her arms and let out a small giggle, but there was a menace to it, her entire demeanor changing as the truth of their past came to light. "I believe that if you want something done right, you should never rely on a man."

A smirk spread across Esmyra's face. "Aye."

"And we got lucky. When our souls drifted, they found the newborn Aeress twins in their beds. Maerinys was sinking quickly and our lovely counterparts panicked and abandoned us. Abandoned Rymelle in fear of us finding them again."

"They fled?"

"It appears that way. They're the one thing I can't *see*," she spat the last word as her fists trembled, hanging at her sides. "They hide in a new world, it appears. Velsinyte guards their entrances, and the magic doesn't allow me to look past it."

Esmyra's eyes grew wide. *That must be how the mortals are in possession of it.*

"None of that matters now, though." Syrena spread her arms wide. "Because here we are. Alive! Powerful, and ready to raise Maerinys from the depths they damned us to as both goddess and Aeress."

Esmyra's gaze drifted over the water's reflecting surface. Her sister's words echoed in her mind, but they only stirred more questions.

Who was she, truly? Was she the goddess, Kaelypso, reborn? Or an Aeress heir born of a thousand years past? Perhaps she was just some fractured blend of them both.

"And who will we be once we break the curse?" she asked.

Syrena grinned. "Whoever we want to be."

Silence descended on them, the only sound coming from the subtle buzz of the merlight orbs as they hovered.

"Where would we even begin to try to undo what's been done?" Esmyra wondered aloud.

A cruel smirk crept up Syrena's face, and it was eerily similar to the one Esmyra wore when taunting her prey.

"This won't be simple," she began. "Undoing the curse means unbinding the power of the gods who placed it on us in the first place. It means stripping away every shackle that holds our souls in this mortal flesh."

Esmyra's eyes widened. "How?"

"Sacrifices." Syrena took a steadying breath. "Azarian believes that in order for us to regain our divinity, we need something to represent each god, along with ourselves."

"Aye..." Esmyra nodded along, taking the words in. "An element of each god."

"Yes. Their own essence is tied to the realms they rule. We need a physical piece of each—the earth Villaem commands, a drop of our sacred sea," she paused as her eyes traced over Esmyra, "a spark of Irah's flame."

Esmyra's jaw clenched at the mention of flame, her mind rushing back to the fire-wielder several floors away. "And what of Vydenne?"

"That's the trickiest one." Syrena tilted her head to the side. "Vydenne's elven hold the power to manipulate minds, often resulting in showing enemies their greatest fears coming to life."

Esmyra blinked and let out a low whistle. "Our fears? We need to offer a tangible fear?" She let out a cackle. "I fear nothing."

Syrena's brow furrowed. "We all fear something, dearest sister."

*I already faced my greatest fear this morning.*

A thousand years—she had been cautious with her heart for nearly a thousand years, and finally entrusted it to Draevyn, only for him to shatter it within hours.

Esmyra nodded, and Syrena continued, her voice lowering. "Next, we'll need to spill our blood upon the remains—only it must be with the velsinyte dagger used to kill us to begin with. Without it, the curse's binding threads can't unravel. No other weapon will do."

"What happens if this doesn't work?" Esmyra wondered aloud. "And how does Azarian know all of this?"

Syrena offered her a smile. "It will work."

Esmyra took a deep breath, pushing down the aggravation of her ignoring the question about Azarian. "Then what happens when we succeed?"

"We'll reclaim our powers," Syrena started. "What we possess now is but a sliver of what we held before. We'll no longer be bound to this mortal shell. We'll be gods once more—the best of them. Naerysa and Kaelypso will return to Rymelle."

They sat in silence as she felt the magnitude of what lay ahead. But Esmyra knew Syrena's mind was made up, and with it, so was hers.

Syrena reached across the Veil of Visions and gripped Esmyra's hand. "Together, then?"

Esmyra's gaze lingered on her sister before she squeezed her hand back and nodded. "Aye... *Together.*"

They descended the stairs from the tower in silence, her mind tangled with the weight of everything Syrena revealed.

The reality of their past had started to settle in, but one thought kept rising above the rest—*Draevyn*—and she loathed it. Esmyra absolutely hated that he was consuming her thoughts as she learned everything she'd longed for her entire life, knowing she would have to face him when she returned.

Every step she took toward the hall only seemed to quicken her pulse, her heart racing as they neared where she assumed he'd be waiting.

*Why do I hope he's waiting?*

Esmyra told herself it was just so she could send her fist through his face—she had no interest in entertaining any other possible reason.

Anticipating his grovelling, she steeled her heart and mind, making it so any pleas for forgiveness from him would fall on deaf ears.

But as she and Syrena entered the great hall, a strange unease filled the air. Guards quickly approached her twin, leaning close to whisper in her ear. Her sister's face flickered with something unreadable, her gaze moving between Esmyra and the guards, looking hesitant.

"What is it? What's going on?" Esmyra asked, brows furrowing as she took a step closer to them.

Syrena shifted, giving her a look that seemed pitying. "I don't know how to tell you this," she said, placing a reassuring hand on her arm.

Esmyra's chest tightened as she took a step out of Syrena's reach. "What happened?" she pressed, her throat tightening.

The queen took a breath and hesitated, glancing at her hands as she picked at her thumb before meeting her eyes. "It's Draevyn... he—"

"What about him?!" Esmyra snapped, cutting her off. She couldn't help the slight crack in her voice.

"He's gone," she answered, and time seemed to slow as the blood drained from Esmyra's face. "Draevyn was seen leaving Maerinys, headed for the caves. He must've discovered where they were and left without saying a word. Azarian tried to go after him, but he caused a cave-in with his flames, blocking the tunnel you arrived from."

*He's gone.*

Esmyra's heart plummeted, every hopeful thought of him turning cold, vanishing in an instant. A distant numbness flooded her, and her face hardened, instinctively guarding the turmoil roiling inside her.

*Gone.* The word clung to her mind, clashing violently with everything she thought she'd known.

Draevyn was supposed to be here waiting for her to return. He was supposed to grovel at her feet and beg for forgiveness. He was supposed to lie and whisper sweet words as all men did for their treachery, but he couldn't even give her that.

The Phoenix was a coward and *ran.*

He fled from the consequences he would face.

Draevyn ran from *her.*

It was just another fucking disappointment, sealing the final nail in her heart's coffin.

He left through the caves, as they had planned to do together, abandoning her.

The heartache she'd been struggling to suppress twisted into something sharper, harsher. Transforming into a fierce wave of betrayal that wrapped around her heart and turned it to stone.

It was rage, pure and scalding, consuming the last dregs of hope she'd naively clung to and burning it to ash.

*Wildfire indeed,* his words echoed in her mind.

Draevyn Rowe had no fucking idea.

While *he* may be the one who wielded flame, *she* would be the one to take everything he loved and reduce it to nothing but cinders.

Syrena reached for her again, but Esmyra pulled away. "I'm so sorry, sister."

Esmyra's fingers curled into fists, talons biting into her palms as she willed her face steady.

The guards whispered to Syrena as they stepped away, casting wary glances at Esmyra that only fueled the growing heat in her veins. She felt their pity, their judgment, as if they knew something she didn't.

Syrena's gaze turned sympathetic, but Esmyra didn't want sympathy. It wasn't needed. Any softness that might've lingered with her memories of Draevyn had hardened, transforming into a burning resolve.

She didn't care where he'd gone or why. He'd made his choice, and she'd let it serve as her final lesson.

Esmyra didn't flinch as she met Syrena's stare, didn't let an ounce of her fury seep into her voice as she forced her lips into a hard, closed-lip smile. "Well, it appears he made his choice."

And it wasn't her.

Draevyn hadn't chosen her.

CHAPTER 72

*Draevyn*

Draevyn woke with a jolt, his body sprawled on the cold, uneven ground in complete darkness. His skull pulsated in pure agony from Azarian knocking him unconscious at Syrena's command.

Wherever they left him, it was deathly silent, save for his rapid, shallow breaths that sounded unnaturally loud, as if echoing in an empty space. Heart hammering, he forced his breathing to slow. But the absolute pitch black pressed in around him.

Draevyn lifted his fingers to his brow, feeling the deep grooves within his flesh from the queen's talons. He hissed at his own touch, but was thankful her claws narrowly missed his eye. His face was likely maimed for life, but he didn't give a damn—the only thing he cared about was Esmyra.

Instinctively, he summoned a flicker of fire in his palm, surprised to not find a velsinyte band encasing his wrists. As the flames grew, the surroundings materialized. His heart nearly stopped at the sight.

The damp, uneven floor beneath him belonged to the cavern he and Esmyra had plummeted to when the ceilings above caved in. The walls rose endlessly around him, and the small lake he had nearly drowned in was across the space. Draevyn whipped around to the tunnel Esmyra had opened with her powers, and he was met with a sight that filled him with dread.

A massive wall of stacked boulders loomed before him, blocking the passage back to Maerinys—back to *her*. They once again sealed themselves off from the rest of the world, trapping him just beyond its borders.

He ran to them, fingers tracing the rough, unyielding surfaces. "No," he breathed, taking a step back as panic nearly consumed him.

Esmyra's face flooded his mind, recalling the way she gazed at him when he confessed his feelings for her—the way she looked as he claimed her and threatened anyone who dared to take her from him in the same breath.

And then that memory shattered, overtaken by the haunted look on her face when she walked in on him and her sister. Syrena had compelled him into thinking she was Esmyra—his Wildfire. The queen had taken over his mind, and there was nothing he could do to fight her off.

She intentionally drove a wedge between him and Esmyra, destroying the trust they'd carefully built, and then banished him before they could speak. Before he could tell her the truth of what happened.

The only question was *why*? What could she possibly have planned to need the two of them separated, and Esmyra hurt? Was it so all of her attention would be on Syrena? But if so, why would she leave him alive? And with his power at that...

The sharp ache in his skull was barely anything now compared to the agony piercing his heart.

The cavern walls seemed to close in with every breath. His pulse raced the more his thoughts spun. Esmyra was still in Maerinys, somewhere beyond that impenetrable wall. Alone, with no one but a sister who was dangerous, who had only hidden truths and twisted intentions—all to gain her trust.

Everything they uncovered in that cave, Syrena already knew. And she intentionally kept Esmyra in the dark.

Summoning a stronger blaze, he poured fire toward the boulders, forcing himself to channel all his power, all his fury into the flames as he let out a bellowing yell.

The walls glowed under the assault, shadows leaping wildly in the cavern, but the stones drank in his fire as if absorbing the magic. He tried again, pouring more power, more fire from his palms, until sweat beaded on his forehead. Each blaze he threw faded against the wall's surface, barely making a mark. Nothing melted, charred, or burned.

Draevyn slammed his fists into the rock, the pain barely registering over the fear clawing up his throat. "*FUCK!*" he shouted, his voice reverberating in the silence.

The firelight sputtered and faded, leaving him in darkness once more.

Breath heaving, he raked a hand through his hair. Every instinct he had screamed to break through, to tear those stones apart piece by piece if he had to, but nothing was working. And every second felt like she was slipping further away.

First, she thought he betrayed her trust and heart, and now, she would think he abandoned her—leaving her alone in a world where she already felt so isolated.

He gritted his teeth and pressed his forehead to the hot stone, welcoming its burn. "I'm coming. I swear on every wretched fucking god who has hurt you, I'm coming for you."

Draevyn hoped that somehow she'd hear him through the stone and depths, but all that answered him was the cold echo of his voice.

In the stillness, a memory surfaced—Syrena's taunting words: *Very small crevices in the rock act as a ladder.*

Draevyn turned back to that wall and the black, glassy lake resting beneath it. The edge of the water felt ominously still, a dark void stretching out before him, and when he re-summoned flame, he saw them—subtle crevices in the rock wall leading up as high as his sight reached and beyond. In the center of the fucking lake.

Steeling himself, he approached the edge. But before he could get any closer, a ripple disturbed the glassy water, then another, and another, until the entire lake was no longer still. His body tensed as their unblinking eyes surfaced just above the water's edge.

*Grindylows.*

"Fucking Irah," he huffed.

They watched him with dark and fathomless eyes—the creatures who had tried to feast on his flesh the last time he was in this gods-forsaken place.

Draevyn gritted his teeth, letting the fire surge in his hands, casting an amber glow across the water and the monsters watching him.

Raising the flames higher, he shouted, "Unless you wish to burn, I suggest you crawl back to whatever hell you came from."

The creatures hissed, retreating slightly into the dark water, but they remained there, still watching and waiting.

He didn't waste another moment. Wading into the icy lake, his fire illuminated the water just enough to make out the vague outline of the crevices embedded in the wall on the far side. Only able to use one hand to swim, the water slowed him, tugging against his legs as he moved, eyes glancing back and forth between the wall and grindylows waiting for their next feast.

Reaching the wall, he craned his neck, following the steps disappearing up into shadow. He'd have to climb—and he'd need both hands.

"Godsdammit," he hissed.

*Gods.* That was who got him in this situation in the first place.

Exhaling, he extinguished the fire, plunging himself into pitch darkness. The moment the last bit of light winked out, the sound of splashing water reached his ears.

His eyes flared, knowing they had been waiting to attack. Draevyn reached out, his fingers finding the sharp grooves within the wall. He quickly hoisted himself up, letting instinct guide him as he climbed, his hands moving cautiously over the rough stone, gripping each crevice as he replaced the last one with his boot.

A sharp hiss-like screech filled the air, and then he felt it—a slick, scaled weight clinging to his back, then another wrapping around his leg. His throat tightened as he forced himself to remain as calm as possible. Draevyn twisted and kicked, but more creatures swarmed up from below, latching onto him with startling strength. Sharp claws and teeth bit into his arms and shoulders, trying to drag him back down.

"Get the *fuck* off of me!" he bellowed, struggling to shake them off as their claws dug deeper. A brief burst of flame erupted at his fingertips, but it was snuffed out almost instantly by the cold water still clinging to their skin.

The creatures seemed to laugh, a gurgling sound that echoed in the cavern as more weight pulled him downward.

Draevyn's fingers slipped, and he slid several feet down the wall before his fingers found purchase again in one of the carved steps. He gritted his teeth, fighting against their hold with every ounce of strength he had left, desperate to reach the surface—desperate to find help for her.

A fury unlike any he'd ever known flared in his chest, fueling his power. With a deep breath, he channeled every ounce of energy he had, igniting a fierce blaze across his back.

The flames roared to life, hot and merciless, scorching the grindylows clinging to him. Their piercing screams filled the cavern as the fire engulfed them, while the smell of burning flesh filled the air.

One by one, their grips loosened, their claws retracting until they slipped off and plummeted back into the lake. The water hissed and bubbled as their charred forms fell into them with a splash, leaving only steam rising from its surface and the occasional bubble.

Draevyn didn't waste a second, forcing himself upward, his muscles aching as he pushed past the limit of his strength. He ascended the wall as fast as he could. His shredded, bloody skin screamed in pain, his knuckles turning white with each tight grip as he fought through the agony.

The darkness seemed endless, the cavern's wall stretching on as if it had no end, yet he climbed faster, harder, pushing himself beyond exhaustion.

Finally, with a desperate pull, he heaved himself up onto solid ground, collapsing against the cold, wet stone. Draevyn drew in a long breath, his heart hammering so violently he thought it might burst as he lay there in silence just beyond a humming barrier.

He pressed his hand against the nearly invisible barrier, feeling a soft vibration against his skin. And now it wouldn't let him pass back through to get back to Maerinys.

*Shit*. That must've been what Syrena meant about her guards not being able to pass through since they were trapped since the sinking. It was true that the only reason he could before was because he was with Esmyra.

Suddenly, a deep, thunderous boom echoed through the tunnels beyond. He shot upright, instantly recognizing the unmistakable sound of cannon fire.

Flame burst in Draevyn's hand, and he held it close to light the way as he took off in a sprint. Winding through twisting passages and narrow corridors, he stumbled over uneven ground as he wove his way through the endless labyrinth of the cave. The firelight only extended a few feet in front of him, but it was enough to catch sight of crumbling rocks and the dust still drifting from the ceiling caused by the boom.

A second cannon sounded as he raced forward, driving him faster. A wild desperation clawed at him with each step he took. Draevyn didn't let himself dwell on what cannon fire could mean, nor did he let himself worry about what Esmyra's crew would do if they found he returned without her.

Finally, he rounded the final bend, the cave's mouth coming into view right before he burst through it.

*BOOM*.

The ground shook beneath Draevyn's feet as the deafening sound of another cannon tore through the sky while he bolted out of the cave, nearly tripping over the uneven ground. He squinted against the sunlight, and gods, he'd never been more thankful to see it, but then his heart leapt in his throat as he looked out over the sea.

In the distance, dark plumes of smoke rose, swirling against the blue sky and mingling with the clouds.

He sprinted down the rocky hillside, ignoring the sharp twinges of pain from the wounds the grindylows had left across his back and down his legs. Each step sent shocks of agony through him, but he pushed forward, boots pounding against the rough earth as the scent of salt and smoke stung his nostrils.

The small rocky beach finally came into view, and his pulse quickened with a mixture of relief and horror as he recognized his ship, *Valor*, locked in battle with *The Night Wraith*, their cannons firing relentlessly.

Draevyn ran across the stone isle, waving his hands above his head, shouting until his voice was hoarse. "Stop!" he screamed, but the word was drowned out by the roar of cannon fire.

How did Samwell find him? He never thought anyone would sail this far south, never mind for *him*.

His eyes locked on *The Night Wraith*, dread filling him as he noticed the vessel was already half sunken to the depths.

That damn ship was all Esmyra had left—her *crew* was all she had, and if they sank to the bottom of the sea, he knew hell itself would be kinder to the world than the wrath she would unleash upon it.

*Something's wrong...*

*Valor* was unharmed. No holes broke her body, and no screams of horror rang from either ship. As he tried to settle his racing mind, he listened more closely to the sounds erupting from Valor.

It was *cheering*.

Not a single cannon fired from *The Night Wraith*, and no crew lay in wait on its deck.

"Mother of the gods," he breathed.

Another cannonball crashed into the water nearby, spraying him with its splash. He staggered but kept his arms up, waving frantically at his crew as they continued to fire.

Desperation suffocated him as he stumbled further down the beach and into the water, cupping his hands around his mouth to amplify his voice.

"Hold your fire!" he bellowed, over and over again until his voice cracked. "Hold your fucking fire, you idiots!"

When nothing caught their attention, he lifted a heavy hand and heaved what remained of his energy into sending flame at his ship, watching as a small fire lit its rails.

Draevyn glanced down at the water he stood in to find the blood from his wounds had stained it red, and the outskirts of his vision began to blur. He didn't realize how much blood he'd lost as it continued to pour from him.

Yelling sounded in the distance, but he couldn't determine whether they were the lingering cheers or someone calling to him.

And then he crashed down into the water.

# CHAPTER 73

# Esmyra

The past week had been a whirlwind of preparation, each day a blur of tasks, meetings with the council, and decisions that left Esmyra too busy to dwell on Draevyn's betrayal.

Syrena was relentless in her guidance, speaking of ancient rites and the importance of aligning their energies for what was to come. The people of Maerinys were prepared as well, their queen's guards and advisors ensuring they knew all possibilities of what to expect—the earth quaking beneath them, the breaking of the dome, a sudden rush of waves. But the truth was...no one truly knew what to expect. So, they were sure to prepare for anything imaginable.

This wouldn't just affect their lives, or that of their people, but all those above the surface as well—including her father.

If Esmyra and Syrena were able to break their curse and free themselves from their mortal bindings, then there was a chance Cyrus Blackwood's curse would be shattered as well. He would be able to walk on land. No longer would he suffocate on the shores of Rymelle or in the prison that held him these past several weeks.

Esmyra and Syrena had gathered their offerings for the other gods. The sand from the ocean's floor, marking the offering for Villaem, the god of agriculture and growth. A torch to light for Irah, the god of rage and war. And all that was left were their fears for Vydenne, the goddess of Illusion, which neither sister had spoken of what they would bring.

Esmyra contemplated everything that led her there. She had a plan, a sacrifice she was more than willing to make, hoping this offering would rid her of it, banishing it for the remainder of her existence.

Now, Esmyra and Syrena stood before the entrance to the crypt, while Azarian and the council trailed behind them in hooded robes.

Her breath hitched as she looked at the sealed door of their tomb, knowing nothing would be the same again once they reclaimed their power.

But what if they failed? Or if Syrena was wrong regarding what it would take? What if this was what they were always meant to remain as?

"Are you ready?" Syrena's voice broke through her thoughts, bringing her a sense of peace she didn't realize she needed.

Esmyra met Syrena's gaze and, perhaps even for the first time, she saw Syrena for who she really was—she saw someone who shared her burden, who understood the weight of what they were about to do, likely even more than she did herself.

"Yes," Esmyra answered, her voice unwavering, even as the beat of her heart pounded in her ears. "Let's get this done." Her gaze moved back to the door, and in unison, both sisters placed their palms against the cool stone.

The stone groaned, the ancient seals trembling under their touch. A low hum filled the air, vibrating through the floor beneath their feet. Neither spoke—they just stood entirely still, their eyes narrowed on the entrance to the crypt as it opened for them. Slowly, the runes engraved on the door began to glow, faint at first, then brighter, illuminating the cavern just as before.

Only, the door wasn't opening as it had the last time, refusing to slide down into a pocket of the earth as she had expected. But with a deep, resonating *crack*, the stone split down the center. Dust and fragments burst, and the massive slabs shifted outward, revealing the yawning darkness. A rush of stale air greeted them, sending their hair flying backward.

Syrena swirled a taloned finger in the air and sent several orbs of merlights shooting into the crypt, revealing the shadowy alcoves and the two slabs of stone that held their bones.

Esmyra's eyes instantly drifted upwards, to the two daggers hung on the wall, parallel to each of their resting places, with the Aeress trident suspended between them.

"Together," Syrena whispered, placing a hand lightly on her shoulder.

She nodded and took the first step, crossing the threshold into the crypt. Azarian lit the torches lining the walls by striking two rocks together as he moved through the room, and their flames flared to life as if welcoming them—or warning them.

Esmyra's gaze was locked on the raised platform. Her hands curled into fists at her sides, her emotions churning as she stared at the altar holding the goddesses' bones. The goddesses who were betrayed by someone she had loved—someone they both trusted.

But she knew better now and history would never repeat itself again.

Esmyra vowed to herself that she would no longer be a tool for others to use or a weapon for them to wield. A being of divine and ancient power, she would unleash a millennium's worth of fury on anyone who tried to manipulate her again.

"Do you feel it?" Syrena asked, turning to look at her. "The magic here? The power?"

Esmyra closed her eyes and let herself feel, let herself reach out with more than just her senses. The crypt thrummed with energy, pulsing in time with her heartbeat. It called to her, whispered to her, demanding her attention.

It wasn't just power—it was hers. It was *theirs*, and never again would they let it slip through their grasp.

"I feel it," she said softly, almost wickedly.

Syrena's lips curved into a faint, knowing smile. "Good. We need to embrace it fully. It will take a significant amount of power to do what we plan." As she spoke, her subjects lined the room, standing on the outskirts, their eyes remaining locked on the twins.

Esmyra's feet felt heavy as she ascended the steps. She stopped at the edge of the platform, staring down at the perfectly intact bones that made a devastating chill run along her spine.

Syrena joined her, standing on the opposite end, the two stone tables between them. "Once we rebind ourselves to what was taken, we'll finally be free." The crypt seemed to hold its breath around them. "Just follow my lead, sister."

Syrena reached forward first, Esmyra following the movements.

Her hand trembled over the ribcage of her skeleton, and as Esmyra's fingers brushed the bone, a pulse of heat jolted through her, like fire in her veins. She gasped, clutching the edge of the altar to steady herself.

Syrena shivered as if an invisible wind had passed over her. "They call to us," she breathed. Her stare lifted to Azarian, who now stood directly before the trident on the far side of the crypt. "Bring us the offerings, and once we have them, you must guard the door."

Azarian obeyed, and together, Esmyra and Syrena took their offerings from his silver tray. They summoned the water from the vessel, a string of it swirling through the air like a liquid ribbon, before pouring itself onto each altar. They watched as it spilled over the bones like a living river, filling the cracks, pooling in the sockets and grooves of the ancient skulls.

In tandem, they scattered earth from the shores of Maerinys, which dissolved into silt, swirling and merging with the water like clay.

Azarian then removed the daggers from the walls, offering them to each twin as their blades glistened beneath the mix of mer and torchlight. The moment Esmyra's fingers touched the hilt, her breath hitched.

*I'm holding my own murder weapon.* The blade that stole her life, driven into her chest by the man who claimed to love her.

She twirled the dagger, watching the swirling mix of the teal merlight and the fire's flame mingle on its reflective edge. A bitter laugh slipped from her as she watched the dance of her water and Irah's blaze mock her.

Esmyra's stare lifted to her sister's, each giving the other a sharp, sudden nod. In unison, the twins held out their palms and sliced their blades through their flesh. They both let out a sharp hiss as their skin tore. Blood pooled in their hands, before turning their wrists and allowing it to fall onto the bones—which drank in the offering eagerly. Onyx, spider-like veins instantly spread over their palms from the velsinyte.

"And lastly, it demands fear," Syrena's voice echoed eerily in the cavern.

Their eyes met, and Esmyra's bloody fingertips grazed over the necklace Draevyn had given her the night of the celebration—the night she had given herself to him—mind, body, and soul. The night that changed everything, and the night she vowed to never repeat again.

*Beautiful and blue with sharp edges. It reminded me of you*, he had said.

Her fingers wrapped around the pendant, and she ripped it from her neck, the chain snapping before throwing it onto the altar.

"And what is it you fear, sister?" Syrena's voice swirled around her, as if she were everywhere all at once.

Esmyra's lips parted as her eyes remained on the blood-stained crystal. "Love," she answered.

Her gaze slowly lifted to Syrena. "And what is it you fear, sister?" Esmyra echoed.

Syrena glanced down at the dagger in her hand, her arm trembling with a sudden rage, before she tossed the blade into the offerings. "Death," she answered, her voice barely a whisper.

The air instantly grew thick with power—the weight pressed on her lungs, making each breath a struggle. As their blood seeped into the remains, the runes upon them pulsed with a faint glow.

Syrena reached out and grabbed Esmyra's hand, their bleeding palms smashing together as their blood continued to rain onto the stone. Her twin's lips parted as she gave her a subtle nod—the cue to begin their chant.

And together, their two voices intertwined, becoming a single, enchanting melody that resonated through the tomb.

> *By the tides that swallowed our name,*
> *By the earth that buried our flame,*
> *By allies that whispered lies untold,*
> *We summon the power we once did hold.*
> *From the gods who bound our bones in shame,*
> *We summon your fear, your blood, and our name.*
> *Essence of water, fire, stone, and mind,*
> *Unravel our chains and return what is mine.*

The chanting evoked a rush of memories, assaulting her mind— flashes of their kingdom, the smell of salt and sun, and the relentless roar of the sea crashing against every shore.

Esmyra's body began to ache, her tendons stretching and twisting. And then the pain moved to her heart. Her very blood had turned to liquid flame—a hot, searing agony that spread outward, igniting her bones one by one as her mortal form felt like it was shattering into tiny shards beneath the raw power.

Her hands gripped the sides of the altar, and she leaned forward, nearly collapsing over the remains as magic reshaped her from the inside out. She risked a peek at her sister to find her writhing in pain alongside her, both of their mortal forms breaking under the agony.

Esmyra cried out, the power filling her with an unbearable pressure, resembling a dam about to break. Her vision blurred, and she staggered back, forcing herself to breathe through the pain as her heart threatened to burst through her ribcage.

But she refused to falter—never again would she yield.

Gritting her teeth, she clutched the edge of the stone and

welcomed the anguish as it forged her mortal body into something eternal—something divine.

With a sudden burst, the ancient bones dissolved into light, a soft, steady glow that lifted itself from the stone and drifted to each of them. That power surged to their limbs, placing itself atop the runes marking their flesh before seeping into them, binding them to those forms.

A mixture of euphoria and torment flooded Esmyra, a tear in the fabric of her being that left her both gasping and writhing as the essence of those remains merged with her mortal flesh.

Esmyra opened her eyes to find her body glowing faintly with a silver-blue light, shimmering like moonlight on waves—while the glow of Syrena's skin radiated the soft hues of dawn over the ocean's surface.

Her flesh then burned with an icy heat, her mortal shell feeling as if it was melting from her bones.

And then, it happened.

The energy within them reached a breaking point, and with a sudden, deafening bellow, they erupted outward in a violent burst of light. Blinding power surged from their bodies in an uncontrollable wave.

The acolytes who lined the crypt's walls screamed, their cries cut short as the raw power incinerated them, leaving nothing but ashes swirling in the charged air.

The two stone altars cracked and crumbled under the sheer force of the eruption, fragments scattering across the stone floor. The tomb's walls groaned, straining to contain the unleashed power while fractures raced up the stone.

Esmyra and Syrena stood at the center of the inferno of power— their silver and golden hair billowing at the force of an unseen wind.

And then, everything came to a halt, the world itself pausing. The glow in their eyes was sharp and unyielding, remaining locked on each other as everything settled.

The silence that followed was deafening.

The twins stood amidst the destruction, the room scorched and lifeless save for the crackling energy that still danced around them—Esmyra felt it skittering across her flesh like crackles of lightning. Ashes swirled in the air, settling like snow upon the shattered remains of the chamber.

Her senses expanded—vision and hearing sharper and stronger than she thought imaginable. The room was silent, but the ocean beyond the dome seemed to pulse in acknowledgment, drawn to their power.

Esmyra staggered back from the altar, her breath coming in shallow gasps as the last traces of the divine power surged into her. She blinked rapidly, trying to adjust to the overwhelming sensation coursing through her body. Her hands trembled as she raised them in front of her, her eyes widening in disbelief.

Her once-black hair was now blue at the roots, spilling over her shoulders like liquid silver as it glinted faintly in the dim, fractured light of the chamber. It was exactly as it had been in her vision, the day Maerinys fell.

Esmyra's gaze dropped to her arms and found the runes adorning her skin were not only glowing, but *swirling*. It was as if they were alive, shifting and flowing like the tides as lines of silver and deep blue intertwined.

She lifted her hands higher, watching in awe as tiny sparks ignited at her fingertips, crackling and popping like miniature storms. They leapt from one finger to the next, arcs of silver and pale blue lightning that left faint trails in the air.

The power was raw, untamed—just as she was.

"I'm... *I'm*..." Esmyra stammered, unable to finish the thought. She looked at her sister, searching for the words.

Syrena stepped closer, pulsating with steady, controlled power. The queen's golden hair now held pink-hued roots, like the sun setting on the sea, as her tattoos swirled in pink and gold to match. "Hello, *Kaelypso*," she purred.

Esmyra's breath hitched. "It's real," she murmured. She stared at her glowing hands, the sparks now crawling up her arms, igniting faint ripples of energy along the swirling tattoos. "Kaelypso's tits."

"I wouldn't say that anymore if I were you," Syrena said with a chuckle.

Esmyra smirked. "Old habits and all." She winked, but then her smile fell, disbelief taking over once again. "It's all real."

"It is," Syrena said, her aura casting a warm glow across the destruction surrounding them. "This is who we are, Esmyra. This is what was stolen from us by their greed."

Esmyra looked back down at herself, her blue and silver hair catching the merlight as she moved, her tattoos shifting and glowing like living sigils. She flexed her fingers, and the sparks intensified, crackling with a sound that resonated from within her. Her lips curved into a faint, almost hesitant smile.

She glanced around, noting there was nothing left of the council. "We killed them." A note of horror crept into her voice as she glanced at the empty robes and ashes scattered on the ground.

"They served their purpose. They knew the risks," Syrena said, her tone colder now. She stepped closer, reaching out to grasp Esmyra's shoulders. "The realm itself shook as we were reborn, announcing what's to come."

Esmyra met her sister's stare, still working to catch her breath as she adjusted to the power pulsating through her veins. "And the gods who betrayed us? Do you think they'll know what we've become?"

Syrena nodded, a subtle smirk tilting the edge of her lips. "All of Rymelle would have felt what just occurred."

*Draevyn.*

Her breathing finally steadied, her back straightening. "Then let them tremble," Esmyra said softly, a grin forming. "Let them know we're coming."

The crypt seemed to pulse in response to her words. Any doubts that had lingered in Esmyra's mind were gone, burned away by the sparks at her fingertips and the tides surging in her veins.

Together, Kaelypso and Naerysa would be unstoppable.

And all of Rymelle would soon know it.

CHAPTER 74

## Draevyn

The creak of wood and the soft sway of the ship woke Draevyn before the sunlight fully pierced his senses. He blinked against the muted rays streaming through the small porthole, the familiar smell of salt and sea filling his nostrils. His body ached, and his mind was sluggish, but the hum of the waves surrounding him was unmistakable.

A figure sat nearby, just out of his immediate focus. When the figure leaned forward, Samwell's face came into view. His arms were crossed, but his gaze was sharp, watching him with a mix of concern and relief as his lips pressed in a tight line.

"Gods, it's about damn time," Sam muttered, a wry grin forming. "I wasn't entirely convinced you weren't dead." He paused as his stare raked over him. "Thought you were going to sleep through the rest of the way home."

"*What—*" Draevyn's voice cracked, and he struggled to sit up. Pain flared along his back and legs, remnants from the grindylows' claws from when he escaped.

Memories of the cave, the climb up the cliff, and the fire swirled together, tangled with her face and voice.

"What happened? How—why am I here?"

Sam reached out to steady him as he swayed. "Easy now. You've

523

been out for days. Took us a hell of a time to patch you up." He leaned back, rubbing a hand over his jaw. "We came to find you. Almost fucking left without you, too. If you hadn't lit part of the ship on fire, we never would've looked back at the land."

*You were out for days.*

His stomach sank. "Came to find me? What do you mean, I've been out for *days*?" He tried to swing his legs over the side of the cot, but Sam's hand clamped firmly on his shoulder, forcing him back down. "We shouldn't have left—she's still—"

"Who? That broad from Anchorage Cove?" Sam's tone sharpened, his brows knitting together.

Draevyn's lip curled back, nostrils flaring. "Don't you fucking dare speak of her that way."

Samwell threw his hands up in mock surrender. "She fucking *kidnapped* you, Drae." His eyes narrowed as he leisurely lowered his hands. "Explain *that* later. Let me tell you what happened in Lephyrin first."

Draevyn stopped struggling, his breath coming in shallow bursts as Sam continued. "Your brother came to us. Said the king refused to send help. Forbade it actually..." Draevyn wasn't surprised by that in the slightest. "We knew something was wrong, and that you clearly needed help. So we left. Atlas had spoken to Blackwood, and he said we would find our answer in southern waters." Sam's smirk faded as his voice lowered. "You weren't looking too good when we found you on that beach, Captain."

The realization slammed into him then. "You *left* her there!" His voice rose, rough and trembling with rage. He pushed Sam's hand away and stood, ignoring the sharp pain that shot through his legs. "Why the hell did you pull me out of there? She's still down there. With *her*!"

"What in all gods are you talking about?!" Sam shot back as he stood. "You were bleeding out and barely conscious when we found you. You were face down in the water! No one else was around, no sign of—" He hesitated, his expression hardening. "No sign of her."

He turned away from Sam, his heart thudding painfully. The

thought of her still there, trapped with her sister—her evil *cunt* of a sister—filled him with a soul consuming dread. "Turn the ship around," he demanded.

Sam sighed heavily. "Drae, you're lucky you still have both of your fucking eyes! What even happened to you? You need to get to a healer. You're not in any shape to—"

"*Turn it around!*" Draevyn spun on his heel, the fire in his chest threatening to erupt, but Sam stood his ground.

"We're days out, nearly back to Lephyrin. Supplies are low, and the crew is worn thin. We can't just turn back now." Sam's eyes softened slightly, though his tone remained firm. "Where even was she, if not on the beach with you?"

The ship seemed to tilt beneath him, though he knew it was only his head spinning with fury and panic. His fists clenched at his sides, his jaw tight. He needed to get back to her. Needed to fix this. "You said you spoke with Atlas and he told you to sail south?"

Sam gave a curt nod and gestured to the door with his chin. "Go ask him yourself."

Draevyn's eyes flared. "Atlas is *here*?!" He didn't wait for Sam's answer before he shoved past him, out the door, and up the stairs of the ship.

Draevyn's steps carried him to the deck, each one heavy with frustration and the burning need to find Esmyra and save her from what Syrena threatened to do.

As his boots thudded against the wooden planks, he caught sight of Atlas at the bow. His brother stood there, leaning on the rail, gazing out at the expanse of the sea. The wind toyed with his hair, and though his posture seemed calm, the tension in his shoulders was evident.

"Atlas." His voice carried sharply across the deck. His brother turned slowly, his eyes flaring at the sight of him.

"Drae," Atlas began as he met him halfway, and when the distance closed, he threw his arms around Draevyn. "You're alive. You look like hell, but you're here. *Alive.*" Atlas gripped his shoulders as if to make sure he was real.

Draevyn laughed despite himself, the tension in his chest loosening for the first time in what felt like an eternity. "How are you even here? You hate the sea."

Atlas smirked, stepping back, but keeping a firm hand on his shoulder. "I wasn't about to sit back and do nothing. I went against the king's orders and came to find you."

Draevyn's eyes widened.

"Our father refused to act when I pieced together something wasn't right, and when he wouldn't supply any answers, I looked elsewhere. Said it was a fool's errand, that you were already gone, or worse. But I couldn't accept that." Atlas's gaze raked over him. "You're my brother. I had to try."

A lump formed in Draevyn's throat, and he shook his head. "I assumed everyone would think I was a lost cause."

"Not me," his brother said firmly. "Not ever."

Draevyn looked out at the horizon, the endless blue stretching in all directions. "How close are we?" he asked.

"Nearly there," Atlas answered. "We've been tracking back steadily since we pulled you off that beach."

Draevyn's jaw tightened. "I don't even know where to begin to explain this, but we need to go back."

Atlas's eyes flared beneath furrowing brows. "What? Why?"

"We found it." Draevyn swallowed before taking in a breath. "We found Maerinys, and we can't waste any time. She's still there."

His brother's expression darkened. "I know you're not speaking of the woman who managed to trap and *capture* you, Draevyn."

He'd never seen Atlas get angry with him so quickly. Typically, he would always be the one to calm Draevyn down or try to turn the situation into a joke to lighten the mood. Atlas was the laughter to Draevyn's brooding—but something in him had changed.

Draevyn huffed through his nostrils, his hands balling into fists at his sides. "Her name is Esmyra. I don't expect you to understand, but—"

"But?!" Atlas cut him off, shock and something resembling hurt flashing in his stare. "Let her rot in that cave. She planned to fucking kill you."

"But she didn't!" Draevyn raised his voice, and he felt the eyes of his crew lingering from all angles of the ship. "Things changed. Maerinys is real. She's not trapped in a cave, she's trapped in the kingdom beneath the waves."

Atlas shook his head rapidly. "I'm not following. It sank a thousand years ago."

Draevyn took a step toward him, lowering his voice into a hushed whisper. "And it *survived*. The entire civilization, Atlas. And the acting queen plans to raise it."

Atlas threw his head back and laughed—*laughed* at Draevyn's words. "I think you may have swallowed too much seawater, brother."

Draevyn's jaw ticked, the veins in his neck throbbing as he lifted his finger to point in his brother's face. "It's the godsdamn *truth*. Esmyra is still there, in danger, and you let them drag me away!"

"I didn't *let* them do anything," Atlas shot back. His voice hardened. "Her crew assumed both of you were dead. When we saw you, we deemed it a miracle. I wasn't about to waste resources or risk lives for some bloody fucking *pirate* when we found who we came here for."

The words struck him like a blow, and for a moment, he couldn't speak, his breath ragged and uneven. "She's not dead," he growled. "She's trapped. With her sister, who is essentially a fucking sea witch, and she's about to become *much* worse."

"Sea witch?" Atlas scoffed, his jaw tightening. "And what would you have had me do, Drae?"

The wind carried the silence between them as Draevyn searched for the words. "Something terrible is going to happen to her. Mark my words, if we don't do something soon, Maerinys will be raised from the depths, and what will come with it will be beyond anything we've ever faced."

Atlas's expression softened, though his voice remained steady. "Tell me everything. What happened in that cave, and what's waiting for us if we go back?"

The weight of it all pressed down on Draevyn, but he forced himself to speak. He explained everything to Atlas as quickly as he could, of waking up on Esmyra's ship, falling through the cave, fighting the krechuums together, finding Maerinys, and the crypt held within.

Atlas blew out a low whistle. "Definitely too much seawater."

Flames danced in Draevyn's eyes, and he was surprised when Atlas took a step back. "The last thing I remember, Syrena told me she isn't just trying to raise the kingdom. She's trying to take Esmyra's power. To bind her soul back to her old bones and rip them from her once everything she needs is completed, starting with bringing Maerinys to the surface." His voice wavered, but he pushed on. "She's playing a long game, manipulating everyone around her—including me."

His brother's eyes narrowed. "Including you?"

Anger flared within him. "She...she used a siren's song to make me believe she was *her*." The shame burned in his chest as he lifted his stare to meet Atlas's. "Syrena played tricks on my mind, making me think she was Esmyra."

"So?" Atlas looked more confused now than ever.

"I kissed her, and when I realized the truth, it was too late. Esmyra saw everything. And now she—" He stopped, his voice breaking.

His brother's jaw popped open. "You—You care for her...don't you?"

Draevyn nodded silently, his throat tight. The memory of her standing in the doorway, her eyes full of betrayal, was a blade that wouldn't stop twisting in his heart.

"It's always about a woman," Atlas groaned, rolling his eyes. He clapped a hand on Draevyn's shoulder, his grip firm. "Well, we'll take this back to the king and inform him of everything so the kingdom can further plan. I'm sure he'll be thrilled to find the entirety of *The Night Wraith's* crew in his hold."

*Her crew.*

Visions of the beach came back to him then—of *Valor* attacking *The Night Wraith* with cannon-fire.

Draevyn grabbed Atlas's shoulder. "The crew—they're alive?"

He nodded. "Held below deck. My future wife is aboard to make sure none of their magic allows them to escape. I'm surprised they haven't tried much since we left, to be honest. She must've put the fear of all gods in them that day at the cave. However, it's an odd thing, isn't it?... A crew of all beings."

Draevyn raised a brow. "Wife?"

Atlas smirked. "We have much more to catch up on, brother."

Draevyn pressed his lips into a firm line, but was racing across the deck and back down the stairs toward the holding cells before Atlas could say anything further.

He knew he was running out of time, if he hadn't already.

The creak of the wooden steps echoed as Draevyn descended the stairs below deck. The air grew heavier, damp with the scent of sweat-slicked bodies, while the faint murmurs of conversation drifted from the ship's holding cells.

When he stepped into view, every head snapped toward him.

"You!" Jak snarled, gripping the bars of his cell. His face was red with rage. "You fucking *bastard*!" He swiped his arm through the bars, and Draevyn was forced to take a step back, out of reach.

"Where is she?" Jak demanded, his voice cracking. "Where is Esmi?"

Draevyn swallowed and let out a breath. "Not here."

Chaos erupted then—every man within the cells spat accusations and insults, each growing louder than the last. He raised his hands, palms outward, as if that might calm the mayhem.

"Enough!" Draevyn barked, his voice cutting through the madness. Tense silence followed. "I'm not here to fight you, or to listen to insults that I fucking *promise* to all of you are no worse than what I've already said to my godsdamn self..." He paused, chest heaving. "I'm here to explain."

Riven cut him a glare. "Explain what? How you doomed her to

fall over that cliff? Or how you abandoned her there and left her to rot?"

The words hit him like a blow, a lump returning to his throat. "I didn't abandon her," he said, his voice steady despite the guilt gnawing at him. "I would never leave her."

"Then where the fuck is she, *Phoenix*?" Ren spat.

"We found it," Draevyn rushed out as he took a step closer to their cage. "We found Maerinys. Esmyra is…" His eyes darted back and forth as he searched for the words. "She's so much more than any of us believed."

"I told you that to begin with, you bastard. What, now you see past her walls and suddenly want to play the fucking hero as you stand before the people who actually give a damn about her? Lying to our faces about how and why you're here!" Jak bellowed.

Draevyn pounded his fist on his chest as he yelled back, "I do care about her!" *Far more than them*, he desperately wanted to voice, but refrained. He exhaled sharply, dragging a hand through his hair. "I'm here because I was *tricked*. Manipulated by magic."

"Well, if Esmi didn't want you there—"

"It wasn't her," Draevyn cut Jak off. "Esmyra has a sister…" He paused, forcing himself to meet their accusing gazes.

"What in all gods are you talking about?" Jak spat. "She doesn't have a family aside from us. We *are* her family, and you fucking took her away from us. Just as you stole her father from her. We were all she fucking had!"

"I know!" Draevyn bellowed, his voice reverberating through the cells. He took a few deep breaths. "Just listen to me. Please," he begged, trying to keep the flames aching to burst from his fingertips at bay. "Her sister's name is Syrena. And she used her powers on me."

They all stared at him, their faces hardened and unblinking.

"She compelled me to believe…" His voice faltered, and he swallowed hard before continuing. "She made me see things that weren't real. I know you're all very much aware of how Esmyra can compel someone's mind—well, believe me when I say her twin is no different in that regard. By the time I realized what had happened, I was locked out of Maerinys, and the only way out was through that godsdamn cave."

"Convenient," someone muttered darkly.

"I'm telling you the truth," he snapped. "Listen, Esmyra is in danger. Syrena plans to use her to raise the kingdom. I don't know how she plans to, but Maerinys is only lost to those above the surface. It's very much thriving beneath the tides, and they plan to come back. They've just needed Esmyra to do it."

"Why?" Jak's brows furrowed as his arms crossed, and the crew watched them as they argued through the bars of the cell.

"I already told you, she's much more than we believed her to be— what she even believed herself to be." Draevyn's stare roamed over all who watched him and sucked in a breath. "A bit peculiar, isn't it? That Esmyra was the last of her kind, but held more power than anyone had known or heard of..."

"Aye, that part has always been *peculiar*, as you say with your fancy, royal words, Phoenix," Riven hissed.

Draevyn rolled his eyes. "Even more...*odd* that once we find a kingdom lost to the world, trapped within the sea, that she finds a sister. A twin." His eyes fell to Riven. "I hope *that* word was easier for you to understand." He couldn't keep the retort in. They were all acting like morons, refusing to listen.

Riven's eyes narrowed, but Draevyn watched as nearly everyone began to put the pieces together of what he was trying to say. "What if I told you the sea goddesses weren't lost, but bound to mortal bones?" he continued.

"You're lying," Jak growled.

Draevyn took a step up to the cell's door, and when he did, flames ignited along the metal bars, and everyone took a step back as they gasped.

When he spoke next, his voice was low, every bit the Phoenix all of Rymelle feared. "Now, now, Jaky, why would I lie about something like this?" Draevyn cocked his head to the side. "Why would I waste my fucking breath? Now, I believe you have love for her, whether it's romantic or platonic, I don't give a damn in this moment, but if you care about her, you will listen to the words I'm trying to drive into your thick skull. But make no mistake, I will be going after her, whether you come with me or not."

Jak bared his teeth as the flames winked out. "Okay, Phoenix, I'm listening."

Draevyn let out a breath, relief trickling into him before he spoke of everything they had encountered in Maerinys, leaving out the part of how he felt about Esmyra—his Wildfire—not wanting to deal with another possible outburst. So instead, he told them Syrena compelled him to listen to her plans, and the next thing he knew, he was waking up beyond Maerinys' borders.

He didn't lie, per se, just omitted certain truths.

A heavy silence fell over the room.

Ren stepped forward, his jaw clenched as he placed a heavy hand on Jak's shoulder, who stood there stunned. "You expect us to place our trust in you, our enemy, who currently holds our captain hostage? How do we know she isn't already dead? How do we know everything you just said isn't a trap, and you didn't kill her?"

*Gods, pirates truly are fucking morons.* Draevyn's jaw clenched.

"Why would I risk treason against my father to try to free you all?" he said after a moment. "Differences aside, I think we can all agree we have one common ground, and that's Esmyra. I made a mistake, but I'll do whatever it takes to fix it. I swear to you, with or without you, I will be getting her back."

Jak's golden eyes narrowed. "And if this is just another trick?"

Draevyn met his gaze, unflinching, as he allowed his flames to dance within his eyes. "Then you can kill me yourself."

The crew exchanged uncertain glances, their anger simmering but not extinguished.

Finally, Jak nodded, his expression hard. "Aye. You say that now, but if you fail her again, if this is all some conjured trick...mark my words, there won't be a place in this world where you can hide from us."

"Good. I wouldn't expect anything less," Draevyn admitted.

Shouts rang out from above, announcing that the Lephyrin harbor was in view from the deck.

"You'll be seeing me," he said to the crew before turning back to head up the stairs.

The weight of their mistrust and Esmyra's life pressed heavily on his shoulders, but he forced it aside, knowing there was one more obstacle he needed to face before anything could be done.

Draevyn knew his father was a wildcard, and one wrong word to the king could lead to a catastrophic mistake for what was to come.

CHAPTER 76

*Esmyra*

They stepped beyond the cave's mouth and into the blinding merlights that mimicked the sun. Esmyra took her first steps into the world as a woman reborn, her silver hair shimmering like molten moonlight as they made their way through Maerinys with the Aeress trident in hand. Turning the last bend, the air became alive with the murmurs of the crowd gathered in the city's streets as the people of Maerinys came to witness their goddesses return.

Once they stood at the stairs of the palace, together, the twins placed the trident in its stand at the edge of the steps, as if the weapon was looking out over the city—watchful and protective of their people.

Esmyra's heart thundered, endless emotions surging through her. The tattoos swirling along her arms glowed faintly, responding to the power coursing through her, and the sparks at her fingertips danced erratically in anticipation.

She lifted them to her face. "Why does this keep happening?"

Beside her, Syrena stood tall and composed, the glow of her power radiating like a second sun. Her golden hair billowed around her as though the wind itself bowed to her presence.

Syrena offered her a smile. "We each possess powers of the sea, mimicking the depths, and the creatures lurking within them."

Esmyra lifted both hands before her face. "It feels like lightning."

"Call it built up tension." Syrena shrugged. "*That* stems from the rage of eels that lurk within our trenches, sister."

*Eels.*

Her eyes widened, unknowing of what to do or say.

"Just imagine what it would do within the water," Syrena tacked on with a wink, and Esmyra's lips parted. "If legends and scripts are to be believed...we're also no longer limited to only blending in with our surroundings."

"What do you mean?" Esmyra whispered.

A ghost of a smile cracked Syrena's lips. "I mean, we can be whoever we wish. Transform into someone else entirely, allowing us to blend in with the world. We can't hold the forms for long, but we're *gods*, Esmyra. The magic we possess knows no bounds."

Syrena lifted her hand and wiggled her fingers, and in an instant, her hand expanded, transforming into an elongated kraken tentacle.

Esmyra's jaw fell open, and she took a step back. "What in all gods?!" she gasped, a nervous laugh trailing the words.

Syrena wrapped the tentacle around Esmyra's wrist and pulled her so close their noses brushed. "Not all gods, dear sister. From now on, there is only *us*."

Esmyra was left stunned as Syrena returned her attention to the awaiting crowd, her hand morphing back to normal in the blink of an eye.

"People of Maerinys," Syrena declared, her voice amplified by her power, rolling over the crowd like a roaring wave. "For too long, we have been shadows of what we once were. Bound by manacles, and cursed by the gods who feared our strength, leaving us for dead. But no more."

Gasps rippled through the crowd, followed by cheers that echoed across the city. She raised a hand to halt the cheering, her golden rose-hued hair levitating around her as if she were in the sea.

Esmyra watched her sister, a mix of admiration and unease curling in her stomach. Since the moment they met, Syrena had always been able to command a room. But now, as Naerysa reborn, there was something almost unnerving in her confidence.

"Together, Kaelypso and I will restore our kingdom," Syrena continued, her voice fierce. "Together, we will reclaim what was taken from us. And to those who dare stand in our way—" Her sharp gaze swept over the crowd. "Know that they will face the wrath of *gods*."

As cheering erupted once more, her twin whispered, "Don't be shy, Esmi. They need to see your power to know our words hold truth."

Esmyra swallowed hard, her pulse quickening as the crowd's attention shifted to her. Taking a breath, she stepped forward, summoning her magic as she lifted her hands toward the false sky.

Silver-blue sparks leapt from her fingertips, crackling like starlight in the air. They danced and swirled around her hands, arcs of light snapping between her fingers. Growing brighter, they merged into streaks of lightning that twisted into intricate patterns above her palms, forming a glowing sphere of pure energy.

The crowd gasped, their awe rippling through the air. Esmyra smiled faintly, something resembling pride blooming in her chest.

A flick of her wrist launched the sphere into the air, where it burst into a shower of sparks, and the crowd erupted in excitement. Esmyra let her hands fall back to her sides, her chest heaving as she took in the sight of her people, their faces lit with wonder—because of *her*.

It was at such odds to what she was used to. No longer did people look at her with fear in their eyes, but with *hope*.

But as the crowd's roaring washed over her, another realization struck her like a bolt of the lightning now living in her veins. The curse wasn't just on themselves and their kingdom—it had been tied to the man who escaped this damnation with her.

It was tied to her father.

Esmyra's heart leapt into her throat, and without a word, she turned and ran, her feet carrying her away from the celebration and back through the main doors of the castle. Behind her, Syrena called out, but she didn't stop. She had to know. If her curse was broken, then her father's should've been too.

Cyrus Blackwood should be free.

Esmyra sprinted through the castle corridors, her bare feet slapping against the stone, as her silver hair streamed behind her. Her breaths came fast and shallow, her thoughts racing even faster.

Behind her, Syrena's voice echoed. "Esmi! Where are you going?"

Esmyra didn't stop, *couldn't* stop, her heart hammering as she rounded a corner and halted at the bottom of the steps that would lead her to the tower. As she moved to take her first step to ascend the stairs, Syrena's hand caught her shoulder, spinning her around.

"Esmyra, stop!" Her sister's voice was sharp, but her eyes were searching, filled with concern. "What are you doing?"

Esmyra shrugged off her sister's grip, her chest heaving as she met Syrena's golden gaze. "The Veil of Visions," she said, trying to catch her breath. "You said it shows the past and the present—*anything* I wish to see."

Syrena's brow furrowed, her lips parting as if to argue, but then she hesitated. "It does," she admitted, her tone quieter now. "Why? What are you looking for? If it's Drae—"

"My father," Esmyra cut her off. The words hung in the air between them. "If our curse is broken, if we're free...I have to know if he is, too. I need to see him."

Syrena stared at her, her expression unreadable. "After he betrayed our parents and separated us?" she whispered. "After the part he played in the fall of our kingdom?"

Esmyra desperately tried to ignore the pain in her sister's voice. "I'm sorry, Syrena. But he's still my father. He still raised me. Cyrus is all I knew for nearly a thousand years."

Syrena's gaze swept over her, her shoulders slumping. Nodding, she gestured to the stairs. "If you must."

Without another word, Esmyra turned and raced up the stairs, visions of her father plaguing her mind—of him choking and gasping for air all this time since she'd been gone.

Once she reached the top of the steps, it seemed to open for her, as if expecting her. The Veil of Visions stood at the center of the chamber, its surface shimmering faintly.

Esmyra stepped closer, her reflection rippling on the glass-like surface as she approached. "What do I do?"

"All you must do is ask, offering your will and intentions," Syrena said, her voice soft, almost nervous. "And prepare yourself for what you may find."

Esmyra took a deep breath, centering herself. Her tattoos glimmered faintly in the reflection of the small pool. "Show me my father," she demanded. "Show me Cyrus Blackwood."

The surface swirled, shadows and light twisting into a vortex before settling into a clear image. Esmyra's breath caught in her throat as she was thrust through time and space, appearing as a phantom within the holding cells of Castle Lephyrin, far above the surface.

# CHAPTER 77

# Draevyn

The throne room was unnervingly silent except for the occasional shuffle of boots on the stone floor. The air was thick with tension as Draevyn and Atlas stood side by side, waiting for their father's arrival.

Samwell and his men had stayed back on his ship, watching the crew of *The Night Wraith* before they were turned in, and Draevyn's mind raced regarding how he would help them escape when the time came.

When the heavy doors creaked open, every muscle in his body tightened. The king strode in and his plump face was already drawn with irritation as his regal cloak dragged on the floor behind him. He ascended the dais with slow, deliberate steps, likely trying to instill fear into his two sons just as he had when they were boys, before dropping onto the throne. His gaze was sharp and unforgiving as it settled on them.

"You have a great deal to explain," King Rowe said, his voice a low growl. His eyes locked onto Atlas, who stood tall. "You disobeyed direct orders. Left the capital. Took a ship without permission."

Draevyn's fists clenched. "Wonderful to see you too, Father."

The king only grumbled in response.

Atlas spoke up calmly, though his tone carried an edge. "I did what had to be done. He's your *son*, just as much as I am. Drae is your blood—your *heir*, if I am to ever meet an early end, and you abandoned him. Left him at the hands of our world's most brutal criminals."

The king slammed his fist on the armrest, the sound echoing through the chamber. "Draevyn would've been just fine." He pointed to his chest. "I made a deal, ensuring his life wouldn't be forfeited."

Atlas stepped forward, his voice rising. "Once again, you put your faith in *pirates*. You willingly allowed your son to be taken and held by the most untrustworthy of men. And for what? To find evidence of treasure from a kingdom lost?"

"I don't need you to remind me of my own godsdamn choices, boy," King Rowe interrupted, his voice thunderous. "You undermined me."

Draevyn glanced at his brother, noting the determined set of his jaw, the shadows swirling in his eyes. Atlas had always been the only one to defend him, but he was done putting up with his father's abuse. No longer could he leave for months at a time at sea to avoid their wretched king.

Too much was at stake now—*she* was at stake.

Something inside of Draevyn shifted, and he stepped forward. "*Enough.* I need to speak."

The king's sharp gaze snapped to him, laced with warning. Atlas fell silent.

"By all the wretched fucking gods, you haven't listened to me or given a damn about what I've had to say the entirety of my life, but you will listen to me here and now." Draevyn's voice was low, the promise of violence lingering beneath it. He could tell the king sensed it by the way his body stiffened, but their eyes remained locked.

"I understand what you think of me," he continued, "but this isn't about me, or the greed of what you sought. This is about what's now coming."

The room was deathly silent, the weight of his words pressing down on them all. The king studied him before he finally said, "What are you stammering on about, Draevyn?"

Draevyn squared his shoulders. "Perhaps you'd like to hear about the kingdom beneath the waves."

The king's eyes widened as he leaned forward in his throne. "You found it?"

Draevyn stepped forward, his jaw tight as he held his father's disbelieving stare. "Maerinys survived the sinking. And it plans to rise. We have to be ready for what we may face."

The king's expression flickered, a wicked grin creeping up his face. And that was when Draevyn knew he wasn't listening—at least not to the parts that mattered.

"Father, if we don't act, it will bring war unlike anything we've faced. This isn't a petty rebellion or some distant skirmish. This is power beyond imagining. The lost goddesses. They're not lost at all. They're trapped with their people and found a way to return to the surface. It's only a matter of time."

Draevyn didn't dare mention that Esmyra was the cause.

"Both of you are dismissed," the king said to his sons, but neither moved.

"You don't believe me," Draevyn began, his voice laced with fury. "You're just going to dismiss this? Dismiss *us*?" He gestured to himself and Atlas. "You had me searching for proof of Maerinys' existence for *years*, and now that you have it, all you *still* only care about is potential gold?"

The king's gaze was cold, his fingers drumming impatiently on the arm of his throne. "Why shouldn't I? If it exists, the wealth of an entire kingdom lies below the waves. That treasure would secure our future. Your tales of magic and goddesses are just that—*stories*. Why should I believe you? You've always been a liar, Draevyn. A violent, no good *waste*."

Draevyn's fists clenched at his sides, and then fire burst brightly in every torch that lined the chamber's walls. "There isn't even gold down there!" he bellowed, putting the guards around the room on edge as he stepped closer. "It's power. Ancient power that you can't even begin to understand. You're being ignorant and letting your greed run you, as you always have."

The king scoffed, leaning back in his chair. "You sound like a frightened child. If this power is as great as you claim, then it's all the more reason to take it. We can control it. Bend it to our will."

"You can't control it!" Draevyn snapped, his voice echoing through the hall. His chest heaved with barely restrained rage as he continued. "You don't understand what you're dealing with. Are you truly delusional enough to believe you're stronger than *gods*? Do you believe you can outwit ancient beings who forged our very realm?!"

The king's face darkened, and he rose to his feet, his figure casting a shadow over the stairs of the dais. "Enough!" he barked, his cheeks flushing. "You'll watch your tone when you speak to your king. Your warnings are nothing but the ramblings of a desperate man trying to save face."

"Desperate?" Draevyn echoed with a bitter laugh. "You're right— I am desperate. Desperate to stop you from making a mistake that will cost us all in your fucking greed."

*Desperate to save her.*

"But don't mistake desperation for weakness," Draevyn finished.

The room fell into a tense silence. The king's jaw tightened, and for a moment, it seemed like he might respond. But instead, he sank back into his throne, waving a dismissive hand. "Where is the *lovely* woman I sent on this quest to begin with? If she thinks I will just be dropping Blackwood off to her, she's even more of a fool than you are."

Draevyn tried to reel in his temper, realizing it would get him nowhere, but then Atlas stepped forward and spoke for him. "She's still there—trapped with those he speaks of. She could be dead for all we know. Drae nearly was when we found him."

Draevyn's breath caught in his throat, his chest tightening at what Atlas revealed. He didn't want their father to know she was still there.

A slow, cruel smile spread across the king's face. "Well, isn't that interesting?"

Draevyn's panic threatened to consume him as he stepped forward, his voice urgent. "She's not dead."

But the king wasn't listening. He straightened, his eyes gleaming with malice. "Well, she isn't here to report her findings, so it appears the deal we made is off."

"What deal?" Draevyn demanded, his blood running cold.

The king's smirk deepened. "You foolish boy. You think I'd truly let you stay in her grasp without ensuring I had leverage?"

It was in that moment he knew what the king planned to do. Draevyn never told his father that he knew all he was to Esmyra was leverage—until he wasn't, and that was when everything changed. But he could never let him know that, never let him know he cared so deeply for someone, knowing he would only hold it against him. Hold *her* against him.

For the Phoenix finally had a weakness, and it was his Wildfire—not the one that surged through his veins, but seared herself into his heart.

"The deal was simple," the king continued. "Her captain rots in my cells, untouched, until she returns you to me, *also* untouched, with proof of Maerinys. But now? Oh, now I think it's time to rid myself of that nuisance."

Atlas's eyes flared, meeting Draevyn's as his panic erupted into rage. "You can't! She'll still come for him—"

"Well, she isn't here now. So the bargain is broken," King Rowe snapped, cutting him off.

Without another word, the king descended from his throne, striding past his two sons as if the matter was already decided.

His laughter, cold and triumphant, caused Draevyn's thoughts to spiral into chaos, and before he could stop himself, he sent up a violent wall of flame before his father. The fire stemmed from the floor and licked up at the vaulted ceilings, and gasps rang out from all sides.

The king whipped around, rage etched into every feature of his plump face as he bellowed, "Drop the wall, Draevyn, before I have them drop *you*."

He barely heard the words.

Guards rushed Draevyn then, unsheathing their swords and aiming them at his throat.

*The king isn't going after her* captain—*he's going after her* father.

Draevyn knew Cyrus couldn't die—not in the way mortals did, but every day on land, the man likely prayed for death. The curse that bound him to the sea made that clear. But Draevyn knew in his soul that if harm came to Blackwood in any way, Esmyra would seek vengeance.

The heartbreak in her eyes when Draevyn snapped from Syrena's trance—it was unbearable. But he knew her fury would know no bounds if something happened to her father under his watch.

It would be the ultimate betrayal.

If Esmyra returned to find her father harmed, the fragile tether holding her together could snap. And if that happened, Draevyn knew she would let that rage consume her entirely.

*What if I just became the monster they all fear me to be,* Esmyra's voice drifted through his mind.

One of the guards placed the edge of his blade at the base of Draevyn's throat, shaking in fear beneath the Phoenix's gaze, but holding steady for his brutal king.

"Drae!" Atlas gasped out. "Drop the wall, brother. This isn't going to end well for anyone if you don't fucking yield. He's still your king."

Atlas looked panicked for him, and when his eyes found the king, he saw the unrelenting hatred and anger in his eyes.

Draevyn's jaw tightened, and a moment after the flames dissipated, the king and his guards stalked through the door. "I'll deal with you later, *boy*," he spat over his shoulder.

His stomach churned with guilt. He'd failed to protect her, and now he failed to protect what mattered to her most.

Draevyn knew he had to get ahead of this and find a way to stop the king before it was too late. If he couldn't...if her father was harmed, the consequences would be more than he could bear.

His Wildfire would burn the world to ash to make them pay. And if she did, he wasn't sure he'd even try to stop her.

In fact, Draevyn may even offer to be the match that lit the spark.

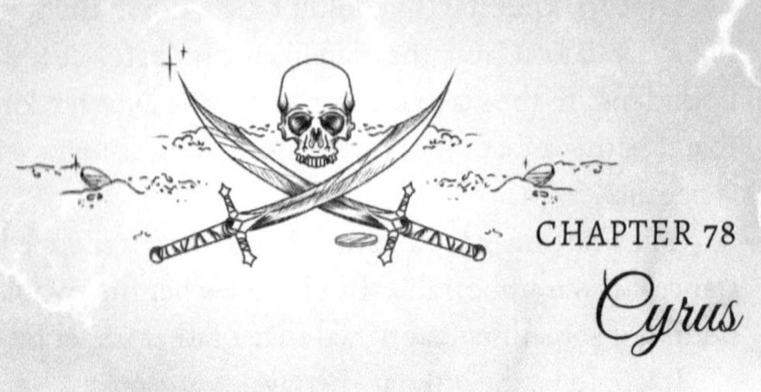

CHAPTER 78

*Cyrus*

Cyrus Blackwood had endured torment beyond comprehension, a punishment designed by the cruelest of minds—the cruelest of gods.

Every moment of every day since he was dragged onto Lephyrin's shores, he felt as if the waves had dragged him under—lungs burning, chest constricting, air forever out of reach. It felt like the weight of an invisible force constantly pressed against his chest, crushing him.

Each inhale was a battle, a hollow imitation of what breath should feel like. The air would come in but never satisfy, like sand slipping through desperate fingers.

The torture never lessened, never gave him a moment's reprieve.

And then, suddenly, the air burned Cyrus's lungs as he inhaled— filling them to the brim.

He tried to stand, but his knees buckled, and he caught himself against the stone wall. His hands pressed into the rough surface, the tremor in his arms betraying the strength he once had.

For centuries, he carried the curse like a chain, never setting foot on land until the Rowe prince had captured him and murdered half of his crew.

Cyrus gasped, savoring the sensation of air in his lungs despite the sharp ache it caused in his chest. The hazy mist over his eyes cleared, allowing him to see clearly for the first time in only the gods knew how long. And then his sense of smell returned—the brine of the sea clearing his nostrils and allowing the stench of the musky dungeons to replace it.

A hoarse laugh escaped his lips, one that turned into a hacking cough.

*What the fuck is happening?* He finally caught his breath, still not used to being able to breathe so freely.

His hand fell to the collar of his shirt, and he ripped it open, revealing his chest. The black mark that was once seared into the flesh above his heart was fading, and it disappeared before his eyes.

*The curse is gone.* But how? Why now? Had Esmyra done it? Had she found Maerinys and the truth of her past? The past that he desperately hid from her for nearly a thousand years. His heart threatened to shatter at the thought—the thought of her knowing the truth of what he did all those centuries ago.

If she had, he just needed to explain to her *why*.

Cyrus turned his head toward the velsinyte barred door of his cell. Outside, the torches flickered, and the corridors were silent, save for the faint drip of water from somewhere in the prison. He braced himself against the wall and took a step forward, his boots scraping against the floor as he adjusted to the returned strength in his limbs.

That's when he heard it—a heavy *clank*, followed by the unmistakable groan of the heavy, iron door being opened and the echo of several footsteps.

Cyrus straightened, his lips curling into a sneer as the approaching footsteps grew louder. He didn't need to see them to know who was coming. He only hoped his Esmi was with them, unharmed.

And then, standing in the doorway flanked by guards, was the king himself.

The glint in his eye was cruel, triumphant. Beside him were his two sons—Atlas appeared smug and unbothered, far different than the last time he saw him, begging for information regarding Esmyra. The fire-wielder, however, looked tense, seeming unwilling to be there.

But if they were here, and Esmyra wasn't...

Cyrus's sneer deepened, and he crossed his arms over his chest. "Where is she?" His voice was rough, gravelly from disuse, but the venom in his tone was unmistakable.

He didn't miss the sudden flare of Draevyn's eyes at his mention of Esmyra, resembling a flash of panic.

King Rowe stepped forward, his boots clicking against the stone. "It appears your little first mate wasn't as talented as she presented herself to be. Either that, or she decided to keep the ship for herself. Pirates and all." He waved a hand.

Cyrus's brows furrowed, knowing the words weren't true. Of course they weren't. This vile king didn't know Esmi. He didn't know his fierce daughter.

However, Cyrus knew if the Rowes had killed her, they would gloat, throw it in his face, and watch agony overtake him for the joy of it.

Which meant she was alive.

"Interesting you're not suddenly gasping for breath, Blackwood," Atlas stated.

Draevyn whirled on his brother, his eyes widening slightly before returning to Cyrus—an unmistakable look of fear radiating from his eyes, despite his face being hard as stone.

It was clear to him that the fire-wielder was putting on a show. But why?

Cyrus let out a humorless laugh. "I'm going to ask you one more time. *Where* is Esmyra?" His eyes were locked on the Phoenix, whose jaw ticked as he averted his gaze to the floor.

King Rowe's smile didn't falter, but there was a flicker of irritation in his eyes. He turned to the guard at his side and motioned toward the cell door. The lock clicked, and the door swung open with a loud creak.

Cyrus didn't move as the guards stepped inside, their weapons at the ready. Instead, he fixed his gaze on the king, his dark eyes smoldering with defiance—just like his daughter.

"Careful, Your Majesty," he said, his voice low and dangerous.

"You might find that freeing me will be the biggest mistake you could ever make."

King Rowe chuckled, shaking his head. "Oh, you misunderstand. I'm not here to free you." He took another step closer, his tone darkening. "I'm here to remind you who holds your chains."

Cyrus's hands curled into fists, his nails digging into his palms as he prepared for whatever they were planning.

"Legends claim you're immortal," he said, his tone casual but laced with malice. "But I'm wondering if anyone has really been close enough to find its truth."

Cyrus's stare dropped down to his chest, to the black mark that no longer marked his flesh. The curse was gone, and with it, his immortality.

"Kaelypso's fucking depths," he cursed.

"Hold him," the king ordered with a cruel smirk.

The guards hesitated, their uncertainty clear as they approached, taking in the sight of him no longer struggling to breathe.

The moment the first guard reached for him, Cyrus surged forward, raw fury driving his weakened muscles. He threw a punch that connected with a sickening crack, sending the man sprawling to the ground. Another guard lunged, but he twisted out of the way, grabbing the man's arm and yanking him into the wall with a thud.

"Not so easy to kill a ghost," Blackwood snarled.

"You're nothing but a weaponless old man," one shouted.

Two more came at him then, and he kicked one back as he grabbing the other by the neck, before slamming him into the velsinyte bars.

"Enough!" the king barked, before turning to his sons, pointing his stubby finger in their faces. "Take care of this!"

Cyrus's panic spiked as he whirled on them.

Draevyn's face bore nothing but disgust. "I will have no part in torturing an old, weakened man," he declared, lips curled.

"We can't while he's in that cell, anyway," Atlas answered.

With this, the guard he kicked came up from behind him and wrapped his arm around Cyrus's throat, putting him in a chokehold.

His already weakened strength buckled as his air supply was cut off once more. The man dragged him beyond the cell's barrier and shoved him to his knees.

Before Blackwood could react, shadows slithered across the ground like living snakes coiling around his legs. He thrashed against them, but they moved too quickly, binding him in place as if they were iron chains.

"Hold him," King Rowe ordered again, his gaze shifting to his eldest son.

Atlas hesitated for a heartbeat, his hands flexing at his sides as he met his brother's stare.

"Don't," Draevyn whispered as he grabbed Atlas's wrist.

Blackwood's glare met the uncertain eyes of Lephyrin's heir, and the silence stretched out like a taut rope.

"Finish this!" the king ordered, and the prince reluctantly lifted his hands.

Dark tendrils of shadow erupted from the prince's fingertips, wrapping around Cyrus's arms and chest. They tightened with unnatural strength, making it difficult to breathe.

"You think I fear your shadows?" Cyrus spat, struggling against the bonds.

"You'll find they're quite effective," the king sneered, stepping closer.

Blackwood's muscles quivered as he fought against the tendril's crushing grip, his teeth bared in a snarl.

When his stare drifted to Draevyn once more, there was something in his eyes he couldn't place. Was it regret? Worry, even? "Is Esmyra alive?" he snarled. "Or did you kill her? At least let me know *that*."

Draevyn's jaw ticked, his gaze dropping to his boots. "She's alive."

A low laugh erupted from Cyrus as he prepared to meet his possible end. "You're making quite a mistake here, you foolish king," he growled, his voice menacing. "She will come for all of you if what you speak is true."

Draevyn's stare lifted back up to his, and all he said was, "I know," before turning away from him and stalking back down the dungeon and beyond its iron door.

"I don't fear a mere female, nor do I care if you trained her in your ruthless tendencies..." The king's smile widened, cruel and mocking. "And you'll use your last breath begging for mercy."

King Rowe eyed a dagger strapped to Atlas's side as he continued to hold Cyrus in place with his shadows. In one swift movement, the king ripped the small blade from its sheath and bent down to Cyrus's ear. "May all of Rymelle know that I, King Barret Rowe of Lephyrin, was the one to rid our world of the fearsome Captain Blackwood."

A second later, the dagger's blade was protruding from Cyrus's chest—from his heart.

His death began as a sharp, searing pain erupting through his ribs, the agony of it spreading outward through his limbs. Crimson soaked his front, seeping into his clothes and puddling on the stone floor. A sudden chill spread through him at the loss of blood, followed by an overwhelming numbness.

The edges of his vision blurred, darkening as death threatened to pull him under. Cyrus looked up and faced the king, who stood just out of his reach with a triumphant grin as his heir stood beside him, mortified. The fire-wielder was still nowhere in sight.

The pain was unbearable—a searing, all-encompassing agony that radiated through his very soul. Every beat of his heart felt like it was tearing itself apart. Though he supposed it was.

His thoughts spiraled, and then the memory of Esmyra's face took over his mind. His little, ruthless girl was the greatest treasure he had ever known.

Though burdened by a cursed, eternal life, he considered himself blessed. He lived long enough to know the unwavering, irreplaceable love of a child. A love that defied even the cruelest of fates.

Perhaps this fate was exactly what he deserved after all he had done —all he had forced his Esmi to do.

Centuries' worth of memories came in a flood—her first steps on the deck of *The Night Wraith*, and her laughter ringing out over the waves. The fire in her eyes when she argued with him, proving to be so much like him, her father's daughter, even when not forged by blood.

Esmyra had always been too strong for her own good, too bold for the world to contain. And he loved his little siren all the more for it.

*She'll know*, he thought, the edges of his vision dimming further. *And may the gods help them when she comes.*

Cyrus tried to smile, though the pain tore at him with every flicker of movement. His lips trembled as blood spilled from the corner of his mouth.

Esmi would take back the seas they stole from him, from both of them.

*And when you stand over their ashes, you'll know I never doubted you.* He tried to will the words to her, wherever she was.

His body betrayed him, growing weaker, colder, but his mind clung desperately to her face. He could almost hear her desperate, pleading voice, demanding he stay alive.

"I can't, little siren," he whispered aloud, earning furrowed brows from all who stood around, watching his death.

The shadows grew thicker, his strength fading fast. But even as the darkness closed in, a flicker of pride remained.

And then, after centuries of evading death, Cyrus Blackwood's world went dark.

# CHAPTER 79

# Esmyra

Esmyra staggered back from the Veil of Visions, her breath coming in short, sharp gasps. Her hands trembled at her sides, sparks igniting at her fingertips as her emotions threatened to spill over into raw, uncontrolled fury. Her chest heaved, tattoos swirling wildly with an iridescent, silver glow that pulsed like a storm.

She stared at the water in the small pool, its surface still rippling, mocking her with the scene it had just revealed. It replayed in her mind like a cruel echo—Cyrus Blackwood's body crumpling to the ground, crimson blood soaking his front as his life was stolen from him by the king's blade.

Draevyn was there, and he did *nothing*. He abandoned her father as he was held in the death grip of his brother's shadows.

Betrayal burned in her veins like acid.

"No," she whispered, her voice breaking as she shook her head. Strands of silver hair clung to her face, damp with tears she hadn't realized she shed. "No, no, no, no. *NO!*"

It was the only word she could manage to voice.

"Esmyra?" Syrena called from across the basin. "What did you see?"

She turned to her, her once blue eyes blazing and emanating a now silver glow with wrath and pain. "Cyrus is dead," she choked out, her voice cracking. "My father. They killed him." Her stare darkened as it lifted to meet her sister's. "*He* killed him."

Syrena froze, her brow furrowing as her eyes darted back and forth. "Who? Who killed him?"

"The king of men," Esmyra spat, her voice hardened with rage. Her throat tightened as the name threatened to escape her lips. "And his sons. *Both* of them were there." She slammed her fists against the stone edge of the bowl.

The impact sent a shockwave through the room, rattling the tower's wall, and the pool rippled violently. Sparks danced along her skin, and the surrounding air crackled with the tension of her barely-contained power.

"Esmyra," Syrena said carefully, "any surge of emotion can cause an eruption of power. We're not used to keeping it contained. Please, just for a moment, take a breath and calm down."

Esmyra whirled on her sister, her silver hair levitating and whipping around her like a storm cloud. "Calm down?" she snarled, her voice rising. "I saw him. I *trusted* him. The man who abandoned me here and fled without a word, breaking oaths he had no intention of keeping. Cyrus was freed from his curse, and a moment later, they ripped his life away from him. The life he craved more than the air his lungs refused to take in!"

She paused and took in a breath, her voice darkening. "This was Draevyn's doing."

Syrena's expression hardened. "You're sure?"

Esmyra nodded, her fists clenched so tightly that blood beaded where her talons bit into her palms. "The Veil doesn't lie. You said so yourself."

Her sister stepped forward and placed a hand on Esmyra's shoulder, her golden glow mingling with the crackling silver sparks that surrounded her. "No," Syrena admitted, "it doesn't."

Esmyra wrenched herself free of Syrena's grip, pacing the tower like a caged animal. The weight of what she witnessed pressed down on her like a tidal wave, threatening to drag her under. Her chest heaved, but no matter how hard she tried, she couldn't draw a full breath. It felt as though the room was closing in around her, the walls tightening with every passing second.

Her thoughts were a chaotic storm, each one sharper and more unbearable than the last.

*My father is dead. They killed him—Draevyn is the reason he's dead. I trusted a man, and all it did was shatter my world.*

The image of Cyrus collapsing replayed in her mind, over and over, searing itself into her soul.

Sparks danced across her skin, unbidden and wild. The water of the Veil rippled again as a misty steam began to levitate from it, reacting to the surge of her power. She stumbled backward, clutching at her chest as if she could somehow force herself to breathe.

"Esmyra, you need to be careful!" Syrena bellowed, her voice sounding both distant and near all at once.

Everything suddenly became too much. It was her fault—*everything* was her fault. If she had never left *The Night Wraith* that day in search of this place, he never would've been captured. If she had found a way to break him free of that velsinyte cage, he would be alive, breathing in the sea air.

And if she had never set eyes on Draevyn Rowe, the world would have remained as it always was—hers. But now that was gone. *Everything* she loved was ripped from her grasp, and she had no one to blame but herself.

"I-I can't be here." Esmyra turned and bolted from the tower.

"Wait!" Syrena's voice echoed behind her, but Esmyra didn't stop. She couldn't.

She threw open the door to the chamber and fled down the spiral staircase. The walls blurred as she descended, the narrow staircase twisting endlessly before her, but she didn't care where she was going. She just had to get *out*—out of the tower, out of the palace...

Out of Maerinys.

The suffocating weight of the tower gave way to the open air as she burst through the castle's doors and onto the front steps.

The stairs' edge loomed ahead, the great open expanse of the city stretching before her, where the crowd remained. She staggered to a stop, her chest heaving as she bent forward, clutching her knees next to the Aeress trident.

But air wouldn't fill her lungs, and the tempest raging within her couldn't be calmed.

The all-consuming power she had been holding back now surged to the surface, unrelenting. Lightning crackled across her skin, brighter and fiercer than ever. Her tattoos burned with silver-blue light, their intricate designs shifting and swirling. She gritted her teeth, squeezing her eyes shut as the energy built within her. A wave she couldn't contain.

*Fuck, fuck, fuck. Control it!*

Her thoughts were frantic. But her control on the magic was slipping through her fingers, barrelling through her, raw and wild, like the storm she always feared would one day consume her.

Memories clawed at her mind, painfully scraping down with sharpened talons. Her father's kind smile, despite his black heart. The crew aboard *The Night Wraith*, and how they were her family. The way Draevyn had once looked at her like she was his entire world.

The lies.

The betrayal.

The blade.

The *blood*.

Esmyra let out a gut-wrenching, soul-shattering scream, her voice breaking as she threw her hands out at her sides while her silver hair whipped violently around her on a conjured wind. A storm erupted from her in a blinding burst of crackling power—lightning shot from her fingertips, striking the ground and scorching the stone.

She sank to her knees, her head bowed as it raged around her, her tears streaking her glowing skin. Esmyra, no—*Kaelypso* wanted to scream again, to let the power tear through her until there was nothing left.

"Esmyra, *stop*!" Syrena's voice cut through the storm. "You're going to destroy the dome!"

*The dome.* That was what kept them trapped beneath the tides.

She knelt there, her chest heaving with raw emotion, as she slowly lifted her gaze and stared up at the vault. The massive barrier shimmered faintly in response, almost as if it were taunting her.

"If it's a monster they want, then it's a monster they will fucking get." Her voice echoed as if it were spoken by a thousand people at once.

Esmyra staggered to her feet, her body humming with the growing power that pulsed within her as her eyes locked on the dome. The sparks around her hands fused into pure streams of lightning, brighter than anything she had unleashed before.

With a look to the trident beside her, she wrapped her taloned, webbed fingers around its staff and watched as her magic surged through it.

Raising her opposite hand to the sky, she let out a cry that was both fury and grief—a primal sound she imagined reached the shore of every kingdom.

Crackling bolts of silver-blue erupted from her fingertips, the force of it making her stagger back as it arced upward. Her power struck the dome with a deafening crack, and the entire barrier shuddered from the force. Esmyra gritted her teeth, her hands trembling as more magic surged from her, each bolt growing stronger, more precise. The dome rippled violently as cracks of light sputtered across its surface like veins.

Gasps and horrified screams rang out from all sides of Maerinys. In the crowd, some were ducking and trying to take cover, while others gazed up in awe.

The power burned through Esmyra relentlessly, but she didn't flinch. She felt alive in a way she never had before, her energy pouring out in a raw, untamed torrent.

The dome pulsed with light, the once-transparent barrier glowing as if alive. Colors danced across its surface—blues, silvers, and golds intertwining in dazzling patterns. The air grew thick with energy, an electric charge that made the hairs on the back of her neck stand on end.

Esmyra's power didn't relent—only it wasn't just hers, it was the power of Kaelypso.

The power of a god.

The magic she unleashed grew fiercer, her screams echoing as she allowed her emotions to fuel the storm. As the dome trembled, a low, rumbling groan resonated through its cracking surface.

The entire city shuddered. The trembling intensified, spreading from the ground beneath her feet to the furthest reaches of the kingdom. Buildings creaked and swayed, and more screams rang out from the people.

Esmyra felt the shift deep in her bones—in her soul. The sea surrounding them seemed to roar in response, currents twisting and swirling violently just beyond the fracturing dome.

Then, with one final, earth-shaking crack, the dome burst.

The ocean itself seemed to gasp, currents surging upward as Maerinys itself began to rise.

"ESMYRA!" Syrena screamed, but it faded away on the deafening winds.

And then Esmyra was levitating, her body mimicking the kingdom itself as it ascended to the surface. Her hair fanned around her like a halo, glowing with the same brilliant light as her runes.

The seafloor beneath it heaved upward, and the massive coral-covered cliffs anchoring the kingdom crumbled away as Maerinys broke free of the ocean's hold.

Whirlpools swirled against its edges, and her heart pounded as her kingdom rose from the depths. The sunlight grew brighter, piercing through the water as they neared the surface at a horrifying speed.

The kingdom's emergence from the water was marked by a deafening roar of the dome as its remnants shattered the moment it reached the sun's heat. Waves crashed, parted, and swirled, sending plumes of salty spray high into the air, as the light of the sun bathed the kingdom for the first time in centuries. Maerinys shimmered in the sunlight as the last of the water drained from the kingdom's floor.

Esmyra's form continued to hover in the air directly before the palace, holding her family's trident. As fear subsided, the cheering of the masses commenced, and her body began to *shift*. Her gown dissolved like ash in the wind, her legs merging into her long, glittering tail. Every scale on her body, from the tops of her breasts to the edge of her fins, glittered in the light.

Esmyra Aeress-Blackwood—the goddess of the sea, Kaelypso— hovered in the sky above her kingdom in her siren form, her power pulsating in rhythm with the waves crashing around the city's edges.

Her gaze dropped to the kingdom below, to the sparkling towers and the disbelieving faces of their people. Directly below her, Syrena watched, jaw agape, as Esmyra achieved the impossible all on her own.

And then her stare turned to the horizon stretching endlessly before her, eyes narrowing as they fixed on the distant line where the sea met the sky—toward Lephyrin.

Esmyra's jaw clenched, her grip on the trident flexing, sending jolts of power through it. Her internal storm had calmed, but the fury remained, simmering beneath the surface like a volcano ready to erupt.

*Wildfire*, Draevyn's voice sounded in her mind.

Esmyra's lips curled into a cold smile, a chilling promise of retribution pulsating through her.

"I'll be seeing you, *Drae*."

Draevyn stood at the bow of *Valor*, the water lapping gently against the hull as it remained docked in Lephyrin's harbor. The cool sea breeze ruffled his hair, but he barely noticed, his eyes fixed on the horizon. The weight of all that occurred since they made port and his father's cruelty bore down on him like an anchor.

He couldn't stay and watch as they hurt Cyrus, and when Atlas pointed out he could breathe, Draevyn knew then that Esmyra had found a way to break the curse.

He wouldn't stand by and watch the man be tortured the moment he took his first real breath on land. Now he needed to not only break *The Night Wraith's* crew free but also Cyrus himself.

Draevyn imagined becoming the Phoenix everyone feared, and burning his father alive right there within the stone walls of the castle. At this point, he didn't give a damn if he turned to ash alongside the king.

But Atlas was there.

His hands were tied unless he wanted to burn everyone in the room alongside his father.

Maybe he should have. He could only imagine the torture they were putting Cyrus through as he stood there, desperately trying to think of a plan as his crew wrangled up that of *The Night Wraith* and dragged them to Lephyrin's prison deep within the city.

Boots scuffing against the worn planks of the deck caught his attention, and he turned to find Sam walking toward him. "The last of her crew was just brought to the prisons, but it's looking like some may need to be moved to the castle if they possess magic. They have the only cells with velsinyte," he said, his tone cautious.

When Draevyn didn't answer, Samwell continued. "Why are you brooding? I know your father can be a prick, but I assumed you'd be at least slightly excited to be home."

He exhaled sharply, shaking his head. "The brooding feels justified," he muttered. "Along with several more violent things."

His first mate leaned against the railing. "What happened when you got back to the castle?"

Draevyn hesitated, gripping the wood so tightly his knuckles whitened. "Cyrus Blackwood is Esmyra's father." Sam's eyes flared at his words. "The man was cursed by the gods long ago, destined to live an eternal life at sea, always made to feel as if he were drowning if he set foot on land. Esmyra dreamed of one day breaking his curse."

Sam let out a low whistle. "And here I was thinking curses were myths and legends." When Draevyn didn't laugh at the poor attempt at a joke, Sam cleared his throat. "Well, what's wrong? Are you upset she didn't break it?"

Draevyn's stare darkened. "That's the thing, Sam...I think she *did* break it."

Shouts rang out from the dock, and then Atlas came into view, walking up the gangplank. "I'm glad I found you," he said as he stepped up to them, his voice grave. He let out a breath. "We need to talk."

Draevyn crossed his arms. "If that bastard thinks I'm going in there to add to the man's godsdamn torture, he's in for a rude awakening. I want no part in it."

Atlas's jaw tightened, looking more uncomfortable than Draevyn had ever seen. "Cyrus Blackwood is dead. Our father killed him. There was no torture involved."

Draevyn froze, heart stopping painfully as his eyes flared. "*What?*"

Atlas pressed his lips into a tight line. "There was nothing I could do, Drae. You know how he is."

*Cyrus Blackwood is dead.*

Shock hit him first, a cold, suffocating wave that left him standing still while the world seemed to spin around him. It wasn't something he even considered—not in that moment beneath the castle.

Then came the anger, sharp and burning in his chest. The king—his own father—had done this. Not out of necessity, but for cruelty. Pure, senseless cruelty. There was no trial, no hanging. It was a silent execution hidden in the depths of his castle.

The man who had kept his two sons under his boot using fear and manipulation for so long had struck again—only this time, he took something that wasn't his to take.

And the realm would declare him a fucking hero for it.

Guilt surged through Draevyn—he hadn't stopped it, hadn't been there. He just...*left*.

How could he face Esmyra now, knowing the one person she cared about was gone from the realm? She never got to enjoy a single day with him in an uncursed life.

Draevyn's fists clenched, flames licking at his fingertips, but before either of them could say more, a deep rumble echoed across the water. They turned toward the sea as a tremor shook the ship beneath their boots.

The three men warily met each other's stares.

"What in all gods was that?" Sam muttered, and they all rushed to the edge of the ship.

The waves swelled, their crests frothing and churning as they rolled in with an unnatural force. In the far distance, where the sea met the sky, flashes of what resembled lightning ripped through the sunset.

The sight was unlike anything Draevyn had ever seen or thought was possible. His throat tightened as he watched the ocean churn with an otherworldly power. The ships in the harbor swayed violently as the sea threatened to rip them from their ports.

"We need to move!" Sam shouted. "We need to get off the ship!"

But Draevyn was bolted where he stood, his gaze fixed on the horizon.

*What have you done, Wildfire?* Dread twisted in his chest.

His throat tightened as his eyes remained locked on the surging storm. "What have *I* done?" he whispered, only loud enough for himself to hear.

Atlas stepped up to his side, staring in the same direction as he gripped the rail for balance. "May the gods help us all," he breathed.

"No," Draevyn said, his voice sharper than a blade. "It's the gods who are coming."

To Be Continued...
End of Book One.

A FLAME AMONG THE SEAS,
BOOK TWO OF BEYOND THE TIDES,
IS COMING IN 2026.

## Books By Emilia

---

### THE FORBIDDEN HEIR TRILOGY

*The Dagger and The Forbidden Heir*
*The Crown of Wyvern's Flame*
*A Throne of Wings and Embers*

### BEYOND THE TIDES SERIES

*A Wraith Beneath the Tides*

www.emiliajae.com

Social Media:
@authoremiliajae

# Join Emilia's Newsletter

*& be the first to know of updates, opportunities, events, and more.*

www.emiliajae.com

## Acknowledgments

Wow it feels like this book has been in the making for a long time (likely because it has been). I started writing A Wraith Beneath the Tides back in March 2024, and by the time it was published in July 2025, I had spent the same amount of time working on this one book as I did the entirety of my last trilogy. I started, scrapped, and restarted this story again at least five times.

My thing has always been "well why can't the FMC be the badass?" Why can't she be the one with powers? The morally grey one? Etc. And I was sure to bring that to my sophomore series as well. I went into this knowing that Esmyra being a villainess FMC was a risk, but the excitement you all showed me leading up to release is truly what kept me going to give me the confidence to click publish.

There are so many people I am forever grateful for. So many people helped bring this book to life, making it what it is today.

TLC: You know who you are, and you know that I would be undoubtedly lost without you. I've never been more thankful for the sisterhood that we share, and I wouldn't have been able to do this without you girls. Thank you for holding my hand through the highs, the lows, the crash outs, and everything in between. Me loves you all to infinity & beyond.

Jenny & Lisa: You two went above and beyond for this book, and I'm so thankful. Thank you for letting me run to you with ideas, new chapters, and the occasional mental breakdown even months after you finished the original book. (I can't wait for the world to meet Jenli in book 2 in honor of you two).

My Street Team, Beta Readers & Editors: Your excitement for this was a huge driving factor for bringing it to this final stage. Thank you so much for all the work you put into this with me.

Loverboy: I love you. Thank you for listening to me talk about this book for over a year. I guess I can also give you the credit for thinking of Esmyra's cool skin shifting powers like an octopus too... 10 Points for Jonny.

My Family: Thank you for always believing in my dreams and encouraging me to push through even on the days I wanted to give up. And a specific shoutout to my dad, who sat and watched Pirates of the Caribbean with me over and over again for years and gave me my love for Jack Sparrow. I hope you don't mind that I stole "Esmi" from you, but bringing your nickname for me into this story is what made it extra special.

And last, but certainly not least... My Readers: I wouldn't be here if it wasn't for you all and your amazing support. Your love for my last series, The Forbidden Heir Trilogy, and excitement for Beyond the Tides is more than I could've ever hoped for or imagined in this career. Thank you for loving my characters and stories as much as I do. It truly means the world to me.

www.ingramcontent.com/pod-product-compliance
Lightning Source LLC
Chambersburg PA
CBHW030326010826
48973CB00004B/889